RYAN KURR

POWDERED OAK
&
SEVEN METALS

A NOVEL

"A triumph, reaching deep into the world of witchcraft and its possibilities. Kurr's second novel is imaginative, with realistic characterization and a true sense of moral code. A gripping storyline, which I dare you to put down once started. His passion shines through, with exquisite attention to detail on subject knowledge, and a deep sense of understanding of the witchcraft community. Expect the unexpected, all is not what it seems. This novel is magical, creative and will fascinate those new to the witchy world alongside the experienced witch community and non-witches alike. In short, a must-read, both enchanting and delicious."

—Laura O'Rourke, *Witches Magazine*

"Ryan Kurr created a beautiful masterpiece that takes you on a journey with unique characters who dive deeper into the world of magic. It's not only a whole new world they explore, but also the depths of their own souls. I loved it!"

—Sandra Szatkowski, owner of *Merenwen's Runes*

"*Powdered Oak & Seven Metals* takes you on a surreal journey through different realms, emotional character arcs and fast paced action that leaves you feeling weightless. In Kurr's second book in the series we dive head first into the fantastical; it's nonstop magical excitement and tantalizing drama that I couldn't put down."

—Cody Tarot, YouTube Content Creator

"*Powdered Oak & Seven Metals* is a wonderful follow-up to *Sage, Smoke & Fire*. The second book of this trilogy was just as magical as the first and what I found most spellbinding was the underlying message that the knowledge and acceptance of oneself, in life and in the practice of the craft, is paramount to becoming more whole as a person and as a witch—that all is interwoven and beautiful, no matter the journey. I can't wait for the final book of this series!"

—Micaéla Royal, Sovereign Witch

"Ryan Kurr's seductive storytelling, bringing us beyond the veil of this coven's practices, is true magic. Traveling through quests and mischief with these maturing witches has broadened my own perspective in a beautiful way. This is a lark of a read for all varieties of witch, magician, mystic, and seeker!"

—Michael Anthony, Modern Thaumaturge @kingoflostwaters

POWDERED
OAK
&
SEVEN
METALS

Copyright © 2021 by **Ryan Kurr**

All rights reserved, including the right to reproduce this book or portions thereof in any form whatsoever, without prior written permission.

Publisher's Note: This book is a work of fiction. Any references to historical events, real people, or real places are used fictitiously. Other names, characters, places, and incidents are a product of the author's imagination. Locales and public names are sometimes used for atmospheric purposes. Any resemblance to actual events, places, people, living or dead, or to businesses, companies, events, institutions, or locales is completely coincidental.

Powdered Oak & Seven Metals/ Ryan Kurr. -- 1st ed.
ISBN 978-1-7347245-3-0 (Hardback)
ISBN 978-1-7347245-4-7 (Paperback)
ISBN 978-1-7347245-5-4 (ebook)

Jacket and cover design by Allison Layman

Map art by Victor Montaghini

Visit the author's website at **www.ryankurr.com**

The wound is the place where the light enters you.

Rumi

Also by Ryan Kurr

Sugar Burn: The Not So Hot Side of the Sweet Kitchen

Sage, Smoke & Fire

For the ones who believed, and helped me succeed
It's pure magic what's been achieved
Together we brought my dreams to fruition
And embodied the spirit of The Magician
Words are thoughts, they create change
Bit by bit, consciousness rearranged
We are not done, there is more to tell
With love and gratitude, we cast the spell

CONTENTS

*Elucidations for text marked with this symbol are located at the back of the book in the Esoteric Compendium.

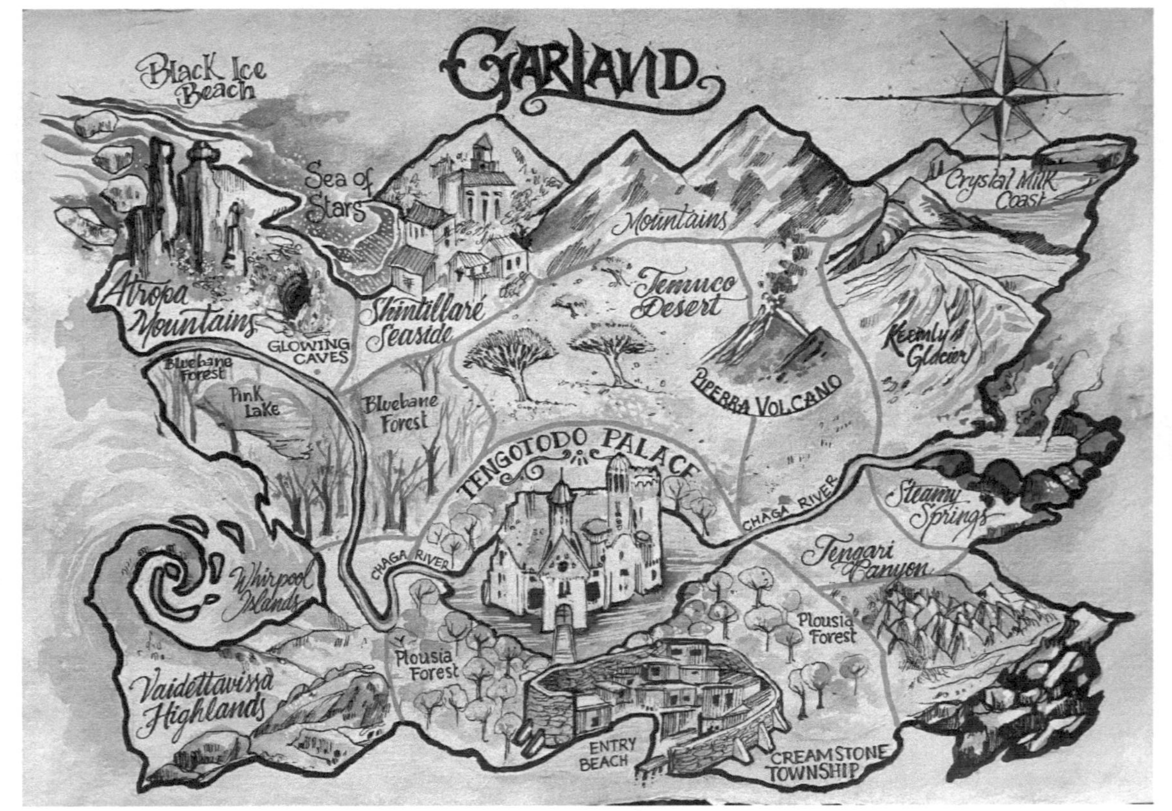

GARLAND
Black Ice Beach
Sea of Stars
Crystal Milk Coast
Mountains
Atropa Mountains
Temuco Desert
Shintillaré Seaside
Glowing Caves
Bluebane Forest
Pink Lake
Bluebane Forest
Keemly Glacier
Piperra Volcano
TENGOTODO PALACE
Chaga River
Chaga River
Steamy Springs
Tengari Canyon
Whirpool Islands
Plousia Forest
Plousia Forest
Vaidettavissa Highlands
Entry Beach
Creamstone Township

POWDERED OAK

&

SEVEN METALS

Småland, Southern Sweden, 1656

Karin had given birth seven times, but had been a mother to no one. She couldn't recall any of her children's faces or explain what had happened to them. It wasn't her fault, she told the court. They were stolen from her, by the very same being that had fathered them. Karin's crime was not neglect, abuse or carelessness regarding her children. She had no proof that she'd given birth to any. Her crime was something the church considered far worse.

Her favorite color was gold, resplendent and luxurious, the color of a life where laughter was common, and rich with the carefree abandon of a spring stream. Where money flowed like waterfalls, always meeting the requests of its owner, and slow-moving time lasted with unyielding deliciousness—as if it had stopped completely—in the everlasting moments of supreme leisure.

While she plucked cloudberries from the bog and tart lingonberries from the forests that spilled down the mountainside, she fantasized about a life dipped in gold, where someone else was the maid. One where she ate the jam instead of made it, and stayed up until dawn, having devoured all the best parts of the day and night. With her fingers stained and pricked from the berry bushes, she dreamed her way through the forest, a habit that had become as routine as her daily chores, past moss-clad stones, patches of wildflowers and loose, wet leaves sprinkled like rose petals along a bride's path.

The wind shifted and laced the tall birch and pine trees with a light foglike garland. The whispering leaves breathed heavily as Karin looked up the path. The life of the forest became unexpectedly quiet as a figure adorned in every shade of gold approached her. The shimmering, streaming, treasure-colored shawls swirled in the air like autumn leaves dancing under the sun. Underneath was a man. Karin wasn't rich or elegant, and the man before her seemed to be both. His steps were light, and his bare feet hardly made an imprint in the dirt. It was the first time she had ever encountered someone in that part of the forest, and her heart skipped a beat when she caught a glance of the man up close. He had the type of features that people paint and sculpt. His hair was as wild as a wolf, with a voice as sweet as a harp's song but strong as oak. He was a poem, one that Karin had never read but instantly swooned before. If words were charms, perfumed love charms dripped from his lips. To say she was enchanted would be to do no justice to the power of his presence. She would have all but collapsed from the sheer sunshine that stood before her if it hadn't been for his gentle hand holding her in place.

When she awoke from a fit, covered in dirt and pine needles, the man was gone, but her memories were not. They had danced and sung and found others to join them. *Where did it all go?* she wondered. What felt like years were merely hours that had been coaxed to stay a while longer, like close friends who linger at the end of a party. It defied logic and all that she knew, but there was no question about it, she knew it all to be true. She had rolled around naked with him under the pines, along the river and in the moonlight The man in gold had given her a child—seven children, to be exact. But where had they gone, and why could she remember being with him, and the children, only every once in a while, like memories slowly bubbling to the surface after a few bottles of wine?

Karin grew accustomed to fits and hysterics as time pressed on and the gold man visited less and less frequently. One day in the buzzing of the forest, she realized that the last time she had seen him was, indeed, the last time ever. She no longer looked for berries to pick in the forest but for the children she was certain she had had, although she couldn't explain how. Bread wasn't baked, clothes weren't washed and the animals weren't fed. Day by day, she dropped chores from her list. She put those extra hours to use and searched in the forest near the farm for her children, children who must be lost somewhere, children without names but who were old enough to stand and speak.

None of it made any sense. Her employer had witnessed Karin's behavior and called her on it one day after there was no morning bread and a few of their chickens had died. Getting to the bottom of it was all he and his wife cared about, as they had lost their patience. They had done a favor for the poor woman who needed a home and a job and had nothing but a few articles of clothing to her name. They had often been guilty of having too good a heart, as some of their neighbors had told them. They had hoped it was an easy fix, something they could rectify with a little time off or perhaps a gift. Who was she calling to in the woods? they wondered. Karin had no friends and spent the majority of her time on the farm if she was not out gathering wood or berries in the forest. It turned out to be an issue they didn't know how to handle, for when they told Karin to be honest, she repeated, "The fairy king took my children."

Her employers were kind people, but they were also deeply religious. It wasn't long before they took Karin into town and marched her to the authorities so she could explain herself. There was no greater sin than having a sexual relationship with a nonhuman creature, for they were all creatures of the devil. They couldn't allow a careless woman to bring demons into their home, and what if she were telling the truth and had given birth to the devil's children? Surely they would come looking for her, or worse, the devil himself would pay them *all* a visit. The laws could be fickle, and although there wasn't a law written in stone that one could not have a relationship of a sexual nature with a fairy, it could certainly be filed under the crime of bestiality.

After what seemed like years—and not the years that flew by like hours that she had grown accustomed to—the court had reached a solid decision regarding Karin Svensdotter. With the counsel of two churches in their region, the court finally announced that they believed Karin had been possessed by Satan and driven mad with insanity. It explained her fits, her hysteria, her blackouts and most of all, her missing children who did not exist. Her employers' congregation closed their eyes on the subject and prayed for her soul to be cleansed and for her to have a miraculous recovery, as they often did. Religious trinkets and symbols of protection were coming at her from every direction from people she didn't even know. Her employers agreed to keep her on staff out of the goodness of their hearts on one shiny, hard condition: that a silver cross be nailed above her bed and never removed.

The gold she had always dreamed of, and had experienced so briefly, was gone. Her favorite color was now nothing but a gray cloud of regret and melancholia. The man, whose name she couldn't ever remember, so beautiful, was no man at all, but a fairy, and from the moment the cross was nailed into the wood above her bed with three solid strikes, she never spoke of him again. Yet on the cooler days, when the fog hung heavily between the spindles of birch, she would see many things other people would miss. The fog knows many secrets of the world and doesn't allow many to see. In the fog, on a frosty day in late November, she saw the flicker of the man's golden robes one final time. Only she believed—she knew—he was not a man but a fairy. Time went on, and what had been gold was now silver and hung above her head, reminding her of what she knew to be true but could never speak of again.

POWDERED
OAK

CHAPTER 1

Colorado, February 2020

The snowflakes looked like tiny blue ashes as they fell in the light of the full moon in Leo. Snowfall always brought Nina a sense of peace, and it fell just in time to help her deal with her stress. Nina had read that moving was one of the most difficult life events, right up there with job loss, divorce and the death of someone you love, but she had never imagined that writing your own will belonged on that list too. The moon in Leo added an underlying electricity to the air, a current of lightheartedness and laughter, which inadvertently created an interesting dichotomy as she selected beneficiaries and chose an executor. Writing the personalized letter to Bisa, which she did next, complete with specific instructions, was a little easier, but unnerving nevertheless.

Nina's dreams the last few nights had prompted her to prepare. The coven was family, and she didn't want things to be any more difficult than they already had been. No one needed any more pain. Unfortunately, she couldn't save any of them from it; she could teach them only that pain was inevitable, but suffering was voluntary to an extent. Nina understood that Mitch struggled with suffering the most, and that Leo was the most addicted to his pain. Bisa could transmogrify her grief, Ollie was adept at identifying and lessening the pain of others and Avery knew that heartache had helped shape her into the woman she was now. They all had their own journey through grief, and she couldn't be responsible for them forever.

The frigid breath of the mountain winds grew stronger as Nina finished up. She looked out the window at the swirling snowflakes now whipping against the glass. For a moment, she recalled her brief time in Louisiana, where she had her first beignet from Café du Monde and the white walls of powdered sugar that wafted from the bake kitchen looked almost identical to the punishing snow clouds outside her window. Nina had been gentle and malleable when she'd first met the coven, but now she was confident and as formidable as the tall oaks in the South, where she had learned how to be a teacher, a position so undervalued and yet so necessary.

Nina closed her computer with a sigh. It was a long twenty-hour drive from Louisiana to Colorado, with a quick stopover in Dallas so they could grab In-N-Out Burger for dinner. She hadn't had an appetite ever since they'd pulled out of the gas station in Kenner by the airport. Bisa had said they should stop for gas later, and Nina wished she had listened to her or things wouldn't have gotten so complicated so quickly. While the rest of the coven ate animal-style fries and cheeseburger combo meals, Nina had run over the events at the gas station in her head.

Leo had pumped the gas as the woman at the pump opposite stared him down. She was the bartender from a dive bar in New Orleans, the bar where a couple of college boys had fought with a man before chasing after him. The man had run out of the bar—as *Leo* had run out of the bar. The bartender was certain it was him, she would have bet her mother's life on it. She may not always remember how to make a Long Island Iced Tea, but she never forgot a problematic patron's face. She had called the police, and they had showed up before Leo had even paid for the gas. In what felt like seconds, they were taking him in for questioning. The officers had smiled and winked at each other as they shoved him into the car, like he was a giant stuffed banana they had won from a tricky game at the state fair. It all happened so quickly for someone so white, Nina remembered someone in the group saying as she watched the cops drive off with Leo in the back.

Nina didn't have a chance to react. Bisa beat her to it, an act that took the breath right out of her lungs, it was so sudden. Bisa jangled the keys to Nina's car, hopped back in the driver's seat and followed the cops all the way to the station. She said only one thing to the coven before she drove off: *Stay here, I won't be long.* Nina didn't know what to do, and there wasn't much she could do. The only thing she wanted to do was trust Bisa. They hadn't prepared for a situation like this and certainly couldn't use any sort of physical magic that would attract attention to themselves or, worse, get them into even more trouble.

"What is she doing?" Nina whispered to herself as she shielded the sun from her eyes and watched Bisa tailgate the police car.

Bisa was right about one thing: she wasn't long at all. She returned, with Leo, in under an hour, something Nina thought even she wouldn't have been able to do. Nina had not a single plan. The only thing she knew for certain was that Leo was guilty and she had no idea what to do about it.

Bisa kept the details of what happened to herself, as if it were something incredibly personal and painful that she didn't want to share. Nina assumed it was shame, but she would never know for sure unless Bisa or Leo opened up to her about it. They had been in Colorado for just over a month and the incident had come up several times in conversation during their daily meetings, but it was never fully discussed in detail. Bisa always shut it down with the conclusiveness of a Supreme Court gavel. She reassured the coven that everything was fine. Her reasoning varied from time to time, sometimes saying everything had been taken care of and other times saying it was all a misunderstanding.

Avery had gotten the hang of what gray answers smelled like, although she told no one about the growth of her power. Bisa's replies struck Avery as being both false and not entirely true, which meant there was a juicy steak of a story behind Bisa's walls. Avery and Bisa had become quite close, so it was a struggle for Avery to not take Bisa's secrecy personally. Bisa was intelligent, and if she kept something to herself, she must have had a good reason for it.

Nina pulled the sheer curtains over the window and slipped into bed. She hadn't meditated, she hadn't called to her ancestors, she hadn't even brushed her teeth, all things that had been a non-negotiable part of her nightly routine. It was just time for rest, a break, and that meant from everything.

CHAPTER 2

Bisa waited outside the police station for a few minutes, building up her nerve to carry out what she had planned in her head. She closed her eyes in meditation until her brainwaves dropped into the alpha state where her magic was the most successful, the most potent. She didn't feel ready, but there wasn't enough time in the day for her to feel prepared; she needed to act. Bisa pushed past her sweaty palms and whomping heart and stepped out of the car, leaving the door open. She pushed her way through the cold doors to the police station and looked around, her mind buzzing with a hundred uncertainties. She found herself part of the majority inside this particular station. She always noticed the whiteness wherever she went, similar to how others noticed whether it was night or day when they looked out the window.

It was damp, and the smell of burnt coffee and mouth breathers mixed with Mylanta and stress hung heavy in the air. But she could still smell Leo…that golden smell that Rosemary described, a smell that was beyond words. As she surveyed the station, she spotted a small Wanted poster of Bowie. She scoffed and made her way to the desk. *Stay focused and calm,* Bisa told herself as she approached the tiny man at the desk. She had survived a lot in her life, and if she just took her plan one step at a time, she could make her way to Leo to retrieve him without anyone stopping her. Her heart began to punch her chest, and sweat began to collect around her hairline.

The cop looked up from his desk, a phone stuck to his ear. "There somethin' I can help you with, ma'am?"

Nina's words raced through Bisa's memory: *Try not to overthink it or rationalize it. Breathe. Listen. Do you hear it? Do you hear his mind?* Bisa stood before the man, her mouth hung open like a floodgate with no water. *It's no different from art. Create change with your intention,* Bisa heard Nina once again. That's when the static started. She fine-tuned the channels of the man's mind until she found the clearest connection, past his mundane thoughts, behind his secrets, underneath all desires, through his hopes, fears and intentions.

"Ma'am?" the cop repeated as he pulled the receiver away from his mouth.

Bisa's eyes closed as she tightened her influence on the man in front of her. Suddenly, all sound emptied from the room as if all life on earth had stopped. She reached up to grab hold of her blue kyanite necklace and rubbed it between her fingers like a lucky rabbit's foot, using it to amplify her psychic connection. As her thumb passed over the rough, bladed sprays of the mineral, the cop's hand dropped from the side of his head and he hung up the phone. His eyes, hollow and receptive—submissive.

Bisa licked her lips, slowed her breathing back down to a normal pace and said, "You have a man in custody here, Leo Sullivan, is that right?"

The man nodded.

"All right. You're going to take me to him, and you're not going to raise a fuss, ask me any questions or allow anyone else to stop us. Do you understand?"

"Yes ma'am!" The cop nodded continually and smiled like a dashboard bobblehead.

Bisa's eyes shot around the room. The other cops looking at her, the clock, the surveillance cameras, the hallways that stretched to areas she couldn't see. Her eyes snapped back to the cop. "Now. Take me now."

Another heavy nod to express his full obedience, and then they set off through the station. She had never been inside a police station, and it was distracting to be surrounded by what felt like a movie set from another time. It was the South, and by now she knew the South was a little slow to catch on to things. She had read everything by James Baldwin, *The Warmth of Other Suns, A Time to Kill,* and *Men We Reaped.* She had seen *Selma* and *My Cousin Vinny,* and lived in Louisiana long enough to understand that modernity and progressive thinking takes its time to arrive in a place like this.

Between the aging carpet and the number of desktop fans, it looked like they were one step away from dial-up internet. The carpet was stained from where a piece of furniture used to be, the chairs were mismatched and a small vending machine cozied up next to the water-damaged walls. Bisa could feel her concentration wobbling as the scent of burnt coffee mixed with the cop's Old Spice deodorant as he guided her through the station. She closed her eyes for a few steps and reopened them with a renewed sense of concentration. The kind that produces boundless opportunities when applied.

They rounded the corner and passed through a door with a sign that she didn't bother to read. The lights became more fluorescent, and the wood paneling was gone and replaced with freshly painted cinder blocks. Her shoes clacked against the newly remodeled floor. The cop opened the door to the room at the end of the hall. Two more cops were inside, but Bisa had already presumed that from shuffling through the man's thoughts, a skill she wasn't sure she had ever had before that moment. She smelled Leo before she saw him, that golden smell that reminded her of the only thing she could compare it to, the Gold Recovery Mask by Chantecaille. For a moment, her time working at Warpaint in Chicago entered her mind, just long enough to remind her of how far she had come and how different her life really was now.

Leo turned around in his chair and saw Bisa standing in the doorway. His brow furrowed as if someone had asked him what the capital of Switzerland was.

The cop who seemed to be in charge sat up in his chair from behind the old desk—a cantankerous man somewhere between sixty and *I'm too old for this shit.* Starched short-sleeve uniform, wet under the arms, a tarnished wedding ring and squinty eyes that had seen so much, they didn't want to see or deal with anything else. "Gator, what in the hell are you doin'?"

"This woman asked to see Leo Sullivan, so I brought her to him like she asked," the naïve Gator said plainly.

"Gator, you dumb biscuit!" said the sweaty, wedding-ringed cop.

The other cop stiffened his spine and pursed his lips in a kind of southern, deimatic behavior as he automatically placed his right hand on the butt of his gun like a natural reflex.

Bisa's hold over Gator was starting to crumble as panic raced through her blood. She grabbed hold of her kyanite once more, inhaled all the ancestral assistance she could through her mouth in a juddering breath and closed her eyes. Like a kitchen grease fire having met water and causing it to spread, Bisa entered the minds of all three cops in the room, and she opened her eyes. Her power of influence was strong and intense. She released her hand from her necklace and exhaled with the satisfaction of the kind of witch she aspired to and knew she could be. With the men under her control, she took notice of the details. The married one's badge read *Captain.* A picture of his wife and a crispy, extremely dead, potted succulent remained the only decoration on his desk. The walls were covered with news clippings from local cases he had helped solve, in addition to twelve photos of him holding prizewinning fish, each with a gold plate engraved with the species of fish and date.

Leo looked at the other cops in the room, waiting for a reaction, but there was none. Bisa had bested them all with the amount of effort it would take to sip soda through a straw.

Bisa took a few steps closer to the captain's desk and stopped. She turned her head to the cop in the corner and met his eyes. Her intention slipped from her mind, through her eyes and into his head, and he dropped his palm from the gun to his side.

"Leo, get up," Bisa ordered.

Leo scanned the faces of the cops, each of them slapped with a vacant expression of someone lost in a daydream. He slid forward off his chair, half expecting someone to tell him to sit back down. But no one did. The chair creaked across the dusty floor and he stood.

Bisa stepped forward into the beam of bronzed light that filtered through the grunge-covered glass of the room's only window. As Leo joined her by her side, she inhaled deeply, her breath creating the sound of a gentle ocean in the back of her throat. The hairs on the back of her neck stood up as if caught in a breeze. "What is he here for?" Bisa asked.

"He's a suspect in a murder investigation," the captain said freely.

"He's not. He's completely innocent. In fact, you've never even heard the name Leo Sullivan before. None of you have," Bisa insisted.

"We haven't," all three officers said in unison.

Bisa tilted her head down, delving deeper into her power, gripping their will more tightly. Suddenly she could hear the incoherent chatter of all their minds, minds that were under her control. None of it made any sense—words and thoughts were interrupted and broken—but she could hear opportunity. Bisa placed her fingertips on the edge of the desk, her hands like small tents. "This investigation is closed. The case is closed. Unsolved. Irrelevant. Gone," she said. She used every possible phrase she could to close any loopholes that would prove to not be in Leo's best interest, in the coven's best interest.

"The case is closed. What do I do now?" the captain asked politely.

"You're going to destroy the case file. Shred everything in it. Any evidence there is, I want you to throw that away too— get rid of it so no one has any record of it. And if anyone else is familiar with this case, you tell them it was a case of mistaken identity and that'll be the end of it." Bisa took a deep breath, the rhythm of her heart normalized and calm, under control. "If anyone asks about this case, whether that be another cop or someone else, I want you to tell them whatever you know that will guarantee it never comes up again. Ever. You can do that, right? All of you?"

In unison like a zombie choir, "Yes."

"You won't remember I was here, or that Leo was here or ever brought in. If you ever see Leo's name again, you do whatever it takes to make sure that the case is expunged." Bisa finally blinked. "One more thing. If I ever need a favor from you in the future, whatever it is, you will do whatever I ask without question. Is that clear? All you have to do is hear my voice and you will obey anything I say, do you understand?"

"Absolutely, ma'am!" said the captain.

"Good," Bisa said as released her grip on their minds.

Leo stood behind her in silence, his golden smell overpowered by the stress-induced sweat that dripped down his temples. He looked at the men's faces one more time. They all looked the same: empty minded, trained, obedient. Leo wiped the sweat with the side of his hand and grabbed hold of the door handle.

Bisa turned on her heels. "Let's go," she said without a backward glance.

A sound of breath, perhaps a sigh of relief, flew out of Leo's mouth as he followed Bisa down the hall. Gator trailed behind them in a waddling penguin sort of way. Bisa knew everything would be fine. She could tell by the looks in the eyes of the other officers in the station and the uninterested glances they made no effort to disguise. Leo held his tongue as they rounded the corner to the front of the building and passed through the earthy stench of burnt coffee once more. Bisa reached into the small glass candy dish at the front desk and pulled out a peppermint as if they had just left the doctor's office. They passed through the front doors quietly, but Bisa could hear Leo's heartbeat thumping behind her in the chasm of her mind. Although she was now fully confident of their escape, she didn't blame him for his level of fear and anxiety. She knew it was the first time he had ever left a police station without suffering an arrest.

When they reached the car, they watched the door to the station for a full minute. No one was coming. They had done it—well, Bisa had done it. Leo had tailed along for the ride. Bisa snapped her head toward Leo in the passenger seat and stared into his eyes with an intensity that could have scorched the sun. He said nothing. Neither of them did. Words weren't necessary. In fact, they would have proven to be of little use to either of them, but especially for Leo. Bisa knew all of it. She knew what Leo had done and what he was capable of, and in that stare, Leo understood that Bisa had uncovered his secrets. More of them. His facial expressions changed with his shifting emotions, beginning with relief, moving through gratitude, flowing into humiliation and landing on cold, hard guilt. Leo broke eyes with her and sank into his seat as Bisa continued to stare at him.

It was a long, quiet drive back to the gas station. Once they reunited with the coven, Leo awkwardly explained that everything was a misunderstanding. Of the two of them, Bisa was the one Nina trusted the most, but Bisa offered nothing. Nina had hoped to squeeze the details of what had happened out of her while in the stuffy cabin of the U-Haul truck, but Bisa remained quiet.

"Is everything all right, Bisa?" Nina asked.

"Yeah," Bisa said, "everything is fine."

It was the way she pronounced the word *fine*, so heavy and burdened in spite of her attempt to disguise her tone, that suggested everything wasn't fine. It just wasn't the time to talk, and Nina would have to wait.

CHAPTER 3

Each member of the coven had changed both massively and subtly since their time in Louisiana, and each in their own unique way. Mitch had begun to withdraw emotionally from the coven and found comfort in the noxious coziness of online anonymity. He wiped his Instagram account clean and started from scratch to make room for pictures of his handmade crochet pieces. He opened an Etsy store and fired up a new Twitter account to promote his work.

Ollie had done the exact opposite: he'd eradicated every social media account that he'd had (and never used) and threw himself into learning more about herbs, plants and how to grow magically altered plants, capitalizing their names out of respect for the natural world.

Bisa had become the prize pupil, studying meditation, mediumship and psychism in her spare time.

It was Avery, the most resilient to suffering because of her confidence, self-sufficiency and acknowledgment of the power of vulnerability, who slowly suffered from a growing sense of perfectionism as her magical abilities grew stronger, came more easily and exceeded her own expectations. Her conscience, once so realistic and trustworthy, now spoke to her in an authoritative language rife with *can*s and *will*s that set her up for unreachable goals. Stronger. Better. More.

Leo was the witch who shifted his daggers designed to devalue others in order to ignore his own shortcomings and turned them toward himself—an act that was both necessary and excruciating at times. Leo did horrible or dangerous things simply because they felt exciting and good. It was a hard cycle to break. Although his redemption teetered delicately on the precipice of power, he had not fallen off quite yet—there was hope, if only a little.

Together, the coven members began new lives in a new place, with entirely new perspectives. Their new home was a massive three-story house at the end of Smoky Quartz Drive in the small town of Nova, just twenty-seven miles west of Denver. The all-black home rested atop a hill of boulders and pine that overlooked Lake Peridot and was hugged by mountains. A single Rocky Mountain maple stood strong in the yard. With the house having been built in 1995, it was a dramatic contrast to the history-rich Barrow House back in Louisiana, where the floorboards spoke and the walls breathed. However, it still had an energy to it, an oldness that had nothing to do with age. The house had no name, other than 444 Smoky Quartz Drive, a small coincidence that only Leo found humor in.

Because of where the house was perched, not all floors were equal. The front door led to the long mudroom and then a short hallway to the rustic wooden staircase that swirled all the way to the third floor, where a chandelier of cascading glass pendants trickled down the center. At the top of the stairs on the second floor one was met with a solid pane of window the length of the wall, a large sunroom painted a hopeful saffron to the left, and a large family room in a timeless, restorative nocturnal blue on the right. Ollie's room, in the same fashion as the Barrow House, was found just off the family room. Bisa and Avery shared the two rooms opposite each other behind the staircase. The third floor housed Nina's room immediately to the left of the stairs, with walls painted a wishful viridian.

The living room, which functioned as their ritual and meeting space, was a rich, earthy plum, its walls decorated with the framed Ab Initio Talismans they had made back in Louisiana. A Bösendorfer upright piano, a shade of matte green so dark it was almost black, rested near the window. The hall by the stairs led to a stained-glass window, with Leo's room on the right and Mitch's room on the left. The door to the kitchen and dining room was next to Mitch's room. The kitchen was smaller than expected, but newly remodeled in a way that made it look older than it was: barn-wood gray tiles, a large fiery copper sink that had only just begun to patina, a matte black faucet and large refrigerator modeled to look like a vintage icebox but with the functionality of modernity. The living room had an inspiring energy about it, as if someone had liquified and bottled the spirit of a hundred muses and sprinkled it from wall to wall. There was a fireplace of selenite with a driftwood mantel, a site that inspired Bisa to move on from macrame to short story writing. A quick writer she was, too, having completed several poems, three short stories and a 35,000-word novella in just under a month. A small balcony ran along the length of the room and overlooked the now semi-frozen mountain lake below.

The best-kept secret of the house was the second, smaller staircase that attached the third floor to a small gabled ceiling loft. Built into the far wall was a solid wood bookcase of black walnut, made entirely by hand by a now deceased local medium who had made a hobby of building furniture. It filled the entire wall, forming a perfect triangle. The shelves held a myriad of books and mysterious relics, and even a copy of *Metaphysical Manifestations and Sharpened Senses,* which, according to the first pages, was the follow-up to *The Secrets of Magic and Other Curious Practices,* the book in the study at the Barrow

House that had charmed Avery. Another tattered buckram cover, this time in euphoric blue, the title in gold, and again—no author.

The house as a whole gave the impression that it had been manifested rather than built, by someone with sharpened senses and curious practices. From the floorboards to the paint, from the layout to the window placement, the house felt like a curated art installation designed by someone who had the ability to transmute emotion and visions into tangible structures to yield an everlasting experience. In a way, it felt like a dream home, but one quite literally of dreams. The ticking of the grandfather clock everyone had gotten used to was replaced with a whisper of wind through mountain pine. Avery joked about it being the kind of thing that luxury candlemakers fashion and name their scents after, but also joked that it would be a candle she would buy. The oppressive southern heat had been replaced by a refreshing and crisp alpine cold, and the buzzing of cicadas by a constantly sung poem of highland birds.

Perhaps it was this new energy that allowed Nina the culinary freedom to experiment in the kitchen. They ordered pizza from Red Pie Pizza the first night, but Nina wouldn't allow that to happen more than once. She spent the next week making sure there was a fresh meal on the table at dinnertime, choosing someone's favorite cuisine each night. On the fifth night, it was Bisa's favorite. Nina searched through some of her cookbooks and made a Forbidden Rice Stir-Fry with Black Pepper Tofu and Crispy Brussels Sprouts*, something Nina was sure would get Bisa's attention because of her love of Asian flavors. Yet halfway through dinner, Bisa had hardly eaten a thing on her plate. By the time she had finally stopped pretending to eat, the food was far too cold to enjoy. Instead, she bit her lip and fretfully rubbed her knuckles with her thumbs.

"Aren't you hungry?" Nina asked. "You haven't eaten a thing since we've been here."

A few moments passed and then Bisa lifted her head, hoping Nina would ignore the lengthy delay of her response. "I just don't feel very well. I think I'm just exhausted—you know, from the move," she said, slightly surprised at the crackling weakness of her own voice.

Nina eyed Bisa's fiddling fingers, her hunched, almost panicked posture like a squeezed stress toy that never regained its original shape. There was a distinct and anomalous blueness to her aura, something Bisa had never succumbed to. She was strong, not easily rattled. Yet something was plaguing her enough to affect her energy.

"Really?" Avery said. "You should have said something. I can whip up a restorative elixir real quick. I have tons of honey I can use; I've been wanting to use that uh…what is it, Ollie, your ginger-fennel powder with ashwagandha? It'll take five minutes." Avery set down her fork, wiped her mouth and waited for Bisa to respond.

Ollie nodded to acknowledge Avery, but his attention was on Bisa. He didn't need to look at her plate of untouched food to know something was off. He felt it, he sensed it—and for a brief moment, he saw it. It was in the subtle ether around her body, as plain as a purple bruise on someone's skin. The unusual, haunted mien was not how Ollie understood Bisa, or anyone in the coven. As he let his eyes slip into a soft focus on the periphery of her body, he was overwhelmed by an unexpected rush of sensation. As quickly as it came, it dissolved, leaving his fingers curled, eyes widened and chest out of breath.

No one had noticed him flinch, apart from Bisa, who looked up at him as if he had blown a gust of air in her face.

He was by no means an expert witch, but from what he had been taught, two words flashed through his mind: *clairempathy* and *clairsentience*. He had been immersed in the world of witchcraft for such a short time, it seemed silly to assume he had leveled up already. But there was no other explanation. He felt what had been poisoning Bisa's mind, but he didn't understand it. It wasn't the stress of the move; he knew that for certain. Within the few moments he made eye contact with Bisa, he tried to decide what to do next with the new information. Was it appropriate to share it? Should he keep it to himself? Just because he felt it—no, knew it—didn't exactly mean he needed to express or act upon it.

Before anyone could say or do anything, Bisa held out her hand in protest toward Avery. "No, no, really, it'll pass. It's nothing that serious." Bisa looked up to Nina, who had been observing Bisa so intensely that it knotted her stomach.

"I finished reading your short story last night," Avery said excitedly.

Bisa seemed uninterested.

"I finished it this morning," Mitch added.

Feeling obligated to engage even though she truly didn't want to, Bisa said, "What did you think?"

"I'm not really much of a critic, but I thought it was really imaginative," Avery said. "I'm impressed, actually. I don't think I've ever read anything like that before. So much detail packed into a short story."

"I thought there was this, like, constant underpinning of meanness to the writing. And like, mean-minded humor," Mitch said softly.

"It wasn't mean! It was honest," Avery argued back.

"I think things can be honest, but like, not be so brutal," Mitch said.

"Honesty isn't always pretty," Avery snapped.

"There was a lot in there that I found really…triggering," Mitch added.

Bisa rolled her eyes for half a second. "*Life* is triggering. I think trigger warnings on art are unnecessary and irrelevant, and don't actually help the people they're meant to help. Life is nothing *but* triggers, and ones we are never prepared for. You can't protect yourself from everything. I get that people experience trauma—I've experienced trauma—but in my opinion, being triggered is the result of a trauma not healed, and avoiding the issue because a trigger warning suggests you should approach with caution only delays your healing. It's not someone else's fault that you were triggered over something you saw, read, or didn't agree with. People apply trigger warnings to cover their ass from someone who wants to blame them for reexperiencing their unhealed trauma."

The explanation got mixed reviews within the coven, but it went in one of Mitch's ears and out the other. "And the whole part about…" Mitch began.

"Mitch, I get it. You didn't like it," Bisa snapped back.

"I'm sorry! I liked some of it," Mitch said.

"Mitch, I don't care what you think or if you liked it, I didn't write it for *you*," Bisa nipped.

"That's a fair point," Avery said. "You can't please everyone. If it's controversial, you've gotta be doing something right! You could make the best chocolate ice cream in the world, but some people just don't like chocolate. I loved it though," she finished.

Bisa scratched her brow and conjured a make-believe headache as she made eye contact with everyone and no one and said, "Sorry, excuse me, I'm going to go lie down for a bit." She rose from her seat, closed the halves of her long, knit cardigan over her chest and headed to her room.

"Is something wrong?" Avery quietly asked Nina.

Nina hesitated for a moment as she stared at the empty stairwell. "No, nothing's wrong. She's just tired. There've been a lot of adjustment in the last couple months. Sometimes it takes time for stress like that to catch up or manifest in other ways. She'll be fine." Nina tickled the remaining bits of food on her plate with her fork, lost in thought. She looked over at Bisa's plate and then stood up from the table. "I'll put her food in the fridge. She can eat it later, if she's hungry after our meeting." She retrieved Bisa's plate and then said, "Please bring a notepad with you to the meeting tonight. I'm going to explain something that you all need to understand really well." She headed toward the kitchen to tidy up.

Leo had finished his plate some time ago and had been uncharacteristically quiet. He stood up from the table without a word and followed Nina into the kitchen. Ollie, Mitch and Avery sat at the table under the light of the hickory branch chandelier with its hanging shards of quartz crystal points, a detail that was one of Ollie's favorite features of the house.

"What do you think the meeting is about tonight?" Mitch asked as he shoved the last bit of black rice onto his fork before taking a look at his scarred thumb, feeling the urge to pick at it.

"She mentioned earlier today that she wanted us to learn about the Union of the Divine Dualities," Avery said casually as she looked at Ollie. "Do you know what's wrong with Bisa?"

Ollie shook his head, but said nothing. He could have answered with a yes, but it wouldn't have been the whole truth. He didn't really know what the whole truth was, he just knew there was one. He collected his silverware and took his plate to the kitchen, leaving Mitch and Avery at the table together.

Bisa wasn't sick, nor was she exhausted; she was concerned. She had lost the ability to feel safe in the coven back at the police station. There were things she could excuse—eating toenails, leaving dirty dishes around and, to an extent, even reckless driving. What unnerved her spirit and chilled her core were the rapid-fire images of actual events that took place in Leo's life. Transcendents were the most empathic witches, but until now, she had believed that their powers were capped at a certain point. It felt similar to when she experienced grief: just when she thought she had finally hit the bottom and it couldn't get any darker, the floor gave way and she realized there were layers upon layers toward a center she couldn't see. Now she realized her abilities transcended a ceiling that wasn't even there. It was a sky, with an atmosphere and a cosmos beyond that—where the limits were only as far as someone had previously gone.

In a traumatizing riot of pain, callous hostility, dangerous risks, lies and rage, Bisa felt, saw and experienced it all. Everything about her current situation suddenly seemed dangerously wrong. Leo had murdered people; she had psychically seen him do it, multiple times. Soon after that flood came the realization that he had magically manipulated Mitch into sex. Some would call it rape, some would call it nonconsensual sex, but either way it was against Mitch's will. Whether it was something Mitch wanted or not, that was a decision for Mitch to make, not Leo. And this monster was downstairs—sharing a meal, sharing a space, privy to everyone's routines, aware of everyone's vulnerabilities.

Bisa's heart raced as awful scenarios ran through her head. Leo couldn't be trusted. How did one trust someone who was so lacking in empathy? Especially now that she knew he was a Corporeal, with powers far greater than her own. If she was only beginning to tap into the galaxy of her abilities, there was no telling what he could actually be capable of. How did one trust a monster like that? Yet, she had. She had found a man—a boy, really—with a monster's toxic talons speared deep into the back of that boy's body. Had he always been a monster or had he been designed that way, shaped that way?

It was then that Bisa slid down a shame spiral as she paced back and forth in front of her long mirror. She could return to her old life if she really needed to. She could pack, sneak out under the safety of night and just leave it all behind. Only there was nowhere to go back to, if she was completely honest with herself. What would she do, go back to her job as a makeup artist? She didn't need to be psychic to know that wasn't the answer. She felt the truth: she was exactly where she was supposed to be, even if it was dangerous. And she was in control of her power, how much it developed, and how well it would serve her—or her survival. There was no going back, but what if staying was the nail in her coffin? Perhaps she would have to tell the coven what she knew, for the sake and safety of the coven.

Bisa decided to meditate on whether it was wise. Since joining the coven, she had found the most clarity in meditation. She had experienced very real changes in her waking life as a result of developing and expanding her inner consciousness and psychic awareness. It was another tool, like a makeup brush, but for spiritual purposes. She smudged her room with white sage, following it with the purifying and joyful smoke of burning sweetgrass. She cast a circle on the floor with slabs of blue kyanite, placing an air plant in the north corner of the circle, a feather in the east, a glass of melted snow in the west, and a lit candle in the south. Bisa sat on the floor, closed her eyes and visualized herself surrounded with white light. Her breathing collected in the back of her throat with each inhale and exhale.

"Aham Prema," Bisa said, no louder than a sigh. The candle flickered, and again she uttered, *"Aham Prema…Aham Prema…Aham Prema. I am divine love."* She then mentally began a dialogue with Spirit. "Body and mind with the truth, what do I need to know about our coven? Tell me, show me, how to proceed. What danger awaits if I expose the truth? For the good of all involved, show me the course of action I should take."

Even after all of her time meditating, she still had moments when she thought, *Am I just making all of this up? What am I seeing? What am I saying?* Meditation was a constant battle, an endless practice, not a mastered technique. Over time the interruptions from her rational mind and ego trying to make sense of something that functioned beyond logic became less problematic. Nina had once told her that if it felt like she was making it up, then it was probably true.

A flash of a moment alone with Nina entered her mind. A training exercise back in Louisiana.

Nina waved her hands over Bisa's head and cleared her crown chakra, like a chef dragging the aroma of a simmering soup toward their nose.

"Psychism is not entirely unique to witches, Bisa," Nina said. "Psychism is a natural gift that every human possesses. Connecting to the spirit world isn't encouraged or taught, but we all have that ability, and we can all excel at it. Someone who isn't a witch could excel beyond our psychic abilities if they devoted enough time to it. Doubting yourself and your abilities is natural, but allowing yourself to be limited by doubt is entirely optional."

Bisa's vision melted as she was pulled by Spirit back into the present with a faint whisper. It was in that gentle murmur that she heard an answer to her questions. She felt it was irresponsible to act without considering the options outside her own perspective. Bisa had grown accustomed to seeing the world through a window of the collective consciousness; it encouraged her to not expect to receive messages as she preferred, but to accept them as they came. And that's exactly what she did: she accepted the message that came to her and decided to act on it. She had to tell the coven what she knew.

CHAPTER 4

Nina had spent the last half hour explaining all there was to explain. Now she paced around the group, her hands clasped in front of her as she built up the coven's anxiety through hesitation. She stopped and stood in the center of the circle, fluffed her curls and then closed her hands over her mouth as if in prayer. A moment of silence.

She began her pop quiz with a velocity that rivaled lightning. "Avery! What's the Union of the Divine Dualities for?" Nina turned and began to walk straight toward Avery.

Avery shifted in her seat and sat up straight. "Um, it's the ritual, the only ritual there is to produce the black hen!"

Nina spun to face Ollie. "And what does the black hen do?"

"It is the only thing that can locate the mineral rafkolite," Ollie said quickly, and then looked down at the notepad on his lap, checking for accuracy.

"Good!" Nina pointed to Leo. "Leo, what's rafkolite for?" she asked sharply.

"Uh, it's uh, it is supposed to create positive vibes—or it *can* produce that when used by the right person."

Nina lifted her outstretched finger toward the ceiling to correct his statement. "The right witch!" She pointed to Bisa next. "Can it do anything else?"

"No one really knows, because no one alive has had any interactions with it. Everything is based on legend. It's rumored to have many abilities," Bisa said freely, her dark secret still in the back of her mind, desperately scratching to find its way out.

"Mitch! Why has no one found it up to this point?" Nina asked.

"Because it's lost?" he guessed.

Nina shook her head. "Avery?"

"Many other witches have tried, but they've either failed or died trying. We're the coven that is prophesied to finally find it," Avery said.

"Correct!" Nina exclaimed. "Ollie, how is the Divine Dualities performed?"

Ollie looked down at his notes, swallowed and ran his finger back and forth across the left page before letting it sail over to the top of the right page, searching for an answer.

"Bisa?"

"A talisman needs to be created before you can even begin," Bisa said, her eyes on the floor, her mind somewhere else.

"Yes!" Nina said. She quickly walked behind the old oak chair Leo was sitting on and grabbed hold of the top rail. "What for?"

Leo tapped his fingers on his notepad, half hoping he would extract the answers straight out of his notes through osmosis. "It allows you to mix the ingredients in the next step. The fairy water or whatever."

Nina moved to the center of the circle and pointed at Ollie. "Ollie, clarify, please."

"A circle must be cast to perform the ritual, and the circle must be drawn with a mixture of stormwater and melted snow that has been infused with a fairy's life force. That mixture has to be combined with powdered oak, but it won't mix unless the talisman is worn."

"Correct!" Nina clapped her hands and then looked at Mitch. "What if the fairy's life force is troublesome?"

"I can't remember," Mitch said with a heavy heart, annoyed at both himself and the quiz.

"Bisa?" Nina said.

"It has to be their own choice. The fairy has to give their life force willingly, or it won't work. They can't be coerced into doing it."

"Right. Next? Anyone?"

Avery closed her notebook and dropped it on the floor beside her. "The circle prevents anyone who isn't pure of heart from entering, so someone really close to Spirit has to be the one to enter."

Mitch rolled his eyes and started picking at his lips with his teeth.

"Good. Then what?" Nina pressed.

Ollie sat forward, feeling the energy of the discussion. "You have to create a cyclone of white light!"

Nina shook her head, spun around in a circle and looked over all their faces. "You're a step ahead of yourself. Bisa?"

Bisa let out a sigh and sat back in her chair. "You have to be invisible. Which is impossible. Well, almost. It can be done, but it's very difficult. You can do it either through aura manipulation or through the use of a rare blend of astral fluids. The types of astral fluids are no longer known, so no one really knows how to go about it that way, and there is no record of anyone having any on hand." Bisa remained concentrated and free from the tension that Mitch was feeling so strongly.

Nina nodded, stopped pacing and stood as straight as the rest of the coven in their seats, apart from Mitch, who was hunched over, trying to hide from being quizzed.

Bisa looked around and saw that all eyes were on her. She released a sigh from deep within her gut and uncrossed her legs and crossed her arms over her chest. "You have to be invisible in order for the spirits that aid in the ritual to actually appear and help you. Once you're invisible, then you create the cyclone of light, which can be done in many ways. You can be a primordial and summon it, or use an incantation. The cyclone of light acts as a sort of primer for the next part of the spell. Next you have to create what is called the esoteric alchemy fire, which will allow the witch to combine the seven precious metals: copper, silver, tin, gold, iron, lead, and mercury, all specifically used for a unique characteristic."

Nina backed away from the center of the circle and sat down in her chair to marvel at Bisa's knowledge of the ritual.

Bisa continued, "The fire has to be manifested by the witch's own will. Once the metals are melted, you must summon the celestial spirits and ask them to solidify the molten metals into a golden egg. This is followed by an incantation: *cogitatio, communicationis, studium, completionem, defensionis, misericordia, disciplinam, patientia, intuitio.* At this point the egg will crack and vaporize to reveal a baby black hen. You recite *crescere, locate,* and wait three days for it to grow and mature to full size. At that point it will locate the rafkolite. But no one knows how that's done or what that looks like, because it's never been done before."

As the coven looked at Bisa in awe, Nina favored her with a string of compliments on her impeccable recollection.

"I don't think I could have said it any better myself, Bisa. I think we've got a Proctor on our hands!" Nina said proudly. "Does anyone have any questions? I know there have to be some."

Leo was the first to jump at the opportunity as his mind was flooded with a few burning questions that needed answering. "Yeah. So, about this fairy shit. Fairies are real?"

"As real as any of you in this room, although in the witch community, they are rumored to have gone extinct a long time ago," Nina said.

"Is that true?" Avery asked.

"I don't know. It might be," Nina said.

"All right, hold up," Leo said. "So fairies are a thing, but they've probably gone extinct, and we need a fairy's life force to complete this ritual? I mean, I don't wanna be a buzzkill, but damn. Doesn't that sound like we won't be able to even do this? Unless one of you happens to be some kind of necromancer, I don't really see us being able to find much of anything."

"I hate to say it," Avery began, "but he's right. If fairies are extinct, then what exactly is the plan?"

"We will find a way," Nina said. "It's not so black and white; there are many paths to explore, many that we may not even know about yet. Maybe it's something we haven't explored or discovered yet. Maybe it has something to do with a different timeline or parallel reality. It would be disadvantageous, maybe even ignorant, to assume that this is the only timeline. Maybe there's another one where a crazy pandemic has destroyed our entire world, or murder hornets have killed us all or people have started worshipping balloons. We aren't performing magic to promote balance during our lifetime or timeline only. We're trying to restore and maintain balance for those to come after we're gone, too. We won't necessarily see all the results of our actions in our lifetime. Balance…It'll never be perfect, it'll never be mastered, but it will be functional. Closure is never fully absolute. Life continues on…even if we aren't there to see, read or experience it." Nina shook her head and circled back to her original point. "There wouldn't have been a prophecy if there hadn't been a way," she said.

"Could it have been interpreted wrong?" Ollie asked.

"What about Leo?" Mitch asked.

The entire group fell silent and hung on the end of Mitch's question.

"What about me?" Leo asked as his brow furrowed.

"Well, you're the Corporeal, right? Doesn't he have abilities that no one else here has? Do we even know what his limits are? What if he's able to do it without a fairy?"

"Come on, Mitch…I could never do anything without you, pumpkin," Leo said sweetly.

A hint of a smile started to form on Mitch's lips. Leo's words were cute enough to warrant a smile, and just insulting enough to pass as the loving banter that had been the backbone of their relationship.

Nina ran over the possibility of Leo being the key in her mind. Mitch had a point: Leo was an entirely new breed of witch with powers unlike any other in the coven—or in the world, as far as she knew. What if he was the key? Perhaps that was why the prophecy named their coven to be the one to find the rafkolite to begin with.

Bisa could feel her heart thumping in her chest. Anxiety bubbled up from her gut as her hands became wet and sticky. *How do I bring this up? What if Mitch is right? What if we need Leo to complete this ritual?* She wondered if anyone else in the coven would have been so conflicted if they had been the ones with dangerous information spinning around in their head like a raging vortex. Nina continued to facilitate the discussion, and Bisa slipped forward to sit on the very edge of her seat. Her mouth cracked open to talk, not knowing what she was going to say.

And then came the smell of something new. It was sulfur, it was cucumber and a few things in between. Bisa lifted her eyes and looked at the coven. She had grown accustomed to how witches smell through Nina's tutelage, so there wouldn't be any cause for alarm were it not for the strange sensation that filled her body and her heart. Maybe she was just overwhelmed with anxiety over what she was about to say and how it would disrupt the entire coven.

She reached up to her forehead and brushed her fingers over her brows, across her temples and down the sides of her cheek. And there it was again. Wafting through the air in faint little puffs, like the smell of baking bread from another room. She inhaled deeply, gathering as much information as she could from the air. It wasn't the coven. It was something else, perhaps even someone else. She couldn't be certain. It smelled like witchcraft, but muddled, like every kind of alcohol behind the bar had been mixed arbitrarily into a bucket without rhyme or reason.

She suddenly felt more than just her own feelings of anxiety. Bisa rose to her feet as a rush of energy ripped through her body. She had already been a little overwhelmed and spread very thin as a result of her psychism becoming stronger. She had pushed herself further and further into her abilities, often ignoring the signs to rest and purposely refusing to tell others no when they asked for her intuitive input. She had essentially done herself a disservice by allowing herself to be spread far too thin, so when that rush of energy filled her body, it didn't ask for permission, and it left her stunned.

When the rush subsided, she was light-headed and could just barely make sense of everything she experienced. Strange foreign memories, heaps of superfluous information, assessments of the past, present and future, the buzzing of love, the stink of hate and vengeance, smells of nature and unidentifiable things, and a sense of anonymous danger. And more, and more and even more. She had no idea where it was coming from or how she was able to sense it so strongly.

"Bisa, what's wrong?" Nina asked as she held her hands out to silence the rest of the coven.

Bisa looked into Nina's eyes, and for an instant, she felt the danger for her. "We did protection spells when we arrived, didn't we? Who did them?" she asked frantically.

All color drained from Mitch's already incredibly pale face, leaving him nearly translucent.

"Mitch? You cast the protection enchantments?" Nina asked, even though she could feel and see the answer to her question before she even finished asking it.

Mitch met eyes with Nina but said nothing. He could feel the searing judgment and disappointment from the coven as a flurry of gasps, sighs and tongue clicks filled the air.

"Quiet," Nina barked.

Avery closed her eyes and tried to use her sharpened sense of hearing. She had been waiting for a moment such as this, a moment to be of service to the coven at a sudden and unexpected time of need. She instantly remembered a passage from the book she'd found in the study: "Divine intervention will naturally occur in states of great peril as a direct result of living truthfully and following one's intuition and listening to spiritual guidance." The mellow pops and clicks of the burning candle wicks like the crackles of an old vinyl record. The winter winds pushing against the frozen glass windows, the quickened heartbeat that thumped inside Bisa's chest. She heard nothing else. She opened her eyes, and then it happened.

A soft hiss of air followed by a dense thud, one that they could feel in the floor through their feet. Then came a distant rumbling that approached with an incessant, hollow sound. A small obsidian sphere no bigger than an eight ball rolled effortlessly as if on a track down the hall and slowly glided into the room. When it reached the middle of their circle, it stopped rolling, the polished surface reflecting the lamplight. Nina shifted her weight anxiously from one foot to the other as she stared at the sphere as if it were a bomb about to blow. She felt the gurgling of her dinner turning in her stomach as worry set in.

"No one move…Stay still," Nina instructed as she held both hands out with her fingers spread, as if they were about to charge forward. A full minute passed as she studied the small, motionless object on the floor, the coven's eyes casting glances at one another as they slowly inched forward in their seats. Nina took a couple of steps, her feet making the softest of sounds on the floor as she approached the sphere. There was an element of familiarity in the sphere, but Nina couldn't place it. She stretched her arm out over it and opened her palm, scanning for any energy she could pick up on. A slight buzzing tickled her palm, like when she had first held a piece of larimar and it had connected to her so strongly that it had felt too hot to hold.

There was a barrier she couldn't get through, a kind of magical enchantment that prevented any dissecting of the object until it was ready to unleash whatever it was intended to do. She retracted her hand and covered her mouth with her fingers as she tried to figure out what to do next. There were no markings, carvings or identifiable designs of any kind; the sphere was as plain as it was black. Yet its pulsating was unnerving and louder than any other crystal, stone or enchanted object she had come in contact with before.

"What is it?" Ollie asked.

When his question went unanswered, he knew something was seriously wrong.

Nina glanced throughout the room, looking for a sign of danger. "Just wait." She kneeled down before the sphere and studied it further for a moment. She took a deep breath, and as she exhaled, the orb began to spin in place like a child's top. That's when she recognized the object before her. She had seen it many years ago. Her eyes widened as bountiful memories came rushing back to her. A curious calm fell over her, but her eyes were filled with an uncharacteristic fire—a lust, even. Leo knew that look very well. He had seen it many times in others, but most of all in himself: the look of someone under the spell of a drug, a hypnotized magnetism nearly impossible to defy. He could see her fingers twitching, her legs beginning to shake and her forehead beginning to sweat. Nina could feel it all happening, but was completely powerless against the influence of the orb. Her brow furrowed as her lips began to quiver. She opened her mouth and tried to speak, but couldn't. Her words had become nothing but a string of stutters.

"Nina!" Bisa shouted as she stood from her seat.

Members of the coven shouted and barked orders as they looked at one another, trying to determine who had the power to break Nina free from the orb's draw.

"Leo!" Avery shouted, anxiously pacing back and forth in front of Nina. "Do something! Can't you do something?"

"I don't know what to do!" Leo roared.

Avery shook her head and dashed toward the orb to try to kick it away, but was sent sailing into the air like a soccer ball. She landed on her side with a loud *whack.*

Leo had his doubts about what he could actually do. He didn't fully understand his powers, but he knew he was capable of some truly elevated magic. He spread his feet and braced himself for any sort of magical counterattack. He thought back to the church, where he had acted on impulse and lifted the car. He could do it again if he tapped into that kind of emotion. A heaviness began to fill his palm as if he were carrying a sack slowly filling up with water.

More shouting, fearful cries and hostile pressure filled his ears as he tried to concentrate.

In the palm of his right hand was now a saturated ball of energy, invisible except for the subtle waves like heat rising from hot asphalt.

"Leo! Do something!" Bisa screamed.

In a single swing, Leo pitched his hand toward the orb and let loose the energy ball he had built up in his palm. He didn't know if that was something he could do or if it worked like that, but he had to try. The waves of energy hit an undetectable barrier and dissolved in a loud hiss. He tried to move Nina with his powers, but couldn't. It was as if she wasn't even there. Leo looked into Nina's eyes. He found himself wishing that he had never been brought into the coven…or better yet, never even known he was a witch to begin with. He felt a lot of pressure, a stinging sense of obligation and a sense of debt that he might not be able to pay back. Nina managed to tear her eyes away from the orb for only a brief moment, and she looked right at Leo. The look in her eyes shared two sentiments: fear and failure. Leo recognized and understood both of those feelings very well, and in the brief moment they shared a gaze, he wished he could help her. But he couldn't. In the flash of an instant he heard her voice inside his head—calm and reassuring.

It's not your fault.

Nina dropped her head toward the orb once more and swiftly reached out to grab hold of it with her left hand. As her fingers curled around it, seared against the surface like a steak onto a ripping hot pan, a burst of energy exploded from within the sphere. An unseen shock wave tore through the room with the force of a car crash, rapidly lifting the coven from the floor and into the air. Their bodies flailed through the room in a mess of whirling limbs as they smacked against various surfaces—some upside down and high upon walls, others stuck to the ceiling, all unable to move or speak. As their eyes reeled from the sudden collision, they looked back down at Nina, who remained unscathed on the floor.

Then, there were footsteps. Slow and controlled, the kind of footsteps one makes when they believe they are in control, even when they are out of control. Nina staggered to her feet, taking a moment to catch her breath as her eyes narrowed to thin slits at the figure entering the room.

Nina nodded as if she had expected this exact situation to come to fruition later on, and here they were, later on.

"Surprise!" Merlot said softly.

Nina took a few breaths, then looked around at her coven pressed against the walls of the room and back at Merlot. "What are you doing?"

Merlot entered the room and stood a few feet from Nina. She was dressed in flowing layers of black silk scarves and wrapped up in an asymmetrical wool coat that draped across her body. A semi-sheer slip dress with metallic threads fell out the bottom of her coat. Her nails, freshly painted a gleaming mulled wine color. She wasn't dressed for winter; she was dressed for death. "You know, Nina, in my book you either survive or you don't. There is no in-between, not if you truly want to live. You and I have been at odds since the day we met. You've grown to believe that I'm *evil*, the worst kind of witch, one who wants to destroy. Our definitions of that word have always differed. I don't know how to destroy; I know how to set people free. Liberation is what I've been after since the moment I came into my power."

Nina took a breath and let out a sigh of disappointment. "Is that what you've come to do, Merlot? Unshackle us? Force us to see *the light*?"

The subtle whimpers of the coven fixed to the walls filled Nina's ears. She could hear them, and every once in a while, she could see them struggle to break free.

"Oh, I don't think you would be able to see my perspective. It's just not in the cards," Merlot said as she took a step closer to Nina.

"The funny thing about that is I tell myself the same thing about you every single day," Nina said, taking a step back as Merlot approached.

"That's probably why we lead two very different types of covens. Well—led."

Merlot's eyes twitched, and then she cracked a smile. "Well, when you assume a leadership role, you're bound to make a few mistakes here and there. Sometimes even members of the Advisory make catastrophic mistakes." Merlot wet her lips like a beast moving in on its prey. "And when those mistakes are brought to light—or, corrected—that's when things get a little messy. Especially when a member of the Advisory is also the

Proctor of a coven. And covens, essentially, are families, are they not? Found families. And sometimes found families overlook the things they don't want to see. Right, Bisa?" Merlot said all this without taking her threatening eyes off Nina. "Oh, that's right, she can't speak."

There were only a few feet between the two when Merlot lifted her hands to her chest and cracked her knuckles one by one.

"Spit it out, Merlot," Nina said. "Enough with the cryptic monologues. What don't they see?"

Merlot whipped her hand ferociously across Nina's cheek, upsetting her footing. Nina stumbled back a few steps and quickly stood straight like an unyielding tree in a storm. Merlot proceeded to advance upon her with a little more haste. Nina shuffled to the side a little to avoid another attack. Merlot stopped in her tracks and stared at her with the sharpness of a blade.

"What don't they see?" Merlot said as she shook her head in pity. "That you're powerless."

Nina grabbed hold of a brass candlestick and flung it at Merlot's leg. Merlot spun away as the candlestick screamed across the floor. She let out a chuckle.

"You're so ridiculous," Merlot said through her giggles.

"I'm a Transcendent, and my powers are more passive—but I have honor."

Merlot clicked her tongue. "Oh, *dulzura*…you think your honor is power?"

"No, my coven gives me that."

"But will they keep you alive? My coven is dead, but I'm still alive. I know danger, I know chaos, I know death. You don't learn to play the game without cozying up to all of that.

But it's dangerous. Do you know how I've managed to live through it all? By taking action. Knowing that power is the key to staying alive. You do what you have to do to get what you want." Merlot began to tread around Nina in circles, making Nina spiral around to keep her in her sight. "Your philosophy and everything you believe and teach your coven is that there are rules for everything. Well, guess what: the rules are incorrect, they always have been. So instead, I live like there are none. Rules are suggestions for insipid people who have no ambition, no determination—for idiots who couldn't imagine a dream world even inside their own dream. Breaking rules are how I've stayed alive, how I've developed my powers."

Avery's cell phone slipped out of her pocket and fell to the floor a few feet away from Merlot. Nina landed a quick shove on Merlot's shoulder, forcing her back just enough so that she could dash toward the fireplace and grab the fire poker. She gripped it, spun around and tossed it toward Merlot, missing her head by only a few inches. Nina dashed to the potion cabinet and ripped open the doors. They hadn't lived in the home too long and hadn't built up much of a supply of defensive potions, nor did she have time to riffle through them. *Where is it? I know it's here!* Nina said to herself as her hands tossed the bottles around in a symphony of clinking glass. There was one stunning potion in there, she knew that for certain, because she had worked with Ollie on it.

After what felt like hours, Nina stopped once she heard footsteps approaching her from behind. She grabbed hold of one of the bottles at random and twirled around, holding the end of the bottle like a baseball bat. Merlot had unsheathed a long, excessively polished dagger with an obsidian handle and acid-etched symbols along the blade. She reached up with the blade and swatted the bottle. Metal screeched against glass as the blade's sharp edge splintered the bottle in Nina's hand, slicing through it completely and leaving a jagged bottleneck behind. Merlot whipped the dagger back toward Nina, moving the tip of the blade closer toward her pulsing neck.

"Don't you fucking move," Merlot hissed.

Nina stared at the tip of the blade aimed at her throat, beads of liquid dripping from the tip like a rabid dog salivating freakishly. The coven, still helpless and pinned to the walls and ceiling, seemed to lose more hope with every passing minute. Even Leo, who had the strongest and most mysterious powers of them all, was helpless. Nina touched her middle finger to her thumb on both hands. She didn't have enough time to slowly dip herself into the state where she could have influence over Merlot, so she performed the one single trick that she had learned but never practiced, one that would allow her to activate her influence immediately. *There is still hope,* she thought.

Merlot cocked her head to the side as if a mosquito had been buzzing in her ear. "Don't you try that shit with me," she said as she drew the blade closer to Nina's throat. Merlot took a ponderous breath and examined the scents of Nina's essence. "You still smell the same after all these years. Weak." Merlot shuffled backward, keeping the blade's edge right under Nina's chin. "What am I doing, you asked? You threatened me…you threatened my coven. You're an obstacle and I'm a vindictive little bitch, you should know that. No more rules. No more Advisory. No more pushback or roadblocks from authority. What am I doing?" Merlot's eyes darted to the members of the coven and then looked straight back at Nina. "I'm liberating you."

Merlot dug her hand into her coat pocket and pulled out a fistful of powder. In a single burst of air, she blew the powder into Nina's face and backed away. Nina coughed and choked on the silvery powder billowing through the air. She heaved and doubled over, wobbling back and forth until she gained control of her breathing.

Merlot turned around to grab the orb from the floor and took a final look at the coven suspended across the room. A few moments later she returned her attention to Nina, who was wiping the water from underneath her eyes. Nina had seen this moment coming, not specifically, but energetically. She had known it was approaching and that there wasn't a way to stop it. Perhaps there could have been a way to delay it, but it would only be that—delaying the inevitable. Only the coven wouldn't see it that way. Nina could have done many things differently, but the outcome would still eventually be the same, she just knew it. It was the reason why she had made out the will and delivered it to her attorney. In the unlikely chance that she could have avoided this outcome, she wouldn't have done anything differently. She just hadn't expected it to happen so soon; that was the only thing she hadn't seen or felt.

Nina's eyelids fell heavy as she accepted what was coming. She wasn't afraid of death, but she was afraid of the pain, and she didn't know how much of it there would be or how long it would last. It was completely out of her control, and there was nothing left to do but wait and suffer the impending doom that had been growing over the last few weeks. Then she heard it, a subtle change in her heart's rhythm, followed by a tight, stinging pain in the center of her chest. Her heart fought against the curse, but couldn't evade its power.

Lub dup…lu…du…lubduplubdup…l…dup…

Nina's heart beat faster, then slower and skipped a beat. She reached up and grabbed her chest, her fingers clawing through her sweater. She could hear a horrible gushing noise coming from inside her chest. Nina looked at her coven one final time, her eyes wet and apologetic. Then a quick vibration like the buzzing of a jackhammer pounded inside her, and she fell to her knees and toppled over to the floor. There was no blood, but there was pain. Physical pain, yes, excruciating even, but the emotional pain of being unable to protect the coven hurt even more. She just knew with every fiber of her being that the coven would succeed, but she wouldn't be there for it. She couldn't help or guide them, or be someone to blame. She was gone.

Merlot tasted the tip of her nail, cocked her head and smiled like an artist appreciating a finished sculpture that had taken years to finish. Her skewed sense of justice was so cold that it could have made the winter envious. Merlot didn't even bother looking at the coven as she pulled out a small bottle from her other pocket. She uncorked it, poured the clear potion over her face and dissolved away. The stench of mushrooms and rotten milk was all that remained.

As soon as Merlot had completely disappeared, the coven peeled from the walls and the ceiling and landed on the floor.

CHAPTER 5

By the time everyone had recovered from their fall, Avery was already at Nina's side, trying to heal her. She placed her hands over Nina's chest and sent all of her healing intentions out through her fingertips. Her palms pressed firmly against Nina's skin, her eyes determined and rippled in red. Bisa jumped to her feet and scurried over to help Avery, whipping off her malachite necklace and slapping it against Nina's sternum. Bisa kneeled beside Nina, one hand on Nina's head, the other clasping Nina's lifeless hands tightly.

"No, no, no, no…" Bisa repeated in unsettling murmurs.

Mitch sat up and watched from afar as Leo and Ollie hovered over Nina.

"Avery, please," Bisa said softly as she closed her eyes and hoped harder than she ever had in her life.

Avery scrambled across Nina's body and repositioned herself at Nina's chest. Her heart thumping in her chest, her face stoic and white. A chain of tears fell out of her eyes as if they had been pushed. Avery let out a sigh and struggled with the looming truth that she might not be able to heal Nina, no matter how hard she tried or what she did. She suddenly felt like a rookie nurse who had been lucky enough to never lose a patient—until now.

"Mitch," Avery said with remarkable composure, "I need your help."

Mitch stood up and stared at Nina's open eyes as if they were ghosts. He had never seen something so empty before, especially something that had once held such abundance.

Avery looked up at him. "Mitch!"

But he couldn't move. He was frozen. A streak of memories flashed before his eyes as he tried to take a step forward. In a second or two, a horrible sense of fear filled his heart, intruded upon his mind and dominated his body. As he stared at Nina, he was immediately transported back to the inside of the Plexiglas box at Edie's church.

"Mitch!" Avery screamed as she moved her hands to Nina's temples.

Mitch panicked, and his eyes flooded with the pain of his past. What was even worse was that in the matter of a moment, he was right back in that box. His skin felt as cold as the winter air outside as the rhythm of his breath rose and fell. Mitch's lip began to quiver, and he brought his hands to his chest, where his fingers tightened into shaking fists. Then the guilt set in. *This is my fault…this is all my fault. I didn't cast the protection spells like she asked me to.* For what felt like hours, he was lost in a spreading pool of hopelessness and danger that swallowed him whole.

Ollie ran over and wrapped his arm around Mitch and drew him close as if he were a warm blanket. Mitch dove into Ollie's chest as his knees gave out under his weight. Ollie twisted his body to catch him, and they collapsed to the floor, where Mitch wailed until his breath became raspy wheezes.

Avery took notice of the situation and returned her attention to Nina. She could feel the healing energy in her hands, but it wasn't working, Nina wasn't returning. Leo kneeled down, and Bisa reached out to grab hold of his hand. Both Bisa and Leo grabbed hold of Avery and formed a closed circuit of energy in a final attempt to save Nina's life.

Eventually, Leo loosened his grip and said, "She's gone, Avery." It was then that Avery let out a ghastly cry. She drew her hands back and covered her eyes. Ollie escorted Mitch to his room and closed the door behind them.

Avery, Bisa and Leo spent the next thirty minutes deciding what to do about Nina's body. Leo, being the most familiar with death, was the most composed. They made the unanimous decision to call the police after they agreed on what story to tell. There wasn't much of a story: Nina had essentially just dropped dead in front of their eyes without any warning, and that was essentially the tale they would tell, without any of the particulars.

The authorities and the paramedics arrived a little more than twenty minutes after Leo made the phone call. It wasn't his biggest thrill to see the police again, especially when they were standing in his home. There was a level of uneasiness that he couldn't quite shake but was skilled enough to hide. The police questioned everyone while the paramedics pronounced Nina dead. The coroner and her team secured Nina for transport. Bisa watched the team carry out their tasks—business as usual. Another body, another trip in the ambulance, another mundane task to finish off the shift. *Numb*, she thought, *desensitized— immune. How strange it must be to be so removed from death, so unprovoked by loss because it's part of your job*. For a brief moment, she even felt envious of them; they were lucky enough to have been spared the emotional and mental anguish that accompanied loss. *Perhaps it's different when it's someone they care for*, she pondered. It was a question she would never know the answer to.

Although there was little need for magical influence over the police, Bisa lightly shifted their questioning just enough to deter them from any unnecessary procedures or questioning, but not enough to impede their protocol. The whole ordeal was wrapped up faster than normal because of Bisa's forced expediting.

When the door finally closed behind the authorities and the house was theirs again, the atmosphere was eerie and chilling. It wasn't from the sweeping gusts of cold air that rushed in through the front door; there was an emptiness, and along with it the gaping wound that a loss leaves behind. The sudden devastation of a life lost brought a lot to the surface for Avery. She didn't really understand how she was feeling or why, and couldn't for the life of her determine why she was suddenly so concerned with what they were going to do for dinner and who was going to cook. After pacing through the house she found herself standing in the kitchen with the lights off, wondering how she'd even gotten there.

Bisa called Rosemary and told her what had happened. She spoke with her for an hour and gave her all the information she needed. It would be a few days before they would be able to determine the cause of death, a superfluous detail that didn't change anything but what Nina's death looked like on paper. She had been murdered, no question about it; it was the biggest murder that never was, according to the coven. Rosemary asked to be kept informed until she was able to get there in a couple of days.

"In the meantime, love—please take care of yourselves," Rosemary instructed Bisa over the phone. "Order dinner. No one needs to worry about feeding themselves at a time like this."

"I'm not thinking about food right now, Rosemary," Bisa said through clenched teeth.

"I imagine you're thinking about many things. Being a Primordial doesn't mean I don't know what you're thinking, Bisa. I can hear it in your voice, and if I were there, I'd be able to smell it on you."

"She's taken everything. She will continue to take everything and destroy everything until there's nothing left," Bisa said before she took a breath to calm herself. "We have to do something."

"We will act accordingly to ensure the safety of—"

"No. She needs to be stopped!" Bisa snapped. "Why didn't she kill us too? Don't you think she might come back and do just that?"

"Acting on impulse is only going to get more people killed. We will address this, and we will be smart, and we will do this together."

"Do you really think that's what Nina would do? She wouldn't have done that. The last time Merlot threatened us, Nina took it upon herself to head straight over to her coven and stand up for us."

"Bisa—that's different," Rosemary said politely.

"How is that different?"

"Listen. I want you to listen very carefully. I understand how you must be feeling, I do. We cannot act out irrationally. We have to be smart. We have no idea where Merlot is, what she is doing, who she has under her command or what kind of power she's tapped into."

"If we can't figure out any of that, then what is the goddamn point of witchcraft?"

"Bisa!" Rosemary shouted. "This is not your decision right now. You are not prepared for this. Your coven is not on a mission for revenge. Not with emotions running so high, and certainly not when one of your bloody witches happens to be an amateur Corporeal with powers that are completely unpredictable and unreliable at best. We will fix this."

Most of Rosemary's words would have fallen on deaf ears had Bisa not picked up on a key phrase. *Your coven*. Was the coven hers now? Was she going to be in charge? Was Bisa the most responsible, the most qualified and the strongest leader? At that moment, she didn't feel like she fit the role. However, there was enough confidence in her spirit that she finally allowed herself to be soothed by Rosemary's words.

"I will be there in three days," Rosemary said. "We can talk more about this, and I promise you, love, we will figure out a bloody plan."

On the third floor of the house, Mitch's anxiety had subsided because of Ollie's tenderness and understanding. Mitch's room was filled with windows, but right now all the curtains were closed and only a single lamp was on in the corner. Tubs of colored yarn lined the walls, crochet hooks were spread across the desk, an unfinished scarf spilled over the edge of the bed.

Mitch was propped up in a pile of pillows on the bed, his knees bent. Ollie sat beside him, watching Mitch angrily pick at the skin around his left thumb in a compulsive fashion. It reminded Ollie of Leo's nail-biting tic, but this was something new, something that wasn't a part of his natural personality; it was something he had developed.

Pick...pick...pick...

Mitch's lap was covered in tiny flecks of skin he'd torn free from his blameless thumb. Ollie looked closer at Mitch's thumb, now raw and red and mostly made up of scar tissue rather than skin.

"Mitch, you're gonna make it bleed."

Mitch stopped picking and hid his damaged thumb under his fingers. There were signs on his index and middle fingers that his compulsion was beginning to spread.

"I can't help it," Mitch said. He felt exhausted, as if he hadn't slept in weeks—which had some truth to it. Between the plague of worrisome thoughts that filled his head and the unfilled Etsy orders, he was a little behind on sleep.

Ollie placed a hand on Mitch's knee to soothe him; Mitch recoiled slightly before allowing Ollie's hand to rest there. "Do you feel like talking about what happened earlier?"

"Nina's dead," Mitch said, *and it's all my fault.* "What more is there to talk about?"

"I mean what happened after that—with you."

Mitch looked up from his scabby thumb as if Ollie had insulted him. After a moment, he acknowledged there was no offense to be taken. He felt his face drain of aggression and begin to flush with humility. "I don't…I'm not sure what happened…It just happened…"

"Does that happen a lot?" Ollie asked.

Mitch hesitated and then nodded.

"I'm sorry that happened," Ollie said, honey sweet.

Mitch fought back a tremor inside his head, a flashback of his suffering that never fully seemed to heal. He felt guilty for feeling so traumatized by it, like it wasn't justified for him to be so sensitive, so affected. His hands fell clammy, and a shiver of gooseflesh rippled down his arms as he choked back the panic attack like a drunk would suppress vomit after a night of heavy drinking. "I don't really…wanna talk about it—right now."

The wind picked up outside, and the closed curtains billowed as if they were haunted. Ollie heard the wind howling and took that as a cue from the spirit world—maybe even Nina—not to press the subject any further. He looked around the room, straining his eyes to their very limits of vision, hoping—no, expecting—to see a vision of Nina. He hadn't seen her, but he felt her.

CHAPTER 6

Bisa woke up very early a few days later. Well, she didn't so much wake up early as she failed to sleep. There wasn't much sleep to be had by anyone in the coven, but Nina's death had hit Bisa harder than she would have guessed. She rose with the sun, its amber light bouncing off the fresh, undisturbed snow and glimmering like stars against a galaxy of white. Bisa stood at her bedroom window, between the glass and the sheer curtain, staring at the rising sun. There was a pervasive grayness in her heart, one that even the cleansing rays of the morning light couldn't wash away. She existed somewhere between numb and shattered, a place where no one feels alive, a place that only ghosts fully comprehend. Only she was breathing and very much still alive, if only in the biological sense.

She took advantage of the rest of the house being asleep and spent thirty minutes in meditation. Even her meditation practice seemed to have plateaued. She let out a sigh, opened her eyes and rose to her feet. Bisa opened her bedroom door and stepped out into the hallway, careful to make as little noise as possible. She was fully dressed and hadn't even a brush of makeup on. She tiptoed up the stairs and found herself at Nina's door. An eerie tawny light rimmed the gap between the door and the floor. Bisa lifted her hand to the silver door handle and her palm froze an inch above it, fingers jittering like the tail of a rattle-snake. An unexpected diffidence ran through her body. She balled her fingers into a fist and gently knocked on the door, even though there was no need. They had kept Nina's bedroom shut, and they wanted to wait until Rosemary arrived before they proceeded inside. But Bisa needed time alone with the room.

Bisa waited a moment, as if expecting there to be a chance that someone might answer. When there was nothing but silence on the other side, she twisted the handle and opened the door all the way with a single push.

The room had life; she could feel it. There was the type of energy of a day interrupted, a schedule in play, a night that hadn't finished yet. A spread of olive-wood runes lay upon the dresser along with a half-empty glass of water. Nina was organized and clean, even when she wasn't, so of course her bed was made and all the clothes in the basket beside it were folded. Bisa was almost disappointed at the fact that Nina was so clean, for the room smelled exactly like that—clean and nothing more, without a single scent that reminded her of Nina. She walked farther into the room and stood next to the bed, where she noticed a sizable box on the nightstand—more of tool kit, really. A silver chain dangled from the opening and had coiled itself into a pile on the nightstand's surface. Bisa reached down and lifted the lid. It was a jewelry-making kit. Inside were all the usual things: hand files, various types and sizes of pliers, mallets, a ball-peen hammer, a caliper gauge, an assortment of sanding papers, clamps and saw blades. Bisa removed the top tray and followed the silver chain inside the box to a newly made amethyst pendant necklace. Instead of guessing about its origin or purpose, Bisa retrieved the pendant from the box and held it between her fingers. She felt a pulse, as if the pendant had its own heartbeat, and then a series of images passed through her mind like a deck of shuffled cards. As close as Bisa had become to Nina, she hadn't known about her recent passion for jewelry making. She saw the art shop in Denver where she bought the kit. She saw her hand selecting the crystal from a bin at an indoor art market. She saw her working through her novice mistakes, endless tries and small successes as Nina taught herself the entire process. She saw the morning she began the necklace, a little past ten thirty, just after a late breakfast, and then she felt it. Nina had made it for Bisa but had never had the chance to give it to her.

Bisa hadn't felt very connected to her powers in the last few days, but now it was streaming through her like a raging flood of electricity. As the surge of information paired with emotion, it began to take a toll on her. Bisa closed her eyes and imagined turning a dial to lessen the intensity of her psychic circuit. She slipped the pendant into her pocket and continued to browse the room. A small macrame decoration Bisa had made hung on the wall near the closet door, which was ajar. She pulled the door open and Nina's robe billowed out, attached to the hook on the inside of the door. Bisa's watery eyes blinked a few times as she caught the scent of Nina that she had so hoped to find. She caressed the robe's soft silk sleeves

(*don't be sad*)

with the tips of her fingers. She brought her nose to the collar

(*please, don't be sad...death isn't the end, Bisa*)

and inhaled more than the familiar smell of a dear friend. With it she captured the memory of Nina's spirit, something she would remember long after the scent had faded from the fabric, when pieces of the pain weren't so tender and all that was left was a memory and the lessons Nina had taught her.

Bisa had known loss—so much loss, so much pain—but the small pendant in her pocket would remind her of all that there was to live for.

A few hours later, Rosemary and Per were on their way to the house after meeting with Nina's attorney in Golden. Rosemary had been designated as Nina's executor and handled everything so the coven didn't have to. When they arrived, Rosemary entered without invitation—not out of rudeness, but out of concern for the coven. A house key in her right hand, a milk chocolate Hobnobs in her left. A plain digestive biscuit simply would not do, considering all that had happened. Rosemary was feeling the stress, and every article she had ever forced herself to believe explained that chocolate helped with easing stress. Granted, they talked about the darker, unsweetened chocolate, not the sugar-laden commercial alternatives, but that wasn't the point. When she saw Bisa upon coming up the stairs, she choked the end of her biscuit down. She could see and feel the pain in Bisa's heart, regardless of how well she was hiding it.

"Bisa, dear, how are you feeling?" Rosemary asked as she walked toward Bisa with her arms held out before her.

Bisa shrugged, gave a feeble smile and closed her eyes. There was really nothing she could say.

"I know that's a stupid question, considering everything, and I don't expect you to have anything to say or anything good to say. You don't have to answer," Rosemary said.

Bisa gave Rosemary a cold and distant hug. "I'm okay. You know…I'm okay."

What an awful year this coven has had, Rosemary thought as she caressed Bisa's shoulder. "I know it doesn't mean much, but I am sorry this happened," she said. "You're very strong, Bisa."

"So what did the attorney say? What happens now?" Bisa said as she backed away a few paces.

Rosemary turned to Per. "Per, dear, would you gather up the rest of the coven? Bring them into the living room. Let them know this is more than just information. We're paying respects to Nina as well."

Per nodded and walked off.

"Respects? What about the funeral? We're not having a service for her?" Bisa asked.

"Of course we are—other people in her life are going to want to attend as well, but we certainly can't be as frank as we'd like during *that* service. This is…for us," Rosemary said. She dusted the crumbs off her fingers and then cleared her throat. "Let's pop into the sunroom for a moment." She lowered her voice. "I'd like to talk to you about Nina's will."

They made their way to the sunroom as Per kept the rest of the coven occupied upstairs with his breakdown of *Game of Thrones*, now that he had finished the series, including his psychological assessment of Daenerys and an alternative ending of his own design, even though he loved the one HBO ran with.

Bisa sat opposite Rosemary on the fog-colored sectional and waited in anticipation.

Rosemary looked around the room for a moment and admired the décor. "I've always loved this room," she said as she gazed over the open bookcase with a collection of hourglasses in various sizes, shapes and colors of sand. She straightened the small vase of fresh silver dollar eucalyptus and then ran her hand over the linen fabric of the sofa. "All those hourglasses are mine. Well, they belong to my family, actually. I don't have the space for all of them, so I chose to keep them here. Some are very old. All antiques, but some—"

"What was it you wanted to talk about?" Bisa interrupted.

Rosemary nodded. "Right. Well, I'll just get right down to it, then." She let out a breath as she sat up in her seat as if about to give a lecture to a class. "I think Nina knew this was going to happen. I don't know if we will ever know that for certain, but she certainly planned ahead."

"Meaning what?" Bisa asked.

"Nina paid for half a million in life insurance money only a few weeks ago. She arranged a will, named me the executor and has left everything to you."

Bisa blinked and huffed in surprise. "Everything? She left me half a million dollars?"

Rosemary's head teetered back and forth. "Well, technically she left you a hundred thousand dollars. Each member of the coven gets the same amount. But she left everything else to you. All her belongings, her car, and this house, apparently."

"Why would she do that? That doesn't make any sense! Are you sure?" Bisa tried to control her thoughts, but her tongue acted on its own and began speaking faster than she could think.

"The house isn't exactly hers to give. Nina clearly forgot that any house given to a Proctor and their coven technically belongs to the Keeper of Books and Assets."

"Which is you now," Bisa said.

"Correct," Rosemary said. "And as the righteous owner of this house, I am going to give it to you. I've already taken care of all the necessary paperwork, and all you need to do is make an appointment with the attorney and fill out some forms, and everything will be under your name."

"What am I going to do with a house?"

Rosemary held her tongue for a moment as she thought about Bisa's question. "Do you not want it? Nina wanted you to have it."

"But why?"

"You don't have to keep it forever, and although I truly don't know what will come of this house if it ends up in your hands, we have plenty of other homes and investment properties across the country, so I'm not too concerned. Frankly, I think it suits you, this house."

Bisa had often thought that a house was something she would never actually own, an elusive and somewhat superfluous luxury that never really felt like it was in her life plan. She thought back to her family's quaint home in Nigeria, where things were functional and minimalistic. That was all she knew and could relate to. The series of residences she had held once she'd arrived in the United States never felt like *home*. Bisa could neither smile nor frown. She was utterly stunned.

Then, a voice from the top of the stairs. "Rosemary?" Per called out. "We're ready."

CHAPTER 7

They sat together in the living room as the bright winter sunlight filled the room and splashed across their laps. Per gathered every large pillar candle and candelabra from the house and arranged them in a cozy fashion around their seats. The flames flickered, yet the air was still. Per had adjusted all the chairs so they formed a circle, as if they were preparing for another magical discussion. Only this was different. Nina was no longer physically present, but her spirit was.

She had asked that before any words were spoken, Aphex Twin's "Avril 14th" be played. Ollie rose from his seat, walked over to the piano and began to play it with as much passion as if Nina were there (she was) watching him. As Ollie continued to play, Rosemary walked around the circle, stopping briefly before each member and anointing their finger with a smudge of her Harmonious Passing Oil* that she had made a couple of days earlier. Notes of lavender, clary sage, lemongrass, marjoram, oregano, rose hips, verbena and rosemary filled their noses. Leo rubbed the tiny bits of poppy and pomegranate seed from within the oil between his fingers.

When the song finished, Rosemary quietly walked over to a small side table and placed a large ceramic bowl on top. She retrieved a silver candle from her pocket, waved her hand across the bottom and melted the wax with the tiny flame in her palm. She stuck the candle into the bowl, fixing it to the bottom, and blew on the wax to cool and seal it in place. Into the bowl, she poured Tree of Life Essence* that she had made from a single leaf from the tree of life in New Orleans, and filled it a half inch up the candle. The members of the coven rose from their seats and simultaneously anointed the candle with the oil from their finger, beginning at the top and ending near the middle. Bisa's wounds ripped wide open as her finger returned to her side. She remembered her parents, and it was so much grief all over again, until she took a deep breath and choked back her emotions.

Ollie, Leo, Mitch, Bisa and Avery joined hands around the candle, and within a few moments the wick caught fire. No one was truly certain who did it—if it was Avery or Mitch or even Rosemary, for that matter—but no one really cared. They remained joined for a minute before they loosened their grip and eventually returned to their seats. Rosemary smoothed her black cashmere dress along her thighs and adjusted her footing before she lifted her chin up high.

"I knew Nina for many years. I first met her in New York, where she said she would always live. I remember asking her what she loved about New York because she was so kind, so compassionate, so uncharacteristic of what people have come to assume New Yorkers are like. She was tastefully unaware of how special a soul she was. She told me she loved the energy there.

"Her modesty was one of her most charming attributes, but also one of her biggest challenges. When she first learned of her powers, she struggled at first, as many of you have. She struggled with accepting them, using them, controlling them and even believing in them. Nina overcame every challenge and exceeded every expectation I had of her. When she became Proctor to your coven, she had a great deal of uncertainty about whether she could lead all of you. But not just lead—care for. This is a coven with a heavy heart today. It saddens me to stand here and mourn Nina's passing as I see what I'm seeing now, the fruits of her compassion in each and every one of you. She has planted a seed inside of you, and that seed has grown. And whenever I look at any of you, I see a little piece of her. I had the pleasure of knowing Nina, but the world has the pleasure of having her live on through all of you." Rosemary cleared her throat. Her mind was as sharp as it had ever been, but her heart was in shambles.

Bisa ran her fingernail up the length of her forearm, snagging the threads of her sweater, wet from the few tears that escaped. "I'd like to say something," she said as she ran her finger underneath her eye. She winced as she stood, clenching her teeth for a moment before composing herself. "When we first arrived, Nina ran us through what she called *celebrations*. I would really like it if we could all say something to celebrate Nina."

Avery began, and talked of how she had learned about balance and harmony from Nina. Ollie praised Nina's uncanny ability to discover and nurture one's individual gifts, beyond the skills of their powers.

Giving thanks and celebrating Nina's life wasn't exactly a radical idea for Leo, but it was still difficult for him to express himself, no matter what it was about. He babbled quickly about Nina's ability to find common ground, but his celebration began to lose momentum when he realized how much he had to be thankful for. Nina had taught him so much, and more important, she had trusted him—believed in him, even when he didn't believe in himself. His voice trembled as he realized all the things he'd done that Nina now knew about—and worse, that Bisa knew about.

"She wanted me to be the best version of myself…because she knew that I could be if I tried." *Only I don't really think I am. I don't know if I ever will be,* he almost said aloud, but it would cause trouble, and he was already in far too much of that. His guilt hurt a thousand times worse than heartache and would have to remain a secret, if that was even an option anymore.

Mitch, still attacking his already wildly scabbed thumb, sodden with fresh blood from all the picking, lifted his head to speak. He doubted he would say something meaningful or heartfelt, or above all—authentic. Mitch looked around the faces staring back at him. All of them were void of judgment and expectations, and for that, he was thankful.

"Nina was a really good leader," Mitch said, unimpressed with his opening. He squeezed and squashed his thumb, trying to encourage the bleeding to stop. "She was a visionary, and I know she sacrificed a great deal for all of us. She didn't care about being in charge. She didn't care about our powers as witches, either, to be honest. Nina led by example, proving that there is power in having compassion. She understood people's fragility. I guess I, like, really think her love language was gifts, because her gift was to give and she loved to be of service, and we all benefited from that. And it came from a really good place."

Mitch was wildly ill-equipped to be giving any sort of emotional speech, but he found the strength to do it, and that surely came from his love and appreciation and respect for Nina. "She was a Transcendent witch, and we all know that with that comes a sort of, like, emotional intelligence that is just a little stronger than other witches'. A knowing or whatever. But that wasn't what made her such a great teacher—a great person, really. She knew a lot of things, and if I were to analyze it, I guess

I'd say that magic can give us knowing, but true compassion…well, that originates from somewhere else. Somewhere magic doesn't touch."

After a few minutes of silence, Bisa said, "I wrote a poem that I'd like to share. I've been writing a lot lately, and the morning after Nina passed, I wrote this." She pulled a piece of paper from her pocket.

We are one,

Ever connected in the multiplicity

of the world's idiosyncrasies.

I now appreciate the sun, moon, earth and all the stars.

You taught us unity, strength and how to extract wisdom from spiritual reservoirs.

Thank you, a hundred-fold, for all that I've learned.

I promise to live boldly and leave no stone unturned.

I hope, in the end, I will make you proud.

I will look for you in every river, sunset and silver-lined rain cloud.

Bisa's lip trembled as she folded the paper back up and tucked it away in her pocket. For a moment, she felt like she was all alone, but a rush of energy filled her, and she instantly knew she was far from alone.

With the celebrations finished and the candle lit, they all let out a breath of relief. The emotional and mental anguish was exhausting, and of course, there would be more. There was still a real service to be held, with real people, ordinary people, ones who knew Nina in ways they never would. Not that any of them wanted to.

Per and Rosemary hung around for dinner, waiting patiently in the living room and watching Nina's gratitude candle burn.

Ollie, Avery, Bisa and Leo were in the kitchen preparing dinner—bucatini all'amatriciana, in honor of Nina. Mitch was in his room taking a nap—or trying to, at least. His anxiety kept him from falling asleep quickly and made getting good rest impossible. Right before dinner he tended to his Etsy orders, packed a few that he had finished early (amazingly) and checked in with his Twitter community. It was so much easier than checking in with the coven.

When the scent of tomato sauce hit the living room, Per and Rosemary had just finished talking about Nina and the future of the coven. Rosemary mentioned that she had spoken to Bisa and wasn't sure how the conversation had gone. It was then that Leo entered the room with two glasses of full-bodied red wine, one in each hand.

"Dinner's about ready if y'all wanna grab a seat at the table," Leo said as he handed them each a glass and then lingered like a bellhop waiting for a tip.

Rosemary could tell there was something on his mind, a question. She flicked her head to Per, signaling for him to head to the dining room without her. Per took a sip of wine, and then another and another as he made his way toward the bathroom to wash his hands.

"Something on your mind, Leo?" Rosemary asked. She took a sip of wine, rolled it around her tongue and moaned in surprise at its deliciousness.

"Huh? No…" Leo said in the most unconvincing way, his eyes wide and inquisitive.

"Oh, come now. I'm old enough to know when someone has something to say."

"All right, fuck it. I wanted to ask you about the Union of the Divine Dualities," Leo said. His thoughts immediately returned to Nina's conversation on the topic, and he tried to think of what he didn't understand or what he wanted to know specifically.

Rosemary leaned her head back and nodded slowly, although she was thinking quickly. She looked at her watch, then toward the dining room, and then she held out her hand and invited Leo to sit for a moment.

Leo sat down, rubbed his hands together to erase the dried bits of tomato sauce, and waited.

"Did she tell you what it was for, how the ritual goes?" Rosemary asked, wiping a droplet of wine from the rim of the glass.

"Yeah," Leo answered.

"So, what is it that you're wondering about?"

"Could she have misheard something? She mentioned something about a fairy. And, I mean, if you had told me something like that a couple of years ago, I would've said you were out of your damn mind, but…I mean, I'm clearly in a very different world now. But fairies? Even if they were a thing, she made it seem like they're extinct. Is that true? I mean, who gave this prophecy? Are they even legit?"

"Her name is Volustina."

"Is or was?" Leo asked.

Rosemary ignored the question. "Her prophecies were never wrong."

"So, she's alive? Or some other fairy is out there…and alive?" Leo pressed.

"To be fully honest, Leo, Per is truly the expert on all things fairy. It's part of his heritage, and he knows way more about it than I do."

Leo nodded and then stood up, excited in the way that only Leo would be at the fact that he was getting closer to something he wanted. "Cool, I'll ask Per."

Rosemary waved her hand. "Wait a minute, just, hang on."

Leo didn't move except to tap his fingers against his leg, again and again and again. His sudden rush of enthusiasm was so strong that he almost felt out of control like he used to, like those times when he'd murdered people without even a second thought. It felt like a new kind of addiction, one that gave him the jitters all the same. For half a heartbeat he pondered why he was becoming obsessed with the ritual, and the moment passed. But then he heard Per's voice in the kitchen, reenacting a scene from *Game of Thrones* at the top of his lungs, and the fixation returned.

"This is something that you are all supposed to do together," Rosemary said. "That really is what the prophecy said. It was divined that this particular coven, that you're a part of, would be the group that would discover the rafkolite." She stood and sipped her wine. "Together," she repeated.

For a hot second, Leo imagined that he had already found the rafkolite, and had been able to do it without anyone else in the coven. His eyes drifted to the empty space around Rosemary's head as he thought—no, believed—that he could do it on his own. After all, why couldn't he? Why shouldn't he? He needed it most, he believed.

"Smells like dinner is finally ready! Come, let's eat. We can talk about this later on," Rosemary said.

Leo hesitated, as if he were going to resist. Rosemary snapped her fingers twice and pointed toward the dining room before Leo turned and headed in that direction. She watched him dissolve around the corner. Her concern bubbled up in his place and festered until there was nothing but distrust and alarm.

CHAPTER 8

After dinner, Rosemary and Per enjoyed a drink near the selenite fireplace. The roaring flames sounded like a raging waterfall, and it was almost loud enough to drown out Rosemary's thoughts.

"Something's wrong," Per said as he studied Rosemary's energy.

"Hmm?" Rosemary hummed innocently. "Oh, I'm just running over some details in my head."

"Care to share?"

"I hate to say it, but I don't fully trust Leo. Something just feels off. I don't know if it's him being a Corporeal or something else. Bloody hell, being a Corporeal is enough to worry about. There's so much we don't know. It's such great, unpredictable power. I don't know if he's the right vessel for it. I know we have no control over that. It's a bit like being left- or right-handed, or hetero- or homosexual."

There had been so much chaos in such a short time, and it was because of Nina that the coven had managed to stay on course. The wind picked up outside and whistled. It reminded Rosemary of the dream she had had the night before, in which she had heard Nina's final breath screech like the winter wind. Was it a message? Was is a warning? Rosemary was never the best at dream analysis, but she knew it had to mean something.

"I have a feeling he's going to ask you some questions," Rosemary said, running her fingers along the rim of her glass, almost making a crystalline song.

"Me? What about?" Per asked. He had information, sure. It was part of his job as a member of the Advisory. But what could Leo want to know that he alone could tell him?

"He's going to ask you about Volustina and the fairies. And I want you to answer him."

Per's eyes brightened, and he nearly choked on his drink from excitement. He loved talking about the fairies. He didn't get to do it very often, and it was a delightful subject for him. "I didn't expect that. I'd be happy to give him a little fairy lesson. They could probably benefit from that, I would imagine."

"If anything seems *off*, please tell me," Rosemary said as she stood up, waved her hand at the roaring fire and extinguished it. She walked away as if she had been sitting there alone the entire time.

Per huffed and rolled his eyes, and took a final look at the smoking pile of burnt wood. "Well, *I* wasn't done enjoying the fire," he said under his breath.

Avery paid Bisa a visit in her room for about an hour that evening after dinner. The conversation moved through three topics: Nina's death, Bisa's state of mind and the coven's goals. Naturally, Bisa was upset and bursting with grief, so much that she vowed to murder Merlot without question if she ever saw her again. It was a state of mind that surprised even Bisa. It felt like someone else, someone who was racked with heartache and exhausted from trying to make sense of it all. She kept it to herself that even she hadn't been aware of how much of an effect Nina had had on her. She hadn't had the chance to say goodbye to her parents, and she couldn't help Nina, and it only left her addled and filled with putrid anger. In a way it made her feel responsible for Nina's death, like she had somehow failed her.

"You don't really believe any of that, do you?" Avery asked sincerely.

But she did, even if it was only the grief talking.

(there was nothing you could've done)

"It can't just…We can't." Bisa struggled with her words as if her tongue had forgotten what language she spoke. "We have the ability to do something about this. I don't trust that this is over. Why did she kill Nina and not the rest of us?"

"Their relationship was complicated. That was some kind of personal vendetta. I don't think she thinks of us as a threat to her plans, whatever they are," Avery suggested.

"Well, she should. The last thing she should be doing is underestimating me," Bisa said, noticing she had mentioned only herself, not the coven.

(this is not the answer)

"I don't care," Bisa said aloud. Avery studied her face, perplexed.

"Will you please do me one favor?" Avery asked, grabbing hold of Bisa's hands in her own. "Before you do anything, will you just come to me first and at least let me know? Please."

Bisa had many talents, and was becoming a very gifted psychic witch with strong powers of influence, but using them on a dear friend was not a box she wanted to tick. "Fine."

Mitch stood in the bathroom, staring at himself in a tiny handheld mirror. He wasn't sure how long he had been studying the emptiness behind his eyes, but at some point, the mirror slipped from his hands and shattered on the white tiled floor.

CRASH!

Shards of mirror spilled out across the floor like fireworks made of glass. Again, memories of his abduction and torture flashed before his eyes. They were gone faster than he could blink, but the suffering remained. His heart raced, and his lungs suddenly forgot how to take in air. Mitch struggled to find his footing and fell against the nearest wall, letting his head slam against it. His breathing became more erratic as he tried to force some sort of control over his body. But he couldn't, not this time. For a second, he forgot that he was a witch, that he was in a coven, and could shout for help. When he thought about screaming out in terror, he knew he would be answered. But he couldn't even do that; his body, his mind, his spirit were all trapped.

Ollie opened the door and rushed inside, stopping in his tracks when he saw Mitch trembling against the wall, wheezing uncontrollably, his hands clawing the tiles on the floor as if he were trying to remove the white from the porcelain. Ollie pushed the door closed and ran toward Mitch. He kneeled down beside him, minding the mosaic of shattered glass. He placed his hands on Mitch's shoulders, then ran a hand through his hair and across the back of his neck, salty with cold sweat.

"Hey, Mitch! Hey…look at me," Ollie said in a soft, smooth tone, almost like a song.

Mitch's eyes closed, as if his body wanted him to see what he was trying so hard to forget. His feet began to slip out from underneath him and move toward the pile of glass. Ollie placed a hand on his feet, holding them in place for a moment and then releasing.

"Hey, Mitch, you're okay. You're okay," Ollie continued. "You're safe, you're at home, you're with me, you're with me." He lifted his hands from Mitch with every breath he took, until eventually he was no longer touching him. He waited for a few moments for Mitch to control his own breath.

"I'm sorry," Mitch said, his eyes wet.

"Sorry? For what?" Ollie asked.

"I feel like I'm crazy," Mitch said, and a couple of tears rolled out. He reached up to feel his heart with both hands to confirm that he was beginning to calm down.

"You're not crazy," Ollie said. He looked down at the mess on the floor and then back toward Mitch. "Cheap-ass mirror, huh?" he said with a smile.

Mitch cracked a grin, even though he didn't want to.

They rested in silence for a minute until Ollie rose to his feet and offered his hands out to Mitch. "Here, have a seat. Wait here."

He left the bathroom for a few minutes and returned with a few provisions. Ollie ran a hot bath and filled it with Epsom and Dead Sea salt, milk powder and baking soda. He opened the small bathroom cabinet and pulled out a tiny bowl and mixed coconut oil with ylang-ylang, lavender, tangerine, geranium and blood orange essential oils. He held the bowl in his right hand and let his left hover above it. His eyes closed, and he charged it with his intentions. When he felt it was ready, he sprinkled it into the bathwater. He grabbed a chunk of amethyst from the shelf and dropped it in next. He rolled up his sleeves and swirled the bathwater back and forth, chanting an inaudible incantation as the wave patterns rolled back and forth like the tide.

Next, he placed a chunk of valerian root, a chamomile flower and a couple of blue vervain seeds into a small pot of soil. Over it, he poured a few drops of a cocktail he made from a harmony elixir, Dark Moon Elixir* and malachite essence.

Ollie was running his fingers across the top of the soil when he heard Mitch sniff behind him. Ollie turned to look, his concentration undisturbed. He stared for a moment, his soil-tipped fingers still connected to the pot. Mitch looked up at him, sniffed and let out a deep sigh. Ollie smiled and returned his attention to the pot. He opened his palm and spread his fingers wide. He closed his eyes and prepared to work his magic. The words came drifting up from his unconscious mind and spilled out of his mouth.

"*Fructus crescere ad sanitatem,*" Ollie said as he connected with the higher consciousness. His fingers wiggled back and forth, as if trying to coax a sprout out of a seed. Again, he said, "*Fructus crescere ad sanitatem.*" When he opened his eyes, a small wisp of steam rose through the cracks of his hands. He pulled his hand back and watched the fingers of steam rise from under the soil. Then he saw it. A tiny dark green sprout poked and prodded its way through the top of the soil and uncoiled into the air. Slowly at first, and then it began to gain momentum. The stalk thickened into a stem, and leaves began to uncurl from the many tender branches that appeared. Once the plant had begun to reach full maturity, a modest twelve inches in height, a single, deep scarlet fruit emerged from the middle of a tiny white blossom. The fruit's skin was so shiny, it looked wet. Ollie plucked it from the plant and instantly the plant died, but the spherical fruit remained fresh.

"Here, chew this," Ollie said as he placed the fruit in Mitch's mouth.

Mitch looked stunned at first, but then delighted as the juicy flavors of the succulent fruit trickled over his tongue. Somewhere between the freshest summer tomato and the sweetest, ripest strawberry, with notes of vanilla and pink peppercorn.

Ollie lit a bundle of dried cedar and cleansed Mitch with the smoke, then lit a frankincense and myrrh resin incense and dimmed the lights. Mitch removed his clothes, unconcerned with being nude and unashamed of his vulnerability, as there was no judgment. Ollie helped Mitch into the bath, one leg at a time, and once he was fully submerged, Mitch closed his eyes.

It was dark. Then there was more darkness, and he fell into a deeper darkness. His eyelids trembled, and his lip quivered. He took a deep breath and then suddenly, the light returned, like the lights in a theater and a show. He opened his eyes and with that his pain rushed to the surface and spilled out into the water. He let out a soft cry, his chest flickering at the outburst as if he had the hiccups. Mitch leaned over toward Ollie, who had been kneeling next to the tub the entire time, and rested his head against Ollie's forehead.

(I told you you're a healer, Ollie)

Mitch cried once more, and then came a breath of relief as Ollie wrapped his arm around Mitch's wet shoulder and rocked him back toward the light.

CHAPTER 9

The next morning, Leo sat at the edge of his bed and outlined what he was going to ask Per. Nina's actual funeral service was two days away, so he wanted to get answers before Per wasn't readily accessible anymore. He was pacing back and forth in his room when he suddenly received a message from Spirit to open the window. It took him by surprise; he hadn't received a message like that in a while now. He obliged, and opened the window. The cool winter air rushed in, the kind of comfortable winter weather that required a light jacket but not long pants. He was listening to the birds sing their songs when a bird landed directly on his windowsill. Not just any bird, a magpie. He knew this magpie, and he recognized the gift in its beak: a thin, four-inch piece of copper wire. It had been so far in the back of his mind, he had nearly forgotten that he had cast the spell to obtain the metals needed for the Divine Dualities ritual. The magpie shook its wings, dropped the wire on the windowsill and flew off into the world, still blithely unaware of its servitude. He now had three of the seven metals. Things were falling into place, quite literally.

After a breakfast of lentils, sweet potatoes and fried eggs (Ollie insisted), Leo cornered Per at the coffeemaker and interrupted him in midpour.

"Hey, Per. Can I talk to you quick before you head out?" Leo asked.

"Sure, what's up?" Per asked as he swirled a teaspoon of cream into the dark depths of his coffee cup.

Leo said nothing, but his eyes swung over to the rest of the coven, hoping to signal to Per that he wanted a more private conversation.

"Show me to your *fika* room!" Per said.

"My what?"

"Never mind," Per said with a smile as he motioned for Leo to show him to another room. Per grabbed his piece of buttered toast with his other hand and followed Leo to the reading loft.

Leo sat in the large blue leather armchair and waited for Per to find a comfortable position in the other one. Patience wasn't something he was used to, and his eagerness was scratching at his throat, ready to unload questions. *Don't seem too eager,* Leo thought, missing Nina a little more than normal now that she wasn't there to keep him in line, which he had hated but also appreciated.

"So, fairies?" Leo said aloud.

"Ah!" Per said as he took a bite out of his excessively buttered and salted toast. "Is that what this is about?" Bits of crusty toast stuck to his bottom lip, and he chewed politely.

"Are there any alive somewhere? We need it as a coven if this prophecy is a thing."

"The short answer is yes, but it's tricky." Per's eyes lit up like an info-geek who is finally asked about their favorite subject that no one ever allows them to talk about for fear they will never stop. "Fairies and witches have a really entwined history. We used to work together quite a bit, both using our skills toward the greater good and trying to maintain balance. This happened all over the world. Stonehenge, for example. Stonehenge is actually a sacred space where fairy and witch magic are bound together to help retain and maintain an energetic balance, almost like how an air conditioner keeps a house cool."

Per sipped his coffee and watched Leo stare at him with tongue-tied excitement.

"Are they like us? Do they just…move around in covens or whatever? Do they have jobs or, *wings*? What about wings?" Leo slid forward on his seat like a child at the top of a snowy hill positioned in their favorite sled, poised for the ride.

"Wings? No. They are not like us, they are very different. They can exist—well, live—only where it is the purest on earth. A place that is essentially or nearly uninhabitable—that is where you'll find the entrance to their realm." Per took a sip of coffee and washed down the last bit of toast. "I hate that word…*realm*. It's so…" he scoffed, "so kingly. They don't care about those kinds of titles. No hierarchy—just fairies. If you're lucky, you might be able to spot them here in our environment when the veil between our two, worlds, for lack of a better term, is a little thin. To be honest, I'm not sure why or how that part works. Sometimes we can see them in our world and sometimes we can't."

"So where are these entrances?" Leo asked.

Per could already tell what Leo was thinking from the excited speed at which he delivered his words. "Entrances to their realm are limited: Angel Falls in Venezuela, the Plitvice waterfalls in Croatia, Tugela Falls in South Africa…" Per looked off into space as if mentally running down a list of locations, like he was being tested. "Nohkalikai Falls in India," he continued, "and the Bermuda Triangle." Per brushed a few toast crumbs off his lap and onto the floor, then looked up, slightly embarrassed at his slovenliness.

"Don't worry about it," Leo said as he waved at the crumbs. "So, we just have to find one of these places and just…what…go in? How does that work? I don't get it."

Per ignored him for a brief second and then said, "All of the entrances were sealed off when large masses of witches self-ishly started hunting down fairies for their life force during the Flaming Flood Era, when rafkolite became more commonly known. The only one that couldn't be sealed was the Bermuda Triangle; nature wouldn't allow it to be closed—something to do with the depth of the ocean and the direction of the tides."

Per continued to ramble on about the history of the Flaming Flood Era, at points even dramatizing the elements of the story for a more exciting delivery. It didn't work. The further Per dug into history, the more Leo tuned him out. Leo didn't care about history. He was tired of the past. He cared about the present, and even more importantly—the near future. Sometimes Per didn't know how to keep quiet, especially when given the chance to talk about fairies. He had grown up hearing about them, knowing about magic and being blessed by originating from two beautiful cultures, alike in rich history with families and witches who liked to share it.

Per continued with his glinty-eyed lesson on fairy history, his voice becoming scratchy and hoarse from all the chatting. "And then in 79 AD..."

Shut up, please...

"Things got really interesting around that time, on November second,..."

Dude, just stop talking...

"in 1773..."

Nina, if you can help me out here, I don't trust myself enough not to make him shut up...

A few more minutes went by, minutes that felt like hours, and Leo was on the verge of murder or dying of boredom, he didn't know which.

"Jasper..."

Leo snapped back into the conversation. "What?"

"What, what?" Per said, kind of amazed at how long he had been talking.

"Who? Jasper? Is that what you said?" Leo asked. He knew that name.

"Yeah," Per responded casually. "It's rumored that he has sort of taken residence in the fairy realm." Per rolled his eyes again. "I need to stop using that word. In Garland! The *realm* is called Garland."

"Jasper the collector?" Leo asked. What he was really trying to do was concentrate on linking a memory to the current information he was being told.

Per's mouth opened in surprise. Leo had done it; he had unintentionally put a stopper in Per's vivacious word storm. "Yeah. How'd you know that?"

Before Per could get a response, Leo stood up abruptly and excused himself. "Can we finish this later? Bathroom."

"Why does everyone keep doing that? Just leaving in the middle of a conversation!" Per set his coffee cup down on the side table in a huff. "It's so rude."

Jasper—the collector, the one who had Leo's soul. Leo now knew a location and a name, and he was sure as hell going to find a way to make it to the Bermuda Triangle. He opened his mouth just enough to show a sliver of his still-nicotine-stained teeth. His eyes became as thin as paper.

(Leo...)

People do change, Leo thought in the deepest, darkest regions of the back of his mind, *except when they don't.* "I'm comin' for you now, motherfucker."

CHAPTER 10

New Moon Meadow was a large circular plot of land covered in yew trees and gardenias with a pond in the center. It was also a natural burial cemetery that catered to both witches and regular humans. No matter what the weather was, it was always just a little warmer on the grounds of New Moon Meadow, thanks to the botanical and environmental enchantments cast by its owner. The sun managed to shine through any clouds, the snow only ever dusted the ground, and it was always quiet. The cemetery, if one could call it that, was forty-five minutes outside of Nova and owned by a woman named Astra Dubois, a close friend of Rosemary's, a teakettle of a woman with stunning black hair streaked with white and a gift for the psychic arts. So gifted that she always wore sunglasses, because the auras of others were so bright, they hurt her eyes. The cemetery was a peculiar spot for someone with such a strong psychic sight, but it also proved to be the most comforting to those who were only passing through. Nina had never met Astra, but she knew Rosemary, and she trusted her completely. That's why she had chosen New Moon Meadow as her burial spot in her letter to Bisa, although it would have been the suggested spot regardless.

The coven didn't attend Nina's funeral service in Denver. They didn't know that Nina. Her parents were already gone, and she had no siblings or close family, so it was easy to inform the funeral director that it was going to be a private burial per her wishes, in case anyone asked. Ollie and Bisa, however, drove into town to wash her body. They prepared a cleansing water to ease her transition from this world to the next. The base was magnolia petal essence, made from the magnolia tree in the backyard of the Barrow House, in which they infused white and pink rose petals, orange zest, malachite, snowflake obsidian and maple leaves. It was far from an easy task, but there was no hesitation in either of their hearts, not even a trace of uncertainty. There was only compassion.

It was a little after noon, the time Nina had chosen for her private burial to start. She had filled out all her pre-need forms between the funeral home and the cemetery, signed every page, paid for every service and described every wish. If she wasn't able to control how or when she was going to die, then she was going to make sure that how her death was handled went according to her wishes.

She had chosen a plot in the far northwest section of the cemetery, a clearing covered in pine needles and encircled by pines and boulders. A little farther in was the pond, still waving in the abnormally warm, gentle breeze. The grounds were silent, and the coven's footsteps were further muffled by the layers of amber-colored pine needles. Astra stood in silence as she opened the back door of the hearse to reveal Nina's body, wrapped inside a fabric shroud and resting inside a lidless biodegradable burial cabinet. It was unlike anything anyone had seen before, beautiful, simple and above all—natural. Leo looked at the burial cabinet that wasn't like what he had come to know as a casket and immediately felt a sense of peace. This wasn't a sterile, impersonal and ridiculous burial chamber that had always scared him for reasons he would never understand. He was the first to grab hold of the wicker handles, and edged the cabinet out from the hearse. Mitch closed his eyes for a moment, as if trying to choke down food he didn't want to eat.

"Mitch, why don't you go wait for us by the burial site, prepare the corners for us," Ollie suggested lightly.

Mitch nodded, apologized with his eyes and made his way to the hollow where Nina would be laid to rest, where he lit a chalice of copal resin at the south end and placed an onyx bowl of spring water in the west, three pheasant feathers in the east end, and a large purple hydrangea in the north.

Ollie, Bisa, Leo, Avery and Rosemary and Per surrounded the cabinet and grabbed hold of the remaining handles. Astra closed the back hatch, switched on her portable speaker and began to play Nina's desired musical choice for her burial, "Andvari" by Sigur Rós. Suddenly, there was a snowfall, light and gentle, like the tiny goose feathers suspended in the air after a pillow fight. There didn't seem to be clouds enough for snow, yet there was some. A reminder to them that so many things made little sense, so many things were beyond their control or understanding.

There was a world of hurt between the coven. The catalyst had been the same event, but it affected them all differently, and they each had an entirely different experience unique to them. Astra followed behind them with a basket of items for burial. Bisa's eyelids were heavier than the cabinet she was helping to carry, yet her heart was heavier still. Their somber march was hypnotic, like a long drive on a highway, so much so that when they arrived at the hollow, they could hardly remember the walk to it. Upon arrival, Mitch retrieved the basket from Astra and pulled out the contents. He scattered fresh green leaves across the top of the shroud and then placed four tools on Nina's chest: a hand-carved wand made of alder wood, a marble chalice, a dagger with a birch handle, and a large, black ceramic pentacle.

"All right, ready? Count of three," Rosemary said.

There was a collective breath as they positioned themselves to deposit Nina's body into the earth.

"One," Rosemary said, checking the readiness of the coven.

"Two," Bisa added, her fingers beginning to loosen their grip on the handle.

(three)

"Three," Bisa repeated after Nina. The blood started to flow back into her fingers as they gently lowered Nina's body into the hollow. An odd feeling of clarity and peace washed over her, even though her hands still shook. Grief was never easy—exhausting, capricious, inevitable.

Mitch managed to satisfy his discomfort and regain some composure, and once again found himself a member of the coven and less of an outsider. He was the first to begin shoveling the freshly turned earth into the hollow. Avery and Ollie followed next. A flock of birds began to chirp and sing as the sun completely broke through the few clouds in the sky. The sweet orangey-vanilla scent of ponderosa pine wafted through the air. Rosemary lit the tip of a rope of braided sweetgrass and waved the smoke over the hollow.

Avery's face was pinched and puckered like she had been left outside in weather that was too cold for ice. All her feelings gathered on her eyelids and dripped down her cheek. She couldn't remember the last time she had felt like this, if she ever had. She had never been to a funeral before and hadn't known how it would affect her. It was easy to assume it would be as episodic as stepping on something sharp and moving on, but that wasn't what she was experiencing. It was so much more than that—dark, and beautiful, melancholic and sticky like the maple syrup on the bottle you didn't know was there until after you grabbed it.

When the hollow was filled, Bisa and Ollie held hands, his teeth clenched as he felt Bisa's heaviness. He gripped tighter, and she rubbed her thumb across his soft fingers as if she were painting a canvas. He caressed her gently with his free hand and released himself from her grip. He kneeled down to the small magnolia tree that had been waiting to be planted. Its roots were bound to the soil in a cylindrical shape. He pushed aside some earth in the center of Nina's grave with his hands and planted the magnolia sapling in the shallow hole.

Avery stepped forward and placed her hands over the freshly planted tree. She muttered a protective enchantment under her breath, no louder than the breeze that whipped through the tall pines. The spell would allow the tree to grow strong and tall, even in an environment that it was not suited for. She understood that type of journey very well, and she knew firsthand that it was possible, with or without magic. She looked up at the swatch of afternoon sky that was beginning to dissolve the clouds. *What a journey this has been*, she thought. As she stepped back and stared at the small tree, her thoughts began to spin, as if she were being dipped into the memories of her entire life.

The song finished, and Astra lowered her head to peek above the rim of her sunglasses. The auras of the coven were a polychromatic storm of colors, most of them bright, some of them dim, all of them active. Bisa's crown chakra was beaming like a water fountain in the height of a summer day. *She is truly something special,* Astra thought. Astra knew that the memory—no, image—of her parents emerged in Bisa's mind, sending her into a storm of silent tears. Her eyes shifted toward

Mitch. She couldn't help but notice the shadowy and dense energy that surrounded him, like a denim outfit soaked through from a sudden rainstorm. She had noticed that he'd started picking at his thumb as the music finished. She studied him a bit further, looking around him rather than at him. The sun bounced across the light ripples in the water, and the world was once again just a little too bright. She adjusted her sunglasses to fit tightly against her face, a habit she had developed in her years of working in the small occult shop in Salem, giving readings out of the dusty backroom with one lamp and ridiculously bright clients.

Rosemary looked up from the gravesite, over the faces of the coven and then into the sunny sky. She took a deep breath and let it out with a sigh of gratitude. A few minutes passed with everyone in silence. Thoughts about what to say began to swell on the tip of her tongue. But she had no other words, not right then, not for the coven. She kneeled down to a small mossy rock near the grave, ran her fingers across the moist surface and whispered to it. Like a baker spreading frosting over a freshly baked cake, she charmed the fronds of moss to grow and twist from the rock and around the base of the tree, like a Christmas tree skirt. For a moment, she thought she heard Nina's voice carried in the wind.

"It was truly an honor, Nina. The magician. You will be greatly missed and forever appreciated," Rosemary added.

And you will be avenged, Astra thought or heard—sometimes she wasn't able to tell. It wasn't always clear where the messages were coming from. She did know that if it felt like she was making it up, it was probably true.

Ollie suddenly felt the subtle shift in temperature, and then the new something that he had grown accustomed to, something that he called static. His eyes fluttered, and he looked around the burial site. He had felt this before, and if ever there was a time for a presence, it was now. In the distance, around other grave sites, he saw others—not people, but spirits. *There you are,* he thought. Then more, through the pines, and others on the other side of the hearse, and another on the next plot over to the right.

He looked toward the lake and there she was: Nina. She stood tall, as if she had grown a few inches since her death, dressed in flowing silk and her wild curls dancing in the gusts of winter air, so warm it felt like spring. His heart began to pound, and he knew it was real. The reality of her passing was finally hitting home. Yet he wasn't sad as much as he was happy to see her in such a glorious way. She smiled, gave him a wink and a nod. He wanted to show the others, but he couldn't. The only person who seemed to know she was there was Astra, who locked eyes (as best she could through sunglasses) with Ollie and smiled. When he looked back at the lake, Nina was gone. His heart dropped. He'd been hoping to get the chance to speak with her, because all the things he wanted to say were burning the edge of his tongue, begging to be said. But it just wasn't in the cards, not right now.

A few minutes later, the snow stopped falling. The coven was making another lugubrious march back toward the car, everyone except Bisa, who had suddenly felt drawn to the silver ripples of the pond.

"You coming?" Ollie asked her.

She nodded and wiped her eyes. "In a minute."

Bisa waited a moment and then started down the pine needle path toward the pond. She crossed her arms in front of her and let out a sigh. A shiver ran through her body and she looked around, not knowing what to expect—perhaps the figure that had been stalking her. Only it wasn't something ominous, it was something beautiful. Her mouth dropped in awe, and the breath was stolen right out of her lungs as she watched a large milky eagle owl soar toward her over the sparkling pond. The owl glided so gracefully that it seemed as if it were flying in slow motion; its feathers, in colors of spun wool and dark leather, fluttered. She stood, stunned, as it approached her. As if by instinct, she held out her arm and the owl took hold of her forearm, mindful of its talons. The owl tucked its feathers next to its body.

At first, Bisa was terrified, but once the bird landed, she wanted nothing more than for it to stay. The contradictory feelings were enough to make her forget about the funeral for a moment and allow her to be present. The owl turned its head toward her and stared at her deeply with its two inky, elegant eyes. They reminded her of the figure in the flowing black robes she had encountered, but these eyes were not those. They were kind, protective and wise. Her totem animal had finally arrived. By the time she realized what had happened, the owl had flown away.

CHAPTER 11

The next morning, Leo rose much earlier than anyone else because there was one more thing he wanted to ask Per. Rosemary had been staying in the sunroom, and Per had been sleeping on the large couch in the family room. When Leo approached the top of the stairs, he noticed the door to the sunroom was cracked open. It felt inappropriate to look, but it felt so deliciously familiar to do something he knew he shouldn't. His eyes peeked through the crack as he walked away just slowly enough to see inside. Rosemary was awake, stretching, or exercising—maybe both? It surprised him to see someone of her age not only so active, but also so flexible, so in control of her body, the kind of control that takes years of discipline to achieve. His curiosity faded quickly as he entered the living room where Per was already up, resting on the couch, watching YouTube videos.

"Per?" Leo asked.

"Yeah?" Per responded, putting down his phone reluctantly.

Leo furrowed his brow as he considered what he was going to do. Was he going to use magic or not? Before he could even decide, he spoke. "Will you help me get to the Bermuda Triangle?" His tone of voice made it sound more like a demand than a request.

Per stared into Leo's eyes and raised his eyebrows. A smile appeared on his face, one that suggested he thought Leo was making a joke. He stopped smiling a few moments later. "Oh, you're serious?"

"One hundred percent," Leo said.

"What do you mean? What do you want to do there? I don't think anyone has even tried to *get* to the entrance for...I don't even know how long." Per shook his head. "What for?"

Honesty rippled from Leo's lips. "I think I have a chance of figuring out this whole Divine Dualities thing. If there's a fairy left, I think I can find it."

"Okaaaay..." Per said. "But you and your coven should be taking on this task together."

"But I want to be the one to do it," Leo said frankly as he sat down on the couch next to Per and placed his hand on Per's knee. "Will you help me?"

The feelings of hesitation and concern dissolved from Per's mind as Leo's fingers curled over his bony knee. Leo hadn't fully intended to force Per into obliging his request (more of a demand, really), but when it came down to it, his ambition took control. He held Per's gaze as his influence, so hot that it melted Per's defenses, took hold.

Per's eyes looked as foggy as the winter storm clouds spilling over the mountaintops. "Of course I'll help you."

Leo nodded, half surprised at the fact that he had forced Per to do something he probably didn't want to do, but also at how easy it had been for him to do it. Then, there were voices. The coven. Leo had to act fast if he wanted to go without the rest of the coven preventing him from doing so. He wasn't entirely sure he knew how to teleport; he just knew that he could do it, that he had done it. For Leo, it was like making hollandaise sauce: he was never really sure if he was doing it the correct way, but he always had a homogenous sauce at the finish.

He grabbed hold of Per's wrist and pulled him toward the window, where they ducked down near the curtains. Leo remembered when he had transported himself somehow during the Mardi Gras parade. Surely he could concentrate and do it again, this time with two people. With one hand holding tightly onto Per's wrist, he closed his eyes, took a few deep breaths and pulled the image of Miami into his mind. He had never been there, he didn't know any landmarks or places of reference firsthand, he just had to wing it. He took one deep breath as the voices from the coven came closer. A second deep breath in through his nose and out through his mouth.

(Leo, what are you doing?)

One final time, he breathed in and exhaled through his mouth as he placed his free hand onto the floor beside his knee. *Bermuda*, he thought. *Somewhere quiet, somewhere unseen. Bermuda, somewhere that I've never been.* At first, he still felt only the hardwood floor underneath his palm, cool and solid. Then came a feeling of water trickling around the edges of his hand. His eyes remained closed, but the rest of his senses were wide open. The cool, flowing sensation around his hand began to fade away, and the hardwood floor changed texture. Suddenly, it was rough and hot. Then, there was noise. Not the expected noise from the coven, or anything in the house at all. It was the buzzing of other people. Leo opened his eyes and focused on his hand on the floor—concrete sidewalk. He let go of Per's wrist and looked around. They were outside, and not in Colorado. Had it worked? Were they actually in Bermuda, or were they somewhere entirely different because Leo didn't really know what he was doing or how to do it?

"Where are we?" Per asked, a little too confused to be concerned yet.

They were at the back of a building, surrounded by trash cans and cardboard boxes. There were no windows, bystanders or even birds. Yet Leo could hear voices. Somewhere close there was a crowd. If he hadn't been who he was, he might have been a little uneasy, but Leo was Leo, and he knew he had gotten them to where they needed to be. They walked alongside the edge of the building to the front of it and arrived at a large street filled with people. Ahead of them was a beach and a small marina on the opposite side of the street.

"We're in Bermuda," Leo said with a smile, half forgetting that Per had even come with him. His body was a little wet from the teleportation, which happens with all sorts of astral travel, but he barely noticed. Leo took out his phone and checked the map, just to make sure they were in the right spot. The little blue dot on his map showed that they were indeed in Bermuda, right across the street from Grimsby Boat Rental.

Forty minutes later, Leo had bribed—perhaps magically persuaded, Per couldn't be certain—a man to lend them a twenty-four-foot Hurricane boat. How Per managed to know how to drive a boat was a question for another time, or maybe once they were already at sea. Leo was eager to be on the water, sailing into the Atlantic, seeing the shores of Bermuda shrink in the distance, leaving all of his failures on the sand. *Soon it will all be in the past*, he thought. He might actually be able to pull all of this off, he might actually have the rafkolite sooner than he thought.

But that wasn't the goal. It never had been. He wanted to be happy. To have the ability to finally be able to experience something that, to him, was the greatest power of all. Besides himself and his own lack of responsibility, it was the next biggest obstacle in his life, the lack of happiness. It haunted him almost as much as the loss of his daughter. Maybe more, if he were to be completely honest. But he didn't need that kind of denial creeping up on him right now. It would only be a distraction, and he refused to have any of those. Not when he was on a boat (a boat!) slicing through ocean water the color of somewhere between paradise and mystic sea glass. The salty air ripping through his wispy beard made him feel like a pirate. For a moment, he was lost in a childhood fantasy. There it was again, another distraction. He needed to focus.

Half an hour later, the world around them had vanished and there was nothing but sea all around them. Sea and the sky.

"How will we know when we're there?" Leo asked.

Per shook his head. "Well, I don't really know for certain, to be honest. This is all kind of theoretical at the moment. I've never been out here before; I don't really know what I'm supposed to be looking for." He looked a little ashamed. He hadn't actually realized that despite all the things he knew about the fairies, he didn't really know much about how to get to their realm. For a second he considered that perhaps that was some sort of fairy magic; maybe people weren't supposed to know, maybe the fairies had made certain that if someone approached their realm, their magic would ensure the trespasser suddenly…forgot.

He swallowed and panicked for a moment, treasuring all the memories in his life that he didn't want to lose. Per let that hypothesis marinate in his brain. It was possible, and he hadn't thought about it. After all, he did know that fairies had a predilection for human memories for some reason he couldn't quite recall. *Oh no…it's happening, isn't it!?*

"What do you mean? You don't know?" Leo asked. "You don't know, like, you don't remember? Are you serious? Now all of a sudden you have dementia?"

I knew it. It's happening. I'm losing my mind…my thoughts…my memories, Per thought.

"Stop the boat!" Leo shouted, holding up his hand.

Per slowed the boat and let it idle. "What is it?"

Leo winced, feeling a strange pulling sensation in his stomach. He looked up at the sky, which was suddenly cold and gray and looked as if it promised a storm. The sea was quiet, eerily so, as if they were in a foggy swamp and not in the middle of the vast ocean. Per walked over to the front of the boat where Leo was hunched over, gripping his stomach. Then Per felt it too, the same nauseating feeling in the middle of his belly. Leo wiped the sweat from his forehead with a rag from the seat next to him. He hadn't felt this sick since the morning after his birthday, the night that he had somehow consumed twelve tequila shots, three beers and a drink that looked like a milkshake but separated his body from his bowels.

Per lunged over the side of the boat as if he was about to vomit, only he didn't. Instead, his and Leo's feet were slowly peeled off the floor of the boat and they were lifted into the air as if picked up by some invisible giant.

Levitation? Holy shit, am I able to levitate now? Leo thought. He was wrong, very wrong, and just didn't know it. He chuckled, thinking he was only getting stronger and his powers were going to be greater than anyone had ever anticipated. But then he saw that Per was floating, too, and his pride deflated instantly and was replaced with fear. What was happening? If he wasn't doing it, who or what was?

The sensation in their stomachs strengthened, and suddenly they were propelled away from the boat. They hung in the air above the open sea, their feet dangling only a few feet above the water. Then it began, the pull. A force that they could only compare to that of a magnet towed them through the air and across the water, away from the boat. They spun in all directions, like a piece of debris sucked up by a vacuum and whipped through the hose into the dirt chamber. They had no idea how fast they were going, or when it would stop, or where they were going. It was like being in space without a suit, or underwater without knowing which way was up.

Per and Leo tumbled and spun as fast as the thoughts in their minds. *What's happening? Are we going to die? Is this the fairies? Do I have early-onset dementia?* It was stunning how one could think of so many things in such a short period of time. In what had been less than a minute, they had been yanked from the boat and had covered nearly half their lifetimes in their own thoughts…as the boat became smaller, and smaller, and smaller. Terror and dread filled Per's thoughts, and the magnetic pull in his stomach was bested only by his fear. It was paralyzing.

They stopped spinning and remained in midair, flailing like fish out of water. They couldn't see the water below them anymore, just gray mist. Had they traveled into the clouds? What was below them? Then, like a chandelier having its cord cut, they fell. Leo used to love that feeling, the immediate sinking sensation he would get on a roller coaster right as it dipped over the edge of an enormously steep drop. It felt like danger, and he loved danger, but this was a little too much even for Leo. He was anxious for solid ground underneath his feet as they fell through the gray fog.

The fog suddenly broke and there was light again. So much light that it blinded both of them. Their bodies smashed gently onto a soft, sandy shore. Wet sand stuck to the side of their faces as they tried to pull themselves out of the beach. Leo opened his eyes; bits of sand fell from his eyelashes as he caught only a glimpse of the world around him. A crashing wave thundered behind them and smashed over their bodies, pushing them a little farther up the shore.

Per spit out a mouthful of sand and looked around, panting. Finally, he remembered. The fairy realm would automatically attract and pull magical people to the entrance of the realm. It was part of the original magic between the fairies and the witches. He would have thought that it wouldn't be active, since all the other access points were closed. But it was. The magnetic pull was still very much operational. It felt like both a good thing and a bad thing. What if other people knew about it? What had become of the fairy realm?

Leo knew with the certainty of his own being that they had made it to the fairy realm, although he couldn't bring himself to say that phrase; it sounded too high fantasy. They plucked themselves up from the beach, dusted the sand off their clothes as best they could and made their way to the tall grass that blew along the dunes ahead of them. When they reached the top of the dunes, they saw that the coast was mostly rock and the small beach was lined with towering, rocky, multicolored cliffs. There was a thin canyon, a ravine that suggested it was more than just a geological formation, it was a corridor. The sunlight showed the magnificence of the cliffs as it splashed across them, highlighting the layers upon layers of time, stacked upon one another like tiers of a cake, millions and millions of years old. Pink and green shale, grayish blue and black limestone, brick-red, mustard-yellow and white sandstone with traces of milky quartz and veins of gold.

Leo and Per made their way through the ravine, slithering through the tight and often unwelcoming pathway. Leo's heart beat faster and faster, excited at the idea of what he would find at the end of it. They didn't chat much. Per just continued to follow Leo as he silently tried to figure out how far the rabbit hole was going to go. He thought all manner of things while they pressed on. Would they make it to where they were going? Where exactly *were* they going, anyway? Would they be able to get back?

"Leo, what exactly are we looking for?" Per asked nervously. "I'm a little worried. I don't know any sort of spell that can get us back to the boat. Can *you* get us back?"

Leo responded only with a shrug. He arrogantly believed it wouldn't be a problem, and he wasn't about to start thinking about how to leave when he had only just arrived. It didn't matter where they were, how dangerous it was or what could happen. He just needed to do what he wanted to do.

The ravine opened up a bit, offering a little relief for Per, who had been growing more and more convinced that they were going to end up swallowed whole by the rocks, like that movie with James Franco he had seen once. Leo stopped in his tracks and listened. Voices. He rushed forward, following the sounds.

"Come on!" Leo shouted.

Per dashed after him, not wanting to get separated. He crashed into Leo a few moments later. Leo's eyes were wide open, his jaw hanging down even wider. The ravine opened up to a sea of a different kind, a grim ocean of tightly clustered shacks and shedlike, single-story structures, no taller than twelve feet high, all humbly made from mud, rock and wood. A muddled jungle of buildings stretching to what seemed to be the end of time. All of it in a state of decay with a sense of despair that hung heavy in the air, one that Leo could feel and even recognize. It reminded him of the tent cities in New Orleans, where he had known a few people, and now in Denver, which had its own growing population of homeless people. He knew that world, he understood it, he empathized with it. He recognized it when he saw it, smelled it, heard it and felt it.

The only thing higher than the sea of shacks was the tall, well-built wall that seemed to enclose the entire city, or whatever it was, too tall to climb and impossible to penetrate. There was no luxury, no quality of life, no joy, but there were people. A pulsating and bubbling community of people all existing within the barracks-like city fashioned from trash and trees and held together with mud and salvaged bits of nature. There was nothing fairylike about it, at least not in the way that Leo had come to imagine. Per, on the other hand, knew for certain that this was not the work of the fairies, even though they were in fact, in Garland, the fairy realm. The nicest thing in sight was the sky above them, a dreamy blue that perhaps was the only good thing to wake up to every morning in a place such as this.

They walked farther into the city, half in awe and half afraid of what to expect. There was no other way to go but forward, and Leo kept moving. The people all looked like them, albeit they were dirty, emaciated and unhappy. But for the most part, they looked, well—human. The people of the city gazed at them in a way that suggested they had seen other people come through that ravine and it was nothing new. Yet they still stared and followed Leo and Per's movements with their eyes.

As Leo and Per walked down the widest path they could find, a monstrosity rose up in front of them from the center of town, a colossal, fifty-foot, twisted black obelisk that pierced the sky. They passed home after home, street vendor after street vendor, and finally arrived at the obelisk. It appeared to be at the city center, if you could call it that. At the bottom, resting against the structure, was a man bathing in the sunlight, or perhaps taking a nap, or more likely, wishing that his life was over. His eyes suddenly opened, and he looked at Per and Leo. A smile appeared briefly on his face as if he had been expecting them. The man stood up and dusted off his robes of gray and brown. They matched his unwashed hair, which was parted and matted down into a sort of hairstyle. The man knew he was unclean, but it was the best he could do. Still, he brushed off his hands and approached them.

"Welcome to the Creamstone Township," the man said, in an accent that neither of them could recognize.

"Where is that?" Leo asked.

The man raised an eyebrow and ran a hand through his hair, scratching the back of his head. "Here," he said.

Leo needed an answer, a real one. But it wasn't working; he had no influence over the man. Leo had felt confident that in a place like this, he would be able to use his powers and no one would think anything of it. It was the fairy realm, after all. But he couldn't do that either. He couldn't do anything. He couldn't summon anything or control anything, and even more importantly, he couldn't get himself and Per out of there if he needed to, like he had planned on doing.

"Is this Garland?" Per asked.

"Yes," the man said as he rolled his eyes. More people looking for Garland, just like the other people. But to be honest, many other people were there who weren't looking for Garland; they had just happened to come across the entrance to the realm by accident and were stuck there. "But this is the Creamstone Township."

"Who can we speak to? We don't know how we got here," Per said.

"I know where you came from, and I know how you got here."

"We're looking for someone," Leo said.

"Who?" the man asked, almost as if he already knew.

Per wanted to stop Leo, but he held his tongue.

"We're looking for a Jasper. Do you know who that is?"

The man laughed. "I knew that was who you were looking for. But that's not me. You can find him in Tengotodo. The palace." He turned and pointed behind him to a place beyond the wall.

"What's Tengotodo? What's past the wall that way?" Per asked.

"That's Jasper's *chateau*," he said in a mocking sort of tone. "I can take you there if you want. But it has to be at nightfall."

"We can't go now?" Leo asked.

"No. The gate is open only at night, Jasper's orders," the man said. Then he paused for a moment and studied them both. "Will you both be returning to your *world* when you're finished here?"

"Yeah, we have to. Why?" Leo said.

"I will show you to the chateau if you agree to take me with you when you go. Do we have a deal?"

There was no reason not to take him, besides, of course, not having any idea how they were going to get back. "Deal!" Leo said quickly.

"Good—follow me!" the man said as he turned to lead the way. He swung his head back around and said, "I'm Henrie!" before continuing on.

Leo leaned closer to Per and whispered, "My powers don't work here."

Per shook his head. "Neither do mine."

CHAPTER 12

Henrie guided Leo and Per to his personal shack. He offered them soup made of dandelion and potato, two ingredients he was able to grow behind his shack. Leo's knee was bouncing with anxiety while Per pressed Henrie for questions about the history of Garland. It was so different from what he had believed it to be. Never in any of his studies had he ever heard of anything even remotely similar to what they had seen. Per had heard that Jasper had taken up residence in the realm, but he didn't really know why, or how long he had been there. Judging from the looks of things, he had been there quite some time and running things just how he liked—unopposed and unchallenged.

"You two managed to show up at a really decent time. It was really messy a few weeks ago," Henrie said.

"What happened?" Per asked excitedly, almost wishing that he had a notepad to take notes.

"The same thing that always happens. People here are upset. We are sick and hungry, and Jasper, well, Jasper is not. People got together at the center of town and formed a protest. They marched to Tengotodo and stood at the gates, yelling their demands, begging to be heard. We don't want much, we just want better living conditions. All you have to do is look around to know that this isn't a fit place for anyone to be living. Jasper has the means to improve things, he just won't."

"Why not?" Per asked, on the edge of his seat.

"He doesn't care. We're nothing. Expendable scum. A town full of scum."

"He didn't do anything as a result of the protests?" Per asked.

Henrie nodded and giggled. "Oh no, he did! He reminded all of us that he is the law and order of this land. He gets what he wants, and if he doesn't get it, he takes it. Anyone who stands between him and what he wants, well, those people don't usually live very long. The whole protest lasted maybe half an hour at best. He marched out to meet everyone, stood right in front of them and covered everyone in the mist of tears."

"What's that?" Leo said, now interested, feeling that there was something unusual about that statement. It sounded magical, and magic didn't work here.

"That's just what we commoners call it. It's some kind of spell he uses. It makes us cough and choke and sometimes bleed from our eyes if we breathe too much of it."

"Like a potion?" Per asked.

"No, no. A spell. Jasper is a witch. He's the only witch who has any powers here in Garland."

"Why?" Leo asked intently.

"I don't know. No one knows." Henrie shook his head before he returned to his story. "Then came the blunt-tipped arrows."

"He shot arrows at the protesters?" Per asked in surprise.

"Oh yeah! He does that a lot."

"What for?"

"Well, the protesters picked a really bad day for the protest. Jasper had arranged for a local artist from the township to paint his portrait in front of the obelisk that day. It interrupted his schedule. So he had his guards shoot through the protesters until a clear path was made from his chateau to the obelisk. They stood guard until the painting was complete. Only one protester managed to get in his way after that. His name was Luca, really nice fellow, never hurt anybody. When the painting was finished, Luca stepped right up to the guards and blocked Jasper's path. He stood there, not in a confrontational way, just a way that asserted the fact that people need to be listened to. It was a completely peaceful manner of protest."

"What did Jasper do?" Per asked.

"He set him on fire."

There was a heavy silence in the air as Leo and Per finally began to realize the kind of person they were after. Per considered that they might not even want to pursue this any further. But they were stuck there for the time being, so what choice did they really have?

"He controls everything and makes sure that he stays in control," Henrie said. "That's why he does what he does to the women every once in a while, so they can't have any children. We're probably due for another round of that right now. That's usually what he does after some sort of attempted revolt or when the population gets too large. He needs us, though. That's why the walls were built. He just needs us to be how we are and nothing more. Some of us don't mind. It's all some of us know."

"Where did you all come from?" Leo asked.

"Same as you, for the most part. People who have been lost or caught in the grip of the Bermuda Triangle. Of course some people are born here, as that's what happens over time in a place like this. Most of us are just like you."

They were there for several hours, so many hours that Per actually managed to take a nap in the corner of the room. Leo was in no mood for sleeping. He was too energized. He thought about what he was going to do now that he realized he didn't have any powers in the realm. Whatever it was, he had to do it with his bare hands. Which he could do—that wasn't the problem. It was the fact that he would have to do it to someone who could use magic.

When Leo had exhausted enough time inside Henrie's shack, he left and went exploring, wandering aimlessly, turning down streets at random, trying to pass the time in any way he could. He didn't know how safe the township was, nor did he care. He could handle himself. It was the only thing that he could do now that his phone was dead and there was no magic, no internet, no porn, no anything other than the sad mess of city before him—that and strange little red-capped mushrooms that grew everywhere.

As he walked through the township, catching the scent of dirt and despair, Leo saw all manner of people. People who looked and sounded like him, and even some who looked better than he ever had. They were a community of people who had been created to be exactly how they were. For a brief moment, Leo considered starting a conversation with some of the random townies, or whatever they called themselves, but he opted to observe from a distance. Whatever their stories were, no matter how interesting they might be, that wasn't what he was there for.

He had to think of a way to not only defeat Jasper, but also find out where his soul was, if Jasper still had it. Leo hadn't actually thought about that possibility. What would he do if he had managed to get all the way to the Tengotodo and Jasper no longer had his soul in his possession? He felt nervous for a hot minute, but then told himself to trust in the fact that Jasper was indeed a collector, and that's what they do. They collect, they don't release. Leo had been a collector himself at times when he was a kid—he knew how that worked. He'd collected rocks in second grade, gum wrappers in fifth grade, and porn in eighth grade, and then he'd decided collecting things was a waste of time when he could just get high. Those days were gone, and unless Jasper liked getting high more than collecting, he still had Leo's soul. At least, that was the story Leo told himself.

When dusk hit the sky, Leo made his way back to Henrie's shack. He was a little more anxious, his shoes were a little dirtier and he was more impatient.

"Everything okay?" Per asked as Leo came through the door.

"I'm ready to go," Leo said.

Somewhere in the shack was the sound of tinkering, and then there was silence. Henrie came out of another room in a fresh set of robes, as fresh as they could be. "Let's go!" he said as he motioned toward the door.

"It's almost pitch black out there. How are we going to see?" Per asked.

"We may not have things like electricity, but we do have other things," Henrie said as he led them out the door and kneeled down next to his shack. His hands ran along the edge of the house, where the mud wall met the ground, until he felt a cluster of the red-capped mushrooms. He felt around for the largest cap, and then clipped the stem with his thumb and forefinger just above the ground. "We have these," he said proudly.

"A mushroom?"

"A mushroom," Henrie said in the dark. "But if you hold it here, and pinch right underneath the cap and crack the stem"—there was a brisk crack and a hissing just before the mushroom cap caught fire—"you have a makeshift lantern."

"They're flammable?" Per asked with surprise. "I always knew about how prevalent *amanita feramignusa* was in Garland, but I never knew they produced fire. Amazing!"

"They grow so fast, and the flame lasts such a long time, that we never have a problem with a lack of light or fire," Henrie said as he pinched the stem a little more and released a little more flame. "Let's go to the chateau, shall we?"

CHAPTER 13

Bisa had spent the majority of the day with her door locked and dividing her time between two tasks, researching spells and performing spells, and she'd had little success with either one. She wanted to find a way to locate Merlot, since the coven didn't seem to think that was a high priority, or one at all. Using her consummate talent and aptitude for bibliomancy, she selected eight books from the shelves in the study and skimmed through them as quickly as she could, looking for a way, any way, to locate Merlot. All of which gave her nothing in return, even though she had been so certain they would. She searched for her in the black depths of her obsidian scrying glass that she'd picked up from a small shop in Denver—nothing.

Bisa then worked herself into a deep trance and waited for a place, an object or even an event to reveal itself to her, something that would help her find Merlot, but again—nothing. She tried spraying her crown chakra with a potion she made to amplify her psychic gifts, loaded with essence of celestite and fluorite and mixed with Fast Luck Oil, but she still couldn't find what she was looking for. The moldavite spell to locate lost people, the chalcopyrite and amazonite pendulum, the prayer to her ancestors and guides—none of them worked. It was maddening.

Merlot didn't want to be found, and she had made sure she wouldn't be. Bisa couldn't decide which was worse, the fact that Merlot had succeeded in staying lost or that the coven didn't seem to realize that she posed dangers far more severe than a single murder. Bisa just knew it. She felt it.

When all of her attempts failed, she rose to her feet, let out a frustrated sigh and walked to the window. Maybe something out there in the snow would have answers, she thought—some bird, insect or fox that would give her the information she so desperately sought. But there was nothing in the cold landscape but the approaching evening. Then something caught her eye. Down by the lake stood a figure, not a man, but something else entirely. She had seen that figure before, the figure with the black glowing orbs for eyes and the flowing robes like liquid turned smoke. Images of the Land of Perpetual Midnight flashed through her mind like flipping pages in a book of illustrations. She felt the eyes staring at her, even from that distance, just as they had before. Bisa's eyes widened, and her breath lost its rhythm. By the time she had blinked, the figure was gone. Her shock was quickly replaced by a gnarling at the base of her sternum. Death was still coming for her. As if she hadn't experienced enough in the last few months. Hollowing grief and inescapable knowingness haunted her—asleep or awake. *I am not letting you take me,* Bisa pledged to herself as she looked out into darkness of night.

Knock, knock, knock.

"Bisa? Can I come in?" Ollie asked.

She walked over to let him in and said nothing as he entered.

"You haven't come out all day. You didn't even eat dinner. I made that sweet potato and lentil thing you like."

Bisa smiled. "*You* like it; I've never liked sweet potatoes."

Ollie furrowed his brow, wondering how he could have projected his love for a dish onto someone else as an excuse to make it more often. He shook his head and then focused on Bisa once again. "Are you all right?" He looked around the room at the various remnants of unsuccessful spells.

"I need to find Merlot. I know the rest of you don't think this is important, and I know Rosemary told us not to look for her, but I can't just do nothing. I can't just wait until she does something else, or kills someone else."

There was a moment of silence. Ollie could tell from the color of her aura that Bisa was growing more and more frustrated as it began to shrink next to her body and emit a reddish-brown, almost blackish tone. He hadn't realized that he was able to see auras until that moment, and he would have been more excited about it if it hadn't been for his concern for Bisa and her state of mind.

"Is this about Nina?" Ollie asked, even though he already knew the answer.

They talked for half an hour about Nina, her effect on them, and the move to Colorado.

Bisa stared into space as she reminisced about a conversation she had had with Nina not too long ago. "You know, she once told me that the reason we're even in Colorado is that something or someone in the mountains here needs release, a part of the prophecy for restoring the spiritual element of balance. Or something like that. I can't really remember. I don't even think she meant to tell me about it, but I had just caught her off guard right after a meditation." Bisa smiled again, only this time it was wide and warm as she thought about that fleeting moment in the past. Even with all the heartache, loss and pain, she was able to smile and find a little peace in the trivial but highly treasured moments in her memory. The corners of her mouth turned up and she felt her spirit lift, if only in an amount too small to measure.

Rosemary appeared in Bisa's doorway oozing anxiety and edginess, like the inescapable spell of the three trailing dots in a heated text message while waiting for a response—the kind that makes you abandon all other tasks regardless of how important they are, even if you're driving. It was that sort of impatience that she exuded into Bisa's already tense room.

"Where is Per?" Rosemary asked. "Have you seen him?"

When they answered no, Rosemary slammed the door frame with her fist. She was exceptionally agitated, especially for someone whose job was to closely monitor mental, emotional and spiritual balance and determine when they have finally equalized.

"What's wrong?" Ollie asked.

Rosemary ignored the question with a shake of her head. "What about Leo? Where is he?"

Ollie and Bisa exchanged a glance and then shook their heads.

"The Symposium room has been destroyed," Rosemary said. "The table is nothing but rubble, and Per missed our meeting."

"Have you asked Mitch or Avery?" Bisa asked.

"I'm about to!" Rosemary said as she stormed out. When she realized Avery wasn't in her room, she headed up the stairs to the third floor. Avery was in the reading loft making an entry in her grimoire with a black ink pen when Rosemary caught her eye. When Avery said she hadn't heard or seen Leo either, Rosemary paced in circles, grabbing at her mouth as if she were going to scream. She turned and opened Mitch's door without knocking. Mitch was sitting on his bed staring into space.

"Mitch, have you seen Leo or Per?" Rosemary shouted.

"No?" Mitch responded as if he were in trouble.

Rosemary mumbled to herself as she fumed down the hallway toward the living room like a tornado of regret and frustration. "Everyone!" she shouted. "I need all of you in the living room. We're going to magnify our energy as a coven and try to get some information from the ether." She moved on down the hall.

Mitch poked out from his room and hovered in the hallway. "I can find Leo."

Rosemary turned on her heels, and the house was silent as she stared at him.

The need to hide consumed Mitch as his eyes met Rosemary's. It was more sudden than his panic attacks and stronger than the physical attraction he had or used to have—he wasn't sure anymore—for Leo. For a hot minute, before Rosemary or anyone else had managed to ask him any questions, he thought maybe he could just run and hide somewhere. In the closet, under the bed, escape the coven and their inquiring minds and go straight out into the snow-covered mountains until he just froze to death and never had to worry about anything ever again.

No more pain. No more struggling. No more self-pity. No more mental anguish. Only relief, a reprieve that would answer the questions he constantly asked himself: *Am I just lazy and senselessly unable to live my life in a different way? What did I do to deserve all that has happened? Why am I so depressed all the time? Why can't I even admit to myself that I'm depressed? Why can't I be better? Why do I keep picking unattainable people? What would death actually feel like? Would it be as liberating as I've always assumed it would be? Is there anything else afterward?*

As his mind raced with thoughts and worries, he suddenly heard another voice inside his mind.

(Only you can fix you, Mitch. You're not a victim. You're light. Be light.)

The voice came and went fast and mixed with his own thoughts so that he couldn't tell if it was Ollie, Nina or maybe even the wisdom of his totem.

"You can find Leo? How?" Rosemary asked. The floor creaked as she adjusted her weight to one foot. Her head tilted back; her eyelids tightened.

Mitch retreated into his room, not to hide like the urge that throbbed in the back of his head told him to, but to retrieve the jar of mother water from his drawer. He returned to the hall and showcased the jar in his hand. "With this."

No one knew how to respond. Mitch had grown more private over time, and no one knew what to think of the small jar in his hand.

"What is it?" Rosemary asked.

Mitch looked around at everyone, trying to figure out how they were going to react to hearing that he had secretly dosed them during dinner one night back in Louisiana. He meant well, and it wasn't anything harmful—it was a protection spell—but still, he had spiked their drinks and let them consume it—unknowingly. He opened the jar, and the air was instantly perfumed with the scent of angelica root and rue. "I made a protection potion. Well, it's more of a locator potion."

Bisa felt a stab of intuition as her eyes looked over both the jar and Mitch's aura. It was exceptionally clear from his fidgeting fingers searching for an itch he didn't have that Mitch felt a hefty amount of guilt and wished he didn't have to admit what he was about to admit. "You gave some to Leo," Bisa said.

Mitch lowered the potion and closed his eyes for a moment, hoping the whole world would have ceased to exist when he reopened them. When his eyes blinked open, he said, "To all of you."

"What?" Avery exclaimed. "When?"

Mitch let out a short-lived sigh. "Last winter. At dinner. I put a little bit in all of your drinks."

There was only the heavy sting of the truth coming to light and the cold wind blowing outside.

"You spiked our drinks and didn't tell us?" Avery exclaimed. "Why the hell would you do that? What if you'd mixed something wrong? You have no idea what it could have done! I mean, I hate to say it, and I'm sure all of us have thought this at one point or another, but Mitch...you're not the most skilled witch." Avery was ignorant of the effect of her callous words.

"I know it worked!" Mitch said in return, his face flushing red with shame.

"You don't know that!" Avery said.

Rosemary stepped forward and grabbed the potion from Mitch's hands, twisting it around to examine the contents up close. "What exactly does it do, Mitch?" She took a whiff of the sweet floral odor escaping from the jar.

"I made it as a way to protect all of us. In case something happened to any of us—"

"Why wouldn't you tell us first?" Avery interrupted.

Mitch swallowed and winced, as if Avery's words singed his skin.

Rosemary held up her hand to silence Avery. "Let him finish." She closed her eyes a little to narrow her vision on Mitch, as if she were trying to see into the depths of his soul. "Go on, Mitch."

"I can determine where someone is, and I can also sense their current emotional state. All I have to do is insert my finger into the mother water and I can connect to anyone I've given a dose to. Well, in theory. I've never actually used it before."

At first, the coven was angry, upset by the fact that Mitch would experiment on them. But the feeling soon faded as Rosemary praised Mitch for his efforts.

"They're right to be upset, Mitch. You should've told them about it or, better still, asked their permission. The coven is about trust, and no doubt that's something Nina tried to instill in you from day one. Potions are nothing to take lightly, and you could have easily killed anyone you gave that potion to." Rosemary stood up straight and pursed her lips. "Yet everyone is still alive. Which leads me to believe that you were successful. So we need to test this and test it now."

Mitch nodded and shuffled his feet, the coven's eyes all studying him as if they were ridiculing him in their minds. He wasn't very psychic, but he could sense that.

"I need you to promise me," Rosemary said before she turned around to look at every member of the coven, "all of you, I need you to promise that from this point on, there will be nothing but trust. We all have to understand that we can't hide things from one another, we have to trust each other, rely on each other and ask each other for help when we need it. That's how we will accomplish all that needs to be done."

They all looked at one another, as if to apologize for any past events when they had taken advantage of, lied to or refused to trust in the other members of the coven.

"Am I clear?" Rosemary asked sternly.

Everyone nodded. All the anger, concern and resentment began to settle, and finally dissolved away.

Rosemary reached into her pocket and pulled out a small plastic bag with a couple of digestive biscuits inside. She bit into one, chewed slowly as if it were a method of grounding herself, and then took a deep breath. "Right. Into the kitchen. Someone grab a map," she ordered.

"Rosemary, it's 2020, no one uses paper maps," Bisa said.

"Oh, bloody hell, I do!" Rosemary said, and she spun around and headed to the sunroom to retrieve her map of Louisiana. "I'll meet you in the kitchen," she said from the stairwell. "No paper maps…Ridiculous," she added under her breath.

She found the coven in the kitchen and unfolded the map on the counter. Mitch poured the mother water into a shallow bowl, eager to see whether he was right to believe that he had successfully executed a potion. He was sure of it—well, almost sure, 99.9 percent sure. He had felt so confident when it was completed, he remembered how it felt. It had to be legit.

Mitch held his right hand over the map and his left hand over the bowl of water. He closed his eyes and suddenly felt a buzzing in his palms. He opened his eyes in surprise before closing them almost as quickly. Then his palms felt a rush of heat, as if the flickering tips of a bonfire were teasing his skin. He closed his fingers into a fist, all except his index finger, which he dipped straight into the water. His free hand swayed back and forth over the map, scanning for Leo's location, searching—divining, for his emotions.

"What do you feel? What do you see?" Bisa asked.

Mitch shook his head, feeling the pressure of the coven's eyes through his closed eyelids. His temples began to sweat, and he could feel a rumbling of panic in the pit of his stomach. *Not now…please.*

Ollie gently placed a hand on Mitch's shoulder and said nothing.

Mitch's eyes closed tighter as he tried to concentrate. His now sweating palms swayed across the map, back and forth, until they suddenly went cold. Ice cold.

"Something's wrong," Mitch said.

"What do you mean?" Rosemary asked.

Mitch shook his head. "I'm not sure."

Avery rolled her eyes.

"It's important that we find Leo," Rosemary said.

"Why?" Bisa asked, now heavily curious to find out what the issue was. Could it be something she wasn't aware of? Did Rosemary know what she knew? She couldn't. If she had known half the things that Bisa did, the conversation would surely have gone differently.

"The prophecy says that *this* coven is the one that will rise up, find the rafkolite and restore balance," Rosemary replied. "Not a single witch, but this coven. Which is why you need to work harder as a group, not split up. Separated, you're vulnerable."

Without warning, Mitch flipped over the map as if commanded to do so, and flattened it out to reveal a large map of the United States, including the Pacific and Atlantic Oceans. Even a part of Mitch wanted him to fail in this demonstration of power, because it would make more sense than actually being able to do something right for a change.

(stop that)

Mitch shook his head at himself and spread his fingers wide over the map. Slowly, his fingers closed and his hand formed an upside-down cup over the map, like a little radio dish picking up signals from the beyond. A hypnotizing rush of energy filled his body and overwhelmed him. He let out a heavy breath as he tried to regain composure.

"What is it?" Bisa asked.

"I can feel him. He's excited. Not excited, but, eager, maybe? I can feel it like it's me," Mitch said as he struggled to control the sensations in his body running wild like a river. His eyelids fluttered on the cusp of opening. His thoughts fell out of sync with his words as he tried to explain how he felt. Mitch's head tilted up, like someone basking in the warm sun through the window on a cold winter day. As his cupped hand passed over the southern states on the map like a heavy storm cloud, it twitched. Like a hummingbird, his hand zoomed to the right and stopped over the ocean. He felt Leo's emotions as if they were his own. He could taste potato and bitter dandelion on his tongue, he could hear the crackling of a flame, and he felt the blissful enthusiasm of a child before their birthday, only not so innocent. His hand, almost as if pulled by a magnet, fell to the map, and he placed three jittering fingers on a space in the ocean.

He opened his eyes, and all his thoughts and feelings were his own once again. For a brief moment he felt a blast of success, and almost smiled. Then he looked down at the map and his face grew cold and stoic. It felt like a stab in the heart. Mitch felt that urge to run, hide and cry all over again. In a matter of seconds he started to descend into a pit of despair as he pulled his fingers from the map. Even when he thought he was successful, he wasn't. Everything he did felt like it was subpar, a failure or some kind of lucky yet unreliable miracle. Success for Mitch was like trying to catch a large butterfly with his bare hands in midflight without spoiling the delicate and colorful patterned scales on its wings.

"There?" Rosemary said softly. "That can't be possible."

"The middle of the ocean? No, it can't," Avery said with growing frustration.

Rosemary shook her head, and looked at Mitch and then back at the map. "The Bermuda Triangle." She pushed herself in front of Mitch and placed an unyielding finger in the center of the triangle. "Here? You sure?"

Mitch nodded, and for a moment, he felt the electric-like surge of doing something right run through his body. "Yeah. Right there. But that can't be right, can it?"

Rosemary traced a triangle on the map with the sharp point of her finger. "It could be. That's the entrance to Garland. The fairy realm," she said, suddenly more anxious than she had been in quite some time.

The coven stared back at Rosemary with stone faces as they tried to grapple with the idea that there was indeed another realm just beyond the veil of the one they knew.

"What?" Rosemary said. "Did you all think that this was the only reality? Seriously? Even after everything you've seen and learned? Bloody hell, children." She suddenly felt more like a secondary school teacher than an accomplished witch. "The quick version of this story is the only one you're going to get. If you want the more detailed one, which I assume some of you may not, you can ask Per. If we ever find him. I'm willing to bet that if we find Leo, we will find Per as well."

Her history lesson started immediately. She made herself a cheese sandwich with a hefty slathering of Branston Pickle, her absolute favorite condiment next to Marmite and Coleman's Mustard. She sometimes ate it with a spoon whenever she was feeling exceptionally bored or depressed. Regardless of how uncertain the coven's circumstances were, she smiled pleasantly after each bite of her sandwich. She paced back and forth, explaining only the necessary highlights that would satisfy the coven's curiosity.

She finished her sandwich after talking about the entrances to the fairy realm, and then started in on the jar of Branston Pickle with a fresh spoon like it was a steaming, fresh shepherd's pie. When the coven was finally up to speed, she wiped her mouth with a napkin like a fancy queen and then tossed it aside. Her eyes caught the clock.

"Everyone get some sleep. We're leaving straight away after breakfast tomorrow," Rosemary ordered.

"Wait, we're not going now?" Bisa asked.

"Of course not! We'll leave first thing in the morning when we have full daylight. If they've been gone this long, a few more hours aren't going to change anything."

A short scoff escaped from Avery's lips.

"Is there a problem, Avery?" Rosemary asked.

"There's no problem. I just hope that by the time we find Leo—if we find him—we won't have discovered that there was one."

Rosemary set her alarm for seven a.m. and met eyes with each and every one of them. "Half past seven, we're leaving. Be ready. I'm going to take you to the entrance of the fairy realm, and we're going to search for Leo and Per, and we are going to find them. Are we all on board?"

Everyone nodded, apart from Bisa. She crossed her arms and pretended to agree with a quotidian sense of normalcy—a skill she had learned working in retail when she could no longer stomach the entitled women treating her like a servant. Bisa clearly had other plans, she just didn't know what they were yet. Luckily, she had several late-night hours to meditate on it.

By morning, at the very latest, surely she would have sorted something out. She would have to. Waiting just felt wrong.

CHAPTER 14

Twenty-something miles away, just outside of Boulder, Nix was in meditative state in a room illuminated by candlelight and the amber glow of the streetlights outside the loft windows. He sat before his altar, a long and slender wooden table covered in a veil of plum-colored lace. Laid out in an orderly fashion was his dagger of silver and bone, a blood-red ceramic bowl of dried mandrake, mullein, and yew, a small black candle anointed in myrrh oil, the skull of a small ram, a single apache tear, and two glass jars, corked and sealed with wax—each containing the soul of a witch.

Nix wasn't particularly proud of killing Blake and Andy, and he would have easily taken more lives if it had been necessary, but his vision depicted that he must. His vision was an old and familiar one, a vision in which he took their lives, used their souls to complete a spell, and forced Death into a human form as he assumed the role himself. It wasn't just a murderous act, it had selfishness thrown in for good measure. However, murder was also necessary, a fundamental part of his journey back to where he had been born—the Land of Perpetual Midnight.

If he had been as juvenile as he was psychic, he would have blamed everything on his parents and their oddball doula. They were the ones who had botched the Child of Countless Charms spell during labor, a spell cast only through a dance of stylized movements and gestures. A ritual that yielded a successful result only if every precise and mathematical movement, every abrupt break and quick spin that transitioned to a frenzied pose, was perfectly executed. His parents had rehearsed for months—nine months, to be exact—straight up until his mother went into labor. However, Nix was ready to enter the world before his parents were, throwing chaos into their plans.

It was just past nine p.m. on a cold night in November 1975 when the labor began. It was also a blood moon, something his parents hadn't planned on or considered important. They knew every delicate finger gesture, every bend of the knee and every twist of the spine, but what they didn't know was how powerful a role the moon had to play.

When Nix's father and the doula began the dance sequence under the moon's sanguine beams, a new set of rules were made. Nix's father had made it very clear that there could be no mistakes, but that kind of perfectionism changes that which is being perfected. He was always a confident man, and he demanded confidence and perfection, especially when he and his wife were attempting to bring their son into the world with exceptional gifts. A confidence stronger than steel coursed through his body, so much so that he performed the dance with his eyes closed.

And then, he faltered. He clapped thrice instead of twice. He no longer heard the humming of the city or smelled the scent of his burning frankincense.

"Diego," his wife's voice spilled out into the unfamiliar air.

Nervously grasping at his earlobes, Diego opened his eyes. A black cloudlike mist evaporated, and he could see his wife and the doula under the bright moonlight. The small blunder had a catastrophic effect on their ritual and had transported them to the Land of Perpetual Midnight. Then, Nix was born. The moment his tiny body hit the air, his entire spiritual makeup was altered, something that witches who dabble in such magic call a dark birth. The living traveling to the Land of

Perpetual Midnight is quite common, but an innocent soul is impressionable—vulnerable, much more than in the living realm. Being born in Perpetual Midnight did have one sole advantage: Death would never come for him prematurely. But that safety would always be paired with a stinging craving to reside in the ether that was most aligned with his spiritual (and now physical) makeup—the darkness.

As soon as Nix was placed into his mother's arms, Diego began an incantation of his own design—more of a prayer, really—to try to reverse their crossing into the darkness and bring them back to the comfort of their own home where they belonged. Diego chanted, his wife bled, the doula cried and panicked. The dark birth was accompanied by a sense of dread, one that Diego couldn't shake. His fingers slipped as he clasped his sweaty hands together in an effort to amplify his intention.

Diego's left eye cracked open, and he peeked at his wife, bleeding and holding their newborn child. Time was running out. Anyone with eyes could see that, and Diego had never been known for his patience but rather for his standard of excellence. It was that very obsession with perfectionism—and perhaps a little desire to correct his earlier mistake—that allowed him to bring them all back to the land of the living, all except himself.

Yet it came with a price. Death was never one for hospitality, but he did like to taunt trespassers into his realm. Depending on his schedule, he could choose when he would come for a trespassing soul. His schedule was light that day, and Diego was a delightful little amuse-bouche. Death appeared before him with the flowing robes that Nix had seen himself wearing so many times in his visions. Diego had cried only once in his life; that moment marked the second.

Death lifted its arm and revealed a single finger of solid bone. Diego repeated his incantations as he stared into Death's swirling black eyes. For a brief moment, Diego smelled the sweet and spicy incense smoke from home, and when he closed his eyes, he could see it burning in the soft light of the blood moon. He finished his incantation with a final goodbye to his wife as he waited for Death to take his breath. He closed his eyes one final time and imagined his wife and newborn child and hoped for the best. Then it was quiet. He waited. *Have I been spared?* he thought. Diego opened his eyes, and then, and only then, did Death take Diego's life.

Nix might have never known the truth of his past if he hadn't been such a dedicated witch so committed to psychism. One hour of meditation became two, two became four, and four became obsession. It was that pledge to excellence, to perfectionism, that allowed him to learn all the secrets of the past. After all, he was his father's son, and anything worth doing was worth doing better than everyone else. So when he sliced open the alligator in Louisiana and divined his future in the entrails that spilled out, he was able to interpret the message without having to intellectualize it. He knew *there will be life…in death* meant he was destined to *become* death. Avenging his father was secondary, and irrelevant. He hadn't known him, he didn't care. It was in meditation that he entered the realms of higher consciousness, connected with his guides and ancestors and learned of his origin, not through the teachers of a perfectionist father who had proved to be anything but perfect.

Nix carried on with his deep breathing, letting his mind wander through the past and present and into the future.

Feelings became visions as he delved further into the psychic realm. He saw his father die, his mother bleed out at the hospital hours later, and the doula suffer a stroke years later as he had seen so many times in the past. He saw that Death was once a witch and pondered whether the Death before that was also a witch. Soon, he would become Death himself and possess the powers of necromancy, powers that would allow him to control and conjure entities that were beyond the realm of natural magic. Powers that could not be controlled—or destroyed—by any witch. Nix would be reborn and shed all the layers of what he once was, and would truly be—perfect. Messages and visions left as fast as they came, like speeding cars on a highway. Then came a voice from the darkness of his meditative state. It was time to begin.

Nix picked up his dagger from the altar, carved a few enigmatic symbols into the side of the candle and drew a ring around the base with a fingerful of the dried herbs and roots. He lit the wick, cupped the apache tear between his palms and held it to his third eye as he repeated a mantra in his mind:

Fiet mortale sit mors,

fiet mortale sit mors,

fiet mortale sit mors.

He felt a gentle stirring between his hands and forehead as the jagged, opaque chunk of obsidian slowly became more and more translucent, like thick fog in a gust of wind. He parted his lips, let out a heavy breath and lowered the stone back to the altar.

A series of lightning-quick visions flashed through his mind. His lips pressed together tightly as the images struck him. This had happened to him many times; unwelcome visions, feelings, energies, emotions had emerged out of nowhere and made themselves known. Often, he wasn't even sure who he was reading, only that he was reading someone or something. It was sometimes like a walkie-talkie—no matter what channel you were on, you'd get a little extra interference occasionally. Yet this particular vision was exceptionally unwelcome, because it showed him his own death at the hands of Merlot. His fists clenched as he watched the vision unfold over and over against the back of his eyelids. He was born to become Death, not meet it. There was no way he was going to allow a rogue witch to get in his way.

Nix lowered his head in concentration and asked for answers.

Body, mind and spirit, show me what I need to know. What is the path to my success? What is the key to obtaining my goals?

The answers came to him in a rush of shapes and colors. He quickly pieced it all together as if someone had narrated it to him like a bedtime story. A storm of solutions whipped through his mind. He learned it all in less than a minute. Bisa was the key. She was the one who had Death breathing down her neck. She was the one with a personal vendetta against Merlot for having killed Nina (news he didn't even know until that very instant).

When the visions ended, he returned to his slow and steady breathing. He knew exactly what he needed to do. It was complicated—well, not complicated, time consuming. Nix opened his eyes and wiped his brow with his sleeve. He looked over at the clock. There was no time to waste. He had a lot of spellwork to do. As he prepared for the next few magical tasks, he understood that what he had been assuming for much of his life was true. Things would all work out—perfectly.

CHAPTER 15

Leo asked, "How much farther? Are we almost there?"

"Almost," Henrie replied. "The moat is right up here." Henrie lifted the mushroom higher in the air as they rounded the corner. A long wooden bridge stretched over a deep moat where nighttime waters flowed far below, the rippled surface shimmering in the moonlight like little stars. At least fifty feet, maybe a hundred, Leo thought. He was never really great at judging distance, but he was good at judging danger, and it looked far enough to kill a person if they fell. At the end of the bridge was a set of thick wooden doors about fifteen feet high.

"This is the entrance to Tengotodo," Henrie said as he led the way across the bridge. The windswept bridge was old, but well maintained, much like the gate in front of them. The palace was built into a mound of rock that jutted up from the middle of the moat. Whether the moat had been man-made was up for debate, but the chateau was stunning. A stark contrast to the Creamstone Township, which reeked of sewage and was so ugly, it hurt to look at it.

Tengotodo was something out of a movie, at least to Leo. He had never been so close to something so opulent. When Henrie had referred to Tengotodo as a chateau, Leo had assumed it was going to be a quaint little wooden cabin nestled into a mountain or in a bunch of trees. It was only upon seeing the outrageous magnificence before him that he realized he had been picturing a chalet, not a chateau. He had driven through the Garden District in New Orleans and the wealthy parts of Mandeville and Slidell, where homes slowly turned into mansions at every block, but he had never seen anything like Tengotodo. It was something straight out of television, something that an heiress would own but not actually live in, a house for someone like George Lucas or Oprah Winfrey, painted in a jubilee of custard-colored hues. A large balcony hung from the second floor, and a massive window. Jasper was clearly a king, there was no other word for it. President, maybe? If they had such a thing, Leo considered.

When they reached the gate, Leo could see that its doors were carved in thousands and thousands of small symbols, all lined up like small bits of computer code. *It looks like* The Matrix, *but magical,* Leo thought.

"How do we get in?" Per asked.

Henrie produced a long metal key the size of a small hammer from underneath his robes. He nodded, and waved the key like he had just won a trophy. The key slipped into the lock. A click, a snap and a heavy, metallic clamoring followed. Henrie grabbed hold of the polished copper ring attached to each door and pulled them open. They proceeded toward the chateau until they reached the front entrance. Henrie opened the front door, and a gust of perfumed air escaped from inside and wafted across their faces. The room was dark, apart from the two standing candelabras on either side of the entrance that were covered in burning mushrooms. Henrie entered first and beckoned Leo and Per to follow with a flicker of his dirty finger.

The hallway was quiet as they slowly followed Henrie into the darkness, wondering where they were going and if it was safe. They passed a section of the hall that opened up to a room on either side of them. They pressed forward, but suddenly Leo and Per felt metal at their throats. Leo's first instinct was to attack, but he couldn't. He had no power in Garland, and he wasn't wormy enough to wiggle his way out of being compromised. Sure, he was scrappy, but he wasn't really a fighter, and he sure wasn't about to start a fight when a knife was at his throat.

Another man stepped out of the dark room to their left, holding a copper blade identical to the one at their throats in his four-fingered hand. His pinky had been cut off during a scuffle the last time someone had been brought to the palace. From that point on, he had chosen to delegate the task of seizing captives instead of risking losing more fingers. It turned out he wasn't much of a fighter either. But he was good at giving orders. He was also known for keeping his promises to the other guards, so when Henrie met him with a nod and an open palm, he knew what was next.

The guard slapped a sweaty handful of copper nuggets into Henrie's demanding hand.

"I told you I had two for you this time," Henrie told the four-fingered man as he picked through the copper nuggets, examining their size. He felt no shame as he looked into the eyes of Leo and Per, now struck with fear. It was a job, it wasn't personal. Leo and Per were nothing more than products being delivered, and Henrie was nothing more than a courier being paid for his services, as he had been many times before. In some ways he was proud of the fact that he was able to persuade the guards to hire him to bring people to the palace.

"So that's how it is, huh?" Leo said. The sharpened blade pressed more tightly against his throat.

Henrie looked up from his pile of copper. His eyes were as cold as his heart was empty.

"What about everything you said earlier?" Per asked. "Don't you want to go back home?"

"Everything I said was true. But there is no way out, no going home. This is home now," Henrie said bitterly. He had been bitter for so long that it made the act of trafficking newcomers to the palace every now and then as instinctual as breathing. Of course he wanted to go home, but that was a distant fantasy reserved for the sleepless evenings when he had no money and no food. Copper was the only metal found in Garland, and therefore it was the most prized element. The constant delivering of prisoners kept him in fresh seeds for his potato garden, and every once in a while, even something a little extra. He had given up on escaping Garland a long time ago, and his guilt had been replaced with the need to survive.

"Go on, now, you've got your copper, now go," the four-fingered man said as he stepped closer to his new prisoners. He was slender and close to fifty, but with the skin of someone no older than twenty. If it hadn't been for the roughly chopped beard and the comet-red scar above his right eyebrow, he might have looked even younger. He could have been someone really sweet under all that chaos on his face, so distracting that it looked like costume makeup. Sweetness was what Per naively hoped for—well, actually, mercy more than sweetness. He had read enough dark fantasy and watched enough television to know that what came next couldn't be good.

Henrie walked past Leo as he shoved his newly made fortune into a small pocket. Leo lunged at him, sending Henrie cowering against the wall. The guard grabbed hold of Leo, shook him like a dirty rag and returned the knife to his throat, this time breaking skin. Leo laughed.

Henrie stopped and turned to Leo. "What's funny?"

"Y'all just wait," Leo said.

Henrie laughed as he left through the gate. "*You* just wait!"

"Where's Jasper?" Leo demanded.

The four-fingered man was struck with confusion. A heavy moment of silence hung in the air as he carefully thought about what to say next. "How do you know Jasper?"

"So he's here? I need to see him," Leo said.

"What are you gonna do with us?" Per blurted fearfully.

The four-fingered man smiled and started to pick dirt from underneath his fingernail with his knife. "Well, that depends. Usually, we eat you."

Horror filled Per's heart, and so did anger as he blamed Leo for getting him into the situation to begin with.

"But we'll let Jasper decide," the man said as he finished cleaning his four fingers.

CHAPTER 16

Bisa opened her eyes and sat up in bed. The house was quiet, but her mind was buzzing. Her dream had been so vivid that she almost thought it had actually happened. She looked around the room to ground herself and then, with perfect clarity, she understood what the dream had meant. It wasn't a dream; it was a message. She knew where to find Merlot, she was certain of it. Bisa removed herself from the sheets and sat in contemplation. Then, after a minute, *I have to go*, she thought. *I have to go now.* She knew the coven was going to look for Leo and Per first thing in the morning, but she didn't have time for that. Considering what she knew about Leo, she chose not to have time for that.

Bisa took the quietest shower she had ever taken, making it in and out in under ten minutes. The image of a location burned inside her head, like a building in the dark illuminated by a bright flashlight. She saw it, but couldn't make out the details. The harder she tried to focus on anything that would give her more information, the more the image became distorted and fell dark. It was almost as if it didn't want her to see. Bisa was going to have to work for this.

"Where are you," Bisa whispered to the image in her head.

The image hissed back to her, like an old steam radiator.

(don't go...)

Bisa flinched at the sudden intrusion.

"Nina?" Bisa asked the voice.

A few moments later, after she held her breath:

(don't go...)

Consumed with grief and frustration, Bisa believed the voice to just be her own thoughts trying to convince her she should remain with the coven because it was the right thing to do. However, the grief that had thickened her skin, chilled her heart and impaired her judgment was in control. It was the grief and the hunger for justice—no, retribution—that drove her for the time being.

Bisa made her way to the mudroom, careful to avoid any sections of the floor that creaked, and retrieved the car keys from the table. She had no idea where she was going. She had to go on pure instinct at this point—instinct and a little intuition.

After she made it to the car, she flipped on the heater and turned it up full blast. She backed out of the garage and made her way to an unknown destination. Bisa didn't care what the location was, who could be there waiting for her or what might happen to her when she got there. The dream had been more than a dream, it had been a psychic gift (*wasn't it?*), and there was no other excuse for it. With her gifts getting stronger by the day, it had to be that.

"First things first," she said out loud. "Where am I actually going?" Bisa released her right hand from the wheel and held her palm out in front of her. She then swayed to the left and then the right. Bisa didn't have time to doubt her decision or her skill, she had to be confident. As her car pulled onto the main road, she closed her fingers together on her raised hand and waited for a sign. *Is this the way?* Bisa asked her intuition. A ghostly flash of the word *yes* ran through her mind, and a wave of heat like breath whooshed against her palm. *Yes,* Bisa thought. She hoped so, anyway, but she didn't have time for hope—she had to be right.

Bisa continued to drive using her hand as a magnet, letting it pull her in the direction of where she needed to be. She drove and drove, sometimes finding herself back in the same place, but she never lost her nerve, not even when she ended up in the parking lot of Costco twice. She knew she wasn't deluding herself. The message was correct, but perhaps it would take a few misses for her psychic hunt to yield the results she was looking for.

Bisa questioned herself only once during that drive. When she hit the turnpike heading into Boulder, she thought perhaps she was being a little too self-involved, running off with the car, leaving the coven to search for Leo and Per on their own…all because of a dream she had had. Bisa had always been a team player as much as she had been autonomous, but the rules had changed because her reality had changed.

At some point between Baseline Road and College Avenue she decided she needed to stop for gas, and that's when she looked up and saw the storefront in her dream, gleaming under the bright morning sun. There were no coincidences anymore; perhaps there never had been. Bisa parked along the side of the street as the *Closed* sign on the shop's door flipped to *Open*. Right then, her phone rang.

Only after everyone gathered in the kitchen at half past seven did they realize that Bisa was missing. All at once, they asked one another if they had seen her, but no one had. Rosemary checked her room to see her door cracked open and her bed unmade. They checked every floor of the house and hollered out for her, and Avery even tried calling her phone. She was nowhere to be found.

Rosemary huffed through the house, knowing full well that Bisa had taken it upon herself to look for Merlot. "We don't have time for this. I'm sorry to say this, but we can't look for Bisa right now." Rosemary's boots clanked across the floor as she ignored the coven's pleas to find her. "Whatever she is up to, she has chosen to do it on her own, and that's her decision. She's not stupid, she is more talented than any of you realize. I'm sure she can handle herself. But as for where we are going and what we're about to do, well…I'm going to need help from every one of you."

Avery felt like she was the only one who cared whether Bisa was okay, whether she lived or died, even though that wasn't true. She had been getting exceptionally hotheaded lately, and her quick temper was on fire. Ollie soothed her with his compassionate and gentle words in the way that only someone like Ollie could do. Rosemary nodded her thanks to him when Avery wasn't looking. She walked over to Ollie's room and closed the door.

"I would have us all astrally project, but I think for the sake of time and the nature of our task, I'll do this instead,"

Rosemary said. "Oh"—she turned to Avery—"be a dear and grab my handbag from the sunroom, will you?"

When Avery returned, Rosemary shuffled through the contents like a raccoon in a garbage can. "Ah! There it is. Lovely!" She closed her bag and threw it over her shoulder. "Now I'm ready."

She beckoned the coven closer and held both hands out in front of her as if she was about to give someone a loving embrace. She cleared her mind, reaching a degree of clarity that would have taken the rest of them nearly twenty minutes. Rosemary squeezed her lips together and began to carve a series of symbols on the roof of her mouth with her tongue, an old way of spellcasting that was lost on the newer generation of witches. When the mysterious symbols were etched, Rosemary blew the enchanted air out toward Ollie's bedroom door. The fingers of her left hand went to the ring of three garnet stones on her right hand, each stone hand harvested from a different member of her family, each infused with the magical blessing of a different coven from a completely different generation. It was this ring that gave her the power to amplify spells, thoughts and intentions along with the ability to create a door to another place out of any door.

In her teenage years, when Rosemary had been given the ring, she had worn it proudly and exercised its power carelessly, as most youngsters would. Now she treated the ring with more respect and used its unique power more frugally because of the price to use its power. The cost of the ring's magic was that every time a door was made, a year was taken from the life of the person who wore it. It was part of the deal with the deity that a member of her distant family had made. It had happened so long ago that she no longer cared to remember. (Perhaps that was the excuse she told herself; maybe she hadn't ever really cared enough to listen in the first place.) Her only concern was that every time she used the spell, she wondered if it would be her last. There was no way of knowing when the ring would collect its final payment and her life would end. But she took a chance and hoped for the best. Surely whatever deity was behind the ring would understand why she had to use it in this situation.

Rosemary held the image of her desired destination in her head. The magic worked intuitively, allowing a door (if there was one) on the other end to be free from the public eye so that the ring and its user would have the comfort of privacy. She gripped the door handle and waited patiently for the thought of her immediate death to be tucked away in the back of her mind. She replaced it quickly with something a little more delicious— her memory of Bermuda. It had been years since she had been there, and as she turned the doorknob, she could smell the tropical air. It smelled the same as it had all those years ago. When the door was fully open, the mouths of everyone in the room hung wide open. It was worth the risk to see the shock on all their faces.

"Isn't that just grand?" Rosemary said with a smile.

The sun was shining bright, the salty-fresh air spilled through the doorway and there was a beach in what used to be Ollie's bedroom. Waves crashed in the distance and rolled up onto the shore.

"Right. Let's get on with it," Rosemary said as she stepped through the door and into eleven a.m.

Mitch started picking at his already bleeding thumb, his anxiety rushing through him. He was the last to walk through the door, stopping in the middle of the doorway to examine both realities. Avery and Ollie gave a gasp of pure delight as they hit the sand. A rush of nostalgia ran over Rosemary as memories of her time on the sea filled her mind. It saddened her a little to know that so much time had gone by since she'd been in Bermuda, but she didn't have time to think about that.

"Now what?" Avery asked as she walked toward the water, mesmerized by what magic was able to do. She didn't even mind the sand spilling into her shoes.

A few beach-loving birds squawked and cooed above them, their wings flapping and carrying them in circles like sharks in the sky.

Caw, caw, caw, caw, caw, caw!

"Now we get a boat and some sunscreen," Rosemary said as she shielded her eyes from the heavy sun. "Someone like me could die without it in a place like this!"

CHAPTER 18

Bisa stepped out into the cold winter air, walked up to the door of the shop and read the name on the glass door: *Oscuro*. She pushed the door open and entered the café just as a batch of heavy clouds covered the sun. Inside, the café was a sleek and surprisingly shiny space, the floors covered in an elegant, coal-colored, diamond-shaped tile, the counters a mix of reclaimed wood and white marble, all set against a wall of brick-shaped tiles, the alter ego of the floor. There was something strange about the scent of roasted cinnamon, toasted masa harina and dark chocolate, something that didn't quite fit but seemed oddly familiar.

Her eyes matched with those of a man in the back corner of the café, and her heart skipped a beat. She knew that man, and as she looked over the features of his face, she also identified that mysterious smell underneath the layers of freshly prepared champurrado. She smelled a witch, and his name was Nix. She strode through the door and headed toward him. He sat completely still, tolerant of her burning gaze. Although she had many questions and even more emotions running through her mind, she bit her tongue and waited for him to speak first.

"Sit, please," Nix offered as he indicated the chair across from him.

Bisa remained still, uncertain how to proceed. At one time she would have reacted hastily, but something told her not to. As she considered the invitation, she also questioned her intuition. What was it that had brought her here? Had she been so obsessed with finding Merlot that she had lost her grip on her psychism? Or was it something else?

"Can I get you something? The Mexican hot chocolate* here is quite good," Nix said as he pointed to the café menu on the chalkboard behind the counter.

"So now you want to buy me breakfast?" Bisa said sharply as she crossed her arms in front of her chest.

"I don't have to buy it. I own the place," Nix said.

"What?"

"This is my café, I own it. I privately invested in the space many, many years ago. It's actually been quite lucrative. Everyone loves hot chocolate, even in the summer. We shake it like a cocktail and serve it over ice. And with a name like Oscuro you can almost guarantee the hipsters and Instagrammers will be all over something like that." Nix raised two fingers to signal the young woman behind the counter. "Two Mexican hot chocolates," he said in a soft whisper. He looked at Bisa once more. "Please sit. If I wanted you dead, you'd be dead by now."

Bisa untangled her arms, placed her hands on the chair and leaned over it in a menacing manner. "Maybe I want *you* dead."

"That's probably true, but you're not going to kill me."

"Why not?" Bisa said softly, yet completely intrigued.

"Because I know why you're here and I know what you want. Why do you think I brought you here?"

"The dream. That was you?" Bisa said, narrowing her eyes.

The milk frother from the espresso machine hissed and whistled as the barista heated the milk and cream. The sudden piercing sound caught Bisa off guard, and she winced.

"Please sit," Nix asked one final time.

Bisa looked fixedly down at the chair. She knew by now that she really had no other choice but to hear Nix out. She had ignored Avery's phone call earlier, and either they had gone to look for Leo and Per without her or they were waiting for her. But she sensed that they had left. So she decided to sit.

"I don't trust you," Bisa said.

"Good. You don't have a reason to, and I don't blame you for that. And I know you must have many questions. However, I can say that the only thing that matters right now is that we work together."

Bisa scoffed and shot him a nasty look. "Work together? You just told me that you know I have no reason to trust you, and then you ask me to trust you. Now, what kind of sense does that make?"

"I know you're looking for Merlot. That's why I brought you here. I'm looking for her too. If I'm allowed to toot my own horn, as they say, I would have to admit that I am not just good at divination, I'm fucking great at it. Most everything I've ever known or learned, I've been able to know or learn because of my dedication to my craft, specifically the psychic arts. I have the kind of perseverance that your coven dreams of having. But you're different, I know you are. And you know that I know that. I wouldn't have been able to connect with you through your dreams if I was lying."

The barista arrived and dropped off two cups of Mexican hot chocolate. Nix thanked her and slid one of the cups toward Bisa. As much as she tried to ignore it, the scent of the hot chocolate was intoxicating—enchanting, even. For a moment she considered that the barista was in on some evil plot and had served her some kind of bewitched potion.

"It's not poisoned. Try it," Nix insisted.

Bisa picked up the cup and held it in front of her face. The rising steam passed over her lips, melting the winter's chill straight off them. "Do you even know how to make this? Can you even work the espresso machine?"

Nix scoffed, "Of course. What kind of owner do you think I am?" He tasted his cup and smiled as he rolled the sweet and mysteriously spicy liquid chocolate over his tongue.

"Good. I'd hate for you to be one of those clueless owners who makes his employees take pictures of him pretending to make drinks when you don't even know how to turn on the machine." Bisa sipped from her cup, waited a moment, and then took a deeper, longer drink.

"I would never. If you're going to do anything, then you have to be able to do it right. No sense in pretending. That's just acting. Not being."

Bisa licked her lips, feeling the heat from the guajillo chili pepper. "Yeah, that's pretty good."

Nix winked at her. Bisa couldn't quite shake a sense of suspicion. She wondered what the extent of his power truly was. She highly doubted it was capped at divination. Clearly he was very gifted. It occurred to her that part of his power might rest in his ability to convince her that he knew more than he was letting on. Bisa didn't have many secrets, but there were things that she sure as hell didn't trust Nix with. Her anxiety began to rise and fall as she tried to decide whether he was privy to information she hadn't volunteered. After all, she knew full well how powerful psychism and influence could be.

Bisa began to press for information—answers, really— about why he had planted the gris-gris bag that compromised their protection spells, whether he was out to destroy the Advisory and why he had murdered Blake and Andy from the Houston coven, offering him the chance to shed light on the situation from his perspective. She quickly found that in addition to his psychic and divinatory gifts, he possessed the gift of gab. There was even a moment when she failed to respond because she couldn't come up with a retort that would get her the answer she desired. *Oh, you're good*, she thought.

"Look," Nix said, rapping his index finger repeatedly on the bistro table, "I know you don't trust me. I also know that Death is coming for you."

Hearing the words from someone other than herself was incredibly disconcerting. It made it all that much more real, and even more—urgent.

"And just like Death is coming for you, Merlot is coming for me. She's already tried to kill me once," Nix said as he adjusted the collar of his shirt.

"Why would she want to kill you?"

"Why does Merlot do half the things she does? She's out of control. But the reason is that she wants to take over the Advisory. Well, abolish it."

Bisa laughed. "I think you've been fired from the Advisory at this point."

"Merlot doesn't know about that. Even if she did, do you think she'd care?"

"Why is this so important?" Bisa asked.

"One's own life isn't important?"

"You know what I mean," Bisa said as she rolled her eyes.

"I've seen what will happen. If she is not stopped, she'll succeed. She'll kill me. Then who knows what happens after that."

Bisa took another sip of her hot chocolate and adjusted herself in her seat. She studied every feature of Nix's face and looked deep into his eyes in a way that finally made him feel uncomfortable. "You know, if Avery were here, she would be able to smell if you were telling the truth."

Nix nodded. "I have heard that about her. However, she's not here. So what choice do you have?"

"Is that why you chose me? Because I wouldn't be able to smell a lie?"

"Again. What choice do you have?"

"What do you propose we do, then?" Bisa said plainly.

"Easy. Your Transcendent powers combined with my Primordial powers; I know a way we can find her. That's the easy part. All we have to do next is stop her."

"And what about me? We save *your* life, but Death is still coming for *me*," Bisa said.

"I can stop it. I've enchanted a stone that will break his connection to you. He'll no longer seek you out."

"Let me guess: I'll just have to trust you."

Nix nodded. "If I die, and I'm telling the truth, then you're fucked. And you know it."

A beam of sunlight broke free from the clouds and filled the front window, illuminating the smoky haze that hung in the air from a batch of smoked guanabana flan that had just come out of the smoker. Bisa took the sun as a sign and decided that she would take Nix up on his offer.

Right then, after another heavy sip of her hot chocolate, she felt the rush of sugar. "I accept. On one condition," she added.

"Naturally."

"You don't harm me or my coven, and you can't spoil or mess up or get in the way of how I deal with Merlot."

"Believe me, I want to stop her as much as you do. My life depends on it." Nix paused. "Have you ever killed anyone?"

Bisa raised her eyebrows and let out a befuddled gasp. "No," she answered, narrowing her eyes suspiciously. "Why?"

"I'm asking because it may be something that comes up. It may be something that you will have to do to defend yourself if we go after Merlot. She's already killed many other people, and we have to consider the fact that I may not be able to protect you."

"I can take care of myself. You ought to be more concerned about me being able to protect you."

"I'm only saying that I know her. I know what she is capable of," Nix said.

"If it comes down to me or her, I can promise you I won't think twice about taking her life to save my own," Bisa said, surprising even herself.

Nix took a couple of gulps of his hot chocolate and then pointed at Bisa's cup. "Be sure you finish that. It would be disrespectful not to."

"I'm not worried about disrespecting you."

"Not me. Cacao is a tree spirit. It's a precious thing to take into your body. Honestly, Bisa, you call yourself a witch."

Before Bisa had entered the shop, she had been certain she was about to see Merlot face-to-face. Now she was just past the point of being uncertain of her intuition. She took a deep breath and rubbed her hands together to warm them up.

"So what next?" she asked.

"We go to my altar, pinpoint where Merlot is…and then we end it."

CHAPTER 19

Rosemary, Avery and Ollie reached the open sea via boat, with Rosemary sailing them toward the boundaries of the Bermuda Triangle. Rosemary looked and felt about twenty years younger, her silvery hair whipping in the cool, salty Atlantic winds. *How I've missed this*, she thought, a smile stretched across her face. Her eyes wide and full of joy, unaffected by the speed at which the wind swept across them. With one hand on the wheel, she reached her free hand into her handbag and retrieved the small rose of Jericho plant she had verified was in her possession earlier. She dropped it into a cupholder beside her and continued to sail.

"Almost there—a few minutes more, I believe," Rosemary shouted over the splashing of the water. "Avery, release the starboard jib sheet! Ollie, you're next, grab the port-side jib sheet and catch that wind."

"When did you learn to sail?" Ollie asked, completely amazed as he wrapped the sheet from the headsail around the winch per Rosemary's expert instruction.

Rosemary grinned even wider. "A very long time ago, longer than I'd care to admit." Time seemed to stop for Rosemary as she reminisced about her past. A soft giggle escaped her. "I've lived a very full life; my advice is that all of you do exactly the same. Time goes faster than this boat." Her fingers delicately caressed the helm of the boat as if it were an old lover. "I had almost forgotten how much I loved sailing and being on the open ocean." Rosemary took a deep breath and looked up to the bright sun and gave her hair a quick brushing with her fingers.

"Who taught you to sail?" Ollie asked.

Rosemary's eyes lit up and her cheeks started to flush. "It was early 1982. I met Morgan Freeman at Paul Newman's birthday party. He introduced me to sailing, and that's when I fell in love with the sea." She took another deep breath and exhaled as she relived the memories.

"Morgan Freeman?" Avery asked, shocked.

Rosemary nodded, and raised her eyebrows. "Oh, I spent a wonderful…" She paused. "...*wonnnn*derful two weeks sailing between St. Lucia and the British Virgin Islands with Morgan, Jacques Cousteau, Prince and Sigourney Weaver."

Avery choked on her sip of water. A few drips rolled down her chin and splashed onto her already sea-soaked shirt. "What!" she exclaimed.

Rosemary laughed as if a joke had been told and she was the only one who got it. Her energy lightened, and her face danced between happy tears and a wistfulness that she hadn't experienced in quite a while. "Prince, you know," Rosemary began, her finger pointed at the coven to make sure they were paying attention (but how could anyone not?) "was—in addition to being an extraordinary guitar player—actually a witch. The original name for *Purple Rain* was supposed to be *Purple Reign*, R-E-I-G-N. Sort of in reference to his rise to the top of the music world."

Rosemary flourished her hand as if brushing away a pesky fly. "Well, that and he considered witches to have *royal blood*, so it was a whole play on words thing, an inside joke." Her face lost all signs of joy in an instant. "Don't repeat that," she stressed sternly. "I'd hate to be sued by Universal Music too. I have enough on my bloody plate with Sony."

The coven sat in confusion, but they were too shocked to press her further.

"Is Björk a witch?" Mitch asked, finally opening his mouth for the first time the entire trip.

"What was Morgan Freeman like?" Avery asked as she fidgeted in her seat, trying to avoid the cold spray of the ocean.

Rosemary had had a crush on Morgan since the moment she'd met him. Back in her youth, she was even more of a spitfire than she was in her golden years. She lifted her hand to her brow and brushed it for comfort as she tried to coerce the reddening in her cheeks to stand down. She couldn't remember the last time she had spoken with him, or even seen him, for that matter. However, even after all that time, the attraction was still there—apparently. She mulled over Avery's question in her mind a few times, trying to figure out how to describe the man she had had a crush on for decades. It only led her to wonder why she hadn't heard from him in so long. What had happened?

A few moments passed. The boat bounced up and down as it busted through some choppy water and sizable waves. Then, it came to her in the fog of the open water that had been sunny and clear only moments ago. *Oh, that's right*, Rosemary thought. She had forgotten about the night with the extra-buttery Chex Mix. A few frivolous drinks under some twinkle lights on the patio had turned into a psychedelic, madcap evening on Morgan's sailboat once they decided to try the chocolate-covered 'shrooms in someone's purse. She couldn't remember their name, only that they had once posed for Basquiat. Nothing out of the ordinary, just your standard hallucinogenic experience. Nobody died. Nobody cried. No one stopped Rosemary from making an uncompromising and, some said, borderline aggressive pass at Morgan either. Rosemary closed her eyes and shook her head as the memory replayed itself in her mind. Needless to say, it had freaked him out, and it soured their fledgling relationship. He never talked to her after that, and it was the last time she mixed 'shrooms with Rum Punch on the open sea.

"So? What's he like?" Avery asked again, desperate for more information.

Rosemary's eyes were busy, her tongue was tied and her mind was misty. "Haven't spoken to him in years."

A few moments later, Rosemary pointed the boat into the wind and ordered the coven members to lower the sails, letting the boat drift in the middle of the ocean. She spit onto the rose of Jericho in the cupholder and looked off into the distance.

"What now?" Ollie asked.

"We wait," Rosemary said. "Be sure to stow away any loose items." She tilted her head back and waited for the magnetic pull that she knew was coming to lift them up off the boat and into the realm. Then it happened—fast. And brought with it all the screams, yells and shrieks of panic of the unprepared coven as they levitated over the open water.

It was dark in the cell where Leo and Per had spent the night. A room of cold stone, barely large enough for either of them to move around, let alone stand up. The only light came from a single mushroom torch on the wall just outside their cell. It had burned all night and looked like a charred marshmallow. Two guards entered the room holding copper daggers that were much longer and sharper than the ones held at their throats the night before.

"Get up, it's time," the four-fingered man said as he unlocked the cell gate.

Leo and Per stood up as best they could and stepped out of the cell.

"Where are we going?" Per asked. His eyelids wrinkled in response to the light pouring in from the open door to the hallway.

"Jasper is ready to see you. He'll decide what happens to you. Or how you'll be prepared," the guard said.

Leo hadn't thought much about how serious their situation was. He couldn't; he had bigger, more ambitious ideas in his head. Yet the reality of their predicament needed to be addressed. Even Leo had to eventually start thinking about how to survive.

The guards stood by the doorway, waiting for their prisoners. Leo looked down and to the right of their cell. Two square holes covered by a metal grate in the stone floor caught the light from the doorway. Leo stretched his neck for a closer look. They were dark and rife with psychological distress that even he could detect. *An underground cell or dungeon, maybe,* Leo thought. The opening was incredibly narrow, and he wasn't sure how deep the pits ran, but he knew for certain they wouldn't be able to turn around once dropped inside. A rush of relief washed over him. He was happy to have been tossed in the cell instead of…whatever that was in the floor.

"If you'd rather stay in the oubliette, I'm sure Jasper will understand," the man said.

Leo and Per followed the men out of the room and into the hall now illuminated by the gleaming daylight. Neither of them had noticed much of anything the night before in the darkness, but now there were no more secrets.

Tengotodo was constructed of wood, earth and local limestone. The walls of the chateau—more of a castlelike mansion, really—were fifteen feet high and made of rammed earth. Its beauty lay in its craftsmanship, with no need for ornate embellishments or designs to signify its opulence. The walls held the heat hostage during the day and released it after the sun had retreated behind the mountains in the distance. The layout was designed in a way that encouraged the winds of the west to flow freely through the rooms and exit the windows in the east.

Being brought to Jasper felt more like being on a tour intended to show off his wealth and furthermore, his power. There was everything inside the chateau, whereas there was nothing in the Creamstone Township. Step-by-step they strode through Tengotodo, peeking into every room with an open door, which was nearly all of them. They passed a room of skeleton keys and polished quartz, then a room of elaborately carved, wooden display cabinets, painted in colors of teal, white and yellow, decorated with chunks of quartz and storing all sorts of strange curios, from beetles to bones.

They rounded a corner and proceeded down a longer hall-way that the four-fingered man called the hall of living landscapes. Spaced out every twelve feet were four, ten-foot-wide openings that ran along the eastern wall. They spanned from floor to ceiling and were bordered with wood frames that, when looked through, gave one a breathtaking vista of the nat-ural landscape. It was fantastic, although inconvenient on stormy days, when the wind pushed the rain inside. Perhaps the reason why the land was so barren was that Jasper had taken it all for himself, Per thought as he slowed down to look out the glassless window. Neither he nor Leo had noticed the six cop-per-and-glass lanterns that hung along the opposite wall, filled not with candles or flaming mushrooms, but gorgeous, irides-cent dragonflies, with violet bodies, wine-colored wings and pearlescent eyes. They fluttered and buzzed with the grace of an autumn leaf descending through a gentle breeze. Suddenly, they heard music.

They passed through an archway of gold-flecked quartz and entered a cavernous room whose ground had shifted from flat, tiled floors to a staggered, cubic path of carved limestone, with stepping pillars both short and tall. Citrus and cherry trees bloomed freely on either side of the path, catching the rays of the afternoon sun through the crystal-clear windows. *How is any of this possible in a realm with no magic?* Per thought as he followed the guards. They pushed against the door that was slightly ajar at the end of the pathway and entered. A large din-ing room was before them. A long wooden table filled the center, covered in mushroom-filled candelabras. In the far cor-ner of the room, a man in a long, burgundy silk jacket sat before a harpsichord. His fingers hopped across the instrument, pro-ducing a melody both eerie and timeless. On top of the harpsichord was a glass bell jar that encased a single milkweed seed, floating as if it had a mind of its own.

"I have the prisoners for you," the four-fingered man said. He knew he was interrupting. "Sir," he added.

Jasper stopped playing and turned his head. His reddish-brown hair shimmered like wildfire under the sun, hiding the features of his face. He rose from his seat and turned to face them, and the back of his coat slipped off the bench and dangled freely. Everything about him looked handcrafted in a privileged sort of way, a style that suggested he had invented the version of himself that stood before them, from the worn, tobacco-colored leather boots to the drapey patterned shirt with a neckline so low, it knew his sternum. Per had seen this type of person at least a dozen times before, perhaps at Coachella, Sedona or some retreat in Tulum. His style and its supplementary ecosystem of exotic jewelry gave him the benefit of looking as gentle as chamomile tea and as approachable as a kitten, even though he could turn on a blink. A Gemini—Taurus rising. He had little patience, but all the time in the world. And there was nothing he liked more than power. And more was never enough.

Jasper walked over to the four-fingered man and slapped him across the face. "Not while I'm playing, you fucking idiot!" He pushed his hair back into place, and they could finally see the man behind the outfit. The cleanest skin anyone had ever seen, with almond-shaped eyes the color of fossilized amber and a nose that people sought surgeons for, the kind that are ubiquitous in places like Los Angeles. He was some version of beautiful that even Leo's fluid sexuality was piqued for a hot minute. It quickly sailed off into the deep regions of his mind moments later.

"I'm sorry, sir! It's only that you asked that they be brought to you when lunch was served."

Jasper cocked his head and looked out the window. "Is it that time already? Well, all right then. I guess we should sit." He still hadn't managed to make eye contact with either Leo or Per. He was the type of person who addressed people only when he felt like it. Jasper returned to the harpsichord and retrieved the bell jar with the milkweed seed and then sat at the head of the table. He set the jar down beside him and leaned back into the dining room chair like it was his throne.

The four-fingered man showed Leo and Per to their respective seats at the far end of the table and then claimed his post by the door. Jasper finally looked up at Leo and Per and studied their faces before offering them a counterfeit smile, yet he said nothing. A band of feet scuffed down the hallway, and a few more people entered the room with copper plates of steaming food, all of them wearing the same grim expression on their faces. *The kitchen staff,* Per thought. What was this place? The plates clinked on the table as the couriers set them down in front of Per, Leo and Jasper. A copper knife and fork followed next.

Leo glanced down at the food: three slices of a tender cut of meat covered in a thin, light gravy, mashed potatoes, a slice of dark brown bread and some kind of mystery vegetable, or perhaps savory fruit. He had worked in kitchens for many years, and even he couldn't recognize what was before him. Steam rose from the plate, and although it was incredibly fragrant, it gave no hint about the sort of protein it was. Now that he thought about it, Leo hadn't seen a single animal since they'd arrived in Garland. Not even a stray, homeless chicken, plucking trash from the side of the street like he had grown accustomed to when he lived in the Bywater neighborhood of New Orleans.

Jasper's lips curled into a smile as he grabbed his fork. He looked up at Leo and Per and nodded. "You must be hungry. Please, don't be shy. I had this specially made just for you two today." The juicy ribbon of meat on his plate was tender enough to break under the gentle pressure of the edge of his fork. He stuffed the meat into his mouth and chewed with a strange gleefulness that made both Leo and Per more uneasy than they already were. When Jasper noticed that he was the only one eating, he stopped chewing, and a darkness fell over his face. "Eat. Drink," he demanded. Jasper held the meat in his mouth until Leo and Per took their first bite; then he continued to chew, and a smile grew on his face as he swallowed. He began to cut another piece, using his knife to smear a mound of potato onto his fork. "Delicious, isn't it?" He waited for a response before he continued with his meal.

Per nodded, and took a sip of his water to wash it down. Leo swished the meat around in his mouth, still unable to determine what he was eating. Even after all these years, he couldn't help critiquing food when he tried something new. *It's seasoned well. They cut against the grain so it's nice and tender. Tastes kinda like smoked brisket,* Leo thought as he analyzed the flavors and textures in his mouth.

"It's good," Leo said to Jasper, and he nodded.

"I always tell Jon—he's the cook—that he knows how to build flavor better than any of the cooks who came before him. So I keep him. I believe this meat is not only grass-fed, but cherry-fed too." Jasper picked up his slice of bread from his plate and held it on display. "You must try the rye bread*. It's my mother's recipe." He rolled his eyes. "Well, sort of. She was so insanely stubborn that she never actually gave me the recipe, only told me the ingredients. I went to this coffee shop in Iceland not too long ago, and they had the most wonderful rye bread. So I've had Jon make a few adjustments here and there. It's almost as it should be. The coffee shop used Lyle's Golden Syrup, which I know my mother never used—we didn't have that sort of thing back then, but like my mother, I'm a little stubborn, especially when it comes to changing up tradition, so Jon made some adjustments for me." He swallowed his food and then lifted a finger in the air as if to make sure all attention was on him. "So, what are you two doing here?"

"You're holding us hostage," Leo said.

Jasper laughed through a mouthful of potatoes. "I meant, what are you doing here in Garland. I hear that it was no accident how you arrived: like so many others, you two came here looking for me. Why?"

Leo looked at Per for assistance. The two shared a moment of angst, not knowing how to answer the question or what would happen to them if they did. They both understood they had no options at this point and could no longer rely on magic to get them out of their sticky spot. Leo grabbed his cup and drank, hoping to buy some more time while he thought of what to say.

Per expected he would be able to come up with something convincing. He was always so good at talking that he figured a convincing story or good old-fashioned lie would roll right off his tongue. What he didn't expect was what flew out of his mouth next. "You have something we need."

Leo looked over at Per, dumbfounded.

"There it is! I knew you'd be polite guests."

Per shook his head at Leo, not knowing why he had volunteered information so easily. His eyes dropped to the cup in front of him. Was it laced with something? *Jasper's the only one with magic*, he thought. Maybe there was a highly potent truth serum in that water. He swallowed, and his eyes scrambled around the room, looking for something else to distract his mind.

Then he said, "What's the milkweed seed for? Is it for inspiration while you play?"

Jasper reached over and placed his palm on top of the jar. "This is Volustina. Well, that used to be her name. Now she's just a decoration. I asked for something that she didn't want to give, so here she is."

Leo's ears perked up. He had heard that name before. But where? He was certain that he knew it. *What kind of a name is Volustina?* he thought. A stream of possibilities coursed through his mind like frames of a film. *Was it Tonya's best friend? Or was it that babysitter I had as kid, the one with a pet parrot? Was it the parrot's name? No, its name was Regina, I think. It had to be someone exotic. Maybe that barfly with the infected piercing? No, that's not it either.* He was starting to stress out, and he craved a cigarette for the first time in a long while.

He repeated the name over and over in his mind until he suddenly found where the memory had been hiding. *Volustina! That's right! That's who Nina said gave the prophecy. She was the one who dreamed about us and knew our names. She was the one who said we would bring the world back into balance, or whatever.* He wasn't completely sold on the reliability of his memory—so many drugs and all—but he felt one hundred percent certain that he was right about this. Then, before he could even think of what to say, he spoke.

"Volustina! She's an oracle!" Leo blurted, just as surprised at himself as he had been at Per's openness only moments ago.

Jasper gasped. "Oh, wow! Look at that! You're famous, Volustina!" He tapped the glass like a child at the zoo, begging to get the attention of a sleepy mammal. "I actually have no idea if she can hear me—sometimes I don't really know the effects of my spells. But I don't care," he added with a smile before he whipped his head toward the jar, only a few inches from the glass. "Shut up, you bitch!" he roared, and then looked back up at Leo and Per and giggled. "Joking! She didn't say anything. She can't talk!"

He laughed again and then his smile arched backward into a pouty, mocking frown. "She's a fairy—the last of her kind. Sadly, the rest were either killed or died in the oubliette before I realized I had gotten to the end of my supply. And being that she was the last of her kind, and she refused me, well…I've got all the time in the world, and now so does she. Maybe one day I'll reverse the spell and see if she's changed her mind yet." Jasper shrugged his pointy shoulders. "I don't even know if I can reverse the spell," he said. His head whipped to the glass once more with a speed faster than his torture was brutal. "Bitch!" he shouted to the jar as beads of saliva sprayed out of his mouth. He laughed again at his own outburst before the novelty of it wore off and he returned to eating as if nothing had happened.

Leo disregarded Jasper's seemingly insane outburst. He'd known lots of unbalanced people, from addicts to chefs, and he'd learned to ignore it, especially when he had other things on his mind. The importance of his quest resurfaced and took priority over everything else, even the current events. He knew he needed a fairy's life force to carry out the spell to locate the rafkolite, the Union of the Divine Dualities. He didn't even need to cast a luck spell before he started his quest. He felt destined to find Volustina. How could he not feel touched by destiny's galvanizing finger when it seemed that his serendipitous journey had placed him but a few feet from the very thing he had been told he needed to succeed? He didn't care about the fairy. He didn't truly care about the success of the coven either, or about being successful. He cared about finally being able to have what everyone else had regardless of class, social status, financial status, or any other modern-day classification—happiness. It meant more to him than anything else, something he felt everyone deserved to feel and experience, even people like himself.

Per continued to shower Jasper with questions out of nervousness because he didn't know what else to do. If they couldn't escape, perhaps he could buy them some time or distract the manic kingpin at the head of the table.

"Who are all these other people?" Per asked. "There are so many in the township. We didn't really know what to expect. I thought there might be *some* people here. I'd heard a man named Jasper had taken up residence here, but that's really all I knew, and I didn't anticipate there would be a whole *community* here."

"And what a community they are!" Jasper said as he sprinkled some flaky salt onto the last sliver of meat.

"How do you keep them all in line?"

"You have a whole arsenal of questions, don't you?" Jasper said playfully, somewhat amused by Per's inquiring mind. He had never seen the truth potion with which he had spiked their water work in such a way before. People usually answered when asked, but they hardly ever prompted conversation, let alone asked questions. He would have to see to it that he made a fresh batch before anyone else arrived in Garland.

Per watched Jasper finish his last bite of food. Jasper, who enjoyed talking as much as Per did, often told people everything about everything. He never worried about exposing too much, because he would kill them shortly afterward. He dropped his fork onto the plate with a loud crash and leaned back in his chair. He crossed his legs and turned his head toward Per.

"I have order because I have their fear. They do something wrong, they get the cell or the oubliette, where they end up begging to die rather than slowly go mad. You've seen both of those already. There are"—Jasper closed his eyes and pictured his chateau—"*so many* of those throughout the grounds. So many that I often forget there are people still in some of them. Well, not alive." His eyes drifted upward and to the right as if he had suddenly seen a ghost in the corner of the room. "But maybe…" It felt deliciously satisfying to consider how much power he had from time to time, how many lives he controlled, how many forgotten people he'd left mentally tortured in dark dungeons to die.

A member of the kitchen crew returned to the dining room with a tray of fresh blood oranges and cherries so sweet, it almost gave Jasper a heart. After a few perfect cherries, he decided to tell them exactly how he kept order, mostly to keep things interesting. Life gets boring when you have everything you need and can take everything you'd ever want.

"Garland is my home. And these people are mine," Jasper said. "The wall keeps them here, which is good, because none of them would have any idea how to survive outside of it anyway. People have escaped, yes, but most of them have been hunted down and killed. The ones who haven't, well…like I said, they won't last long outside the walls." Jasper bit into the top of an orange and then dug his finger into the serration he had left behind with his teeth. He ripped the peel off in such a hateful way that if the fruit could have felt his malice, it surely would have been traumatized. "You saw the obelisk in the township, yes?" he asked.

Per and Leo answered with a nod.

"It's beautiful, isn't it?" Jasper slipped a bit of orange into his mouth and began to chew. He stopped when no one answered. "Isn't it?" he shouted.

"Yes," Per and Leo answered.

Jasper's eyes burned into them for a moment before he returned to his fruit. "It's enchanted. If anything happens to me or the obelisk is damaged, hmm, how do I say this. If I die, well—the obelisk explodes and it will rain heads, legs, arms, tits and cocks until there are nothing but ghosts. Think of the biggest fire you've ever seen; then picture something fifty times bigger than that. No one wants that kind of death, even people who hate their lives don't want that kind of death." Jasper picked up a cherry and chucked it across the table, hitting Per in the chest. "Now, tell me, are you a witch?" He smiled maniacally.

"Yes," Per answered quickly and without restraint.

"I *knew* it! I could smell it on you. I may forget a face from time to time, but that smell is haunting." Jasper pointed to Leo. "You, though…I don't know what *you* are."

"But witches don't have power in this realm," Per butted in. "How do you?"

Jasper shook his head. "Just special, I guess." The truth was, he didn't actually know and he didn't know why he was special either. All he knew was that it worked in his favor and eventually, that was all that mattered. Every other random witch—and not many came through Garland—was powerless…except for Jasper. "You said I have something that belongs to you, yes?"

"Yeah. I want it back," Leo said, his eyes cold. Even though he had absolutely no power in the realm, his tone, like that of a scrappy bulldog, falsely suggested otherwise.

Jasper stood up and took a few steps closer to Leo, closed his eyes and began to surf through higher consciousness. When he returned a few moments later, his eyes flashed open. "It's your soul, isn't it?"

Leo stared in shock. A flood of validation and excitement rolled over his body in a slow, tempestuous wave. He couldn't answer, but he didn't need to, because his eyes revealed more than any amount his limited vocabulary could offer.

"Every once in a while, the perks of being a Transcendent witch make the party so much more exciting." He took a few steps back with a tight-lipped smile, pleased at his own claircognizance, something he didn't exercise nearly as often as he should. Like with ordinary physical exercise, he always felt much better afterward. Jasper indicated to his guards with a nod for everyone to follow him as he turned toward the door. They walked out into the hall, turned a corner and walked down another, to the second door on the left—the room of souls. He had never intended it to be a room of souls, but like when a junkie takes that first hit, they're hooked—some say for life— Jasper was a lifer when it came to collecting things, especially souls. Something about the way they buzzed inside their little clay jars, like a prisoner's scream from the oubliette, begging for mercy—he loved that sound.

Jasper led them through the arched doorway and down the stone stairs into the room of souls where a comfortable cellar-like temperature hung in the air. The stones in the floor had been harvested from the cliffs near the shore and meticulously placed. Stone pillars rose into a vaulted ceiling where a large chandelier of burning mushrooms filled the room with a mellow orange glow. The walls were spotted with small cubbyholes, each showcasing a single jar, each unique in shape and color yet all relatively small, and each containing a soul. The exquisite jars kept the imprisoned soul hidden, but they couldn't silence their cries that all together sounded like a swarm of bees. It was a room both mysterious and beautiful, but disturbing at the same time.

"This room is one of my favorite rooms in my entire home. Do you know why?" Jasper asked as he raised an eyebrow. When no one responded, he continued. "I love the sound the souls make. Like a distress signal." He held out his arms and wiggled his fingers as he copied the sound. "Bzzzzzzzzzzzzzzzzzzzzzzzzzzzzzzzzzzzz," he mimicked, with a racing heart and eyes void of focus. "I can almost feel their sound—their cries—in my chest. The sorrow and torment in that whirring, it's legion. That sound is like a warm bath." Jasper looked at Leo. "How many souls do I have?"

Leo looked around the room without a clue. He wanted to hold his tongue, but he couldn't resist. Words were being forced out of him like toothpaste being squeezed out of the tube. "I don't know."

Jasper's indifferent expression quickly spun into madness and he shouted, "Guess!"

"Five hundred. Maybe," Leo said.

Jasper laughed. "Maybe!" he confirmed. "I don't actually know. I've lost count." At some point he had stopped counting and just kept collecting. "Which one of the hundred-something jars do you think contains *your* soul?" he asked.

Leo looked unsettled. He had come so far, and what he had been looking for all this time was right in front of him somewhere—he just didn't know where. If only he could use magic, then surely he'd be able to find just what he was looking for. The guard at his back pushed him forward into the center of the room.

"I have so many as it is, maybe I can part with one. If you can find it," Jasper said tauntingly. "Pick a jar, any jar."

Leo let out a deep, heavy breath as the pressure to make the right choice welled up inside of him. He had never been known as any sort of overachiever, unless it meant achieving a great amount of nothing. Actually, that wasn't entirely true: he seemed to have a natural ability for spellwork and magic, even when he didn't try. It came as naturally to him as breathing. Only that wouldn't serve him now. He had to make the choice on instinct alone, and he had to make the right choice.

Leo looked around the room, a room that offered little hope. He took a few steps along the wall, examining the jars. Tall ones, short and fat ones, glazed green, black, brown and many bold combinations. *How the hell am I gonna choose?* Leo thought as he continued to browse. None of them felt right, and even if they had, how was he supposed to judge based solely on the jar itself? He crossed over to the other wall and was met with the same dilemma. They might as well have all looked the same.

Leo ran over tactics in his mind. Maybe he could do something that would help him figure it out, something primal, instinctual, something that had nothing to do with magic at all. A few memories bubbled up in his mind. Maybe he could lure it somehow. Or maybe he could trust that divine intervention would intervene and a miracle would unfold right before his eyes. Another minute passed, but there was nothing but a room full of choices and a choice yet to be made. He stared deeper and deeper into the void, slowly slipping away from any sense of hope.

Then it happened. He suddenly saw the color blue—or was it red? He had the overwhelming reflex to investigate the first wall of jars once more. He turned around and looked. He could almost see the word being spelled out in his mind. B-L-U-E. Each letter taking shape, like a recently demolished building in reverse. He scanned the wall, searching, hoping, almost praying. At first, he saw only a mob of jars, which, as he tried to inspect for clues, only became a mess of colors and shapes and an overabundance of options.

He let his eyes drift to a soft focus, the kind that Nina would have instructed him to do during a meditation. Out of the corner of his eye, he saw the faintest hint of blue. He turned his head to see. A stocky, shiny blue jar with an obsidian lid stared back at him from the mess of cubbyholes in the wall. It would've been easy to miss among the hundreds. He took a step forward, and as his foot met the stone floor, the buzzing in the room came to a grinding halt. Leo took a few more steps toward the jar. He didn't know what he felt, but it didn't feel *wrong*.

Jasper stepped up next to Leo. "It seems like you've made a choice, yes?"

Leo didn't even bother looking around at any other jars, out of superstition that he might jinx his decision, his one and only chance to get what he had come here to get. He nodded, and pointed at the blue jar. "That one. The one with the black lid."

Jasper walked over to retrieve it. There was a magnetism to it, and it nearly jumped toward Leo when he picked it up from its resting spot. Jasper knew Leo had chosen correctly; he could tell from the exuberance of the soul inside. It wanted to be back home. But a soul that could be found was a soul that Jasper didn't want to part with. He'd never meant for anyone to actually claim it; it was more of a gesture. The fact that Leo had actually chosen correctly not only irritated him, but also excited him. He had been pretty bored for a while now, and this was just the type of excitement he was looking for, the kind that involved additional torment. The kind that could be served only by denying someone exactly what they sought. Jasper signaled to his guards with a flick of his head. Suddenly, their cold daggers were at both Per's and Leo's throats.

"It looks like you may have chosen the right jar," Jasper said, stepping only a foot away from Leo. He brought the jar closer to Leo and watched it jump from his hands like a frog trying to escape a predator's grasp, only to reach out and snatch it before it got away. He did it again, and then again, the lid clinking shut under his fingers each time.

"I picked it fair and square. It's mine," Leo said from behind the cold edge of the copper blade.

"I feel kind of foul, having you for lunch and not even knowing either one of your names," Jasper said, blind to Leo's growing animosity and deaf to his demand. His eyes tapered nearly to a close. "What are your names?" he said, unsmiling.

"Fuck You, that's my name," Leo said.

Jasper laughed, and analyzed the features of Leo's face as if capturing a mental picture of it before mutilating it, which he was on the edge of deciding whether to do.

"He's Leo," Per said after a short gasp of disbelief. "I'm Per. Like the fruit."

Jasper nodded. Then he froze. His eyes changed to Per. "Per?" he asked.

Per bobbed his head and repeated, "Like the fruit."

Jasper raised his eyebrows for a moment before letting them furrow. "Per, Per, Per," he said out loud to himself.

Leo studied Jasper, taking notice of his sudden change in energy. He looked back at Per, then back at Jasper. "Do you two know each other?"

"Per..." Jasper said as he looked to his guards, as if they would know. "I know that name." He turned his head to face Per and looked him in the eyes.

Per smiled shyly—nervously. "Well...I don't know *you*!" he said with an anxious giggle.

"Per Kaji?" Jasper asked. His eyes lit up like lightning in a midnight storm.

Leo's face curled in confusion and he turned to Per, who was just as surprised as he was.

"Four-Fingers, bring that chair from the hall," Jasper ordered.

The four-fingered man left briefly and returned with a wooden chair. He slammed it down behind Per and stood guard.

"Sit," Jasper ordered.

Per looked around, searching for help that wasn't there. "But I don't wanna sit," he said.

Jasper blustered over to Per and slapped him straight down into the chair. "Sit down, you stupid *witch bitch*!"

Per, who hadn't been in a fight his entire life, thought for a moment he might die, the pain was so intense. He wondered how anyone could ever be in a fight and last more than a few hits. It suddenly made all the film and television he had watched seem incredibly unrealistic. He could barely see straight after a slap, and in films, people would headbutt each other, get stabbed in the side or punched in the face twenty times and go out for ice cream a few minutes later.

Jasper towered over Per, leaning his head forward just enough to show how serious he was. "I don't know you, but I know *of* you. And if you are who I *think* you are, you're part fairy. Which means I need your life force. And you're going to give it to me."

"Fairies? I don't know what you're talking about," Per said with the most simplistic witlessness he could conjure.

Jasper struck him across the other cheek with the quickness of a threatened rattlesnake, grabbed Per's chin with one hand, forced his head straight, and pointed a stern finger with his other hand. "You belong to me, this is my fucking house, I tell you what to do and you do it! When I ask you a question, you answer it, do you understand?"

Per nodded as he looked into the dark and fanatical eyes staring back at him.

Jasper cocked his eyes toward the four-fingered man. "Four-Fingers? Remind me to make my next batch of truth potion three times as strong so that it lasts longer."

"Yes, sir!" Four-Fingers said.

"Now, about giving me what I want—" Jasper began.

"I don't know what you want me to tell you," Per said foolishly.

"Shut up!" Jasper shouted. He turned to Four-Fingers, grabbed the knife from his hand and kneeled down next to Per. "I know that's a lie. I just know, so there's no sense in trying to trick me. Lie to me again and this dagger will slice you open and whatever spills out I'll wear as a bow tie. Now, I'm going to ask you again…"

"I—I…" Per stuttered in a whisper.

Jasper nodded and smiled. "Per…I'm speaking," he said condescendingly with an incredible amount of calm. He continued to nod, and followed it with a few contemptuous blinks. "The last person who lied to me escaped! I told everyone that I hoped he was practicing how to sodomize himself on a mountain peak, because whenever I caught him, I'd strap him to my freshly oiled Pyramid of Perjury! Do you know what that is, Per? It's not a chair like this one you're in now! It has three legs, not four, and they form a pyramid with a *ripping* sharp point.

"Do you know what I did? I found that liar, suspended him in the air and lowered him down hour by hour, bit by bit onto that point. He fought back quite a bit. It turns out he hadn't been practicing after all." Jasper laughed. Then his smile curled downward. "So I tied weights to his feet. And then he sank lower, and lower, and lower, until it ripped him in half. Do you want to sit on my Pyramid of Perjury, Per?" Jasper laughed again before Per could answer. "Alliteration! Did you see what I did there? I didn't even try! I love it when that happens." His face fell serious again. "Do you want that, Per?"

"No," Per answered.

"Good," Jasper said softly, his voice delicate and no louder than the humming of souls. "I'd hate to have Four-Fingers drag that crusty ol' thing out of storage just for you. Now, I've got some crucial needs that need satisfying here. So when I ask you a question, I want you to answer me straight away." A moment of silence passed as Jasper stared into Per's eyes. Then, like lightning, he shouted, "Understand? Huh?!"

Per nodded as his eyes began to well up with fear.

Jasper nodded back, and in one swift swing, he plunged the dagger into Per's thigh, just above the knee. Per roared out in pain, his arms flailing, his hands shaking.

"So, stop that wailing and answer my question…Four-Fingers, take that fucking dagger out."

The four-fingered man unsheathed the dagger from Per's leg, and a stream of blood cascaded from the wound.

Jasper paced around the room, lost in his own thoughts for a moment. Then he began to speak, before Per even had a chance to divulge any information at all. "I hate fairies. I fucking hate fairies. It's their defiant nature. Defiance for the sake of being defiant. The catch is that I need fairies. Well, only one, for a very…special ritual."

Leo suddenly figured it all out, and he watched the realization spill over Per's face as well. Jasper had been looking for the rafkolite, probably for quite a long time. Now Leo was fully invested, even more than before. He had competition, and that competition had already stolen something precious to him. He wouldn't allow Jasper to rob him of another valued treasure.

Jasper pointed at Per. "And you see I'm just naturally really great at divination. And one sunny day, I tapped into the divine and I learned—I *knew*—that Per Kaji would have the life force of a fairy but none of their powers. Apparently it has been diluted down through the ages, and now he is just a witch. I saw that you would come to me, and I've waited for so long for you to arrive, and now, here you are. So give me your life force, and give it to me willingly, or both of you will die." Jasper was nodding as he spoke, and then he smiled. "You'll give it to me, yes?"

Per shook his head. "No. I won't." He knew what would happen if he gave his life force willingly, and especially to a monster like Jasper. He wouldn't have it. If that was the last and only defense he had, he would suffer the punishment for it. A brave thing to decide for someone who could barely handle being slapped.

Jasper took the dagger from Four-Fingers once more and speared it up into Per's uninjured leg at an angle. The blade hung at a thirty-degree angle, and then fell slowly as his flesh gave way underneath the weight of the blade.

After a few minutes, Per finally managed to catch his breath enough to speak. "You're Finnish, aren't you?" His legs were soaked with blood, his pain was immeasurable, and yet some-how, a man stripped of all magical abilities, with two stab wounds and his death in the very near future, suddenly had the upper hand.

A flat, confused look crossed Jasper's face. He was of Finn-ish descent. It had been so long since he had thought about his origins that he had nearly forgotten his own heritage. He had grown accustomed to not having to worry about small, trivial details. When one has magical drugs and a room full of souls at their disposal, time, age and identity become superfluous. Fi-nally, he nodded, curious to see where the conversation would lead.

"It's one of my many talents," Per said. "I can usually spot an accent, even if someone has lost it. But it's not your accent that gave you away. It's your stubbornness. You're so uncom-promising." He took a moment to collect his breath as a sudden rush of pain swelled in his legs. He wiped his brow and pulled back the sweaty wisps of hair that had glued themselves to his temples. "I'm Swedish. Japanese too. But mostly Swedish, because that's where I grew up. Spent time in Finland in my early teens. When you grow up around cold, stubborn people, one of the best things you learn how to do is deal with stubborn, uncompromising people. You learn how to play the game after a while."

Leo's face was the blankest it had ever been. He had no idea how to react and no idea why Per was saying the things he was. Sure, Leo had some crazy ideas to get out of a jam every now and then, but they usually made some kind of sense. He couldn't find sense anywhere.

"You should know," Per said as his shaking hands hovered over his wounds, wanting to touch them but afraid to cause more pain, "that Finnish people came from fairies."

The notion was so outrageous that it looked as if the information went in one of Jasper's ears and out the other.

Per nodded, ignoring the searing pain. "Finland was first populated by fairies some hundred and thirty thousand years ago. And fairies are often impulsive and nomadic, and characteristically…very stubborn. If you ask a fairy for something, chances are, you aren't going to get it. They like having things their way or on their terms. They're historically very open-minded and nonjudgmental, but definitely a no-rules, anti-authority type of species."

Per closed his eyes for a moment and took a deep breath to quell the throbbing, gushing wounds. He opened his eyes again, somewhat refreshed and empowered. "Then the first settlers arrived, the Finns, and the fairies were very sexually experimental during that time. By the Viking Age…true blood

Finns were nearly wiped out by fairies, and most of them didn't even know it. Not many Finns were pureblood human. Those pretty almond-shaped eyes? Fairy eyes. Those stubborn fairy genes, traits, are still just as stubborn as they were hundreds and hundreds of years ago. All those fairies you killed after they refused to give their life for you…are probably your distant relatives. Your ancestors by blood…are fairies! And one of the staples of the Finnish diet, ruisleipä, is an old fairy recipe. Your mom was making fairy food. So now, knowing that I'm just as stubborn as you genetically, am I gonna give you my life force willingly?"

Jasper grabbed his heart with his hand and laughed. He and Four-Fingers shared a glance, and then he laughed a little more before turning completely sour. He looked at Leo and down at Per and his bleeding legs. The room fell quiet, and there was only the dark sound of blood dripping and pooling onto the stone floor.

Drip…drip…drip…

Jasper stepped over to Four-Fingers and held out his palm. Four-Fingers offered him another copper dagger, but Jasper waved it away like a pesky fly. He snapped his fingers. The man knew what that meant. This was serious—no, personal. He didn't just want to kill Per, he wanted him to suffer until the only options were to give Jasper what he wanted or die. He wanted to cause the kind of suffering that he would enjoy watching. Per had managed to do something that no one had been able to do in a long time: he had seeped into the crevices of Jasper's weak spot, something that was unforgivable to someone who always came out on top. It was a win that he couldn't afford to not steal back through any means necessary, even if that meant he had to besiege, maim and kill to regain his triumph.

Jasper had access to magic and could rain cruelty in any number of ways: a potion, mental torture that cooked Per's brain until it was as tender and lifeless as steamed cauliflower, or perhaps a whisper of influence that would force Per to take his own life in some dark and horrific way. Only, Jasper wanted to prove he was in control and that *he* would have the last word. The best way to do it was to *not* use magic. He would beat Per, all in the name of making sure everyone knew who had the bigger dick.

The guard revealed a three-foot copper bludgeon attached to his belt. He unhooked it and handed it over to Jasper daintily, as if it were a precious Samurai sword. The scent of skillfully built malice filled the room, a smell so hateful, it could have blistered one's skin. Jasper had executed many people in his unnaturally long life, and he had grown quite good at it. He took a step closer to Per. The fingernails of his right hand glided down the bludgeon, creating an eerie, hollow, metallic ringing. His eyes looked up from the weapon and directly at Per. Another step.

Jasper's excitement began to simmer inside his chest, creating a sinister hint of a smile on his face. He looked over Per's body, one that housed a fairy life force that he still believed he could coerce him into giving naturally. Right then, he remembered the last time he had been so riled up, when Volustina had denied him her life force. He had made mistakes that time, given in too quickly. He would get what he desired this time; it was written in the stars, he told himself. Another step. His intensity rivaling volcanic fire. Per grew squirmy and frantic. Leo tried to dash out of the guard's grasp but was restrained and brought to his knees with a swift kick to the back of his legs.

A gust of wind blew in from the hall, warm and sweet from the flowering fruit trees around the corner. It rushed over Per's face, and for a moment, he accepted that he was going to suffer. A strange calmness fell over him. That's when he finally looked at the bludgeon in Jasper's hand. Seeing it as a death sentence for the first time.

Another step.

Jasper pointed the end of the bludgeon at Per. "Last chance. Will you give me what I want?"

Per licked his lips and thought about all the different ways that he could say no, all the clever retorts that he had seen in all the films, brilliant television shows and books that he had read in his life, but finally settled on a mouthful of spit, not words. He spat. A large and heavy wad landed on Jasper's thigh.

One final step.

Jasper shook his head and wanted to smile, but instead he furrowed his brow. He had truly thought that Per would give him what he needed. He pursed his lips, gripped the bludgeon like a bat, and saw Volustina's face. He swung, and with a low clunking noise, Per's jaw flew to the side. A train of blood spatters and a few teeth chugged across the room and landed on the floor.

"Still no?" Jasper asked.

Per had no intention of satisfying Jasper in any way whatsoever. He remained silent.

Jasper swung again, this time from the other direction. More blood. More life. He repeated, "No?" The red-stained bludgeon met Per's already busted face once more. Leo shouted for Per and Jasper to stop. He tried and failed once more to escape the clutches of his captors. His arms were twisted in a painful pose behind his back.

"No?" Jasper shouted as he swung, again and again, oblivious to the fact that there could be no answer, even if Per had wanted to oblige. He was gone.

Jasper dropped the bludgeon and ordered one of his guards to clean up the mess. He asked Four-Fingers to escort Leo back to the cells for now. As they left the room, Rosemary, Avery and Mitch, escorted by four guards, approached them.

"We found these three on the shore during our patrol. Seeing as it's harvest season, we brought them straight here for you," the tallest guard said, a champion of a woman with sea salt–crusted hair and a scar from her lips to her earlobe like a comet in the night sky. She was clearly in charge because she deserved to be—she'd earned that spot.

Leo's eyes lit up. He was so numb with shock that he barely even felt the dagger at his side and the guard's viselike grip on his arm. *How did they get here? Did they come to find me?* he thought.

The tall guard shifted her weight to one side and studied her three captives. "There were four of them. One of them got away as we were entering Tengotodo."

Jasper was unconcerned. People hardly tried to escape anymore; it was a choice that always ended in them wishing they hadn't. Those brave (stupid) ones who did try to escape were always found, usually within the first couple of hours. It was only a matter of time.

Ollie? Bisa? Please don't let it be her, Leo thought.

"Put them in the cells," Jasper said as he approached Mitch, who had been twitchy throughout the entire encounter. "Except for this one." Jasper hardly needed to use any sort of clair to see inside Mitch's mind and spirit to know it was severely damaged. But he did anyway, only for a moment. It was like taking a tour through a war-torn country still in the middle of a battle. It was fascinating to see the devastation, and there was nothing more delightful than dropping a bomb on a burning city just about to collapse. He lifted a steady hand to the side of Mitch's head, dug his fingers through his hair and caressed his way to the back of his head. "Put him in the oubliette."

Ollie expected that he would be captured or killed within a few minutes of his escape. He also thought that the rest of the coven would be right behind him as he ran—only they weren't. He ran toward the one familiar thing that made him feel safe: greenery. A copper dagger followed him in the air and landed in the footprint he left in the soft ground beside the walls of the chateau. He ducked into the heavy garden of shrubs, trees and strange plants that adorned the left part of the palace. The safest thing, once he realized he had been separated from the coven, was to try to make sure he knew where they would be taken.

He followed a path just outside the small garden and ran down the length of the wall to a balcony he could easily scale. He took hold of the divots in the wall, grabbed the posts in the railing and pulled himself up and over. Ollie glanced back through the posts like a caged bird, making sure he was in the clear. For a moment, he thought he was, but a single guard was already rounding the corner, tracking his footsteps. He held his breath and looked around. There were no guards anywhere to be seen, but there was a way inside, an open set of French doors, fashioned with copper handles and curtains fluttering in the breeze. On his hands and knees he crawled to the entrance, scouted for danger and went inside.

Ollie found himself in a gallery of paintings. Still lifes, murals, landscapes, some larger than his own bed, some more beautiful than most museum pieces. All of them were outshined by a single portrait of a man with eyes that sent chills into Ollie's soul. The portrait was so outrageously large that it covered the entire wall. The painting's background included the obelisk they had seen in the center of town. *This must be his place,* he thought. Among the paintings was a display of knives, daggers and other random spearlike weapons, crusted with blood, stained with the energies of battles too old and anonymous for any textbook in history. He grabbed a modest dagger of black and silver and held it close. There were three other doors to the room, and with no real way to determine where to go, he listened. First he heard footsteps, then chatter from another room. He tested the limits of his human sense of hearing and mixed it with his natural sense of intuition and chose the door on the far right.

With a growing sense of urgency, Ollie passed from one room to another, amazed at his own stealth. He avoided all eyes, heard all conversations and moved toward the front of the chateau. He hid behind a regal chair and a massive plant and watched as a few of the house staff members and guards recruited more cronies to help find the missing prisoner—Ollie. They had instructions to bring him directly to the cells. After they dispersed, Ollie snuck out of his hiding spot. He slithered along the wall, moving like rain on a leaf, until he caught a guard by surprise. It wasn't just the guard he surprised; Ollie was surprised, too—at himself. He pressed the dagger to the man's neck.

"Where are the prison cells?" Ollie whispered.

The man started to yell for help, but Ollie kneed him in the crotch.

"The cells, where are they?" Ollie asked again.

After the man recovered from the pain, he told Ollie everything he needed to know, but now what was he going to do? Ollie dragged him across the room, his arm around the man's neck, pressing against his throat. When he reached the window, he snatched a piece of rope that held the curtains back, cut a slice of material from the curtain and stuffed it into the man's mouth. He shoved the man to the wall, wrapped his hands around his back and tied his wrists with the curtain rope. He found a closet nearby and shoved the man inside, locked it, and blocked it with a nearby table.

Ollie continued into another room, its deep red walls covered in a phantasmagoria of animal horns, antlers and taxidermy. Hundreds of amputated horns from all manner of creatures: goats, antelope, deer and rams. Some were curved or spiraled, and others were screwy, or scimitar shaped. Carefully preserved bodies of wildlife hung from the walls in between the horns. There were no large animals or wildlife of any kind in Garland, not anymore. Jasper had seen to that by harvesting and hunting every species to extinction just for food. He now dined on a different meat.

Through a heavy wooden door, Ollie entered another room, one filled with dozens and dozens of jars on wooden shelves. A work desk ran along the length of one wall, covered in pots and messes of herbs and strange liquids. It reminded Ollie of the potions, elixirs and essences he made from various plants. Only this room, this strange apothecary, had a much more sinister energy. On his way to the door on the opposite side of the room, he read the labels on the jars, hoping to find something he could recognize, and possibly use. He didn't have enough time to browse, however, so he came up empty-handed and proceeded through the other door.

Then, Ollie heard screams. He was certain they belonged to Mitch. He continued farther, slinking through the rooms and long halls like a shadow. There seemed to be endless doors and places to hide, and every time he saw a group of guards, he was able to pass by them without any trouble.

Ollie followed the sound of Mitch's screams, past rooms and plants, seeking cover behind large pieces of furniture, heavy curtains and strange statues. Finally, he tracked the screams to their source. He peeked around the corner and saw a single door guarded by a man with greasy hair, cleaning the dirt from under his fingernails with the tip of a dagger. He was no more than five feet away, and Ollie had no idea what he was going to do or how he was going to do it. Then, the guard answered that question for him as he turned around to the cell door and pounded on it with his filthy fist.

"Shut up!" the guard said as he pummeled the door.

Ollie seized the momentary lapse in the man's watch and in a single, swift attack, grabbed hold of the dagger and wrested the man into a chokehold. The guard reached his hands up to Ollie's arm, desperately trying to pry it off with his fingernails, struggling for breath.

"Stop!" Ollie said softly. "Open the door." Ollie started to panic, thinking that, eventually, his luck had to run out, especially if he didn't get through the door and out of sight.

The guard let out a few garbled words and pants of air. Ollie loosened his grip—just enough. "It's locked!"

"Where's the key?" Ollie said.

The man took a few wobbly steps to regain some balance, and then said, "My underwear."

Ollie frowned, thinking that he had misheard him. "Bullshit," he said, disgusted. "You put the key in your underwear?"

"I always do, I swear!"

"Get it, now! Open the door!" Ollie ordered as he rolled his eyes. He lifted the dagger and put it to the man's neck. "Open the door, or I'll cut your throat." If someone had told him earlier that day that in a few hours, he would be threatening to slit someone's throat, he would have laughed. Yet here he was, holding a quivering dagger to a stranger's throat, making demands like some kind of desperate criminal.

The man reached into his pants with one hand and pushed his bits aside with a forceful but careful shove. He retrieved the key along with a stray pubic hair and pushed it into the lock. The door creaked as it opened a few inches. Ollie kicked it with his foot, and it swung into the wall with a crash. Ollie saw Leo, Rosemary and Avery all rise to their feet. He looked down to the oubliette next to their cell where Mitch continued to scream, oblivious to Ollie's rescue attempt.

"Let them out," Ollie ordered as he looked behind him, caught the door with his foot and swung it closed with his heel. He tightened the blade against the guard's throat as he unlocked the cell door. The door swung open and Mitch screamed even louder, scratching at the walls only a few inches from his face, with nowhere to go, nowhere to sit and nowhere to move. It was the equivalent of a full-body, stone straitjacket, and he was going insane. As horrid as being buried alive, only with a little more hope.

Ollie ran over to the oubliette and lifted the metal gate off the top. Mitch screamed and screamed, a hurricane of tears and fears.

"Mitch! It's me, Ollie! It's me!" He offered his hand to Mitch. "Mitch, look at me!" Ollie shrieked, finally getting his attention, stopping Mitch from gale-force cries and splintering his fingernails against the stone wall. Ollie reached down, grabbed hold of Mitch's hands and pulled him out.

Leo rushed out of the cell and landed a punch straight in the center of the guard's face. The guard fell back onto the floor, clutching his nose. Fury seized Leo almost as quickly as blood rushed out of the guard's nose. The guard crawled back on his hands and knees as Leo approached him, fueled by darkness and rage, but mostly inconvenience. Leo threw another punch as the guard rose to his feet, but the man dodged out of the way. Leo would have to do this the old-fashioned way: no magic, no supreme advantage, just brute force.

The guard hurled a few punches that struck nothing but air. Except the fourth punch, which slapped directly into Leo's palm. Leo's eyes were wide and bulging. With a twist of his arm, he bent the guard's arm around like a twisted crank, and then he kicked the man's knee, cracking the joint. When the man buckled over, hobbling over his busted knee, Leo drew his leg back and with a momentous kick punted the guard's head into the stone wall, cracking his head.

It was the crack that echoed through the room that instigated Mitch's panic attack. He saw the Plexiglas box hitting the floor at the church once more. He couldn't tell himself that he was safe, that he wasn't at the church anymore; he wasn't—he was somewhere far worse, and he knew it. And all of their lives were in danger. Mitch chewed his lip, lost in his own hell. It wasn't until the coven was halfway down the long hallway and three other guards were chasing after them that he realized he had unknowingly stayed behind. He shivered and threw himself against the coldness of the wall.

As the coven ran past a crossing of hallways, they split up when a few other guards came rushing at them from another direction. With eight guards and surely more on the way, and five of them, they were outnumbered. Everyone was lost. All of them were pursued.

Avery found a quiet hallway and pushed her way through a heavy door. The sound of her racing breath nearly drowned out the herd of footsteps she could hear down the hall. They were still coming. She took a moment to collect herself and realized she was in a dining room. Her eyes sprinted over the room, taking in every possible place to hide—only she couldn't find one. She considered hiding under the table, but knew that they'd surely find her if she hid there. Avery couldn't rely on her muscles any more than her magic, so she couldn't move the harpsichord and hide behind that either. The only real option was to keep running.

In the split second before she began to run, she thought about the strange metaphor that was upon her. She thought about her purple notebook, her old boyfriend, her chocolate-bar lighter and the endless traveling she had done after she had left it all behind. All of the moments of the past made her consider how unimportant they were now, which only inspired her to consider that maybe there wasn't such a thing as time, and maybe everything was just something that happened, and people only force moments into significance. Maybe she had always been one of those people who thinks too much, to the point that the subject she was thinking about no longer had any relevance. She rolled her eyes at the irony that running and running had gotten her to where she was now, and that her only option, if she wanted to continue living, was to keep running. She darted across the dining room and passed the little bell jar with a floating milkweed seed inside. It puzzled her, but she had no time for puzzles. What she did have was a mob of guards chasing her down and fire in her blood.

Avery found her way into the kitchen as the guards entered the dining room and searched for her, first under the table. The racing footsteps started once more, coming for her faster and faster. Avery scampered through the kitchen, past the pots and large wooden prep table with large knives and cleavers strewn about the top. It smelled of roasted meat, starchy potatoes and fresh herbs, although none of those things were in sight. There was a door on the far left and one on the far right. She was closer to the right door, which she took as a sign. Avery ran toward the door on the right, slipping a little in a puddle of soapy water that had spilled from the sink. She shrieked as she flailed and caught her balance before running again, like an Olympic ice skater who had botched a landing and just kept skating and smiling, even though they knew it had cost them the medal.

She opened the door and found herself in what would have been a walk-in refrigerator if she had been anywhere on earth, but she was somewhere very different. It was cold, like a barn at the end of autumn, and before her hung, upside down, six bloody human bodies. Each of them naked, their feet bound with rope, their throats slit and a bucket beneath each one to catch the blood. Avery tried to gasp but couldn't; the smell of death and blood was too overpowering. She looked down at her feet, the tips of her shoes covered in a few splatters of blood. Suddenly a vision of the past filled her head, so fast that it almost knocked her off her feet.

She was twelve, and it was late autumn, and the barn smelled just like this. She had known her father was a hunter, and she hated it as much as her mother did (she always suspected that was one of the reasons for their divorce). She encountered the awfulness of it only once. Dinner was ready—

Bacon and Eggs Soup*—and Avery went to find her father. The barn was the first place she looked, and it was the last time she ever went looking for him in the fall. She opened the barn door, and the first thing she saw were two deer, strung up and hanging, their fur saturated with blood, their tongues hanging out of their mouths. She stared into the cold, dead eyes, ones that had no idea they were about to die. Her body ran cold, her heart raced and she had nightmares for months.

Avery shuddered, horrified at a ghastly realization. These people, whoever they were, were food. They were being eaten—*cooked*. People from the Creamstone Township? Unfortunate people who had somehow found themselves on the shores by accident? It didn't matter. Avery didn't want to be next, and she had to keep running. She slipped past the bodies by running along the wall to the door at the other end with her eyes closed. Her heart was drumming, her hands were shaking and her skin was icy, even though she had been running. She had to find the rest of the coven—they all needed to leave.

Leo and Ollie had bulled their way through a few rooms and found a small passageway where they hid for a moment.

"Can you get us outta here? Transport us or teleport or project us?" Ollie whispered urgently.

"I can't, dude; none of us can. Witches don't have power here. I've tried!" Leo snapped back. He still felt weird calling himself a witch.

They followed the passageway until they reached a stone staircase that twisted around like a cyclone. Leo led the way down the steps as they raced to the floor below. At the bottom of the staircase was a large open archway, like one in a museum leading from one exhibit to another. They spilled through the archway and into a massive room filled with strange, abstract sculptures. They paused for a moment to listen. There were no guards. Leo looked back up the steps and listened. He couldn't tell, but he assumed it wouldn't be long before the guards found them. They had to keep moving.

The room—more of a gallery, really, lit by streams of daylight that flooded through the canopy-covered skylights—was decorated with still-life and landscape paintings. It also housed several glass display cabinets, each one containing various objects and artifacts, all random, all from various parts of the world, both modern and ancient. The case closest to Leo showcased a boomerang, a Greek pyxis with concave sides, an Aztec stone carved with hieroglyphics, a ceramic equestrienne figurine from the Tang dynasty, a small Egyptian amulet from the Ptolemaic period, a Spanish cup-hilt rapier, a bronze-and-silver ring-headed brooch with elaborate filigree patterns, and a gold wolf figurine no larger than Leo's palm.

Suddenly, Leo remembered his little side quest of collecting metals. Sure, he had cast a spell to basically serve him with the metals he needed, but he couldn't resist taking matters into his own hands when they presented themselves so suddenly. With hardly a second thought, or even whether it would draw attention to him and Ollie, Leo elbowed the glass and shattered it. He waited for the large pieces to fall and then reached in and took the wolf statue.

"What are you doing?" Ollie scream-whispered.

Leo said nothing, but hushed Ollie with his hands, as if his voice was louder than the shattering glass. He slipped the wolf figurine into his pocket and looked around the room. There was only one other exit. "Through there?" Leo asked as he pointed toward the door.

"Shh!" Ollie said, holding his finger up to his lips. He hesitated for a moment. "I hear them, they're coming. Let's go!"

They ran through the gallery and toward the door. When they reached it, they looked behind them. The guards were coming.

Rosemary found herself running alone in a hallway, but running calmly. She came to a standstill at the intersection of two hallways. She spun around, deciding where to go next. Suddenly she heard footsteps. Rosemary turned her head to the left and saw a gaggle of men running toward her. She stood long enough to count. *Five more*, she said to herself before she turned down the hallway to her right and entered the first door she saw. As she slammed the door shut, she realized there was no lock, and the shuffling of their feet and angry voices grew louder.

Every once in a while, Rosemary praised her good luck. She liked to jokingly blame it on a spell she had done in her thirties, much in the same way that she blamed the limited run of OK Soda and its high caffeine content for her not being able to get a good night's sleep since the summer of 1993. The room wasn't so much a room as it was an armory. Swords, spears, shields, armor, daggers, exotic whips, morning stars and staffs of all lengths and materials. There were twenty copper daggers, at least. But it was the thirty-five-inch scimitar with a brass-and-silver handle and a polished sphere of turquoise for the pommel that seduced her. *That'll do*, she thought. She pulled it from its resting place on the wall and familiarized herself with its weight.

She hadn't had a proper fight or even a good spar in perhaps thirty-some years, and the five guards who busted through the door with their daggers at the ready were about to let her know if martial skill was just like riding a bike. She had confidence, striking confidence, especially when it came to a weapon. It was in her blood. Rosemary may have been a tad rusty, but she had bested many with a sword, and when she threw a punch in a melee, the person often didn't get back up for more.

The first guard, the woman with the scarred face, charged. Rosemary took a few steps back as the guard jabbed her dagger and met the scimitar in a clash of metal. Rosemary swirled her sword and sent the dagger to the floor. Catching the momentum like a tornado, she spun and slashed her sword against the woman's leg, ripping through her skin. The guard toppled to the floor. A second guard, a woman half the size of the first, struck her dagger against Rosemary's bloody sword.

A third guard raced in behind the second, and Rosemary quickly parried an amateur attack, dodged another from a fourth, backed away and spun her sword to deflect every stab, slice, thrust, lunge and blow. Rosemary pushed back, and with a swish and flick of her wrist, sent a dagger clear across the room. The guard, now defenseless and armed only with his bare hands, dispatched a series of martial blows. The fifth guard had circled around, hoping to get an advantage, but was met with a stunning kick from Rosemary as if she had seen the attack coming. Rosemary danced across the floor with her sword and sliced through the scarred woman once more as she passed by her, all while deflecting every attack.

At some point, Rosemary realized that although her heart was young and fierce, her body was not—she was a bit rusty. The sneaky guard cut at her and landed a superficial slice on Rosemary's arm, causing her to drop her sword. She snuck out of the danger zone just as quickly as the guard had crept in for the kill. She ran to the closest wall as she reached into her pocket and retrieved a small vial. She spun around, and whipped the bottle at the closest guard's feet, where it exploded on the stone floor. The guard flinched as a large flash of blackness erupted from the spilled liquid on the floor like a sack of black salt shot with a bullet. In the flashiest of flashes, the man dissolved into ash, instantly incinerated by her Black Death potion that was to be used in case of emergencies only. She had hoped it would take a few of them out, but her luck seemed to be running a bit short. Two down, three to go.

Rosemary wrestled a large bullwhip with a spiked cracker off the wall, and inadvertently liberated a steel chain whip with a diamond-shaped dart at the end as well. There was about twenty feet between her and the guards when she said hello to her new weapon with an introductory warning crack. At the height of the thunderous noise, the guards dispersed like water droplets on a hot griddle. In a blinding flurry, Rosemary unleashed a burst of rhythmic sonic boom cracks, splitting one guard's chin into shreds of red and disarming another.

She flashed toward the center of the room as the whip sailed high above her, and snagged one of the lit mushrooms from the chandelier. She twirled the whip round and round, sending shafts of fire out around her as the guards advanced. Rosemary planted a foot in front of her, firmly snapped her arm and let the fire loose toward her attackers. One guard tried to turn away, but the whip was too quick, and it cut through the side of his leg. The flames from her whip traveled quickly up his cloth armor until he was engulfed in fire. The man staggered and reeled in a whirlwind of nightmarish screams. He tumbled onto his knees and then to the floor, tangling himself in the whip.

One of the two remaining guards flung a candelabra at Rosemary, nailing her, just barely, in the side. She grunted and swayed. The other guard seized the opportunity and attacked with his dagger. In a shockingly intense tussle, they matched each other's attacks, strike for strike, until she misjudged one. She flew back with a kick to the stomach and rolled across the floor, catching the chain whip on the way back up to her feet. The two guards closed in on her, and she threw the whip out in front of her like a cowgirl with a lasso. It wrapped around one's neck, and with a sharp tug, she dragged him off his feet. His face landed squarely on her sharp knee, knocking him out. As the final guard approached her, with much more caution than before, she slithered the chain whip back up to her hands, the metal dart at the end hanging in the air. The guard gripped his dagger with both hands like a sword, ignorant to the fact that he was in a room full of actual swords at his disposal. But Rosemary required full, undivided attention.

Rosemary moved closer, spinning the chain whip in hypnotic circles that clinked and jingled like the set of prison keys the guard was so familiar with. She advanced faster, passing the whip back and forth in front of her, letting it dance off her arm in a menacing trance. She spun round and round, letting the chain catch and release from her neck, taunting the guard. Finally, she took a break from the fancy flamboyance and built up some more momentum. A spiral on the left, the right, and then straight into the guard's head, crushing into it.

She watched the last guard fall before she wiped the sweat from her brow. After a cursory glance around at the damage she'd done, a mess of blood and broken bones, she took a deep breath. The sight of the blood on the floor reminded her of the blood that flowed through her veins, the blood of her ancestors—warrior's blood. In her old age, she sometimes forgot the origins of her blood, like a disconnected millennial forgets that a chicken was a live animal before it was wrapped in plastic at the supermarket.

Rosemary paused on the memory of her mother tucking her into bed and telling her stories of their family's nomadic lifestyle. Stories of her great-grandparents and their renowned fighting skills, how they traveled the world and paid their way by taking jobs from whoever needed a battle to be won, or whoever could pay their hefty price. People sought them out; their reputations as superlative warriors preceded them wherever they went. Everyone knew they were worth every silver penny, because when they accepted a job, it was because they knew they would win. Whether Rosemary liked it or not, she had a warrior's heart that pumped legendary blood, and victory was the only choice she had. When her family became magically inclined, the fighting had tapered off but never fully dissipated. There would always be a primal urge to battle and train, even if eventually it was employed only to stay fit.

Rosemary herself was a part of the latter philosophy. She had taken some basic self-defense and martial arts as a child, received a black belt in tae kwon do in her teens and a brown belt in Brazilian jujitsu in her twenties, won a few competitions, and been given a handcrafted *tantō* by her instructor. She had always wondered if she would ever get a real chance to exercise what she had learned instead of it being pure theory. She had finally been tested and could cross it off her list. It wasn't the first thing on her list, but it wasn't the last either. However, even though she had bested a room full of guards, she was still a little disappointed that she had never gotten a chance to spar with Nicolas Cage, who showed off his black belt at his after-party for *Kick-Ass*. She had always wanted to see if she could land a good punch.

Rosemary picked up one of the large copper daggers and left the room to find the others.

Mitch snuck through every corridor like a secret avoiding being brought to light. He wasn't sure where he was going, but he knew that if he stayed frozen in fear in the hallway, he would surely die. His only method of survival was to move in the direction that the voices weren't coming from. There wasn't much of a plan, and he hadn't thought about what would happen if he did actually escape. Where would he go? What would he do? He was literally powerless.

He pushed open a large wooden door—a piece of art, truthfully—with hand-carved positive and negative reliefs of a blooming tree. His fingers passed along the finely detailed wood-grain branches on the door as if he were a snake on a live branch. Before him was a large botanical garden twice the size of their house. A large, domed glass ceiling covered the space like a clear blanket. Plants and trees were all around him, small shrubs and saplings, tall grasses and towering leafy trees with vines and flowers.

Mitch took a breath of relief. If this had been a normal garden in a normal place under normal circumstances, he would've wanted to craft a few of his colorful tree sweaters for the skinny tree trunks. Then he heard what he had been trying to avoid—voices. A few guards poked out from behind the trees with a mushroom lantern. He turned to leave, but guards were already arriving farther down the hall. There was no other choice but to keep going. Keep going—or die. Mitch dove to his left and took cover under a large monstera the size of a car. His thumb twitched, begging to be picked. He closed his eyes and tried to overpower the sense of dread that was slowly filling him. All he could do was fantasize about making it out of the room alive. If the past year had proved anything to him, it was that fantasies can become reality, albeit dark.

He opened his eyes and crept around the plants and through the room, crawling, kneeling, standing still. Bravery and confidence didn't come naturally to him, not even when they were necessary for his own survival. He bit his lip so that he wouldn't cry. He didn't have time for that, and he knew it. It didn't mean he couldn't shiver with fear or anxiety; about that he had no choice. His heart was pounding so hard that he was sure one of the guards would hear it, like banging water pipes in an old house. So he continued to choose bravery, because the other option was a road straight to death, and the farther into the room he made it, the more obvious that fact became. Mitch peeked out into the middle of the garden and took count of the guards. He lost count at five, because after that he started to picture how they were going to kill him if they caught him. It had to be something horrible, some kind of long torture—and probably the worst kind of mental torture, and probably after physical torture.

As if prodded by a hot poker, Mitch bolted across the dirt path and into a cluster of tall grass and lavender, and pressed himself to the ground. He lay there for a minute, as flat as dirt, listening to the chatter and shambling footsteps of the guards hunting for him. All they had to do was comb back a plume of grass and they'd see him sprawled out and vulnerable like a spatchcocked chicken. Mitch thought about rotating on a spit and being roasted over a fire like some kind of medieval meal for the guards. He sprang to his hands and knees and scurried through a veil of ivy and into more trees. With shuffling feet too inept to remain quiet, he followed a twisty path between the trees and tropical plants that gilded their trunks until he reached a wall of heavy vines. It seemed simple enough. *Stay out of the middle of the garden,* he told himself.

Mitch tried to dumb down the situation and tell himself it was just like a tricky level in a video game, something that required a high level of stealth-skill like *The Last of Us*, a game he loved but also hated because of how much anxiety its authentic sense of realism evoked. Maybe he could apply the same sort of logic to his current situation: just run straight to the destination and survive, or possibly be killed staying in the shadows until the time was right. Sometimes he would miss valuable items in the game because of that strategy, but at least in the game, he could restart the encounter. That wasn't an option now. He was almost angry at how unprepared he felt. Finishing the game should have given him an edge in a predicament like this, he thought.

Mitch peeled back a thick leaf with his shaking finger and peeked out into the room once more. He could see the way out now. Then, a guard passed in front of his field of view, so close that they almost introduced themselves. Mitch released the leaf and ducked back into the lush maze of vegetation. He pivoted behind a tree next to the vines and held his breath. He took a single step, and the ball of his foot met a branch that snapped under his weight.

Crack!

The breath inside Mitch's lungs was desperate to escape, but he couldn't allow it. Now there were whispers, and then there was more indistinct chatter. Mitch turned his head and looked back through the leafy overhang that fell from above. The guard stood right where he'd been moments ago. Mitch glanced toward the exit and listened to the guard creep through the leaves, like a cat that had just discovered a cornered mouse. Two other guards arrived behind the first one, each holding a dagger and a flaming mushroom. Then, a rumbling of thunder echoed throughout the garden. Mitch looked up through the trees and saw that the ceiling was covered with a mass of dark gray clouds. *Clouds? Inside? A watering spell for the garden?* Mitch guessed, mouse-quick.

Jasper had enchanted the glass-domed space with a storm spell. It happened once every night, and was a way to tend to his lush landscape without dedicating his precious staff to it. A rumble of thunder ripped through the air as a bolt of lightning met the ground behind them and took the guards by surprise. Lightning by spellwork was still lightning, and it could still crack as loud as a firecracker. The guards flinched, and Mitch took his chance. He threw himself into the heavy vines and forced his way through them, his heels digging into the ground as he pushed forward.

On the other side of the vines was the wall of the indoor garden, and alongside it was a narrow pathway that led to another wall near the exit. It was all he could do to not tear down the path and scurry toward the exit, but he knew for certain that if he did, he'd be caught. His thumb began to itch. His consciousness formed a haunting mantra that repeated

run…run…run…

He took a few steps down the pathway, ducking behind the tall grass.

The cuticles of his torn thumb burned and called out…

Pick…pick…pick…

Like being hypnotized by a long, empty highway, Mitch found his way down the path, but he didn't really how he'd made it there…

Pick…pick…pick…

He could smell his own sweat now and feel it pooling under his arms, running down his chest, and around his neck. It almost reminded him of camping with Leo in Louisiana, the mixture of swampy hiking sweat, rain-flooded dirt paths and sultry, humidity-kissed greenery. Only now it carried the immediate threat of a painful death, and not from an alligator or wild boar, but from a gang of men crazy enough to torture him in ways he couldn't think of.

Mitch hopped around the last stretch of shrubs until he was only a few feet from the doorway. He could smell a little bit of hope on the air wafting from the exit. Then a voice, softer and more confident than the monstrous and monotonous droning of his own that chanted and commanded him to *pick…pick…pick…* interrupted.

pick…pick…

(RUN!)

Without even checking to see if it was safe, Mitch bolted from the mass of ferns near the wall and slipped through the door as the guards continued to search the vines. He melted into the darkness of the hallway…

pick…pick…pick…

And for a moment, the only thing he wanted to do more than keep running was cry. He did neither of those things. He stood there in the darkness and watched the guards search for him in the trees. He reached his right hand over to his left and picked at his thumb with the nails of his right thumb and middle finger.

Over and over, like the tide rolling in and out. Then, a softer voice that was not his own, shouted.

(RUN! NOW!)

Mitch stopped his relentless picking and ran down the empty hallway, his feet pounding against the stone floor.

Leo and Ollie made it into the front hallway. They had a clear shot straight to the front door.

"There's the door! Come on!" Ollie said quietly.

They had started to run toward the door when they heard shouting and screaming. Avery spilled out into the hallway in front of them with a tall, slender guard right on her heels. He charged into her and wrestled her to the nearest wall. The guard reached down with one hand and unsheathed his dagger from his side, but Avery knocked it out of his hands with a slap. The guard slammed her into the wall and gripped tightly around her neck. Avery's fingers scratched at the man's arms as her torso squirmed against the wall. She grew panicky as the amount of air she could inhale dwindled. If she had been able to do any kind of magic, the guard would be bubbling in flames by now— but she was defenseless. Her eyes caught movement that fell just out of her range of vision, and she assumed the worst. *More guards. This is it*, she thought.

Suddenly she was free from the grip, and she doubled over and coughed air back into her lungs. Leo grabbed hold of the man's neck and dropped him to the ground, where his tiny head smashed into the floor. A stain of red marked the floor as Leo drew the guard's head back by his greasy hair and violently drove it into the ground a second time.

Avery grasped at her throat as she realized what was happening.

"Come on! We need to leave now!" Ollie said urgently.

"What about the others?" Avery said.

"We can come back, but we have to go!" Ollie snarled.

And then Leo suddenly realized something that rattled all of their exit plans—he couldn't leave without getting his soul and the milkweed fairy. After all that he'd been through, he sure as hell wasn't about to just leave it all because some assholes with daggers stood in his way.

"You guys go! I'll find them," Leo said as he pushed on both their elbows and ushered them toward the door.

"What? Alone? No!" Avery said.

Leo rolled his eyes. "We don't have time for this! The longer we fight about it, the less chance we've got!"

"What if they're already dead?" Ollie suggested.

Leo shook his head and shrugged. "Gotta make sure they're not." He noticed the blood on his fingers and wiped them on his pants as he turned around. "Go!" he yelled as he ran off down the hall.

Ollie and Avery left through the front door and out into the empty entryway of the chateau. A large boulder was only a few skips away, right near the bridge, so they found shelter behind it and waited for Leo to return—hoping that he would.

"What if he doesn't come back?" Ollie asked. "I mean, how long are we supposed to wait? What if they're dead and he just goes and gets himself killed trying to save dead people?" He ran his hands through his hair, so nervous that his teeth were chattering.

"They're not dead. Leo's gonna get 'em. He will," Avery said, reassuring herself as well as Ollie. "I should have gone with…" she added softly under her breath.

"No, we'll wait for them to come back," a voice came from the other side of the boulder. Jasper's voice. "Well, I will. You'll be dead by then."

A wave of sickness fell over Avery and Ollie, who realized they had walked right into a trap.

"I haven't had to work this hard since I started making other people do the work for me," Jasper said. "So now that I've had to go through all this trouble, it'll be really quite nice to watch as you both walk off the cliff." And right then, Jasper exercised his power of influence over them and turned them around to face the edge of the cliff.

CHAPTER 22

Avery and Ollie took a step closer to the edge, their wills bent in Jasper's favor. He didn't rattle off an unnecessary speech, one that would add suspense and delay their deaths. Jasper wasn't like that. He did what he wanted, when he wanted, and decided that he'd done enough talking for the day. Since the last person who had talked a little too much had ended up dying, he thought he might as well just skip story time and jump right into the death scene.

They continued to walk until they met the bridge, and then they crossed over onto it and stood in the middle. With a quick flourish of his head, Jasper made them begin walking toward the edge of the bridge. Slowly, rich with satisfaction. They couldn't scream, they couldn't wiggle their way out of his grasp, and ordinarily, they wouldn't have even known what was going on, but Jasper had evolved a little beyond traditional influence. He was able to allow his victims to be fully aware of what was happening while under his spell—it was more fun that way. He could watch the fear build in their eyes before ultimately watching it drain out after he had played with them long enough. Like animals at a meat factory, slowly approaching the moment where they receive a nail gun to the head or are strung upside down and have their throat slit. They knew it was coming, and there was nothing they could do…except take another step forward. And another. And another.

Ollie's eyes darted around in fear, hoping that by some miracle he would be able to do something—anything! But he couldn't. All he could do was keep walking leisurely toward the edge. They were getting close enough to see into the chasm and sense how much time they would spend in pure agonizing fear as they plummeted to the water far, far below. It would surely crack their bones, possibly kill them instantly. *But what if it doesn't?* Ollie thought. What if he ended up a soft heap of broken bones and blood too damaged to move but too strong to die? Would he just end up floating in inconceivable pain until he eventually drowned? How long would those moments be, suspended in air before he crashed into the jagged rocks and water below? *Does time slow down for the skydiver who finally realizes their parachute has malfunctioned?* Ollie pondered as fear and speculation drained all color from his face, traumatizing him even before anything had happened. He suddenly felt a wave of emotion that wasn't his, but Avery's. He could feel her panic as well, even hear her thoughts as a result of simultaneously being under the same spell—her screams reverberating off the walls of her mind. Her mind suddenly detached completely from the chaos and terror around her, clearly from feeling she had no other option left but to succumb to her demise.

A dagger came soaring through the air as Rosemary jumped out of hiding and ran toward Jasper. But the sound of her footsteps gave her away before she could sink the dagger into his back. He turned around and shielded himself with his arms just before Rosemary crashed into him, and they tumbled to the ground under her momentum. They scrapped on the ground, rolling around like a couple of pit bulls in a dogfight. Jasper knocked the dagger out of her hand, and it sailed through the dirt. Rosemary looked into his wild eyes, which seemed to smile back at her. She glanced up at Ollie and Avery, who were still approaching the edge of the cliff. He hadn't loosened his grip on them yet. Rosemary couldn't lose, she just couldn't. She grabbed hold of him tightly and kneed him in the groin. Jasper let out a gasp that sounded more like a laugh than a moan of pain. It was almost as if he was enjoying the fight.

Avery and Ollie continued to walk, a little faster now. So close to the edge they would soon fall off.

Rosemary fumbled her way through Jasper's grasp and landed an elbow into his chest. It wasn't enough to stop him. Like the pit bull with a taste for blood on his tongue that he was, Jasper snarled as his arms shot out like bullets, grabbed hold of Rosemary's hair with his vise-grip fingers, and jerked her to the ground. He climbed on top of her, a leg on either side of her body, pinning her like a set of crocodile jaws. He reached down and tangled his fingers into her hair, lifted her head, and slammed it into the ground. Rosemary bellowed as Jasper knocked her head into the rocky ground once more, punishing her for attempting victory. Blood oozed out of a jagged cut on the side of her head, matting her hair.

Rosemary balled her fists, ready for another round as Jasper loosened his trap-like legs from her side to reach for the dagger on the ground. He leaned over, and Rosemary twisted her way out from underneath him as his fingers clasped tightly around the handle. Rosemary knew she had two choices: run and try to save either Avery or Ollie, or continue to fight and possibly lose them both.

Two steps away.

Rosemary let out a heavy breath, because she knew there was truly only one option. She had to stop him. She sprang to her feet as Jasper prepared to plunge the dagger into his target.

One step away.

Rosemary saw Leo running toward them in the distance. He would never make it in time. Then right as Jasper swung forward, Mitch jumped out from behind the boulder with a large rock.

Leo's eyes widened, knowing what would happen if Jasper died: the obelisk would explode, killing everyone in Creamstone, including all of them. "No!" Leo shouted, hoping for a miracle.

Mitch saw everyone and everything that plagued, haunted and tortured him all at once as he rushed forward feverishly with the rock. Jasper turned around and met the jagged edge of Mitch's rock, and a small spray of blood freckled Mitch's face as Jasper fell to the ground, addled and bleeding. The rock shook in Mitch's hand as he darkened, mad with desperation and anxiety. He towered over Jasper in a shaking mess of erratic breaths and ferocious sobs. They were all still there. Jasper was severely wounded—but not dead. Avery and Ollie were released from Jasper's influence and anxiously began scurrying away from the edge.

Avery lost her footing and slipped on the gravel beneath her feet. She tumbled forward and rolled over the edge, and let out a shrill scream as she reached out for something—anything—to hold on to. Her frantic fingers grabbed hold of the side of the bridge as her eyes flared with panic. It was too much to look down, so she could only look up and scream. Ollie ran over and grabbed hold of her. With a few strong heaves, Avery emerged from the edge, safe but distressed.

Leo ran up to Mitch and pried the rock from his stiff fingers and tossed it aside. Jasper was still alive, for now.

"It's okay, you're okay," Leo told Mitch, who looked like he was about to either vomit or faint. Leo ran his hand down

Mitch's spine and cupped his lower back. Ollie and Avery walked over and stared at Jasper's wound. He moaned and writhed on the ground—still alive.

"Come here! All of you! Grab hold of me," Rosemary ordered. She pulled a small rose of Jericho out from her pocket, similar to the one she had left on the boat. She cupped it in the palm of her right hand, spit on it and performed a series of gestures over it with her left hand. She stared into the rose and held the image of the boat in her mind as she uttered, "*Reditus.*"

The rose of Jericho bloomed like a chrysanthemum flower in a cup of hot tea and then caught fire. In what seemed like the light from a nuclear blast, the flames erupted and sent out a pale green shock wave of energy that passed through them and transported them instantly back to the boat. The half of the rose of Jericho talisman left on the boat burst into flames and disintegrated on their arrival, completing the spell. Either Jasper's descent into death or the use of a magical object rather than her own magic had allowed the talisman to work, Rosemary couldn't be sure, but she was certainly relieved.

Jasper spat as he tried to utter a spell, but he couldn't wrangle his tongue to form the necessary words. He no longer felt the searing pain of the gash in his head; what he did feel was dread. There was no one to help. Guards were no longer under his control, and he was alone. He rolled to one side and slowly pushed himself up from the ground, leaving a small pond of blood behind. He stumbled forward a few steps, and thought he heard a voice, but there was no one. He looked into the distance toward the township and squinted through his blurry eyes. The obelisk, albeit fuzzy and doubled, was still standing. He was still alive. Jasper wanted to look back at Tengotodo one final time, but as he turned to look, he succumbed to the weakness in his legs and fell back to the ground.

A vulgar and tasteless stream of obscenities filled his scattered brain as he stared into the sky. After so many years of getting everything he wanted through tyranny over honor, bullying instead of decency, he finally seemed to have gotten the dose of karma that had been building up over time, waiting to strike. Jasper, with his endless list of loathsome acts and a vocabulary that translated only to *me, me, me, I want, I want, I want, more, more, more,* finally seemed to have lost his power. The fat cat with all the cream had finally been left outside to starve.

As his soulless body bled out, a salty tear streamed down the side of his face. When it hit the ground, the obelisk exploded in a hell-like eruption and turned it all to ash.

CHAPTER 23

Bisa and Nix located Merlot's whereabouts with a considerable amount of ease. Between a locator incantation and a little pendulum scrying on Bisa's part, they had her coordinates mapped out within minutes. Bisa thought that it came almost too easily, but she didn't have time to worry about something like that. She had other things on her mind. If she knew where Merlot was, then she had a fight to start.

Nix offered to let her drive so that she would feel more comfortable and to help her establish a little trust. Thirty minutes later they were in the mountains, a gloomy, overcast sky above them. After a twisty ride uphill, they found themselves at a small clearing with a tiny house in the distance.

"That's it. That's where she's been hiding out," Nix said.

"It's so isolated; it doesn't look like there's anything else up here," said Bisa.

"Well, that's just how she wants it."

"Won't she have set up some kind of protection spell around the house? Surely we can't just walk right in."

Nix shook his head. "Oh no, she has a few enchantments up. I can feel it. Park here, turn the car off." He flung open the door into the cold mountain air. "But lucky for us, she's a shitty enchantress when it comes to protection spells."

Bisa took a few steps toward the house, a cabin-inspired home painted a deep wine red. "I can feel it. I don't think it's letting me close." She tried to take another step. "It's like I can't even move toward it."

Nix let out a breath. "You can't," he said as he pulled a little piece of folded paper from his pocket. "Not yet!"

"What's that?" Bisa asked as she moved closer to inspect the small parcel.

Nix unfolded the paper to reveal three strands of hair.

"Is that Merlot's hair?" Bisa asked as she surveyed the strands and then looked back up into Nix's eyes.

He nodded and smiled, pleased with himself.

"Where did you get it?" Bisa asked as she furrowed her brows.

"From her head, obviously," Nix said. What he failed to reveal was that he had taken them when he'd attacked Merlot's coven. She had managed to escape with all but three hairs that Nix had ripped from her head.

Bisa was back to not trusting Nix. She was smart enough to know that those hairs could only have come from a scuffle, and if not from that, he had deliberately taken them without Merlot's knowledge. He was shady, and she knew it for sure. What she didn't know was what he was up to.

Nix wrapped the strands of hair around his index finger and pulled them tight with his other hand. He whispered a mantra over the taut hairs, and they vibrated like the singing strings of a harp catching the breeze from a nearby open window. When the humming stopped, Nix pulled and snapped the hair. He looked over at Bisa and wiggled the loose hairs off his fingers. "We can go in now," he said with a smile.

As they walked toward the house without any resistance, Bisa shook her head. "How do you know so much?"

"I read books. What I don't read, I make up. Magic is learned, and what you don't learn, you create."

"Well, what if what you make up doesn't work?"

"Then you try again until it does."

Nix took a deep breath and exhaled. "She's not here, I don't smell her."

"Your senses are that keen?"

"Keen enough to know she's not here, but someone else *is*." Nix walked ahead of Bisa to the door, an act that put Bisa at ease. She liked being able to see him at all times. The door was unlocked, and with a twist of his wrist, Nix turned the doorknob and entered the house. Bisa hung behind a few steps, watching his every move.

The house was quiet and warm. An arrangement of pink and white grow lights lit the room and illuminated a corner filled with various plants. A massive cactus towered over them all, its thorns only inches away from the ceiling. Hand-dyed silk sheets hung from the ceiling, creating a makeshift canopy that covered a small wooden altar along the far wall. The air was thickened by the sweet smoke of burning amber resin. Suddenly the sound of footsteps could be heard from the other room. Bisa tightened her fists as Nix took a step forward.

A young boy entered the room, still rubbing the sleep from his eyes. Then he froze in his tracks and stood there with wide eyes, rapt and nervous, but curious. Merlot had warned the young boy that there were people who would hurt him, people who *wanted* to hurt him; she had instilled the idea that if anyone showed up without her, he shouldn't trust them, no matter what they said.

"Hello," Nix said to the boy, who was no older than twelve.

The boy said nothing, but returned a fraught glance. His fingers twitched like a junkie's.

"We're looking for Merlot," Bisa said. "Is she here?"

That was all the boy needed to hear to suddenly feel claustrophobic in his own skin. *Merlot was right—they've come for me*, he thought, suddenly triggered by a fabricated threat, one put there by Merlot—intentionally.

"Who are you?" Nix asked as he concentrated on the boy's aura. Everything was going according to plan so far; everything that he had foreseen was playing out in front of him perfectly. It was all the reassurance he needed to continue with his plan—even if it would hurt. He could handle a little pain. When the boy didn't respond, he knew it was time to take a step closer.

The boy was instantly filled with dread, and with a paranoid swish of his hand, he pulled a chair from across the room and placed it in Nix's path.

Nix pretended not to smile as he stepped back and dug into his coat pocket. "Take this," he whispered to Bisa. "If he attacks, throw this bottle at his feet. It won't hurt him; it'll only stun him." He slipped her the small vial and returned his gaze to the young boy. "You have a wonderful gift. We can help you understand it." He moved closer.

"Who are you? Why are you here?" the boy said.

"We're friends of Merlot's," Nix said with as much warmth as he could muster.

"She's not here," the boy said as he took in an eyeful of his two unwelcome guests.

Nix licked his lips. "We've come to help you. All you have to do is tell us where she is."

"That's a big lie," the boy said crassly.

"No, we're here to help," Nix repeated, moving closer still.

"You're lying," the boy said without fear because he knew he was more powerful. "I can smell your lies."

Nix hadn't anticipated that. He started to tremble as his plan started to become incredibly fragile. Every single thing he had done for the past few years had been part of an intricate and slow-paced plan, a house built nail by nail. To a hammer, everything looks like a nail, whether it's a screw, bolt, person, plan or young boy. Nix's house was almost finally built. After years of carefully hammering nails, he wasn't about to let a rusty one prevent him from hammering it into place. His eyes filled with tears of excitement and replaced the dread. He had seen it all, everything—almost. He had felt it all, right up until this point. The moment of truth.

"You don't even know what I can do," the boy said. "I can snap your neck if I want. Don't come any closer. I'll do it!" He tensed every muscle in his body as if he were bracing himself for a tidal wave.

"Whatever you've been told…is a lie," Nix said as he took a risky step forward.

Bisa stood in the background, watching the events unfold, her throat tied tight in a knot. She fingered the tiny bottle in her hand. She didn't know what the bottle would do. *Can I trust that this will do what he says it will?* Bisa thought.

Before she could come up with a solid answer, she had already thrown the bottle on instinct as the boy launched Nix across the room with a schooled gesture of his hand.

When the glass broke at the boy's bare feet, his eyebrows gathered in the center of his forehead as if he had suddenly seen visions of hell. He reached up and clutched his chest with his soft hands and tugged at his shirt as his heart pounded wildly to a permanent halt. The boy's knees buckled, his eyes released their heavy gaze on the world around him and he collapsed as if his bones had gelatinized. Bisa caught her breath and looked to Nix, who was dusting himself off. He rushed over to the boy and kneeled down beside him while Bisa hovered in the background.

"You said it would stun him; is he dead?" Bisa asked uncertainly.

"Only knocked out," Nix said.

Bisa walked over and stood above Nix. "I could've handled that on my own. I should've just taken control to calm him down." She took another deep breath and watched for signs of life in the boy's chest. "He's not breathing, Nix!"

Nix held up his hand as if trying to calm a toddler's tantrum. "It appears that way. That's how the potion works. I should know, I formulated it myself. Trust me."

"I don't," Bisa said sternly. She continued to wait for the boy's chest to lift with breath, but it never came.

"Like I said, what choice do you have at this point? We don't have time for this, we need to find out where Merlot is. Our best chance now is for you to try to look into his thoughts and figure out where she is," he said quickly.

Bisa scoffed. "I don't know how to do that! How do I do that? She could be anywhere. We don't even know if she's coming back!"

"She'll come back. She wouldn't leave a Corporeal boy all by himself. Once we know when she'll return—and she will—we can decide what to do next. Now come on!" Nix forced Bisa down next to the boy on the floor.

"What am I supposed to do?" Bisa asked.

"Put your hands on his head and concentrate. Close your eyes."

"Is this even something I can—"

"Not if you don't try; now try!" Nix ordered.

Bisa looked up at Nix one more time, and Nix placated her with a nod. She shook her hands to free them of any unwelcome or undesirable energy she had picked up, took a deep breath and placed a hand on either side of the boy's head. Her eyes closed as she began to concentrate on the task, which seemed ridiculously out of her skill base. She tried listening to the vibes, but there were none. *Just something new, that's all. I'm just learning and practicing something new,* she told herself, slowly becoming more and more confident that she would succeed. But nothing came. No abstract thoughts, sounds or visuals; she couldn't sense anything but an overwhelming absence.

A rustling caused Bisa to flinch and to open her eyes to a paper-thin slit. At first, she thought it was the boy rousing from the spell, but he was unnervingly still. She closed her eyes once more, waited for a moment, and then released her hands from the boy.

"I can't do it," Bisa said as she turned to look at Nix.

A puff of powder powered by Nix's breath rushed from his palm and into her face. She tumbled back onto the floor, coughing, and squinting her burning eyes. The stinging sensation froze her eyes closed as the texture beneath and the temperature around her—changed. It felt like dying, or what she imagined it would feel like if her body had suddenly seized up and stopped functioning. She clawed at her eyes, desperate to see as they watered uncontrollably.

Then, as quickly as it had happened, the burning stopped. Bisa opened her eyes and looked around. She was somewhere entirely new—no, different. She had been there before, she felt it. It was the same blackness, the same darkness as where she had encountered the figure in the wispy, flowing cloak—the figure with the black, glowing orbs for eyes. Her skin turned cold as a chill ran down her body. She was in the Land of Perpetual Midnight. The sky was empty, the air was quiet.

Her eyes adjusted, and she finally discovered herself standing in the middle of a long wooden bridge. It was too dark to see how far down the drop was. *Maybe there isn't a bottom*, she thought. Bisa stood for a few moments listening to the sound of her breath in the stunning silence around her. *What do I do?* Both ends of the bridge looked exactly the same, apart from one significant detail. She narrowed her eyes and forced her vision to see beyond its limits, like a patient desperately trying to make out letters on a Snellen chart to avoid having to have a prescription. At first it was just blackness, but then slowly, ever so slowly, the void began to fill with shapes. Like smoke from a fire, the shapes billowed out to reveal the figure she had seen before—the figure with fingers of solid, sharpened bone, bone that had scratched her. In that moment, as the glowing black eyes began to spin, she understood that the figure—was Death.

Bisa's lips quivered, and her eyelids crawled back from her wide eyes as she watched Death glide toward her. She took a step backward as Death approached faster and faster. There was nothing she could do, except turn and run. Bisa geared up and spun on her heels to dash to the other side of the bridge. It was like a wolf chasing a rabbit. She ran as fast as she had ever run in her life, and still, Death trailed behind her as if tethered to her waist. Her legs burned as her feet pounded across the wooden bridge, like a mallet continually striking a twisted, funereal xylophone. She couldn't look back. If she did, she just knew it would be over. Bisa focused on the end of the bridge. It was getting closer now. She could feel the presence of Death practically breathing down the back of her neck.

As she approached the end of the bridge, Nix appeared out of the darkness and blocked her path. A rush of emotion passed over her, and she couldn't determine which was the lesser of two evils: Nix…or Death. Bisa ground her teeth and plowed forward, determined to cut through Nix like a sharp blade. She could tell he was casting by the movements of his hands and the shifting of his lips, but casting what…she didn't know. Nix scattered a powder along the edge of the bridge in front of him and backed away. Like a runner taking a final leap toward the finish line, Bisa jumped toward Nix and away from Death. As her body crossed over the powder, she was transported back to Merlot's house, where she tumbled straight into the altar along the wall.

Nix had planned for this his entire life, and now here he was, finally face-to-face with his destiny, with Death. His lips curled into a smile as he watched Death's speed grind to a stop. His spell had worked. Nix had managed to actually summon Death. Granted, he had done it in a roundabout way. Every book and every witch he had ever met had told him the same thing—there is no way to summon Death, no way to cheat or outsmart Death.

But Nix had found a way. He was as cunning as he was insane, yet that came second to his tenacious grit. It took effort, a lot of it, but through a strange hodgepodge of mystic preparations, he had ended up being the only person to cheat death. It was a strange kind of magical alchemy, and the gamble had paid off—well, so far anyway.

It had all begun with meditation, and dedicated meditation. Hours and hours of it, until eventually, after mixing meditation with psychism, he had pieced together exactly what to do and how. He knew that Death was after Bisa; she had been marked. The trick was how to summon Death to her. Death comes for everyone, especially those who trespass into its realm. But Death can be found only if it wants to be, and it had evaded Nix repeatedly. So Nix had devised a spell that would make Bisa magically irresistible to Death, like a piece of raw, bloody meat thrown into a pit of hungry lions. And Death had taken the bait.

It had never been about Bisa, it was about his date with Death. Nix had traveled through the Land of Perpetual Midnight, mapping it out over time. When he stumbled upon the bridge, he knew he had found the right spot. The only problem was that the mishmash spell he had created would work only if there was one other human body, not two—so he had tweaked the spell and arranged for Bisa to act as bait and only as bait before being sent back to the house.

Nix ran warm with excitement and let out a shuddering breath. Death stood before him on the bridge, bewildered and stunned. Then Death's glowing eyes began to spin with rage, and the billowing streams of fabric seemed to grow longer and wider. Nix felt a bead of sweat emerge on his forehead, but he knew he couldn't be afraid. He had come too far to succumb to terror and intimidation. After all, this was his home.

Nix unsheathed a small black candle that had been anointed in Black Arts Oil and rolled it in a variety of crushed herbs and plants from his coat pocket. He had prepared the candle ages ago and kept it safe for years, to be lit at this exact moment, a moment that he knew would come if he just believed hard enough. Yet, to be fully honest with himself, he also knew it would take more than just *believing*; it would take a great deal of effort and hard work on his part. Years of it. It all lined up, and he was about to see the fruits of his labors and how rewarding they were. Like a witch had told him many years earlier, some of the best spells are the ones you create yourself.

Nix waved his hand back and forth over the wick of the candle, lit it with a lighter, and watched it flicker to life. He waved his hand faster and faster next to the candle, continuing to fan the flame of what he had named his Transmogrification of Death candle.

Death writhed before him, twisting around like a fly under a magnifying glass, caught and tortured under intensified sunlight. A horrific, sharp shriek filled the air. The screams of a thousand souls would be like the chimes of an ice cream truck compared with the sound of Death dying. Around and around Death spun, twisting and dissolving in a combustion of flashing lights, wet, slushy sounds and ghastly smells—until Death was what it had once been…a human body—a witch. The glowing eyes were soft and white, with rings of green, as green as green can look in the blackness of night. Death was but a mere shadow of what it had been moments earlier.

Nix stared down at the body sprawled out before him: blade-thin limbs, and eyes full of time. Suddenly the body began to decompose as quickly as a flame ignites. Nix took a step closer as the body spontaneously combusted in a puff of smoke that rose into the air. Pieces of flesh dropped toward the earth in ashy flakes. Even the ashes looked old, as if they contained centuries and centuries of secrets. Then all was quiet and there was nothing but Nix, a pile of ashes, and the dark, heady stench of a burned mystic. Nix kneeled down before the ashes, almost reluctant to touch them for fear that it might have all been a dream. But when he reached down and grabbed a handful, his fear dissipated. He hadn't anticipated ashes, but he was thankful, because this saved him a step. With maniacal glee, Nix scooped up the ashes with both hands, dipped his tongue into the pile and swallowed a mouthful.

It was done. He had become Death. He was home. Right then, a gust of wind passed over the ashes on the ground and revealed a large sickle.

SEVEN METALS

Rosemary brought the coven back to shore, where she used the power of her garnet ring once more to create a door back to the house. After they took a few moments to catch their breath in the living room, Rosemary asked Leo to explain once more how Per had died. It was after hearing the story for the second time that she realized she was the only member left in the Advisory—well, excluding Nix, which went without saying. She called for Bisa and noted that she was still missing.

At the edge of the room, Mitch stood near the wall, trembling like a whipped dog. Ollie could feel the darkness that enveloped him before his eyes saw it. He brought Mitch to a chair and cleaned the spatters of blood off his face with a wet rag. It was like cleaning a fragile piece of porcelain. When Ollie closed his eyes for a moment, he could feel the rushing rivers of trauma running through Mitch's body. There wasn't a violent bone in Mitch's entire body, so when he had struck Jasper with the rock, it had torn his already broken spirit apart and left it a bruised purple. Ollie knew he couldn't say or do anything other than just be present. Sometimes that was enough.

When Rosemary had taken a seat and stared into space, Leo saw it as the perfect time to inquire about one of the two things he had in his pocket.

"Rosemary," Leo said as he walked over, "what can you tell me about this?" He pulled out the milkweed seed that had been tucked away in secret.

Rosemary's face knotted up. "I don't understand what you're asking," she said.

"Jasper had this in a jar. He said it was a fairy. That its name was Volustina."

Rosemary's eyes brightened, and she sat up in her seat as if someone had poured cold water down her back. "What?"

"Volustina," Leo repeated.

"No, I heard what you said. I just can't believe it." Rosemary studied the milkweed seed for a moment and then spoke. "He told you that this was Volustina? You heard him say that? This *seed*…is Volustina?"

Leo shrugged. "Yeah."

After she demanded that Leo run through the story from beginning to end and regurgitate all that he could remember, she clasped her hands together as if in prayer and kissed them. She smiled as she took an expedited tour through the most recent of current and past events. Everything had happened in a way that validated the eye-roll-inducing saying that she would see on greeting cards, bumper stickers and kitchen magnets: *Everything happens for a reason*. She had always hated that saying, albeit understood it, but now she made a certain amount of peace with it. Even the parts of the past that were horrible and unfortunate had a part to play in Volustina entering their lives. If Nina hadn't died, if she hadn't ever met Merlot, if she hadn't been a part of the Advisory…if she hadn't been a witch—would any part of the prophecy have come to pass?

As she revisited the emotional landscape of the past, she understood that even the events that were dark and unpleasant had been necessary to bring about balance. It was one thing to understand that balance was something to be achieved, but it was quite another to comprehend that balance was something that was temporary, just as darkness is temporary—that it will never *stay* in balance. Even at her age, with all the wisdom she had collected through the years, she was still surprised to learn that she could develop a deeper understanding of something. She had always understood the concept of balance, but it finally made sense to her beyond an intellectual sense. Balance *was* that endless act of back and forth. Of course the goal was for them to achieve energetic balance, and it was necessary, but it would never remain forever. That was growth, that was expansion, that was balance.

Rosemary scolded Leo for acting alone and then gathered the coven together and told them the news about Volustina. Part of her wanted to find Bisa first so she could share it with everyone at once, but she couldn't wait that long, and she hated having to repeat herself. An hour later, she had explained what she needed to do and all of the provisions she would need. Reversing a transformation was something that no one in the coven could do. Leo would have been the first choice, but he wasn't sure he could do it, and Rosemary didn't want to blow the only chance they had. They needed someone whose specialty *was* transformation, a skill that they were known for. It was the only way they could essentially guarantee that everything would work out. Rosemary had invoked spirits into her aura four times in her life, so she had grown beyond it being an experimental procedure. She was more along the lines of a young surgeon who had performed enough operations to feel comfortable doing them, but was still waiting for the day when they lost a patient. Frankly, she had secretly been enjoying the level of excitement and she wasn't about to say no to more. Things hadn't been this exciting since Morgan Freeman.

Into a cauldron she mixed balsam fir, peppermint, the dried petals of the common snowdrop and a chunk of amber resin. She crushed and ground the mixture together with a pestle and combined it with a blend of cornstarch and eggshells. Rosemary treated spells, rituals and magical handiwork like recipes, and there are many ways to make marinara. She opted for the quick and dirty method, which would essentially give her close to the same result (with perhaps some unwanted side effects), only she wouldn't have to write anything or waste valuable time letting something charge under the sun.

Rosemary poured the powder into the shape of a sigil on the floor and stood in the center of it.

"Hand me the candle," she said to Ollie, and then shoved a cherry into her mouth and chewed it to release the juice. She swallowed the pit but stored the juice in her cheek. Ollie handed her the lit candle. She lifted the flame to chin level and concentrated on it until it had flickered to a standstill. Her eyes closed and she began the incantation.

"*Invoco te, Circe,*" she said aloud. Then twice more in her head, each time swishing the juice around in her mouth and over her tongue. *Invoco te, Circe…Invoco te, Circe.*

Then the deep silence arrived, the moment when spirits are invited and drawn to a physical body, until the sound of a second heartbeat is heard thump-thump-thumping alongside the spellcaster's own. Rosemary remembered all of this, even though it had been quite some time since her last invocation. *Next should be the heat,* she thought. It came. A cocoon of warmth covering every inch of her skin. One major difference between her hasty recipe and the more traditional method was that hers involved a breath of fire, as she liked to call it. She opened her eyes and looked into the flame. The somewhat bland juice of a cherry out of season still ready on the tip of her tongue. She swished her cheeks and spat with all her might into the flame. Her juice-laden spit met the fire and ignited into a roaring fireball. The powdery sigil beneath her feet shuddered like a pile of rubble in an earthquake.

A silvery haze rose up from the sigil, and shimmered with flecks of purple and green as it surrounded Rosemary. Not everyone could see it happening, but Ollie, the highly sensitive witch, could. His eyes lit up like those of a young child marveling at bursting fireworks for the first time as he watched the energy cloak Rosemary from head to toe.

A few moments later, Rosemary stepped off the sigil and set down the candle. She felt like a new battery, one that had all the power and knowledge of Circe: a trivial goddess to some, but a magnificent enchantress in truth. Circe, both the daughter and the transformer, the nymph and the witch. Her aura had been blessed, but Rosemary knew she didn't have long. Her expedited spell would burn bright and quick. Sure, there was a chance that the borrowed power would be a little sloppy, but it was better than the ham-fisted attempt that Leo would have come up with. Changing a milkweed seed into a person—fairy—wasn't something to leave to a newbie.

Rosemary took a moment to relish all the gifts that rushed in: the ability to speak ancient Greek and Latin fluently, the encyclopedic knowledge of herbs, plants and how to combine them, and, most importantly—the divine power of transformation. She stood in silence for a moment until Leo placed the milkweed seed on the floor in front of her. With her aura coalesced with that of Circe, she was ready to begin. Rosemary rubbed her hands together briskly, and Ollie watched the energetic mist spatter from them. When they were primed, Rosemary gracefully lifted her left arm in front of her and flourished her wrist, ever so slowly. Next, she raised her right arm in a circular, slow, whiplike motion, tangling with the left but never touching. She continued to twist, unravel and undulate her arms together—seductive and hypnotic, like a spider spinning a delicate web. Rosemary ended with her hands outstretched before her, fingers spread, palms open to the floor.

The coven was quiet, the wind had stopped, and a gentle snow began to fall outside. A fresh, earthy scent filled the air as Rosemary began to hum. Low at first, then higher to an entrancing ring. She stopped abruptly, and her eyes focused intensely on the milkweed seed. The world around her seemed to melt away as she channeled Circe's power. She felt the warming sensation of the energy in her mouth, like fresh ginger on her tongue. After a few moments of deep breathing, Rosemary released a few words too faint to understand.

The seed swirled up from the floor as if caught in a breeze that wasn't there, until it hung in midair under Rosemary's spell. Another whisper, another movement. The seed rolled, and its feathery tips spread into the air like ice crystals forming over a wintry window. It began to morph and unpack itself, like layers of an onion, or years in one's life, changing, evolving. Rosemary's hand quivered, and the seed mimicked the shake. Her borrowed power was already running low, and she wasn't even sure if there would be enough left to finish the transformation. The seed, or mysterious hybrid plant and animal object that it was now, fell to the floor.

"Leo," Rosemary called out softly as she shifted one hand out toward him.

He stepped forward, reached up and pressed his hand against hers without hesitation and without instruction.

Nothing happened. Frustrated, Rosemary slid her fingers between his and locked hands with Leo. The ringing returned, followed by a sharp rustle as the seed rose from the ground and unfolded over itself like water at the top of a fountain. Both Leo and Rosemary could now taste their blood running down the back of their throat. Too much energy was being used, too much, too fast. But there was no other choice.

The seed unfolded to reveal a human figure resting on the ground. Rosemary released her grip from Leo, and the pulsating shock ripped through both of them as the power was untethered. And not a moment too soon, because Circe's spirit faded away only seconds later.

The seed had become a full body. They lay out on the floor, shiny and wet, like a brand-new baby. Their eyes fluttered open as they began to establish a relationship with the eyesight that had been stolen from them. The almond-shaped eyes explored the faces around them as they blinked away their hazy confusion. They looked like a woman and had female genitalia, but they also looked like a man—but were they either? A mixture of watery softness, rife with emotion and creativity, and structured, bold, fiery and strong, rampant with confidence and charisma.

Avery ran to get the closest blanket and wrapped it over the person's body, careful not to get too close. The person coughed a few times and released a fury of emotions. They erupted into tears, sobbing hysterically for a moment before switching to a strange cackle, and ultimately ending up in a rhythmic pattern of deep breaths, gasping at the body they had forgotten they had. Their fingers scrambled along their face and arms as they inspected them. They paused for a moment and then looked up at Rosemary, their eyes blitzed with adrenaline.

The coven was too mesmerized to speak. Their mouths hung open in surprise as they tried to make sense of something they had thought existed only in the movies but looked better and more realistic, like the puppetry and special effects of the eighties that were abandoned when CGI took its place and spoiled everything.

The room had gone quiet once again apart from the deep, labored breathing of the naked being who sat before them.

In…out…in…out…

A final dribble of blood oozed out of Rosemary's nose and hung on the ridge of her upper lip. She threw her head back and wiped her nose with the back of her hand before she stared into the person's eyes. Only she was not a person—she was a fairy.

"Welcome back," Rosemary said gently, "Volustina."

CHAPTER 25

Volustina was older than the human species and any of their languages. Volustina was a fairy, a spirit of the earth and nature itself. The fairies' realm, Garland, existed on a plane within the natural world, making them the original inhabitants of the earth before the very first humans sprang into existence. Volustina was the oldest fairy of them all—the mother (and father). Their origin story had always been a mystery, even to themself; it was as if they had always just—been. Volustina believed the fairies had arrived along with a shower of meteorites that, upon collision with the earth, created entrances into the additional layer of existence now known as Garland, a large island with a plethora of dramatic landscapes and geological contrasts that varied between regions.

The fairies had a particular way of living their lives, back in the beginning when time and place were of little importance. They invented skills as they dedicated their lives to the connection between all things on earth. The fairies used the land and protected it simultaneously. They knew the importance of nature's cycles and the role they played in keeping it in balance. When the fairies took from the land, they asked permission from it first. The fairies gave as much as they took, because balance was work. They made it common practice to take only what was necessary and always leave some behind. It was part of their spiritual and genetic makeup to tether the energy of the natural world to their own and function as one. It was through that process that nothing was wasted and there was always something left for others, whether fairy, animal, plant or insect.

The bond between nature and fairy was based on mutual respect. Respect went a long way, and the earth rewarded them with its continual bounty. This primal connection to and respect for nature was stored in the very blood of their bodies, and it was passed on through generations and generations of fairies through their cellular memory.

What nature didn't provide, they made or built—if they needed or wanted something: furniture, shelter, community. Together, they were able to make the impossible possible. Collaboration allowed them to evolve as they learned from one another. Community was the key, an ideal that they would impart to the witches later on. They planted the first seeds and knew how to grow all the food that the earth provided. They were self-sufficient; they spun their own cloth and silks and dyed them with the blood and juice of the earth's fruits and flowers.

Volustina embraced the rich abundance of creativity nurtured by generosity of spirit and created their own musical instruments and textiles—Volustina's favorite pastime was playing the hand harp. Fairies by nature were great musicians, and many popular melodies had come from them. Craft by craft, skill by skill, they developed into magnificent creators and lived artfully.

The fairies were natural teachers, and they loved to teach as much as they loved to learn, whether the student was fairy or human. As the fairies evolved with nature, humans chose instead to evolve with power. Fairies were the ones who enchanted the earth to link humans to its energy, giving them magic, making them witches. Humans quickly became the majority. The fairies were being outnumbered and outsmarted technologically, something they couldn't and wouldn't compete with, because it was so against their own nature. Volustina had hoped through enchanting the earth that humans would learn to value their world and live as they did, in balance, with respect for themselves, their environment and those around them. The enchantment was partly a selfish act, because Volustina had an itch they needed to scratch. Their passion to live a full life with respect to both the world and their spirit led Volustina to grab life by the horns and ride it, respectfully, throughout time. But before they would embark on their wonderful adventure, they wanted to see all of Garland one final time.

They took a Garland horse and rode west through Plousia Forest, where the scent of rain-soaked mushrooms perfumed the forest floor. The forest led to the Vaidettavissa Highlands, where they spent endless amounts of time rolling through the grassy hills. Farther west was the Whirlpool Islands, where the water mysteriously swirled as its currents spiraled in toward a small islet full of berries. They spent the night there before traveling north, through Bluebane Forest and by Pink Lake. They said goodbye to the glowing caves and their friends at Shintillare Seaside, and soaked in the views from their cliffside homes. Volustina traveled through Temuco Desert, where the sand and spiked trees cast a spell all their own. They rode up to the summit of Piperra Volcano and admired the lava that churned inside one final time.

Heading farther east, Volustina watched the sunset on the Crystal Milk Coast, where the water was inexplicably white in the evening sun. Down through Keemly Glacier, where the songs of ice and snow reminded them of just how much bigger nature was. They ate a handful of snow, creamy and sweet. Next, they enjoyed an afternoon bath in the Steamy Springs, using the silica-rich mud to soften and nourish their skin for the journey ahead. Their journey ended with a ride through the strangely beautiful and barren Tengari Canyon, a place that always seemed to inspire deep thought. It was there that they decided it was time.

Soon after Volustina made the decision to see more of the world, they had a premonition, a message straight from source energy. Although Volustina was an active oracle and received many messages from the higher consciousness, one in particular seemed crucially important to pass along. They told the fairies about the rafkolite and those who were destined to find it. The names they divined made no sense, but often things lack sense when logic is not involved—yet they knew that that shouldn't suggest there was no truth in their prophecies. Volustina abandoned their home of Garland in search of experiencing the entirety of the human world. The humans—the witches, rather—continued to use their gifts to tilt the energetic scales of the earth, keeping both the earth and the plane of Garland safe.

There were many, many years of harmony, until, of course—there weren't. A human witch is still a human, and humans are fickle. The knowledge of rafkolite spread, the desire to find it became obsession, and soon afterward, some witches abused their power, as humans tend to do. The Flaming Flood Era began, and fairies were hunted by massive groups of witches for their life force, so they could attempt to find the rafkolite for their own selfish reasons. The witches attacked the fairies with waves of fire that flowed like lava, trapping them with nowhere to go but into their captors' arms. The witches hit village after village, hideout after hideout, the earth and Garland, taking every fairy they could along the way.

As more and more fairies were hunted, the witches experimented more with their powers; their practice became reckless—unstable, even. Whereas some witches desired power, others wanted satisfaction and pleasure, and plenty of it. Under the full moon in a circle of roses and pearls, a witch attempted to summon Pan and Hedone using fairy's blood to become a wildly desirable, fantastic and undeniable lover. It might have worked, except the witch misjudged the spell's effects, chanted the mantra incorrectly, and made numerous other blunders, forcing the spell to morph into a radical form of contagious magic and metastasize to one of the nearest fairies. That fairy instantly became more indulgent, a trickster, a deceiver, more like how people think of fairies when they think of them now. That fairy, now wildly contagious, traveled back to the fairy realm, where the contagion spread to most of the fairy population. The infected ones, drunk with ecstasy and high on madness, traveled to the human realm out of impulse to cause chaos in human life. They were to blame for countless missing children and the growing number of people who went missing while taking a lone walk down an empty path. Which only gave the witches more reason to hunt them down.

Eventually, the fairies closed all the entrances to their realm, apart from one that could not be closed because of a random, ecological idiosyncrasy. The witches who desired power never kept it; the ones who fought for balance survived, along with Volustina, who had avoided the front lines of the Flaming Flood Era.

Although fairies have the ability to change sex at random, or to remain completely nonbinary, Volustina chose to spend several millennia as a female at the height of their lengthy sexual peak. Volustina then switched to a male in 3561 B.C., then back again to a female in 79 A.D. after some of their sexual energy caused the eruption of Mount Vesuvius in Italy and buried the city of Pompeii. Later in 1651 A.D., they changed back to a male and had a particularly tricky sexual relationship with Karin Svensdotter while spending time cultivating bilberry bushes in Sweden. After some drama there, Volustina switched back to female in 1657 and had a wild relationship with a man they couldn't remember the name of in 1658, before ghosting him in 1691 for Sven Andersson.

When Volustina outgrew themself once again, they relocated to France in 1773. It was there that Volustina befriended Marie Antoinette at her eighteenth birthday party. The two became the best of friends—instantly. They spent endless days and nights drinking hot chocolate together and gossiping at Marie's private château, the Petit Trianon. Volustina decided to leave abruptly in 1777 after having a premonition while staring at the full moon during a walk through the gardens of Versailles.

Life would change for Volustina shortly afterward, for what is another millennium later when one has been around since before the word existed? Science began to replace what was once ancient belief, and people believed in fairies less and less as their population dwindled. Humans inadvertently transformed fairies into fiction, where they were able to exist safely and free from annihilation.

Sometime between harvesting silk and sealing the entrances to Garland, they acquired, developed, and expanded the ability to erase and steal humans' memories and use them to live a little longer than their already surprisingly long life. The fairies knew trade and cooperation—not currency, except for memories. Volustina's philosophy was that memories were of the highest value because they lasted longer than the actual experience itself. They weren't always reliable, but they were precious all the same. Memories of a life as endless as time were the only thing Volustina had left after Jasper turned them into a milkweed seed.

CHAPTER 26

Bisa gathered her thoughts as she stood up from the floor. The tumble into the altar left a few broken bowls, a disarray of herbs, and a small cut on her forearm. A trickle of red oozed out and dripped onto the floor, but she hardly noticed. Her mind was still reeling. After a few deep breaths, she realized she was back at Merlot's, and she was alone. Bisa gave the house a final search before she walked outside. The cold winter air had grown frosty, and there seemed to be an energy in it that made her uneasy. Carried on the wind, a train of whispers passed before her.

(home...go home...now...)

She paced across the front of the house for some time, gazing into the thin blanket of snow on the ground like a sheet of lace. The whiteness of it burned into her eyes and even deeper into her mind as she reflected on the events. It was so silent, not even a bird was in the air. Everything was hushed, like nature had grown tired of its own creations. Everything but the whispering wind that carried a voice with cold breath.

(home...)

Bisa took one final look at the house before she walked to the car. With her hand on the door handle, she looked up to see a car driving along the road before it steered out of view. She hoped for a moment that it would be Merlot so she could follow her just like they did in the movies, but would Merlot really drive a Ford Escape? Bisa got into the driver's seat and sat in silence. She needed some time to think. *Why would Merlot be hiding out in the exact state that we chose to relocate to?* The thought spun round and round in her mind as she tried to come up with a reasonable explanation. It could have been any number of things, but it couldn't be coincidence, it just couldn't—could it? Her eyes continued to look over the house and the land around it, hoping that if she looked hard enough, the answer would come to her.

Bisa looked down at the wound on her arm, which had already stopped bleeding. *It has to be some kind of preordained thing*, she thought. She closed her eyes and searched through the hive of memories in her brain, hoping to find something that would make sense. Suddenly, air filled her lungs in a quick huff as she landed on a theory. The memory was hazy and fragmented, but she remembered enough of it. Bisa rubbed the side of her forehead and drowned out the humming of the car, the whirring of the soft wind and even her own heartbeat. *Nina knew something, she felt it. Nina chose Colorado based on some kind of divine knowledge or intuition. Was it because of Merlot? Did she pick up on some kind of psychic signal? Did Nina know Merlot was here? Maybe it was all just blind luck. No, there was nothing blind about it. She was a Transcendent witch...She was a seer, even with her eyes closed.*

A stretch of heavy thought later, Bisa pulled up next to Nix's shop. She squinted and tried to make out the dancing shapes behind the counter. Then she used her third eye. He wasn't inside. With the only choices being to head back home or back to Merlot's, she chose to listen to the muffled voice that breezed past her in the wind, and headed home.

As she passed into Nova and made the drive up the mountain toward the house, she suddenly found herself shivering as a feeling of dread flickered through her. It felt like a shock and looked like the bright, blinding light of a camera flash. It was disorienting enough to cause her to swerve just a little off course—not something someone wants to do while driving in the mountains in winter. Nevertheless, Bisa pressed her foot into the gas pedal.

She ripped to a stop in the driveway. The rhythmic voice that had been following her had finally stopped. Either the spirit had run out of breath or she had made the right choice and arrived on time. *I hope so.*

Bisa stepped out of the car and looked up at the house. She didn't need any sort of clair to know that something was going on in the house, some kind of…anxiousness. She could practically see it, the feeling was so strong. She wet her lips as she pressed on toward the door, wondering what she would encounter.

CHAPTER 27

"And it seems that karma finally caught up with Jasper after all this time," Volustina said as they blinked away the memory of their time as a milkweed seed. After a moment, they looked up at everyone, all engrossed and stunned by the story of their life.

Avery shook her head and played with her necklace. "So, fairies have never had wings, like ever?"

Volustina hinted at a smile, but then shook their head. "No."

Rosemary took a bite of a chocolate-covered biscuit. "How did Jasper find you? Fairies were supposed to be extinct. What caused him to go looking for you, do you know?"

Volustina nodded. "I do. It's all because he read Charlotte Brontë and Hugh Miller's *The Old Red Sandstone*. He was a Scottish geologist and passionate folklorist. Hugh had described encounters with fairies...*me*, specifically. Jasper tracked him down, inquired about how to find the fairies and where he could meet one. Hugh didn't want to give details to anyone, but Jasper threatened him. He said that he was a powerful witch and would curse him with a sickness spell that would eventually kill him if he refused to help. Hugh told him what he knew, and Jasper cast the spell regardless. He suffered a long time, the entirety of 1856, to be exact. It all started slowly with unbearable headaches, then the curse moved into his psyche, and he began to have delusions and horrible visions and was plagued by voices. It tore him apart until all that was left was the screaming choir of his own madness and depression. He took his own life.

"Jasper, on the other hand, followed the trail to a painter who was known to paint portraits of fairies. I always knew letting myself be captured in the spirit of brush and pigment was a mistake. From there, one clue would lead to another, and another, until eventually he found me. Jasper was a magnificent tracker. But he never got what he *really* wanted. And that's how I ended up in such a state, cursed and indestructible."

"And you can change sex? Are you male or female?" Ollie asked.

"We don't—*I* don't—identify as wholly male or female, masculine or feminine. I exist beyond that kind of dualism." Volustina looked at Ollie directly. "You do too."

"I call myself a he?" Ollie said in a way that sounded like a reminder.

"It doesn't have to be constrained to whether you are biologically male or female. It is who you are, how you function. Your species have both of those energies." Volustina looked off into the distance for a moment and grew sad. "There's so much hatred here. So little understanding, even less empathy. No one is listening." Volustina closed their eyes and took a breath, pained by the state of the earth. But they had no time for heartache and sorrow. They opened their eyes. "Humankind is stained by the ignorant, the foolish and the supercilious. Only those of that frequency belittle, condemn and fear what they simply don't understand."

"Wasn't that confusing? Changing back and forth from male to female?" Leo asked.

Volustina shook their head. "It was liberating. Gender isn't limited only to the norms that the world has set in place. It wasn't confusing or traumatic. The only traumatic thing would be to deny someone's expression by trying to make them feel that what they feel is wrong. What's confusing is how the world believes things are only one thing or the other. You're not the same person with the same ideals as you were when you were a child, are you? It's the denial of expression and creation that's one of the many causes of chaos and destruction. To conserve for the sake of conservation out of respect for tradition is precisely that...not growth. Life needs to grow and change to survive, to be free. Tradition is a cage made of antiquated ideals—protection of the belief that things should always remain the same based solely on the argument that they have always been that way. Just because something has always been a certain way doesn't mean that it's right."

Avery eyed Volustina, still focused on Jasper. "What did he want from you? Why would he go through so much trouble just to find you?"

"Not me, a fairy. Any fairy would do," Volustina said. "I was just the one who was easiest to track. I had been more places, met with more people, left more traces."

Avery repeated, "Okay...so what did he want from you?"

Volustina could feel the intensity of Avery's words, but she didn't understand it. They looked at Rosemary. "He asked me to give my life force to him so that he could use it to find the rafkolite."

Rosemary nodded as she connected dots in her head. "And you refused," she said.

Volustina nodded. "I could *feel* his intentions. But that wasn't the only reason I refused. I knew that I had divined that there were other witches who were destined to find the rafkolite. It was called something different so long ago, there isn't a word for it in any language on earth." Volustina pronounced a word—no, made a sound that was something between the falling of raindrops and the ringing of a brass bell. "That's what we called it before science gave names to everything." Volustina adjusted the oversized hand-knitted violet mohair sweater courtesy of Mitch's wardrobe. "It was you that I saw. All of you. If I was going to give my life force to anyone, it would be the ones who were destined to have it. And here I am. So many lifetimes since then."

Leo's heart skipped a beat. He didn't know what he was going to say or do, but he needed to ask what Volustina intended to do. He made a mental note to figure out his plan, but first he would ask Volustina the important question. "And will you give it to us?"

The coven looked at Leo, wanting to judge or reprimand him for asking such a blunt question—but they themselves were wondering the same thing. They cast their gaze to Volustina and waited for their response.

They pulled their knees to their chest and hugged them close. "When the time is right, I will not hesitate to give you my life force."

Leo nodded. *I'll remember that you said that*, he thought, half anticipating that Volustina would go back on their word when the time came. How easy would it be to just give up your life to people you don't even know? Suddenly, Leo found himself stuttering over his own tongue as he tried to craft what he wanted to say. "What happens to you? Do you die?"

"I will be gone, yes. We never really die."

"Fairies, you mean?" Leo asked.

"Fairies. Humans. We are all energy, and energy never dies, it just moves from one place to another."

Ollie slid down on the ground next to Volustina and kneeled by their side. "You're okay with that? Giving up your life?

You've lived for so long. And you only just now became a whole body again."

"The universe is bigger than any of our lives, even mine," Volustina said. "I know there are parts to play and sacrifices to be made. I understand the consequences of my choice, and I will make that choice regardless, because I know what the result will be if I do."

Rosemary tilted her head back. "Which is what?"

"Balance," Volustina said as they flashed a tranquil smile toward the coven. Then, as if suddenly reminded of the details surrounding the divine prophecy, they said, "Although I know many things, and Spirit has shared many things with me over time, I cannot know all." Volustina's voice lowered, somber and concerning, as if coming straight from the source. "Someone in this group, one with an unpolluted and pure heart—only they will be able to enter the circle cast in the ritual."

Leo's heart sank as Volustina's words cut through him like the sharpest of knives. He knew for a cold, hard fact that if his heart was anything, it was not pure or unpolluted. Leo ran his rough fingers over his face and stroked his beard. He knew that he had to think outside the box if he was going to find a way to make this work for himself. It was like trying to fry an egg when the gas and electricity had been cut off. He needed to think more like Rosemary, who would have told him you don't need either to cook when you have a fire. For a few moments, he lost himself in his own self-induced hopelessness, and then he spoke. "What if none of us has that?"

Avery rolled her eyes. "Always. Always the doom and gloom."

Volustina's eyes drifted to the wall in the background, with the collection of framed Ab Initio Talismans on the wall. Their breath seized in their chest as they lost themself in the abstract designs of the ink that seemed alive through their fairy eyesight. Volustina was shaken to their very bones by the talismans, which were more than unique visuals; they were a language beyond words. Volustina let out a breath of air and was caught somewhere between wanting to laugh and needing to cry at the profound beauty of the universe and its ability to continually surprise them. They finally managed to blink after nearly burning the image of the framed talismans into their eyes.

"What is it?" Rosemary asked.

Volustina continued to stare at the wall, mesmerized. "You made these?"

Everyone looked at the talismans on the wall. They looked like they always had to the coven, ordinary and half forgotten. Not a single member of the coven had used them as they were meant to be used, or even thought about them since they'd created them together.

"We all did. Back in Louisiana," Ollie answered, feeling a buzz that was causing the hairs on his neck to rise.

A thousand memories coasted through Volustina's mind as they remembered bits and pieces of history and the tiny details of the prophecy. They stood up and walked over to the wall. With their eyes racing over the splotches of ink, they explained. "These have a purpose beyond their intended one. They're instructions—more exactly, directions."

The coven closed in behind Volustina as they continued.

"These are directions to an object, another talisman of sorts. One that holds a very rare and great power, that of invisibility. I never knew the location of this talisman; I only knew of its existence. You have given me a map. No one on earth could have found the talisman, or the rafkolite, for that matter, because it's not actually in this realm, it's in Garland."

Rosemary placed a hand on Volustina's shoulder. "I knew the ritual involved invisibility, but I never knew how that was possible or how anyone was going to achieve it."

"Why?" Leo asked quickly.

Volustina continued to study the inkblots and flecks, reading them. "Invisibility isn't something that comes incredibly naturally. It was something that we were never able to fully control. In the beginning, I was able to give many gifts to the world through magic, but my transformation has changed me. It has robbed me of the ability to give or produce any other gifts. It all makes so much sense now."

Avery gently pushed Leo out of the way and stood next to Volustina. "Why do we need to become invisible?"

Volustina finally turned to face them all. "Once the one who has the purest heart enters the circle—"

"—the spirits necessary to complete the ritual can be conjured or will show up only if the person calling them has made themselves invisible," Rosemary finished.

"Correct," Volustina said softly. "They want you to play in the shadows, in their playground. They risk too much by materializing in full form. Spirits can be fickle. There are ways to forcibly create invisibility through alchemical means and aura manipulation, but it's an extremely complicated science—an understanding of and respect for not only esoteric chemistry but also atmospheric pressure, the being's aural makeup, astral fluid and their physical and spiritual state. It's very sensitive work, so cryptic and encoded that the very act of deciphering the exact science to succeed was far too laborious for most people to attempt. But done correctly, it illuminates the space around a body with an energy that obstructs others from seeing them."

"Like…sunblock," Avery said.

Rosemary shook her head. "But surely *someone* had to succeed. Someone made the talisman."

"Oh yes, someone succeeded and even managed to enchant an object to give the possessor the power of invisibility. The universe is vast, and it's ignorant to assume that no one figured out the process. I'm sure whoever made the object wasn't the only one." They took a deep breath as long as their life was long. "It was as if you were destined to rescue me," they said, looking at Leo, and then back at the wall. "Destined to see this so that I could demystify it for you." They let out an astonished *hmm* before they gazed out the window. "One can always rely on divine intervention arising as a result of following the path of Spirit. To live intuitively, and to accept what is, is to experience the blessing of source."

Mitch looked up from across the room, still sitting in his safety blanket of a chair. Ollie caught his glance, and the two shared a moment without words. Ollie could feel the trauma dripping off of Mitch like some kind of pungent sweat. He had no idea what it would be like to have to kill someone, even out of necessity, but he didn't have to know what it was like to understand the impact it had. Ollie walked over and stood next to Mitch, placing a hand on his shoulder. Mitch trembled underneath his touch for a moment before he relaxed. Ollie stroked the back of Mitch's head a few times as Mitch gave in to the influence of Ollie's empathetic care.

After a short discussion about where the talisman was in Garland and whether all or some of them should go find it, they decided it would be best to wait until Volustina had full strength again. The metamorphosis had sapped their energy and made them a little hazy and weak, something that Volustina assured the coven would last only a few days at most. Rosemary sat back down in a chair and retrieved another chocolate-covered biscuit before she reiterated that it would be in their best interest not to return to Garland so soon, considering the events that had just taken place.

Just then, they heard the sound of the front door open and close. Bisa had finally arrived back home, sporting a now-crusted cut, exhausted and completely conscious of how the coven would react to her absence. When she entered the room, Leo was the first to look at her, mostly to make sure she was okay. Her arrival brought about a sudden wave of relief as they all realized she was more or less safe. As if Leo could protect her from the entire world. When their eyes met, he knew that she felt differently about him, even if she didn't know exactly how. When she turned to head to her room, Leo finally realized that he had completely forgotten that he had his soul in his pocket. Here he had thought that taking a break from weed would strengthen his memory.

Rosemary rose out of her chair and followed Bisa to her room, where she insisted on hearing where she had been and what she had done. Bisa explained what had happened between her and Nix, spilling every detail. Ollie guided Mitch back to his room and set him up on the bed, tending to him like a nurse would a patient. He found Avery and recruited her to help him start dinner. Ollie hadn't thought about it before, but as they were preparing the marinade for the Piri Piri Chicken*, he decided to see what adding a little enchantment would do. It was Avery who gave him the idea, inadvertently, after she reminisced about how her father always made her guess what the special ingredient was when he made dinner. "Wuv," he would say, in an attempt to be cute—usually on the days when he was hunting and wanted to counter Avery's sour feelings about him killing deer. If Avery's father could add wuv, Ollie could certainly add something to help Mitch relax.

The spicy, zesty smell of charred Fresno peppers and dry-roasted garlic married with smoked paprika, fresh thyme and cilantro delivered an abundance of enchanting smells with a vinegary bite throughout the house and into Leo's room. It was enough to whet his appetite, but not enough to distract him from fiddling with his soul. He hadn't thought about what he was going to do with it once he got it. It wasn't like a package of ramen with instructions on the back; this was his *soul*.

He browsed through the books on the shelves in the library nook, but nothing was useful. He even tried to Google the answer, almost thinking he might find something helpful: a witch forum, some socially inept thirty-nine-year-old witch with colored hair and an online diary of her emo musings and entries on how to fuse one's soul once you lost it. He didn't find anything, apart from that exact description of someone on Twitter, masquerading as a witch. All that searching and where did it get him: right back in his room staring at the jar.

He frowned as he stared at the jar. *What do I do now?* As he waited for answers and ideas that never came, he wondered what would happen if he actually was able to match his soul back to his body. Would he finally be complete? Would it feel like home? *What if it doesn't? What if I get my soul, which is something I didn't even know I needed, and it turns out to be different? Or what if it isn't good enough? What the fuckitty fuck do I do when I finally get what I think is supposed to make me like everyone else, and I'm still not satisfied, and I still can't feel happiness? What the fuck do I do then? Will I know what it looks like when my needs are met? Am I even…satisfiable?* He glowered at the jar and contemplated just breaking it and slitting his wrists with the shards (but not really). Leo thought he could do anything, now that he knew what kind of witch he was. Corporeals were supposed to be great. But he wasn't.

After dinner, Leo went to sit with Volustina by the fire. He realized that he needed to ask the being who knew the most about the world. It came as a crushing blow to learn that although Volustina had an answer for him, it wasn't the one he was looking for.

"In all my time on this planet, I've never come across any one object or magical process with the power to fuse one's soul to one's body after it has been lost and found." Volustina turned to study the emotions on Leo's face. "The only thing that I know for certain would do that is the rafkolite."

"How do you know?" Leo asked, unsatisfied. It seemed too mysterious for them to know all of its properties.

"I just do."

It was just that kind of woo-woo, bullshit, 900-number psychic hotline answer that Leo never loved, but…what choice did he have?

CHAPTER 28

The bliss that Nix felt was so palpable that he almost thought it had all been a dream.

He chortled. "I did it," he said softly to himself as he looked at the darkness all around him. It was as if everything had been illuminated by some unseen light. Wisps of air swirled in the sky above him. The silence called out to him now in whispers, delicate and seductive, whispers that carried instructions for him to pick up the large sickle in the ashes. His eyes dropped to the sickle, and he suddenly felt a sense of peace return. Now that his spiritual makeup was back where it belonged, where it felt most comfortable, he finally felt what he had been looking for his entire life—a feeling of home.

Nix kneeled closer to the sickle. He could feel the energy it gave off, like the vibrations of a tuning fork so strong, they could break glass. Closer and closer he leaned, his hands stretched out before him, ready to receive the scepter of Death. It was about time, too. He was exhausted, trying to pretend to be someone he wasn't, constantly hiding who he really was and what he really wanted. He remained true to himself, but only in secret.

Nix would soon be able to leave all that behind—the shame, the lies, the life of someone he truly wasn't—but most of all he would finally be able to add necromancy to his list of magical skills. It was something no witch was ever able to practice; their powers fell short right on the cusp of achieving such a thing. Now he would be able to conjure and control entities that were beyond the realm of natural magic, spirits that couldn't be controlled or destroyed by any other type of magic—apart from his own. The only kind of magic that rivaled the power of Death was the power of Life, which he had no ties to.

Every part of his life was about to change. Not only would the sickle allow him to practice great powers of necromancy and live endlessly as Death itself, but he would have control over an entire realm. He could rule over his world as he saw fit, shaping and molding it to his liking, making and changing the rules to suit himself. Combined with his very powerful Transcendent skills, he would be the king of a kingdom shrouded in darkness. Above all else, the true reason behind his intentions was that by becoming Death, he could avoid it and all the cold, paralyzing horrors that came along with it. He had already decided that he would take advantage of his new power and deliberately snub his duty as Death.

His fingers curled around the black handle of the sickle, which he expected to be icy cold. Instead, it was warm. Pure, unadulterated joy surged through him as he plucked the sickle out of the ashes. He rose to his feet and marveled at the shiny new tool in his hands. It was surprisingly light, like an empty snail shell. All at once, he felt his stomach turn, and he sensed something was wrong. He eyed the sickle up and down, from the formidable razor-sharp blade flecked with the reflection of the stars above to the bottom of its black wooden handle. The pain in his stomach grew stronger. He thought he was about to vomit, but swallowed his spit.

Nix opened his eyes wide and let out a cough. The overwhelmingly warm sense of calm was gone, replaced with the coldness of pain and shadows. His hands began to fuse to the handle as if welded by fire, but he could not let go. He swung the sickle to the left and then the right, but it would not release from his grasp. Nix shook his head, took a deep breath and hoped for the first time since he had succeeded in achieving his goal that it was all a dream.

Right then, the sickle stung his palms. It felt like a million bees stinging all at once in the same spot. His eyes began to water as he began to buckle under the pain. There was nowhere to go and nothing he could do. A sizzling hiss filled the air as the sickle glowed red hot. Then it happened: all at once the sickle infused him with the death of every human who had ever died. But it was more than that. The sick irony was that humans begin to die the moment they are born. Then came the crushing rain of emotional suffering and mental anguish of all living beings. It snaked through his body, and the voices, screams and cries of billions of pained and passed souls deafened him. His heart fluttered and pounded, his insides pulsed and ached, and his legs failed to support the heavy weight of unfathomable pain that hailed down on him. Hours, years, centuries, millennia, and ages of pain, sorrow and savage misery passed in a frame of immeasurable time.

And when the unbearable assault on his heart finally passed, he was consumed by a permanent state of mourning—a haunting feeling that was so unequivocally cold that it could freeze time. He understood everything and everyone, he felt the past, present and future as if it were as tangible as the tool in his hands. In the flicker of an instant, he knew who and what Death had been all this time—a witch. He knew it but didn't understand it. The only thing he could make sense of was that he now knew what it felt like to die, and he did, only to be reborn.

Nix had half expected something like this to happen. He had expected there to be some sort of phoenix-like episode, an initiation to his powers. But this wasn't that. There was no ownership or free will, and he was most certainly *not* in control. His vision blurred as he blinked the water from his eyes, now slowly liquifying into swirling orbs of black light. He twisted his hands free from the sickle as he took a few steps back to collect himself. When he could see clearly again, the ashes at his feet were already swirling around like dead leaves caught in a breeze. He watched them rise on their own and fill the air, until they cocooned around him, sticking to his body, stripping him of his clothes and giving him a new skin.

His face was no longer a face—expressionless as an empty void. His clothes had become robes, with wisps of black, foggy vines that billowed in breeze that wasn't there. Nix—no, Death—retrieved the sickle from the ground and held it willingly between his bony fingers, realizing that living as Death and harnessing such a power comes with a hefty price, one of eternal servitude until the end of time. Or until another witch assumes the unlucky role. His body and soul now possessed the ability to be millions of places at the same time, but the body and soul were no longer his to call his own. He would have laughed at the cosmic joke that he had played on himself, if it had been something he could do. Nix had found what he had been looking for, only it didn't look anything like what he had expected. He was relentlessly determined, uncompromisingly stubborn, exceptionally talented, yet completely naïve. He was home…but now a slave—forever.

CHAPTER 29

The next morning, Avery woke up in caretaker mode. She was the first to the kitchen, and by the time the sun spilled over the mountains, she already had coffee made, banana pancakes* prepped and a winter breakfast hash that was accidentally vegan cooked. She hadn't fully decided to go meatless; it was more of an unconscious suggestion that manifested often enough to feel deliberate. It was the perfectly fried potatoes with mushrooms and roasted red peppers that brought Volustina crawling into the kitchen. Something about the potatoes, something that was always being prepared in Garland, reminded them of home, in a dark, twisted kind of way that they would hope to erase. It wasn't the potatoes that bothered them, it was the man who grew them. An entire community had close to nothing but potatoes and dandelions, whereas Jasper at least had other things.

Volustina was still a little weak and their mind a little jumbled from the transformation. Plagued by a bout of sporadic nausea, Volustina started off slowly with a glass of tepid water.

"How are you feeling?" Avery asked with a set of raised eyebrows.

Volustina pursed their lips. "Not amazing. It'll just take some time before I'm back to normal—whatever that looks like."

Avery couldn't help but try to heal Volustina's vitality. She placed her hands on Volustina and got to work. Before they knew it, five minutes had gone by, and then it was ten more, and still there was no change. Avery's best efforts fell flat on the fairy. It was the classic situation of *it's not you, it's me.* Only in this case, it was true.

"Thank you for trying," Volustina said. "I didn't think it would work. It was never something we developed…We never anticipated that witches would ever need to use their powers for our kind. The magic works a little differently."

Avery frowned a little, disturbed that there was something that she couldn't do, yet again. She felt as if her powers were slipping, at least the healing ones.

"It doesn't mean that healing isn't happening!" Volustina said as they cupped Avery's hands with their own. "It could just be a very, very slow process. So slow that it actually looks like there isn't any change happening at all."

Ollie went to check on Mitch in his room, where he had sequestered himself in some unhinged corner of social media. Ollie hovered by the door as he watched Mitch furiously type a response to a Twitter post. Mitch had been trying to process a mountain of overwhelming emotions that he didn't know how to climb. He was the climber stuck at the base without a rope or gear, looking up at the summit through the fog. He was lost, and it was as inarguable as noticing that his thumb had scar tissue. The issue wasn't that Mitch was suffering, it was that he was addicted to it. Mitchism, a novel strain of self-loathing and trauma, had taken over him, desperate to remain broken—and the light, now exceptionally difficult to see, couldn't break through the darkness to show him the way out.

Ollie felt the surge of panic rise in his stomach, but it wasn't his, it belonged to Mitch.

"What are you doing?" Ollie asked.

"Everyone is such a fucking asshole. I hate the internet," Mitch said as he resumed typing, so irate that he had twelve typos in a single sentence.

Without warning, Nina walked up next to Ollie. She stood by his side until Ollie finally became aware of her presence. They looked at each other but didn't say a word. They didn't have to; he knew what her message was. She was guiding him, supporting him, encouraging him to use his tremendous gift of emotional healing with Mitch.

Ollie walked over to Mitch with his hand outstretched, fingers quickly curling in and out. "All right, gimme your phone and five minutes," Ollie demanded.

Mitch broke away from the heated Twitter exchange and looked up at Ollie. "What? Why?"

Ollie just wiggled his fingers more aggressively. Mitch handed Ollie the phone as if he already knew the reason why he wanted it. Ollie sat down on the bed and began scrolling through the Twitter exchange, clicking on a profile here and there, scrolling some more, and then returning to the stream of tweets. Three minutes passed, and Ollie knew he didn't even need the full five.

Ollie locked the screen and looked up at Mitch. "Mitch, what are you doing?"

"What?" Mitch said, ready to defend himself.

"This person is clearly disturbed, and you know that. You can't argue rationally with an irrational person."

"Did you see what she said? It doesn't even make sense! But now all these other people, who clearly don't get what's going on *either*, think I'm an asshole. It's fucked up. It's them, not me! They're all crazy!"

Ollie revived the phone and opened up an Instagram profile. "Mitch. Seriously? You're really threatened by this? You're upset that a twentysomething, quote, *spiritual influencer,* who has more pictures of his shirtless torso than episodes of his podcast, insulted you on Twitter? Do you really think they matter? What they say matters? Do you really care what all of these people think about you?"

"Yes!"

"Mitch…buddy, humans are the buckthorn of the earth."

Mitch stared back, utterly perplexed.

Ollie shook his head in the most loving way possible, and waved Mitch's phone back and forth. "This isn't real. These people, these internet people, don't know the truth. It's impossible to know anyone's truth unless you're actually that person. People are so complex that you can never truly know why someone does or says something, so why engage? And it doesn't matter what you post, *someone* will have something negative to say about it. Do you know what they're doing on the internet? They are there to judge and to be looked at, because everyone wants to be seen. They all want the *like.* So many people are like this, and they will find, attack and criticize people like you because it makes them feel better. That's why Avery and I deleted all of our accounts. I try to keep a pretty clear channel, and social media wasn't doing me any favors."

Ollie set the phone down on the bed, scootched closer to Mitch and turned his head to face him. "You don't need to defend yourself. You don't have to make it your job to shut them up. All you have to do is ignore it. Don't let it hail all over you, because that hail will sink right in there"—Ollie lifted a finger to Mitch's heart—"and that will make you heavy and dark, and you already struggle with being heavy and dark." Ollie took a breath. "And I'm not saying that you have to *not* ever care what people think either. I wouldn't think you were human if you somehow managed to do that. These people and their judgments and opinions of you don't matter. It doesn't matter if they think they are right or not. Let them trash you, let them roll around in their own shit and drama. They don't know you. They don't care about you. It's just negative energy. Negative, sticky energy that rolls around and wants to infect all that sticks to it.

"Don't take what doesn't matter to heart. Don't try to analyze hateful words until you can't even text because your hands are shaking from anger. The whole world isn't going to like you—that fact applies to everyone. People like me, who are here to help you out of the dark, that's what you have to focus on. And I'm right here, right now, and I'm not going anywhere." Ollie hesitated for a moment. "Mitch, I know you're upset, but I don't think it's this that you're hurt about. I think it's something else." He knew it was something else, and Mitch knew it too.

Mitch suddenly burst into tears. Ollie took his hand and cupped it in his own, shielding him from his over-picked thumb. Mitch then unleashed another round of tears as he clenched his fist tighter in Ollie's palm, causing his cracked and wounded thumb to ooze a little blood. His emotional and mental wounds were fully open, and now Ollie needed to treat them, heal them, until they were nothing but scars too small for concern.

Ollie laid Mitch flat on the bed as he whimpered from the emotional release. Ollie wasn't really sure what he was doing—it was more of an experiment—but it felt right. He was going to attempt to make Mitch feel better by showing the power of his own vulnerability.

Ollie positioned Mitch on his back and instructed him to close his eyes. He could hear the noise that filled Mitch's head, knowing it was partially to blame for his suffering, as he let it consume and define him. He rubbed his hands together vigorously and charged them up.

"I get anxious and depressed every now and then, too," Ollie said freely. "Some of it stems from the whole adjustment to becoming a witch and the fear that came with it. Uncertainty. But sometimes the thing that you're most afraid of is exactly what you should be doing. You have to rise above the noise in your head. If you want to grow beyond it, you have to break through the walls of the container." Ollie stretched his arms out a few inches above Mitch's body and began to slowly pan his hands from Mitch's head down to his feet, scanning the length of his body, feeling for hot and cold spots in his aura, searching for blocked chakras. He held his hands like little radar dishes and passed them over Mitch's chest as he said, "Pain of any kind…is inevitable," then his abdomen, his navel, and finally just below it, resting over his closed sacral chakra, "but endless suffering is voluntary."

A tight pressure began to build underneath Ollie's hands, like a balloon filling with water. He cupped his hands even more as the pressure continued to build. The pressure came with heat, and turned his hands so hot, they could have melted cheese. Even as the pain slipped into his wrist and then up the length of both arms, he never had so much as a finger twitch. The searing pain continued. A single tear dripped out the side of one of Mitch's closed eyes, and slid down and hid in his hair.

Ollie looked into the horizon of Mitch's body. "Why are you addicted to staying in this…" he stuttered to find the right word, "headspace? I don't mean to diminish your feelings, I really don't. But you're not dead. You have a lot to live for, and you're just wasting so much time and energy, keeping yourself in this prison when there are so many other things that need and deserve your attention more. You need to love yourself, appreciate yourself, nurture yourself and those relationships that lift you up, not drag you down. And you need to believe that you deserve all of that. It's as simple as that. Accept that you do deserve it."

Mitch jerked up from the bed, as if his chest were tugged by a string wrapped around his heart. Again. Ollie closed his own eyes as he felt and saw all that was inside Mitch's head. The pain, the fear, the dissatisfaction and perpetual melancholy, the trauma and the monster that held on to it.

(I'm so proud of you, Ollie…)

Time seemed to stop in that moment of energetic release as Mitch finally embraced his pain so he could release it. Suddenly, they were both still, locked in shock as the bubble of pain that hung in the air between Ollie's hands and Mitch's body—popped. Mitch's cheeks were wet with tears, and the room was hot and dry, like an oven that had just been switched off. Ollie called his hands back and sloughed away the quagmire of unwanted energy.

As Ollie leaned back, Mitch took a few deep breaths, still paralyzed from the flood of emotion. He fell asleep right there only moments later—and this time, he dreamed only good dreams, ones that came from a place of newly found peace, and even more significant—acceptance.

When Ollie returned to his room, he immediately noticed a shuffling sound. The sheer curtains billowed in the breeze from a window he hadn't opened. Something was behind them, something that the outside light outlined in hazy detail. He pulled back the curtains, and there before him on the window-sill was a small, yellow sunburst bearded dragon staring back at him. A full minute passed as he stood there frozen in shock. He wanted to smile, but he couldn't; he was too bewildered. The tiny reptile was amazingly still as it gazed back into Ollie's eyes. It then bobbed its head up and down a few times, inviting him to come closer. *My totem*, Ollie thought. He had never been a lizard person, and usually the thought of being near one brought only feelings of fear. He had avoided lizards and similar creatures his whole life, ever since he was twelve and a monitor lizard in science class had escaped from its cage and chased him out of the room.

The lizard bobbed again. Ollie was still a little paralyzed and still held a grudge against lizards, which only encouraged him to resist the dragon's invitation even more. He rubbed the stubble on his cheeks and for a moment heard the sound of his own advice, words that he had said to Mitch only minutes earlier. Ollie looked a little closer at the dragon and examined the beauty of its skin, a jubilee of radiant yellows. He extended a shy finger toward the dragon and let it quake in the air between them. With a slippery flick of its forked, tacky tongue, the dragon licked his fingertip. *Look at you, being all brave,* Ollie said to himself, surprised that he didn't even flinch. All tension dissolved from the room, and the dragon suddenly jumped out the window. Ollie rushed to the sill and surveyed the area, but it was gone.

CHAPTER 30

Later that afternoon, Volustina found the internet—specifically, Google. The best way to catch up on lost time. In under an hour, they learned that ice was melting and the world was getting warmer, and it immediately triggered a vision—a wasteland of skeletons—if the coven didn't succeed. Article after article, they learned about modern-day society. *The world can't sustain itself with the practices they are using*, they thought. *Why are they not sapping the abundance of energy from the sun, the wind and the water? They take, and give nothing back. Leave nothing. It's about money and wealth and power. Still. So few care enough because the only thing that matters to most…is if they can have more.*

A little while later, Leo found Volustina by themself recuperating in the family room. They weren't entirely alone; they had made a new friend: PlayStation 4. Volustina started out playing *Resident Evil 7*, but deemed it too dark for their psyche. They found first-person shooter games insufferable, and didn't appreciate how mean players were in the online chat. A happy medium was achieved with *Limbo*, which they had completed earlier that morning. Volustina had moved on to *Uncharted 4* after teaching themself how to Google something and reading all the praise for Naughty Dog games.

Leo sat down next to Volustina. "Hey, can I ask you something?"

Their fingers mashed on the buttons. *Click, click, click, click, click, click, click, click!* "Yes, you may," Volustina said, eyes fixed on their Nathan Drake making a climb up a wall.

"Where can I find the talisman?" Leo asked as he began to judge their game play.

Volustina tilted their head a bit, but still kept their eyes on the screen. "It's in Garland."

"Where, though?"

Volustina took a deep breath as they pondered the consequences of giving him and him alone information about the talisman without the rest of the coven present. "It's in the northwest corner of the island." They managed to sneak a glance at Leo without letting Nathan lose a life. "You'll have to follow the Chaga River northwest, until you reach the Glowing Caves. Pass through them, and then Atropa Mountains, until you reach Black Ice Beach." Volustina hit Pause on the game, realizing that this was a serious question. Leo was planning to go there as soon as possible, and probably alone. "Find the tallest hill on the beach and climb those cliffs. There will be a hole at the top of the hill—Mokara's Crater, we called it." Volustina stared into Leo's eyes until they melted into the hazy images of his near future. "You'll find it there."

Leo was almost a little disappointed. He had expected at least a little bit of a fight, a little bit of *You can't go alone* or something like *It's too dangerous!* But Volustina offered neither of those options. They managed to crack a smile, though, as if they knew something he didn't.

"How long will it take to get there?" Leo asked, realizing that he hadn't even thought about the logistics behind his operation.

"If you found someone or some*thing* to take you there, you should be able to reach it by nightfall."

Leo was about to launch into a whole defense about why he was going, but Volustina stopped him as if they already knew what he was going to say before he said it.

"I know that you're choosing to go find the talisman…alone. I also know that I can't stop you."

"Yeah, but you're gonna try, aren't you? Or tell someone? You're not just gonna let me go…right?" he asked, still wanting that fight, no matter how big or small it was.

Volustina shook their head. "I won't stop you. It's not my place." Volustina broke their focus and stared off into space. Their eyelids twitched for a moment, and then they were consumed with sadness, the face of someone who had just received the news that a family member had passed. "I couldn't follow you there anyway." They closed their eyes and focused on the visuals in their head. They saw the crater, and it was covered with a colossal infestation of reddish-brown algae, inside and out. "The crater is toxic to me now." Volustina opened their eyes and shook their head. "I have seen it. Just now. I should have known, I just never expected it to happen so soon."

"It what?" Leo asked.

"Garland's ecosystem is very sensitive, more so than yours. The increase in human population because of Jasper has altered the environment. I could sense the changes; I just didn't know how drastic they were. The lifestyle within the Creamstone Township caused the temperature to rise just enough for the bewalembu to overproduce."

"What's that?" Leo asked, suddenly worried but also kind of excited. Still such a danger whore.

"It's an algae. Native to Garland, yes, but still toxic to fairies. Just because it's our realm doesn't mean that everything is safe. The township created the perfect environment for the bewalembu to bloom, mutate and spread. It can be fixed if Garland is allowed to heal, but it will take some time for it to return to normal. But I certainly can't go with you now. We can't risk it if I'm the last fairy left and you need me. Fairies are so sensitive to it that if I get too close, or inhale too deeply, any number of things could happen. Fairies have had their hearts stop, their lungs collapse, they've had horrible head pains and rashes for days before they just simply perished. It is safe for you, but not for me."

"Well, fuck."

Volustina placed a hand on Leo's rough knuckles. "You must be careful. Jasper is gone, but he wasn't the only threat. He had enemies—the Medeans. In the past, a group of people escaped the township and set up their own society. You must avoid them. Anyone left in Garland is a friend to no one."

A chill ran through Leo, and he wasn't easily chilled. He furrowed his brow as he pulled his hand out from under Volustina's warm touch.

"You won't have any power there. Remember that. Don't let that hot temper mix with arrogance. It will only cause you to fail."

"*You* could help me. You're a…*fairy*…right?" Leo still had trouble using that word. It sounded so ridiculous.

Volustina cracked a tiny smile. "You don't have to use that word. We've been called many things."

Leo shook his head, realizing that maybe they had some sort of psychic power, a clair of some sort. Or maybe they were just really good at reading people. Either way, he still wanted to know what powers they had. In Garland, he would be powerless, and relying on offensive behavior and foul language wasn't exactly going to save him from having his throat cut, or whatever the Medeans were going to do to him if they captured him.

"My energies aren't fully restored," Volustina said. "The transformation took a toll on my body and my energy." They paused for a moment. "How will you get back?"

Leo realized he hadn't thought about that part at all. "Well, fuck, I'm glad you said something. I don't know?"

Volustina nodded encouragingly. "Yes, you do. I think the rose of Jericho spell should suit your needs well." They returned to their video game with a click of the controller. "I'd get going if I were you," they added with a polite nod.

Leo turned around and saw that Mitch was coming into the room. He could smell the sweet, buttery aroma coming from the freshly baked, warm chocolate chip cookie* on the porcelain plate in Mitch's hand before he saw it. He turned to greet him. Normally, Leo would have taken the cookie without asking and just walked away. But he had bigger treats on his mind. After Leo checked in with Mitch to see how he was holding up, mostly just to not look like a complete asshole, he scurried away, half relieved that Mitch hadn't responded with the truth. If he had, they both would've been there until sundown. But Mitch hadn't come to chat to Leo, and he didn't care where he was rushing off to, he had come for Volustina.

Mitch walked over to Volustina and sat down on the couch next to them. Volustina wanted to be annoyed at yet another interruption, but they couldn't be. Instead, they just clicked Pause one more time and gave their full attention to Mitch, who deserved it, even if he didn't believe it.

"I brought you a cookie," Mitch said.

"That's for me?" Volustina said with a wide-eyed smile on their face.

Mitch nodded and offered the plate. "Yeah! Avery baked them. I think she likes to bake when she's stressed out."

"Well, you're very kind," they said as they lifted the cookie from the plate and studied it. They stuck their nose above the gooey piece of chocolate and sniffed. "I've never smelled anything like it."

"You've never had a chocolate chip cookie before?"

"I've had cookies before, but not one quite like this." Volustina sniffed again. "Brown butter. Dark Muscovado sugar. An extract of vanilla she made herself…and two kinds of salt."

"You can tell all of that from the smell?" Mitch asked, astonished.

"Smell gives me pictures sometimes. I can see the bag of sugar she used; I can see her browning the butter. I guess I'm slowly coming back to normal." They took a bite of the cookie and let out a hoot of pleasure as the buttery, sweet cookie softened over their tongue. "That is a positively sinful cookie."

Mitch's stomach turned into a knot. The easy part was over. Now he had to do what he had come to do. "Can I ask a favor?" he asked in the humblest way possible.

Volustina swallowed their first bite and took an even larger second as they said, "You may."

Mitch's eyes were suddenly filled with gravity, and he instinctively reached over to pick at his thumb. "You can…erase…memories, right?"

There, he'd done it. He'd asked. Now he could take a breath.

Volustina slowed their chewing as they looked deep into the joyless eyes looking back at them. All at once, they knew everything about why Mitch was there. They had been so distracted with the cookie, so buttered up (which apparently was the point) that they hadn't paid attention to Mitch's energy.

"That is something I can do, erase memories and the feelings attached to those memories, yes," they said, nodding and gazing into his next sentence.

Mitch stumbled over his words. Any words that he couldn't say fell out of his mouth and onto his thumb, where he ripped them from his skin. His heart began to race, and tears began to form under his eyes as the whites turned red. "I can't live like this anymore. I can't live with these feelings. It's like poison, stinging me from the inside out, all the time." He gasped some air into his lungs and choked back his emotions long enough to continue his request. "I feel like I'm never going to get over this."

"What's this?" Volustina asked as they put their hand on Mitch's head to pet his hair.

"Everything. I'm just in so much—pain—all the time. I can't shake what's happened, and it just replays over and over. I feel like I just do everything wrong. Shouldn't I be better off than this? Is there something wrong with me? What am I doing wrong? I feel stuck. I hate that I can't be better. What if I don't know how to…*be*…*better*? Sometimes I wonder if I'd just be better off dead." Mitch sobbed and wiped his nose with the back of his hand, and a bolt of clarity struck him. "I love beginnings. I get bored with the middles. I hate endings so much that I get stuck in the middle…fantasizing about another new beginning. That's not working anymore."

Volustina knew that Mitch was in the throes of a deepening depression, and it pierced their heart to see it spill out like this. They also knew what was best for him, even if he didn't.

"Oh sweet boy," Volustina said as they wiped his tears, "I know this is hard. I would never suggest anything different. Don't let anyone tell you how to grieve, or how long it should take or what it should look like. Sensitive people often live in a world of wounds only they can see."

Mitch wiped his own eyes and looked straight at Volustina. "Will you help me? Please, just take it from me. The memories in my head, you can make them go away. Just take them, please. I don't want to live like this anymore. I can't."

Volustina cupped his hands in theirs. "Mitchell," they said as soft as spring rain, "no."

He stopped sobbing. A look of shock fell across his face.

"I will not take your memories. They are what make you who you are. And you will get through this, even if right now, it feels like you won't. But you will. It's only time that will help you. And yes, it is work, and I know you feel like a hot knife is endlessly slicing through your heart. But it's the only way you will ever be what you desire to be. And I would hate for you not to learn how to become that. Because that's strong and beautiful."

CHAPTER 31

Leo changed out of his heavier winter clothes and into a T-shirt and jeans. The rose of Jericho plant that he had prepared to get him back safely was left on his nightstand. He grabbed a shabby old red backpack from his closet and filled it with all the things he thought he might need: the jar with his soul, a primed and paired rose of Jericho, a few fruit-and-nut bars, two bottles of water, a utility knife, a chocolate chip cookie and a lighter. The truth was, he didn't know what he would need, any more than he knew what he was doing or where he was going. As he zipped up his backpack, he felt the familiar sting of excitement, one that he would get before doing anything dangerous. Only this wasn't about cheap thrills to pass the time, this was something much more than that.

He closed his bedroom door and next, his eyes. His breathing grew deep and long as he stood magnificently still. Leo visualized Garland at first, but then more specifically the spot in the Bermuda Triangle where he knew the entrance was. If it didn't work, he would end up drowning out in the middle of the North Atlantic. Dangerous. Loved it. Lived for it. He began to lean back. Like a plank of wood falling to the floor, Leo dropped through the air and dissolved through a pocket of unseen energy just above the floor.

He opened his eyes after the initial swoosh of energy passed, and soon realized he didn't quite have the greatest understanding of his powers yet. Leo was still a little too cocky, a little too arrogant. Everything around him was gray and foggy, and there was nothing solid underneath him. He looked down at his tattered pair of Vans and saw the surface of the ocean some indistinct number of miles away. His skin was wet, as though he were in the middle of August in Louisiana.

He found himself hanging out the bottom of a cloud with a set of feelings that he normally associated with parts of his past. He was nauseated and sweating, and his breathing was erratic. He didn't know what he was about to feel—the junkie nightmare. Only he was sober, and he had no idea how far that fall was, or if crashing into the water would kill him. *Would it?* His heart skipped half a beat and then began to pound as he watched his feet dangle thousands of feet above the water…And then he fell. Faster and faster, tumbling toward the open ocean. Suddenly, he felt the magnetic pull. It slowed his momentum just enough for him to make sense of which direction was up. *It worked,* Leo thought as he gave into the magnetism. Shortly afterward, he felt the squishy sand cushioning him underneath his feet. He'd made it to the beaches of Garland.

He traced his footsteps from the first trip, and found himself not in the Creamstone Township, but amidst another type of vast ocean, one of rubble, ash and charred bones. The obelisk had exploded and left nothing behind but debris and the heavy stink of death. He'd never seen such devastation before, at least nothing that didn't involve water. Having lived through Katrina, he knew water very well and how much of a bitch it could be.

Just twenty minutes later he managed to reach the Chaga River. Leo had purposely not thought about how difficult this task might be without magic or any sort of help. For a brief moment he considered how stupid it was to attempt, and even hated himself. Why couldn't he just ask for help? Why did he need to do this alone? The moment passed when he realized how much of a piece of shit he'd really turned out to be. He had chosen to do this alone because he held his needs above everyone else's. He wasn't trying to be horrible; it wasn't like he didn't care *at all*, he just cared about everyone else *less*.

Leo didn't want to admit it, but he felt his choice was justified. After all, no one else had to Google "how to trigger happiness chemicals, life hacks." He had tried fistfuls of dark chocolate, he couldn't run because he would get winded, essential oils smelled good but that was it, and there were only so many small tasks he could finish. None of them offered the super-boost of dopamine, serotonin or endorphins that the internet told him he'd receive. Searching for the talisman alone wasn't a fuck-you to everyone else, it was more of a belief that he deserved something more than they did.

He reminded himself of that as he followed the river, realizing that even though he hated himself for feeling that way, he was doing it regardless. But he was proud of himself for at least acknowledging how awful he was. He certainly deserved some credit for admitting it to himself, *right*? It wasn't like finally admitting that he didn't trust people whose hair he never saw because they always wore hats; this was a big deal. At least, he repeated that to himself as he followed the river. It helped the time pass. As beautiful as Garland was, he still had the nightmarish thoughts of his own psyche to deal with.

Leo hiked over to the edge of the river to rinse the sweat off his face. He realized he was moving at a slow crawl. He had to go faster than this. He looked behind him. He could still see the rubble of the township, but there was also something else. A small, weather-worn rowboat. He rushed over to examine it. The boat was a humble thing, with splintered oars and sun-beaten seats that buckled in the center. It stayed afloat and there were no holes, and that was all Leo needed.

He stepped one foot into the boat and pushed away from the shore with the other. He wasn't the most athletic person, but he began rowing regardless. Leo started off strong, with a steady pace and a firm grip on the oars. It took all of six minutes before he needed a break. His calloused hands could take it, but his muscles couldn't. As he took a few moments to catch his breath and coast north with the river's current, he soaked in the beauty around him. The forest on either side—thick with thousands of dark trees, with blue leaves, all reaching high into the sky from a meadow of blue flowers that rippled in the breeze. They reminded Leo of the wolfsbane that Ollie grew for magical purposes, the ones he'd been told never to breathe, touch or even look at. Which, naturally, only made him want to do it even more.

Right when he got his stride back, he stopped rowing as the forest opened up to reveal an enormous lake in the distance on the shore at his left. He smiled, and his eyes widened with surprise. It wasn't just any lake; the water was pink. Bright pink, like the candy aisle at the drugstore a few weeks before Valentine's Day. Leo laughed as he marveled at the sight that instilled enough childlike wonder to make him forget that his arms were sore. He wondered what else was on the massive island and what kind of trouble he could find.

Leo refreshed himself in the river and then continued rowing. He was starting to stink, and sundown was maybe an hour or two away. He had to be getting close. The rowing was wearing him down, and every stroke was less powerful than the one before it. Then, his ears perked up as the quiet of the river grew louder. He squinted and looked as far up the river as he could see, and then he saw it. A cascading, whitecapped rapids, bubbling, frothing and roaring like a beast. Leo was no stranger to a boat or to the water. He had taken his old canoe out into the cypress swamps that ran through Tickfaw State Park, but those were different. Those waters were still, dark and threatening because of the water moccasins and gators that slithered through them. The waters ahead were angry all on their own. The anger had a short wick. It didn't look like the path through the rapids was very long, but it was just dangerous enough to set him on edge.

He stopped rowing, pulled the oars into the boat and used one as a tool to push himself away from the boulders. Then he entered the rapids in a quick dip over a small waterfall. Water sloshed inside, and the boat spun around like a car on ice. Chills rippled through his body as he began to think that he might not be up to this task. He instantly regretted coming alone. However, it was too late for any of that now, too late for wishes and *if I had only*s.

The boat swung out of his control and was ripped away by the current, slamming into a jagged rock. The front of the boat fragmented into pieces as the water rushed in to carry him out. He took in a heavy breath and plunged into the water headfirst. Then everything was muffled, reduced to a haunting hissing noise as the water poured onto itself. He broke the surface by what seemed to be blind luck, but only for a few seconds before the current sucked him back under. The cycle repeated twice more, until a piece of the boat knocked into his chest and forced him out of the rotation. Everything was murky and brown, a mixture of powerful water and stirring sand.

Leo held his breath for as long as he could, flailing his arms and legs, hoping to catch on to anything solid. He opened his mouth, but was just shy of breaking the surface, and he drew in a mouthful of water. *This is it*, he told himself. *All this for fucking nothing, because you just can't help yourself. Because you're a piece of shit. You probably deserve this.*

Then something wrapped around his forearm, and the next thing he knew, he was on the shore, coughing up everything he had drunk. For the first time in his life, he thanked God, even though he had never really believed in him…it…whatever God was. He certainly had been opened up to a whole new set of rules since Nina entered his life, and he knew there was something bigger out there, whatever anyone chose to call it.

After he stopped coughing and could finally make sense of where he was, he found what—who—had pulled him out of the water. Three men, none of them friendly. One of them stood over Leo, highlighted by the sun, and knocked him out cold with a club.

When he regained consciousness and opened his eyes, he was met with a pounding pain in his temples. One eye was bruised and swollen, and there were voices all around him. His vision was still a little blurry, so the voices were nothing but shuffling shapes. It was then he noticed that his hands were bound and he was tied to a post. The sweat that ran down into his mouth wasn't sweat at all but his own blood as it trickled out of a gash on his forehead. *This would happen,* he thought. *I would get saved from drowning only to end up being held hostage by...*he didn't know. Who were these people? Leo peered into the back of his eyelids as a rush of pain came searing from his head. Then he remembered. Were these people the Medeans that Volustina had warned him about?

Finally everything started to take shape, just as the rest of his senses returned. The air smelled like fire and blood and hot feces, even with the sun hidden behind a sky of gray. He looked around him and saw that he wasn't the only one—or thing— tied up. Erected around the firepit were four posts, and he was tied to one of them. The others held a large blackbird, a fish gasping for air, and a relentlessly white man. He had never seen anyone whiter than Mitch before, and this person was so white, his skin was almost translucent. His hair was void of pigment, and the only color came from his eyes. Whether this person was some sort of natural albino or magically altered, he would never know. What he did know was that the Medeans were about to start some kind of ritual, and they were all part of it.

Leo looked around the group, counting about thirty or so. Men and women, all with the same wild, cult-y eyes. He dealt a storm of fuck-yous to the Medeans in his head because he was still too exhausted to do much else. There was no telling what they were going to do, but judging from the sharp, makeshift knife that flickered from the cloaked man's hands, it wasn't go- ing to be pretty. *You bastards*, he repeated to himself, desperately trying to blame them rather than himself. He was the one who had ultimately gotten himself in this position. He had just *had* to do it his way, he'd had to do it all by himself because his needs were more important. After all he'd been through, he still hadn't changed enough to make a big enough difference. Even when he thought he had. Leo considered that it could be one of those things that would offer him some re- demption, something like two steps forward and one step back.

Then the chanting began. Softly at first, and only by the one who wielded the shiv, then the rest of them followed suit, until it became a dark drone of prayers, wishes and demands. The leader lifted the knife to the air, and the group silenced.

Then he spoke. "We call upon you now, Shuterra…"

"Shuterra," the group whispered in unison.

If Leo hadn't been so terrified, he would have laughed. They looked like cultists pretending to be witches pretending to be possessed.

The knife swayed back and forth in the air like a metronome keeping rhythm to some kind of twisted song. "Our blessings have arrived. We thank you for your gifts and your lessons, and for showing us the way. We give to you our offerings of flesh and blood. The time is now. Come. Appear. Empower us." The man revealed a bone from within his cloak and set it upon the ground. "We will serve you and you will serve us, and we will devour Jasper and reclaim your world. We are one. Accept our devotion. Be our salvation."

It clicked right then and there. They had escaped from Jasper and wanted him dead. Only that wasn't the crazy part. As Leo listened to the man praise the bone on the ground, he realized that they believed the bone was from some mystical god they were aiming to resurrect to save them all. Leo didn't need to be a Transcendent to know they'd lost their shit. And then he realized that he might be able to convince them that what they were doing wasn't even necessary—Jasper was dead.

"Hey!" Leo shouted. "Hey, yo! He's dead, dude!" But no one was listening. He tried to wiggle free, but the rope was tight. He yelled again and again, "Jasper's dead, you don't have to do this, he's dead, he's dead," until *dead* no longer sounded like a word in English.

The leader was immune to Leo's cries. When insanity takes over, it takes over. Leo would know. He might not have ever tied people up or threatened a bird with a shiv, but he'd done some wild shit.

A quick-footed cultist ran up to the leader's side and offered him a large machete. With the blade next to his lips, the man closed his eyes and began to recite the words he believed to be passing over his eyelids. Only they weren't words; it was a river of rapid sounds, clicks, whirrs and unintelligible phrases that danced off his tongue with urgency and conviction. There was so much faith, so much belief and intention in the man's voice, it was almost as beautiful as it was frightening. It sounded bloodcurdlingly ancient, but also completely invented, like reading the rainbow or verbalizing sacred geometry. For a second, even Leo thought maybe these people knew something he didn't. Who was he to judge, criticize and tell them their god didn't exist? He had shat on magic before learning that he himself was magic.

Then, in a powerful swing, the man sliced off the right hand of the albino man, right at the wrist. Leo's eyes flashed open, and the headache he had was suddenly the last thing on his mind. Leo had broken down chicken before, many, many times back when he was a line cook, so he naturally assumed what would happen next. And he was right. The man chucked the hand into the fire like a piece of battered chicken into a deep fryer. The albino screamed until he passed out. Leo rescinded his previous thought about trying not to pass judgment. Praying to and communicating with Spirit was one thing, slicing off a man's hand like a chicken leg was something else.

A whole novel of thought rushed through Leo's head as he tried to calm himself down. He tried to concoct a way to escape just so he wouldn't freeze up with panic. He couldn't do any magic, so he resorted to wishes that he could only hope would come true. *Please! Someone help me! Help me!* he shouted. He was so struck with fear, he couldn't tell if his screams were in his head or out loud. For the first time in a long time, he was scared for his life. He thought about Bisa, and his daughter, Krystal, and Nina, and all the people he'd let down and could never make amends to. How could this be it? *I always knew it was going to end like this…*

The leader dropped the machete and caressed the knife, and with another coldblooded stab, he stuck the fish.

He just shanked a fish! Leo screamed in his lead. *Nina…what do I do…*

With the fresh blood still glistening on the tip, the man slowly walked over to the post with the bird.

Leo closed his eyes as sweat began to bead up on his forehead and mix with his crusting wound. *No…not the bird, that means I'm next…* His breath filled his lungs as he tried to collect himself. He huffed and puffed, trying to clear his mind. He could hear the chirping of the bird…until he didn't. Still, he kept his eyes closed and concentrated on anything but his reality. His hopes and wishes turned to prayers, and prayers turned to a request, and the request became a call. *Please, help me…just this once…save me…protect me…protect me…Spirit…*

Leo crushed his eyes together so tightly that he started to see spots, familiar purple ones. He heard the man's footsteps approaching. He didn't want to see what happened next, so he kept his eyes closed. Then, the footsteps stopped, and there was another noise. A growling. At first, he thought it was his imagination, or some sort of episode, the kind one experiences right before they die, but he was still very much alive. Leo creaked his eyes open and peered around. Hanging on the periphery of the group was a large wolf. Its teeth bared and lips quivering, but not at Leo—*for* Leo. He knew this wolf. His totem.

The leader spun around and grabbed the machete. He was stocky and muscle-y like a bulldog, but his hands quaked. Faster than any animal Leo had ever seen in the nature documentaries he used to fall asleep to, or any vampire in any film he'd ever seen with faster-than-light vampires, the wolf jumped. When Leo's eyes finally caught up with the wolf, it had already torn out the leader's throat. By the time Leo blinked, it had found another victim. Again, and again the wolf made its rounds, biting through flesh and tearing through necks. It moved too fast for Leo to follow, because it was beyond movement, it was disappearing from one place and materializing at another. It happened thirty-three times, until the entire cult was nothing but a pile of bloody limbs and open throats.

Leo squirmed and pulled himself out of his restrains. When the carnage was over, the wolf stood still with its eyes fixed on Leo. Thoughts swam through Leo's head. He was almost dizzy from trying to follow the bloodbath. There was a strange kind of submission behind the wolf's eyes, as if it had done it all out of love. Leo put aside his doubts, scruples and cheeky thoughts until all that was left was an abundance of awe and gratitude. What does someone say to someone—or something—that has just saved their life in ways that were unimaginable? There were no words, and none were needed.

The wolf approached Leo, passing through blood, limbs and dirt, until it stood only a few feet from him. They studied each other, as if communicating in some subtle way that needed no explanation. Leo reached a shaking hand out and rustled his fingers through the wolf's fur. He smiled and let out a breathy laugh, thick with wonder. He had never in his life felt so con-nected to nature, to Spirit, to something greater than himself.

A few moments later, the wolf pulled away and scampered off into the trees, where it vanished instantly as it brushed past the tall grass and foliage.

CHAPTER 32

Leo continued on, fueled with even more gusto than he'd previously had. When he reached the edge of the mountains, he saw that there was only one way into them, through the glowing caves. There wasn't a trodden path, and he had to maneuver through boulders and rocks as he hiked inside. He didn't see any flammable mushrooms nearby, and he hadn't thought to bring any, because, well—Leo, but he didn't need any. As he walked farther away from the mouth of the cave where the light of day guided him, the cave provided him with a new kind of light. He followed the strange blue-green glow coming from around a corner, and a calm rushed over him. When he rounded the corner, he found himself wrapped in a rich turquoise light, like sun through a shard of sea glass, that speckled the ceiling of the caves like the stars of the night sky. Silk-like threads hung from above like strings of pearls and beaded drop lines on a wedding cake. Leo marveled at the majesty of it, almost wanting to look for a constellation in the animated bioluminescence. It was humid and quiet, like being in a womb, and the walls were covered in moss. He immediately thought back to his time in the temazcal where he had transformed in complete darkness. Now, there was light.

The next thirty minutes were a blend of amazed stares, shuffling feet and neck twists as Leo took his own self-guided tour through the caves. He thought about Bisa while under the shimmering chandeliers of charlatan stars, and wished he could share them with her.

When he reached the end of the cave and spilled out into daylight once again, he found himself in the middle of the Atropa Mountains, a stunningly vast range of tall pillar-like spindles of black sandstone and milky quartz that were dressed in moss and speared the sky. It looked like a rain forest on acid. Granted, he'd never been in a rain forest, but he had taken acid, and lots of it.

He followed the only logical path, a trampled dirt route through the rocks and lush foliage that covered the ground. It was a tropical paradise with its own ecosystem apart from the rest of the island. Leo restlessly flitted through the mountains, staring up into the cloud-frosted tips every few steps.

When the path shifted a little downhill, he parked himself on a boulder and had a lunch of bottled water, a cherry almond bar and a fat chocolate chip cookie that left his fingers buttery. He stuffed the trash back into his backpack, careful not to leave any litter behind, something Ollie would have surely gotten on his case about if he'd been around. When he plucked the backpack up from the ground, he noticed the soil had become sandy. *I must be getting close,* he thought as he pressed farther on.

Ten minutes later, he found himself at the base of a large hill covered in prairie grass. He took a few steps up the hill and looked to his left and then his right. He was in the center of a curve of undulating hills. The air had changed. It was significantly cooler, and fresh. Leo looked back into the Atropa Mountains behind him and knew he was in the right spot. Mokara's Crater should be at the top of the hill he was ascending, if he remembered correctly. As he neared the top of the hill, he could see the beach that stretched out along the other side of the hills. Miles and miles of black sand, spotted with huge chunks of pale blue ice that glistened in the light like wet diamonds.

I've gotta get back in shape, man, this is ridiculous, he thought as he finally reached the summit of the hill. At the top, the air was cool and crisp, a refreshing and welcomed treat now that his shirt was soaked in sweat and he could hardly breathe without wheezing. There had been so much magic lately that he had forgotten he was still…human—ish. Ahead of him was a large mound of rock covered in bewalembu. The closer he got, the more pungent the bewalembu became. It was all around him, covering the peak in ghastly piles. It was worse than Volustina had made it out to be. It glistened like a wet, sticky pile of pasta, and produced a horrific, sickening smell akin to rotten eggs and decayed flesh. Leo covered his mouth as he gagged on the foul odor. His eyes followed the clumps that formed at the summit all the way down the other side of the hill, where the bewalembu spilled onto the beach and suffocated the shore. The ocean's vomit.

A few moments later, Leo peeled his hand away from his face and noticed the crater. His heart soared as if he had already found the talisman. He found his footing among the slippery algae, and peeked into the depths of the crater. Leo looked around the summit, but there was nothing but bewalembu—no flammable mushrooms.

"Shit!" he said, completely frustrated with himself. He hadn't thought about what he was going to do once he arrived. What was he going to do down there in the dark without a light? Then a second conundrum plagued him: how was he going to get down? Leo had done many risky things: climbed the rusty coasters at the abandoned Six Flags at night, shared a needle with someone he didn't know, and picked a fight with a canebrake rattlesnake just because he could, so diving into a cave didn't really chill any bones. He just had to figure out how he was going to pull it off.

Leo murmured to himself for a good five minutes before he picked up a long, slimy strand of bewalembu and tested its strength. *This'll do*, he thought as he ripped up a long rope of bewalembu from the crater's edge and readied himself on the rim of the abyss. As he leaned back over the blackness, he muttered a few more words of encouragement to himself. His feet slipped a little on the bewalembu, and he slammed into the side of the crater. A stream of *fucks* flew through his head as he gathered control over his rope. Leo had never been so humbled in his entire life. For once, he finally stopped talking shit. A few deep breaths and mental psych-ups, and he began to descend into the crater. The air felt cooler as the world became darker. He looked up to the round, moonlike opening above. It reminded him of the time when he'd been higher than high and thought that the moon was the opening at the top of a straw and he was at the very bottom just waiting to be slurped up. He wanted to laugh, but he found that dangling who knows how many feet in the air curbs your sense of humor a bit.

The farther down he went, the more his mind raced. When he could finally see a bottom, he felt a little relieved. He had forgotten that he had an enchanted rose of Jericho, so he started to wonder how he was going to be able to climb back up the rope. A little childhood trauma crept out of the depths of his mind and forced him to remember third-grade gym class and being the only boy who couldn't climb the rope and ring the bell at the top—or the easier cargo climbing net, for that matter.

When his feet hit the bottom, he was relieved to see several flammable mushrooms around him. He picked up the largest one he could find, squeezed it and took a moment to let his eyes adjust. Leo's hands were red and swollen, his shirt was soaked through and his heart was thumping so hard, he could feel blood pulsing in his earlobes. He slowly spun in circles and looked into the darkness. The cave mushrooms were exceptionally bright, bordering on white. It was a smaller crater than he'd expected; he could see the walls.

He took a few steps into the cave, and then his breath was stolen straight out of his lungs. Against the wall, half buried under a pile of rubble, was the silhouette of a familiar demon. It was too clean for a cave—it was as clean as he remembered. He took a few steps closer, bringing the mushroom's light. Fuzzy, chocolate-brown fur, a fluffy white belly, an oversized jet-black nose and shiny eyes. It looked smaller than he remembered, but the little stuffed koala bear had always looked big when Krystal hugged it.

Leo's skin began to crawl, and he went ice cold. A hundred memories of his daughter with her favorite stuffed toy flooded his mind, but it was the shock of seeing it at the bottom of the crater that choked him. He kneeled down before it and placed the mushroom on the ground. It even smelled like Krystal, a childish mix of pink erasers, play dough, Popsicles and straw-berry bubble bath, a personalized potpourri that existed only in memories he had forgotten.

He reached out to grab it with a shaking hand. As his fingers sank into the plush toy, he closed his eyes and released a single tear. When he opened them, he was no longer at the bottom of the mysterious crater, swallowed in darkness. He was back in Krystal's room. He gasped and dropped the koala bear. Leo gazed around the room nervously. It was exactly as it had al-ways been in his mind, so much that he wondered if he was actually there. Was everything just some crazy, drugged-out illusion? Maybe he had taken one too many drugs and had only now come out of it to find himself standing in the middle of Krystal's room. Suddenly, nothing made any sense and he questioned everything—but really, what was the change there? It had to be real. It smelled like baby lotion, he could hear the cars driving by on Palmisano Street, the room was filled with toys, rattles, dolls, green stuff, pink stuff. He remembered that his daughter had always liked rattles more than stuffed animals, until one day she decided the opposite. That's when she and the koala became inseparable. She took it everywhere, even into the closet, where she would sometimes spend the night in a fort Tonya helped her build.

Leo turned toward the closet. The door was shut. It was shut only if Krystal was hiding in her fort. Suddenly, everything fell quiet. No more cars, not even the whirring of the air conditioner, only deafening silence. Apart from the crying from the closet. Leo looked at the door, now incredibly uneasy, almost frightened. As he crept closer, the cries became louder and deeper until they grew into the wet, snotty, inconsolable wails he had never known how to handle. When he reached the closet door, the crying intensified.

Leo suddenly felt a surge of panic. What was on the other side? Was it his daughter? If so, why was she crying, and could he make it stop? He couldn't before…Why would he be able to now? He felt suspended in time, caught in a monstrous loop of violent, dreadful bawling. Then, as though ripping off a Band-Aid, Leo grabbed hold of the door handle and whipped it open. He gasped and let out a blubbering howl as he glimpsed his daughter inside the fort, bloody and broken. Her cries gave him an intolerable chill. He backed away in horror. He could see all of her wounds, where every bone had broken. Leo glanced behind him and found himself staring into the headlights of his old car.

Another sharp, ear-splitting scream came from the closet, and Leo turned to look, even though he didn't want to. The dread had nearly swallowed him whole. The car horn blared endlessly, the cries rose to shattering heights and there was not a single place to run. Finally, his eyes found the bedroom door. He hesitated for a moment, frozen between the horn and the cries like a vise of nightmares. His calloused hands covered his ears, but he found no relief.

A few agonizing and exhausting moments later, the decision finally came. It rose up from inside him like a jack-in-the-box, and he gave in to his weakness. He forced himself to run to the door. He pulled and pulled, so much that he thought it was going to shake right out of the frame. But it wouldn't budge. Leo had never felt anything so horrible. This was worse than any withdrawal, any depression, any death. It was all of it, yet none of it. His fists met the wood over and over, and then with one violent tug, he opened the door and fell through the doorway.

He arrived back in the cave with a loud crack. Confused and broken, Leo looked down at his hand. He was holding a paper-thin shard of black marble, no larger than a silver dollar, shattered into a myriad of pieces. He closed his hands over the pieces and cried. Perhaps his daughter would have been able to forgive him for, well, everything, but Leo couldn't forgive himself. It was one thing to feel the shame, but having to face it honestly turned out to be the one thing that was too dangerous…even for Leo. Everything resurfaced, all at once, even the things he thought were too trivial to remember, or forget. He fell to the floor, clutching the shards of the marble talisman in his hands. All he could do was cry and shake his head, and wait for his pain to subside.

A half hour later, the tears stopped, but the shame wouldn't quit. So he just learned to live with it in the same way that he had been. When he opened his hands to examine what was in his grasp, he noticed strange markings on the shards. He brought them closer to the light of the mushroom on the ground that was still burning, so he could examine them. When he rubbed his fingers across the symbols, everything suddenly made sense, as if the symbols had spoken to him, explained to him exactly how he had failed, a magical by-product of the enchantment. The koala bear had been the talisman he'd been looking for all along. It was enchanted, charmed to take the shape of whatever symbolized a person's greatest regret or shame. If he didn't confront it and tried to leave, as he had, the talisman would shatter—irreparably.

Leo dug into his backpack and pulled out the rose of Jericho he had saved for his moment of victory, which was now the sad opposite. He spit on it, and performed the gestures he'd seen Rosemary do. With the image of his room somewhere far, far away from where he was, he gazed into the rose and said, "*Reditus*."

Just as before, he passed through fire and space and found himself inside his room.

CHAPTER 33

Leo waited until after a dinner of Curried Cauliflower with Yogurt Sauce* to break the news to everyone. Everyone was upset; no one was surprised. After he mentioned that Volustina hadn't stopped him, everyone shot them a look. No one could be angry with them, but it also seemed like a slap in the face, considering the actual prophecy had come from their lips.

When he arrived at the part in the story involving his daughter, he rushed through it. There was no way in hell he was going to relive that experience *a third time,* swathed in guilt, shame and misery. A summary would have to suffice. He wasn't about to risk having everyone else find out what he had discovered about himself in those few short minutes of horror…that he was *still* a wretched person, and he couldn't even face up to it and redeem himself. Would he ever be able to? Would anything he did ever make up for his cowardice? Maybe that's all he truly was…spineless and pretending he wasn't.

He wanted to be the piece of sand caught in an oyster that eventually turned into a pearl. One of Leo's top ten wishes was that people would see him as more than just what he had done, because he knew that when they looked at him, that was all they saw. He just wished they saw that there was more to him than that—at least he told himself so. Even he didn't fully believe it.

The room was thick with loathing. The only chance that they had had was gone. Leo had blown the one and only chance they had had to find the rafkolite. It caused a great deal of commotion among the coven. It didn't make any sense. Could Volustina have been wrong?

Leo escaped the hostile room and fled to the comforts of his bedroom, where there was nothing and no one. No one wanted to go to bed angry that night, but they did, apart from Volustina, who had passively observed the entire conversation from the corner of the room.

(Bisa...)

It was three a.m. when the snow stopped falling. Bisa was tossing in her sleep, tangled in the sheets. She was somewhere between dreaming of enlightenment and feeling the weight of everyone. It was in this space that she heard the voice that woke her.

(Bisa...)

With a gasp, Bisa snapped up from the bed and opened her eyes wide. She flicked on the lamp, and its light painted the floor in tones of amber, washing away the gentle blue of winter that scattered across the snow and into her room. When she realized it must have been a dream, she swung her feet out of the bed for a silent moment of meditation. She rubbed the back of her neck, suddenly incredibly awake.

(remember...)

The voice whispered again, stronger and more familiar. Bisa found herself looking around the room as if to find someone hiding in the shadows. It wouldn't be a stretch—that kind of thing had happened before. But the voice wasn't malicious, it was helpful. *Remember what?* Bisa asked herself as she squinted. But in those moments, the moments that she tried so hard to unriddle the puzzle of what to remember, she realized that by striving so hard to find the answer, she was only detaching herself from it. A moment of reflection calmed her mind, and she knew—she *felt*—that the answer was already available to her, as it always had been. Just as time itself was an illusion, so was the idea that she needed to search for an answer.

She liberated the key from deep within her mind as she allowed herself to let the falsity of not knowing dissolve. A conversation with Nina entered her mind. She allowed her eyes to commit to a soft gaze into space as she coaxed the memory from her storage chest. Her mind focused next on Rosemary. She had mentioned something about being invisible too. Then, after she willed the answer to reveal itself, she remembered. Invisibility could be achieved through aura manipulation and mixing astral fluids. But was there such a recipe? Everyone in her magical circle seemed to suggest that no one really knew how that kind of alchemy worked. Everyone…except one person. Evan. He called astral fluid AFD, as if it were some kind of street drug that sold for a hundred bucks a gram. If anyone had that kind of skill, surely it was him. She didn't know much about drug dealers, but she knew how to trust messages from Spirit. As she evoked the memory of Evan's place of business, with all its wires, stacks of books and a catastrophic system of organization, she trusted the vibe she got.

Bisa rose from the bed and got dressed. She quietly crept through the house and found her way to Leo's room. She pressed her ear to the door to listen. After all, Leo was unpredictable and could be doing any number of things at any time of the day—or night. When nothing but silence was heard, she snuck into his room. The smell shocked her: it actually smelled clean. There were no clothes on the floor, or boxes of cereal, there was no hoard of dirty dishes. In the past it wouldn't have been her first choice of where to spend time, a room perfumed with dirty socks and Cap'n Crunch–crusted bowls. Now at least he had graduated to a Glade PlugIn.

Bisa glided across the open floor and caught a glimpse of Leo in his bed, a bundle of sheets rising and falling with his heavy breath and a bare leg hanging out over the edge. There was no telling where he would have Evan's business card, or if he still had it, but something told her that he did. Leo was the type of person to say he would never buy drugs again and then never delete their hookup's number from their phone—you know, just in case. Bisa held out her dominant hand and closed her eyes. *If Evan's card is still here, where can I find it?* A warmth filled her palm and tingled like it had fallen asleep. She scanned the room until she finally felt a ping as she passed over the bedside table.

Bisa crept over to it and noiselessly opened the top drawer. She turned to the bed and tried to see through the thickness of the dark. She could see the sheets rising and falling in time to a soft snore. It was too dark to see into the drawer and she debated turning on the lamp, but she didn't want to risk it. She ran her fingers across the top of the table and found a bundle of sage. Her fingers rustled through the burnt edges as she searched for a nearby lighter. *Would he even need a lighter? He can light it himself. Please let there be a lighter.* Her pinkie finger knocked into the smooth shaft of a tiny lighter. She made a flame with a quick flick of her thumb and held her breath. Leo was still undisturbed, fast asleep.

Bisa cupped the flame with her free hand and dipped it closer to the drawer, skirting Leo's face. Sunflower seeds, playing cards, loose change, three old vapes, a garnet stone, a pair of dirty socks (*there they are…*), four random keys—none of them to a single lock in the house—three pens, a journal (*interesting…*), a few sticks of palo santo, small tapered candles in various colors, a dollar bill, and Evan's business card. She plucked it from the drawer and headed back to her room.

When she arrived at Evan's house, she had all sorts of questions that challenged magic. *How is this place still here? Who pays the rent or the mortgage? Doesn't anyone else ever ask any questions like this?* Magic often prevented questions of that nature from being asked to begin with, because someone manipulated it to be that way. Sure, maybe no one ever knew about this house because it was so rural, but there was no doubt some kind of enchantment on it that allowed it to remain forever a place of mystery.

Bisa approached the red door and entered the house. It was the smell that scared her, so putrid that she could hardly breathe. The living room was swarming with flies. She looked over to the shape that was Evan's rotting corpse. As if she were being led by someone other than herself, Bisa scurried past the body and through a door she hadn't noticed the first time she was there. She slammed the door behind her, locking out fumes that had already marinated the walls of every room. Bisa opened the window and pushed the shutters out into the world. There were bottles, a sea of bottles, some labeled and some not.

Bisa groaned at the sight of countless bottles and grew sick with impatience, as if the stench wasn't enough. *It has to be here somewhere,* she thought as she eyed the bottles in the cabinet closest to her. For a few minutes she was filled with nothing but pessimism, maybe a side effect from being in Leo's room even for that short time. It was only half past four by the time she had browsed nearly every bottle in the room. She had opened, smelled or read the label of every bottle she could. She felt like one of those dramatic, entitled shoppers who came into Warpaint back in Chicago, the ones who wanted a miracle product that did everything, that gave full coverage but was also insanely sheer and lightweight, and it had to be nude, but also had to be peachy or coral, and they needed to have a full face—applied by her, without an appointment and also free of charge. It was a stressor that only someone who has worked retail during the holiday season in the beauty industry would identify with, and one that had clearly left scars.

Then she thought about where she was now, *who* she was now, and she was proud of herself, even if she hadn't found what she was looking for. The final shelf held a collection of three bottles. Two of them were empty, and the third was corked and sealed with silver wax. She picked up the third one and examined the matter inside. A glittery, ghostlike, prismatic fluid that gently swished like the waves of a calm sea. She wiped the dust off the label with her thumb. It read, *astral invisibility*, and below that, *alchemized: 31st of March 1727*.

CHAPTER 34

Ollie had woken up early to make breakfast, one that Volustina could eat since they were what Ollie classified as an ovo-lacto vegetarian. The smell of sauteed mushrooms and swiss chard with harissa-smothered potatoes filled the kitchen. He had just finished up the buttery soft scrambled eggs when everyone piled into the kitchen, including Bisa. Even though she had had only a few hours of sleep, she didn't look like it. Her eyes were ablaze with satisfaction. But she wasn't ready to tell anyone that she had just solved their invisibility problem. *Not yet*, her vibes told her.

Volustina was dressed in a mixture of Avery's and Mitch's clothing. As they started breakfast, a vision bubbled up in their mind. Then they spoke. "The one named Nix." A pause. "He's gone."

"He's been gone for some time now," Rosemary said. "What do you mean, gone?"

Bisa knew instantly. Whatever plan he'd had hadn't worked.

"He's no longer on this plane. He's fallen into Death," Volustina said. Yet no one seemed to understand how literal they were being.

Rosemary sat in silence for a moment, then cut into her breakfast. "Well, he was dead to me anyway after the position he put me and this coven in. Saves all of us having to worry about him or what he was up to. Serves him right."

The topic bounced around the table for a few minutes, yet Bisa said nothing. Eventually the topic faded away faster than a celebrity blunder on social media.

"I hear you have quite a gift with the elements," Volustina said as they took a bite of potato, spicy and crispy on the outside, soft and creamy on the inside.

Avery smiled, but then her expression transformed into confusion. "How'd you—"

"But you have trouble with air," Volustina said. "Electrical currents…lightning."

Avery nodded. "I do. I mean, I can do it. Conjure it. Produce it. Direct it, even." She shook her head. "I just…can't always control it."

Volustina looked deep into Avery's eyes as if reading something written on her irises. A few moments later, Volustina nodded. "Rosemary, may I borrow your ring today? I'd like to take Avery somewhere to help her understand the spirit of lightning."

Rosemary waggled her head back and forth, clearly undecided about how to answer. She was about to explain her hesitation right after she swallowed her food, but Volustina already knew what she was going to say.

"Nothing will happen to it," Volustina said. "I will be more than careful. I know you've never lent it to anyone, and I do not take that responsibility lightly. I know it's precious."

Rosemary knew there was no real reason to argue. After all, Volustina was the one who had divined the coven into existence from who knew how many years ago. Surely she could trust them when they said it would be safe. "Where will you go?"

"Kabare, Democratic Republic of the Congo," Volustina said lightheartedly, as if it were the Cheesecake Factory.

Avery's heart skipped a beat, while Mitch's sank a little.

"Wait, what?" Avery choked.

Volustina nodded. "It's one of the biggest magnets for lightning. That area is prone to incredible lightning storms…like the dramatic one that's happening right now. The best way to harness and understand something is to study it, speak to it, not control it."

Rosemary cleared her throat, removed her ring and reluctantly handed it to Volustina. "Please be back by eight. We're having dinner at Ruby's."

"Is that a place or a person?" Ollie asked.

"Both!" Rosemary answered. "Ruby owns a dim-sum restaurant, and she serves the most delicious Butter Dumplings*. Her daughter Grace runs the apothecary next to it."

"Are they witches?" Ollie asked.

"They are indeed. The smallest coven in the States. Ruby was formerly a Proctor, but we reached an agreement to relieve her many years ago. It's insanely rare for members of the same family to share the active witch gene, but there it is! I want to run a few things by her about possibly assuming a role in the Advisory, and I figured it would be helpful for you to know a few other like-minded people."

After breakfast, which Avery finished in a matter of minutes, they fashioned a protective amulet from some string and white cloth containing a quartz crystal and some dried mistletoe they borrowed from Ollie's growing collection of plant matter. It would allow Avery to observe the wild lightning without being endangered by it.

"When we return, I'm going to give my life force to you," Volustina said.

Avery stared in shock. "Me? Why me? When? Right when we get back?"

Volustina grinned. "Not *right* when we return. But something tells me I need to offer it to you. I know you need it for the ritual, and I wanted to let you know that it's yours."

When they finally opened the door to Kabare, Avery had to shield her eyes from a series of lightning strikes. Volustina seemed immune to the brightness. They moved through the land, guided by Volustina's keen sense of the natural world that allowed them to receive information clearer than any satellite. After some time, they stopped walking and started observing. Volustina held Avery's hand as they watched lightning strike. Avery's hands were as hot as the ground where the lightning struck. Her mind was swollen with excitement but soon overwhelmed with knowledge.

Volustina's hand had a stunningly calm effect on Avery, one that worked its way through her blood and into her heart. It changed the way Avery saw the world and understood it, especially the chaotic lightning before and all around them. Within a few moments, she had slipped into a deep meditative space, one that allowed her to see, hear and read the truth of the natural world. It reminded her of the feelings of clarity and enlightenment that she had experienced one summer when she and a friend had spent the afternoon high on molly. All the fog had lifted, the veils had dissolved, the truths had been unearthed and patterns were exposed. The sounds of crashing electric spears ripped through the air, but all Avery heard were teachings. The amazement on her face melted into understanding.

For the better part of the afternoon, Avery experienced neither hunger nor thirst. She was completely satisfied from the lessons of nature. Even when she had learned as much as her brain would allow, she and Volustina stayed under the storm, watching it streak the sky with spears of white and violet. They talked like the oldest of friends would, and for a moment, Volustina saw a glimmer of their old friend Marie Antoinette. They didn't question it, thinking that maybe a part of Marie was in there somewhere.

It wasn't until seven o'clock that they returned and dressed for dinner. Rosemary happily accepted the ring back with a smile and ushered everyone toward the door. She didn't want to be late; she could practically taste the buttery dumplings on her tongue. Bisa stayed behind and opted to catch up on some sleep, even though she anticipated she would end up staring at the bottle she had chosen to keep a secret.

Forty-some minutes later, after passing two lakes, and a bend through the mountains had erased all forms of civilization, they arrived on the twelve acres that belonged to Ruby and her daughter Grace. A large gazebo-shaped building stood at the center of the property. Ruby's, a quaint restaurant with windows on all sides, was surrounded by hills of rocks speckled with trees and a crescent-shaped lake that hugged the back courtyard. Nestled into the rocky hill was Ruby's personal home, an even simpler structure, one that let the splendor of the environment take the spotlight.

"I can't wait for you to try her food. I've been dreaming about it all day," Rosemary said as she practically left everyone behind on her way to the door.

When they entered, the air was fresh and gently spiced. The restaurant was mostly empty of patrons but full of good energy. A small fountain bubbled away near the door, the windows were draped with dangly plants and votive candles decorated each table.

A woman strolled out from the kitchen sporting a huge smile. She was a beanpole of a woman, beaming with cheerfulness, with a voice as soft as the mountain snow. When she saw Rosemary, she hurried toward her, ponytail bouncing, her arms stretched wide, ready to give and receive.

"I'm so happy you're here! It's been forever!" Ruby said.

"Far too long," Rosemary said as she gave Ruby the warmest of hugs that she could conjure from her usual English reserve.

"Ready for dumplings?" Ruby asked as she tickled Rosemary's elbow.

Rosemary pretended to roll her eyes. "Do you even need to ask?"

Leo had already decided that he liked Ruby and that he believed she was as nice as she seemed. It was uncharacteristic of him to trust his first impression of a chef, but maybe witch chefs were different.

Mitch had been trying to resist picking his thumb in public, but he couldn't help himself, and started the moment Ruby arrived. Ollie stood close by, as if he could feel Mitch's anxiety rising. Avery and Volustina were taken by the views.

"You remember Grace," Ruby said as she pointed across the room to a younger version of herself, only with pinker cheeks and a pair of glasses. A sweet-natured, aging millennial who always let calls go to voicemail only so that she could text the caller back.

Grace waved from afar.

Rosemary introduced the coven to Ruby one by one, celebrating each of them in a way that allowed them to be seen as individuals. It was the kind of thing Nina would have done and something that Rosemary wanted to adopt. Partially out of respect for Nina, to reinforce that closure isn't absolute and that her spirit—her legacy…story, hadn't ended.

"And this must be Volustina?" Ruby asked.

Volustina reached out to hold Ruby's hand and cupped it within their own. "So happy to meet you, Ruby!"

Ruby looked over Volustina with a childlike sense of amazement. "Wow. A real fairy. How beautiful."

Rosemary quickly hushed Ruby with a hiss and shot her a stern and penetrating eye. "Ruby, not so loud. Don't say things like that in public!" She looked anxiously around the restaurant, checking to see if any of the six diners had heard or even cared about what she had just said.

Ruby rolled her eyes. "Oh, Rosemary, if anyone did hear that, they wouldn't even think to believe for one second that I meant fairy like…*fairy*."

Rosemary gave her best cross face. "We don't know that. Especially with everything that's been happening, we can't be too careful."

Ruby's eyes began to drift away. "Okay, fine. Stop scowling at me," she said, never losing her twinkling playfulness.

Ruby showed them to their table along the window at the other end of the restaurant, the one with the best view. Grace finished texting and ran over toward Rosemary, her long, fine hair fluttering behind her. She hugged Rosemary in her chair, resting cheek to cheek for a moment as she lovingly swayed Rosemary's shoulders back and forth.

"Hi, Auntie," Grace said.

Not her aunt.

"I watched your *ASMR French Palm Reader* video last night," Rosemary said. "It hit all the ASMR triggers! Delicious tingling up and down my spine until I just fell asleep. It was a euphoric experience. You're so good at role play. You could be in Hollywood, or better yet, Netflix. HBO, even!"

"Did you like it more than the *Spanish Candle Maker*?"

"Yes!" Rosemary exclaimed.

"Did you watch the *Interstellar Rock Painter*? Or *Eye Exam with Boston Accent*?" Grace asked, pleased with herself, knowing that all the hours spent on nailing foreign accents and procuring obscure props was worth it to at least one person.

Rosemary nodded. "I did, but I preferred the *Vegan Candle Whisperer*, or even the *Sustainable Graham Cracker Maker*. What are you working on next?"

"I'm trying to finish the *Sixteenth-Century Apothecarist* video," Grace said, smiling. "Which is really just a way for me to multitask."

"How do you mean?" Rosemary asked.

"I'm experimenting with an eyesight potion because my prescription is getting worse and I hate wearing contacts, so I'm just filming myself making the potion, but of course, no one knows that." She finished with a smile larger than the one she'd started with.

"Are they really getting that bad? What are you using? Maybe Ollie can help—he's become quite the botanist," Rosemary said as she waved toward Ollie.

Grace leaned in and whispered, "Baiji dolphin essence." The guilty expression on her face and the caution in her voice only made everyone at the table more interested. "They're technically extinct, so it's blind luck that we've happened to have some of it lying around. I found it in my grandpa's house after he passed. I have no idea where or when he got it." She suddenly felt the need to justify her usage, as if someone in the group was an outspoken and confrontational member of an animal rights group. "But I *do not* condone the use of animals for magic without their consent!" She then descended into a panicked defense of using animals for magical purposes, which, strangely enough after three full minutes, had everyone thinking a little differently about consent with all living ingredients. Except for Ollie, who was the first of all of them to ask plants for permission before he used them.

Ruby returned with a few books in her hand. "Here are the books you asked about."

"Oh lovely!" Rosemary said as she accepted a stack of three books, all old and tattered.

"The purple book is the one that talks about the Union of the Divine Dualities, the red one has everything you could ever need to know about the order of balance."

"What about this one?" Rosemary asked as she dusted off the front cover of a brown book with a mysterious symbol on the cover, embossed in gold.

"That one is sort of a collection of all mystic things. I've had it forever. Thought it might be of use to you. It mentions Corporeals, shape-shifting, soul fusion, things like that."

Leo's ears perked up, like those of a dog who'd heard a bag of treats being opened. Rosemary shot a glance toward Leo out of the corner of her eye and quickly tucked the books into her bag. "Well, I don't know about the rest of you, but I am ready to savagely destroy some dumplings!"

When the first set of dumplings arrived ten minutes later, nestled into a tantalizing smear of gochujang crème fraiche, showcased on rectangular gray plates, Rosemary's eyes began to water just as much as her mouth. She loved only two things absolutely in her life: Morgan Freeman and Ruby's dumplings. They looked like little pieces of sculpture, and they were.

Rosemary held a special place in her heart for them, which may have affected how much she raved about them. It was the amount of time, thought and love that went into Ruby's food. The ingredients came from their nearby farm and gardens—everything from the plant-derived brines to the eggs. But it wasn't just Ruby's philosophy about food and her respect for it, it was how she managed her staff, or rather elevated—encouraged—them. They weren't expendable slaves whom she had come in and do whatever she wanted, they were a community, another kind of coven, in a way. Every cook in her kitchen had had little to no training, and she encouraged success through compassion and by providing a nurturing environment rather than a place of hell, like nearly all the restaurants Leo had ever worked in. Ruby was able to charm people without magic, and she felt an obligation to do her own part in helping to promote balance, even if it was only through food and leadership. Both had value.

With dancing eyes, Rosemary lifted a dumpling with her chopsticks, dipped it into a shallow bowl of soy sauce and popped it into her mouth, undeterred by their steamy hotness. Her eyes relaxed into a languid gaze as her tongue explored the carnival of flavors that followed. As she rolled it over her tongue, she savored and analyzed all the individual flavors: garlic, toasted sesame, napa cabbage, ginger, scallion, onion, and so many other delicious tastes.

Several more plates followed: mapo tofu, xiao long bao, sweet potato and kale jianbing, curried mung bean bao. Avery didn't rag on Leo for something (anything), Ollie and Volustina chattered endlessly about their passion for all things green, and Leo felt he might be finally growing up, because he didn't force a fart the entire time. Mitch, however, was picking not only at his food, but also his thumb, carving away at his torn cuticles under the table and after each bite. He wanted to enjoy it, he really did, he just—wouldn't (couldn't?).

The restaurant emptied, and the staff cleaned up and left. Rosemary caught Ruby up on all the drama before Grace took the coven on a tour of her spice shop and apothecary next door. When they reached the back storage room, they stopped to ask about the strange setup in the corner.

"That's where I do all of my ASMR filming. It's like my little movie set," Grace said as she giggled and adjusted her glasses. She talked a little about where she got all of her props and how much effort really went into each "production." Ollie had taken a particular interest in the apothecary cabinet along the wall. The bottles used for props were not props at all; they were actual potions, elixirs and ingredients. They exchanged a few words about elixirs and flower essences before he caught a glimpse of a small brown vial. He fingered the tag and noticed the emblem of a dolphin on the label.

"Oh, careful!" Grace said as she gently touched Ollie's shoulder.

"Is this that essence you were talking about?" Ollie asked as he stared quizzically at the contents.

"That's it," Grace confirmed. "It smells nasty. Smell!" She uncorked the bottle.

Ollie turned away, instantly repulsed.

Grace giggled mischievously and recorked the bottle. "Isn't it gross?"

Ollie continued to make retching noises as he waved the tang out of the air.

"I love a good *bad* smell," Grace said. "It's like someone threw cheese into a medieval toilet."

"Grace!" Ruby called from the short hallway that joined the restaurant and the apothecary. "Did you ever finish that defensive potion?"

After a pause, Grace responded, "The salt one or the basil one?"

"The black pepper and nettles one. I wanted to give some to Rosemary, remember?"

Grace turned around to face the display of bottles, her eyes wide and her fingers fluttering irrepressibly. "Umm..." she hummed to herself as she surveyed the collection. Finally, she found it resting on the table. "Yeah, I've got it!"

She brought the jar of incredibly thin handblown glass to Ruby.

"Thank you!" Ruby said, checking to make sure the cork was in tight.

"What's this now?" Rosemary asked.

"I wanted to give you something, because you're right, it's not exactly safe out there. I know you have a lot on your plate with the coven, so I wanted you to have something for a little extra peace of mind. It's like a witch's pepper spray. Grace has been working on it for a couple of weeks. Ideally it'll do the trick if you ever get into a pickle."

"Is it dangerous?" Rosemary questioned.

"Only for witches. I don't know how she came up with this formula, but it completely removes all powers of anyone within a few feet. It reacts with magical auras. Grace wasn't able to do any sort of influence for a few hours, and she usually has no problem at all. So be careful."

Grace said her goodbyes to the coven, closed up the apothecary and headed home to edit her latest video. Ruby still had some office things and last-minute prep that she wanted to get a jump on for the next day, so she called it a night. She flipped the music back on with a tap of her phone, and "Excessive Moonlight" by Indian Jewelry boomed from the speakers. She disappeared through the kitchen doors as the coven prepared to leave. Rosemary and Leo turned off the front-of-house lights and waited by the door for everyone to get their coats on.

Avery, Mitch and Ollie were a cluster of whispers at the table. Mitch slipped on his coat and hid his thumb under his fingers. As Avery and Ollie tried to press him to let them know if something was wrong, Rosemary remembered that she had noticed something was off with Mitch, too, even with the supreme distraction of Ruby's endless supply of dim sum. She wasn't the warmest of witches, but she did care, so much so that she had been dividing her attention between dumplings and Mitch all night. Maybe it was that distraction that allowed her to miss a lingering energy in the air, one that she should have recognized. Or perhaps all the blood was rushing to her stomach to digest the food baby that she now had.

"Everything all right?" Rosemary asked with one hand on the front door.

Avery glanced over her shoulder to her and Leo. "Yeah, we're coming."

Rosemary swished the pepper spray potion in her hand, as if on instinct. When the group was halfway to the door, she opened it and took one final step as a sharp dart of white-hot lightning pierced the front of her head and flashed out the back of it in forks. The dark room was filled with a blinding strobe of silver as the sound of nature's fury boomed in a violent crack. The walls shook as Rosemary fell lifelessly to the ground like a discarded marionette at Leo's feet where the potion bottle had shattered.

Merlot rubbed her fingers together as if dusting off crumbs, her eyes wild with borrowed magic. She strode toward the restaurant like an unchallenged champion, her silhouette lined by the moon. Leo scrambled to say something, anything—but he couldn't. The potion had rendered him powerless. Merlot stabbed her hand toward Leo, and a spear of lightning missiled straight into the ground. It landed a good ten feet from Leo, too far to be dangerous but still too close to feel safe. Leo fell over his feet and crawled off behind the bar. He knew that last beer had been one too many, but had no idea the potion had temporarily sapped him of his powers. The coven scattered like rats into the dark dining room. Mitch darted under the closest table, too scared to run farther. Avery, Volustina and Ollie ran toward the kitchen, where Ruby clutched their shoulders.

"Bisa?" Merlot called out playfully as she stepped over Rosemary's body and into the restaurant. The dining room was dark, but illuminated with fear and confusion. The music spilled out from the kitchen like a soundtrack and came in waves as the doors swung back and forth. "Bisa!" Merlot shouted, and she scowled into the darkness like a church-perched gargoyle.

With hardly a second thought, Avery pounced out into the dining room and grabbed hold of a tray table. Her fingers plump with fire just burning to be released from her skin. She set fire to it and then swung it toward Merlot. It sailed clumsily toward Merlot in shafts of orange and yellow. Merlot crashed it midair with a rope of lightning and wind, using her free hand to send Avery zooming into the side of the bar.

"Bisa, just come out, or they will all die in slow, horrible ways while I force you to watch. No, you're a Transcendent: I'll make *you* make *them* kill themselves. How about that?" She waited for a moment and listened to the heavy panting and murmurs from under the table. "Or you can come out!" Merlot was juiced up, so much so that her mouth was practically frothing with electric mania. Her breath hot and sulfurous.

Ruby shouted from a corner, "What do you want?"

"Bisa. Bisa. Bisa. How many times do I have to say it? She killed my Corporeal. You think I don't know her smell? My witch nose is basically a master perfumer right now. Maybe I'll start my own fragrance. Call it Witch's Blood…drain Bisa's blood and use it as a heart note, or something like that." She zapped the floor once more. "I needed that witch. I know you all know how rare and legendary Corporeals are, and that bitch stole the only one I have ever found." She spun around on her heels as she talked, like a tornado alarm in the summer. "Do you even know what that means? What they can do? The impossible. More than any of us could on borrowed powers. Think of all the people who could be resurrected! And—"

She stopped abruptly. She raised her head and nuzzled the air. Merlot sorted through her mismatched thoughts until she finally identified the scent, the one of a Corporeal. Her heart beat so fiercely that it sang like a choir at the golden odor in the air. She shook her head, not wanting to believe her luck. "You're a Corporeal." She ignored the others and walked toward Leo's hiding spot. Her eyes glazy and blazed with ecstasy. She sniffed again, like taking a long line of cocaine, and exhaled. Merlot finally cracked a smile as her anger began to dissipate.

(now)

Avery heard it in her head. She rose to her knees with an aching back and spit the hair out of her mouth. She wailed in

pain as she swung her arm like a bat and sent a gust of air ripping toward Merlot.

Merlot felt the intention, lightning-quick, and caught Avery
gearing up out of the corner of her eye. Faster than Avery could
assault her with the wind, Merlot returned her astral body to her
physical one. Merlot left empty-handed, but with her eyes on a
new prize.

CHAPTER 35

Mitch was shaking again, and more than his thumb was bleeding. Ollie rescued him from underneath the table and sat him down in a proper chair. Mitch could take only so much, and everyone thought he was going to crack if he hadn't already. He may have been trembling, but his mind had switched off, whisked him away somewhere else. It was like having one final tequila shot, the one that makes you sick and black out, the one that erases everything after it slides down your throat.

The dining room lights switched on, and there were voices all at once. Everyone spoke out of turn and over one another as they tried to determine what to do next. Volustina ran their fingers over Rosemary's solar plexus, feeling for any energy that was left behind. They didn't want any more chaos than there already was, and dealing with another lifeless body wasn't a step toward stability.

Avery suddenly appeared at Rosemary's side, opposite Volustina.

"What do we do now?" Avery said, panicked but trying to hide it as best she could.

Ruby shoved herself into the middle of the group, corralling the coven toward a table like a bunch of spooked sheep.

Leo sulked down over his knees as he sat. He glanced over to where the defensive potion had shattered at his feet, realizing only now that it had deadened his powers. For how long, he didn't know, but he would have been lying if he'd denied being more worried about that than anything else. He looked around the room, checking to make sure that no one there was in his head. They were so preoccupied that no one noticed Leo trying to make something magical happen. Anything. A flame, the candleholder move, bring Rosemary back to life with only a strong-willed intent. None of it worked. For a moment, he almost felt humbled, mortified…embarrassed to be so human again. Then, he saw it. Between the collective haze of grief and the shock of a violent surprise attack, he saw—opportunity.

Leo walked over to Rosemary and acted how he believed he should be acting to blend in with the rest. So when he kneeled down, supposedly to see whether Rosemary was dead or alive, he was really reaching a sneaky hand into her bag to retrieve the brown book with the strange symbol. The book Ruby said contained information about soul fusion. Any information was more than he had. It could be less than a sentence, and it would still put him closer to where he wanted to be than he was at that moment. In a series of camouflaged gestures, he slipped the book under his coat.

Ruby split her attention between Rosemary's body and the shaken witches. When the time was right, she walked over to see Rosemary, really see her. She wanted to scream, to grieve on the spot, but even that didn't feel like it would be enough. Instead, she melted away to the first feeling that showed up— numbness. Ruby kneeled down at what was left of Rosemary's head. She stared at the still smoking remains that had been sliced and cauterized by lightning. She was suddenly blinded by tears until they poured out of her eyes and down her cheeks. Guilt paid her a visit as she remembered how she had downplayed Rosemary's alarmist attitude earlier. Her mouth was filled with words she wished she had said instead, words that wouldn't make any difference if they were uttered now.

Avery looked over at Ruby for guidance, as Volustina had yet to respond. "Ruby, what do we do? I don't…I don't know what to do!"

Ruby shook her head, and her words broke up as she tried to speak them. "I…" Suddenly memories flooded her mind faster than she had ever experienced during any meditative state. They were powered by grief and the potent fire of unexpected loss.

Ruby began again, "I…I…thi…"

Memories of Rosemary dropping everything in her life to spend a week with her when her father passed.

"I think we…"

A memory of the morning she woke to find a brand-new telescope and an official, framed certificate of an unnamed star assigned to Ruby in her name, simply because she'd casually mentioned that she had always loved astronomy. It was something she had said only once but had felt a hundred times. The telescope and certificate were next to a pair of teal hiking boots with gray laces. Although she'd abandoned hiking once the restaurant opened, she'd repeatedly told Rosemary it was the only thing she loved most besides her daughter Grace. The boots were still in the box under her bed.

Ruby restarted once more. "I think we…"

It was June 2, and she was thirty-five, suffering from a broken heart for the first time in her life. She applied for Proctor of Colorado and met Rosemary, who instantly bonded with her in a way that she had never forgotten, because that bond saved her sanity. It wasn't the wine, or the endless conversation where they each saw the universe behind their eyes, they just understood each other. People thought Rosemary had a stiff, cold English heart, but that wasn't the woman she knew.

"We should…" Ruby said before a groaning sound rose from her throat, the sound of someone trying to find light where there is none.

"I know what to do," Volustina said. "I know where she needs to be." They removed Rosemary's garnet ring from her finger and slipped it onto their own. "Avery, will you assist me, please?"

Avery looked down at the ring on Volustina's finger. "Where are we going?"

"To take her body to where she left her heart," Volustina said. "Snowdonia."

Volustina calmly soothed the minds of the coven with only a few words, and assumed the role of the decision maker for the time being. Volustina grabbed Rosemary's bag with the books and handed them to Ollie to take back home—that's where Volustina was sending them. They used Volustina's ring, seeing—knowing—that the ring's price was something that they wouldn't have to pay, at least not until it was used more than ten times. But that was more than they needed. Volustina found the closest closet and engaged the ring. They didn't need instructions for it. Volustina knew many things; their mind picked up information preemptively more accurately than predictive text.

Volustina held the image of the room they knew best. They pulled the door open, and before them, outlined by the door like a framed portrait, was the coven's living room. With the coven's heightened protective enchantments in place and their increasingly high levels of anxiety, it was the safest place for them to be right now. The coven needed safety, stability and the comforts of "home," whatever version of it they had. Whatever that looked like now with so much missing. It was beginning to feel more like an address than a sanctuary.

When the door closed behind them, they stood in the dark, shaken and distraught, except for Leo. Not that he didn't care about Rosemary—he didn't *not* care—but he had seen and dealt out enough death to know that it wasn't something to linger on. Not unless you really care about that person. And Leo had felt that only a few times in his life—maybe just twice.

Ollie turned on the lights and tried to escort Mitch to his room, but he was already halfway there. Bisa turned the corner with a cup of tea at her lips. She had felt the energy in the room before she saw them, and they didn't have to say a single word. She sensed all of their emotions and mental statics all at once. She was so absorbed that for a moment, she didn't even realize that some people were missing.

Bisa swallowed a sip of tea and gave a worried look. "Where's everybody else?"

Leo turned to Ollie and asked, *What should we say?* just from the look on his face.

"Where's Rosemary? Avery?" Bisa asked, growing more aware that something awful had happened.

Leo then remembered that Merlot had come looking for Bisa, and he had a question that would be even more complicated to answer. "What did you do?"

The next door that Volustina opened revealed a wall of snow. Avery and Ruby didn't understand, but Volustina did— they had been there a few times in their life. Where they were going, there was no physical door to receive them.

"It's all right. There is no door—so we must pass through snow," Volustina said.

Avery gave Ruby a puzzled look, but Ruby was still too busy drying her eyes to care much.

"Can you harness the air?" Volustina asked Avery. "To support her body and carry her through to where we're going?"

Avery hadn't thought about using air in that way before. At first, she wanted to say no, but she decided she would try. Whether by trust in herself or guided by Spirit, possibly even encouraged by Nina—she coaxed the air to gather beside Rosemary and slide underneath her like a spatula slipping under a slice of pie.

"Good. Now, tether it to you, like you're pulling a rope," Volustina instructed.

Naturally, Avery succeeded. She tried not to be overjoyed, given the circumstances, but allowing just enough joy in took her mind off the fact that she was holding a dead body, albeit through magical means. It was a fine line between remembering the deer and letting Rosemary fall, and appreciating that she was a gifted witch and keeping Rosemary under control.

Volustina nodded gently and beckoned Avery and Ruby to follow them through the snow. They stepped forward, their hand stretched out before them until it pierced through darkness. The rest of their body followed. They entered horizontally, but came out on the other side, reaching up out of the ground like a vampire from a grave. Volustina adjusted to the change in gravity and pulled themself out of the snow. Their arms and knees covered in a light dusting of snow, hidden in the dark blue of what was now 4 a.m. halfway around the world in Wales.

Avery's hand cut through the path Volustina made and climbed into Snowdonia. The air instantly woke her up, but she never lost control of Rosemary. Volustina helped her up from the ground and heaved her to her feet, where she hovered Rosemary to a soft spot in the snow. Ruby came next, seemingly unfazed by the transition, still stung by grief.

"You had best give us some light, Avery," Volustina said as they delicately caressed Avery's shoulder as to not disturb her concentration too much. "The sun won't be up for another three hours, and we won't get far in the dark."

Avery looked out into the solid fog and saw only a couple of feet ahead. She turned to Volustina. "I can only create fire. I can't control it."

Volustina smiled. "Hold it in your hand using air to support it so you don't burn yourself. No need to release it."

Avery crafted a precious ball of fire in the palm of her hand and illuminated the darkness around them. Volustina watched Avery as she guided them down toward the lake. When they reached the shore, Avery turned to Volustina. She had been concentrating so hard on trying to multitask that she hadn't considered what they were going to do once they got to their destination. It sent a chill down Avery's back to think about how they were going to deal with Rosemary's body now that it was time.

Volustina laid Rosemary into the shallow edge of the cold, black lake.

"Make a plank of ice for her to rest on," Volustina said as they positioned Rosemary's arms snugly against her sides.

Avery dipped her fingertips into the freezing lake and crystalized the water underneath Rosemary's body. Moments later, Rosemary rested upon a raft of ice. Avery stood back and took a deep breath. She suddenly realized just how lost and vulnerable the coven was. They had no one else to ask for help, no other masters to turn to with questions. Nina had always told them that there were no masters of anything, only people who knew more than someone else. Yet, even that didn't ease her mind. She had already said goodbye to so many people in her life. Some goodbyes were premature, others were necessary, and some were unexpected or long overdue. She had said so many goodbyes that she was pretty good at them by now.

But Avery was still trying to figure out how to say hello to the new world she was a part of now, one that was as beautiful as it was dangerous, a world that seemed to take as much as it gave. As they pushed the slab of ice out into the water, she said goodbye. She looked up at Ruby and shuddered at the grief and pain in her face. Perhaps Ruby would be the next mentor. Avery didn't know what to expect anymore, any more than she knew what was going to become of the coven.

Avery used the density of the fog to push the slab out into the middle of the lake. When it reached the center, she looked out into the world around her. The fog was thinning, and she was able to see the outlines of the mountains that surrounded them against the starry blanket of the early morning sky.

She was so lost in her thoughts that she couldn't recall when Volustina had asked her to set the raft on fire; all she knew was that she had. Out in the middle of the dark lake, Rosemary quickly dissolved into swirls of hot yellow and orange. Avery suddenly felt incredibly sad as she realized just how lonesome Rosemary's final goodbye was.

Avery turned to Volustina. "What about her family?"

Volustina looked to Ruby. "Her family is here. She's not alone."

Ruby released her tears with a newfound sense of peace. "She is exactly where she wants to be."

Rosemary had devoted so much of her life to service within the witch community that it felt unfair to Avery that she should end up alone on a block of ice, burning away in the dark morning hours in the middle of an isolated lake. But none of that mattered. Rosemary was beyond all that now. Her physical self, the part of her that had been so in love with Snowdonia, was now able to live within it, become part of it, forever.

Somewhere above the snow-dusted mountains, a peregrine falcon called out. Avery chased the sound of the funereal squawks until she found it descending toward the burning plank. They watched the bird missile closer to Rosemary's fire, until it disappeared entirely with a flap of its wings. *Rosemary's totem*, Avery thought. It only made sense. It was just as fierce and majestic as she was.

CHAPTER 36

When Avery returned to the house, a heavy tension hung in the air as thick as the fog she had just left behind. She found the coven in the kitchen, apart from Mitch, who was in the quiet of his own room. When Avery's eyes met with Leo's, another shiver ran through her as she witnessed his death inside her mind. She had seen it all before in a dream. When Leo asked why she was staring at him, she saw the dream once more. She gasped and tried to disguise it as delayed grief. She hadn't thought about that dream since she'd brought it up to Nina back in Louisiana, nor had she really tried to make much sense of it.

Is Leo going to die? she asked herself as she tried to look as normal as possible, whatever normal even was. *Is there such a thing? Was there ever?* She wanted so badly to ask Nina, or even Rosemary, about the dream and what it could mean. She was never one for dream interpretation, regardless of how important they seemed. For a moment, Avery worried that she was starting to develop into a cynic—a *real* cynic, not a cynic who secretly hoped for the best. Someone like Leo. She took a few steps away from Leo, as though his energy was rubbing off on her.

"Bisa's got something that'll make someone invisible," Leo said. He almost said *to make me invisible*, but caught himself.

"Since when? Where'd you get that?" Avery asked.

Bisa let out a frustrated and exhausted sigh. "From someone who deals in that kind of thing. It doesn't matter. What matters is that we have what we need."

Ollie looked into Avery's energy and leaned against the wall. "Everything okay? Rosemary…"

Avery nodded. "It's done." She looked around the room and ran her fingers through her hair and under her brows. "Where's Mitch?"

Ollie shook his head. "He's not great. He's in his room." There was a pause. "I don't know how much more of this he can take. I think it's a little more than he bargained for."

"Ollie, at this point, this is more than any of us bargained for," Avery said. "None of us asked for this. I think the only way for things to start getting back to"—she struggled with her tongue as she tried to spit out a word that felt silly to utter now—"*normal* is to do what we're supposed to. You know, setting things back into balance. Then, working on finding the rafkolite and really making an energetic difference."

Volustina glanced at each member of the coven before they spoke. "She's right. The more time that passes without these acts being performed, the more difficult they will be to actually achieve."

Leo decided to test the weight of his true intentions on the group. "Do we even need to bother with that shit right now? Nina's dead. The Advisory's gone. If there is another kind of Advisory somewhere, we sure as fuck don't know about it. Maybe we should just focus on what we know will really balance all this shit out. Right? Shouldn't we just find the rafkolite and not even worry about all this other shit? It all kind of seems like some kind of useless side quest in *Zelda* right now." Leo pointed at Volustina. "Aren't you the one who…oracled…that we *would* find the rafkolite?"

The aggressive question didn't seem to bother Volustina one bit. "You aren't performing magic to establish and promote balance just for the remainder of your lifetime; it's for those who come after you as well, and those after that, for however long the world lasts. All worlds end, everything eventually ends, but if you always strive to maintain balance, the world may just last a little longer, lives may be enjoyed a little longer. Life is meant to be lived."

Leo rolled his eyes. "Sometimes I wonder if we should even be worrying about balance at all. Our world is so fucked up. Most people I've ever known haven't really *enjoyed* their life. Why are we supposed to risk our lives so that someone else can enjoy their day?"

Volustina sat in a chair at the table. "The world isn't lost forever. The way you live now isn't carved permanently in stone. It may feel like it, it may look like it, but life as you define it, as you see it, as you live it, is all a choice. It is crafted from a series of choices that humans have made throughout time. I've spent very little time on...the internet...and it's amazing. Amazing in the sense that I can see that humans have the power to change those choices that are doing more harm than good. Technology doesn't have to be just machinery, it is knowledge. What good is knowledge if you refuse to recognize that the initial, old ideas are no longer working, or that they don't work at all?"

"I didn't build any of this!" Leo said. "I was born into it, and now I gotta do all this shit to try to survive. How does someone enjoy life when the whole world is a setup? Look at our government, that's a hot mess. Politics, religion, education, all of it. No one listens, no one cares, no one actually wants to compromise on anything, because the system works...*for them*!"

Bisa looked at Leo with a fierce intensity. "Not everyone is going to admit or even realize everything is broken. The only time things ever change is when things hurt. That's how things get better. Change doesn't *feel* good. But someone must be strong and brave enough to challenge what doesn't work."

Volustina smiled so faintly that no one noticed. "That's what creates a collective choice. Nothing will be perfect, nothing is. There will always be…" they paused and considered all the auxiliary factors at play "…evil. It's not about trying to cleanse and reinvent the world, it's about building an environment that counteracts the system that aims to destroy those who are deemed unworthy. Environment is energy, energy is thought, thought creates awareness, and awareness produces acceptance, which is really just another word for balance."

Leo became more agitated and paced back and forth. "So, what do we do? Just blow up the world and start from scratch? Will that get the balance we're looking for?"

"It's about choice. A choice needs to be made to create the kind of pressure to transform and remodel the way life is lived. Pressure creates diamonds. Nothing is built overnight. Everything takes time. The purpose isn't to destroy or abolish the shadow…but to integrate it, to meet it. It is an ongoing spiritual maintenance."

Leo looked like he was going to scream. Being told that something great—that he felt he deserved—would take a shit ton of time wasn't something he wanted to hear.

Volustina stood up abruptly and retrieved Rosemary's bag with the books. They flipped through the pages until they found what they were looking for on page 126. "This is it—the ritual you must perform to begin the restoration of spiritual balance." They tapped the page and looked to find the most receptive eyes in the room. Bisa retrieved the book and read through the ritual with Ollie and Avery at her side.

After they read through the ritual three times, Bisa folded the edge of the paper over to mark the chapter and closed the book. "We need to do this soon."

Ollie looked up in alarm. "Why?"

"I don't know. I just feel it," Bisa said softly. But she did know. She knew that change was upon all of them, especially her, and it wasn't going to be easy. Bisa could feel something beginning to sour and curdle, and realized that it was the parts of her former self. She had one major part left to confront. A habit, a fixation, an addiction, a weakness that stifled and obstructed her growth—her feelings for Leo. Her life had been split between things she understood and things she couldn't explain—but felt to be true. The bond she had with Leo was toxic, and she had become increasingly aware of its toxicity. Yet she couldn't explain how or why. She didn't know what the immediate future held, or what the world would look like as they continued down the path they were on, but she did know that she wouldn't be able to fully commit to her own growth if Leo remained a constant in her heart for reasons she couldn't explain or justify.

"The time has come," Volustina said as they handed Rosemary's ring to Ollie and then approached Avery. They stood before her, stoic and still. They stared into Avery's eyes, and right then, Avery knew what was coming. Volustina closed their eyes gently and nodded. "I'm going to give you my life force now. I have played my part here. The rest is up to all of you." Their voice held the emotions of eras upon eras of change. "I give this to you willingly."

"What will happen?" Avery asked. Part of her didn't want Volustina to give up their life, but she knew that it was supposed to work out like this. It had to.

"Hold out your hand," Volustina said as they held out their own. Volustina wrapped their fingers around Avery's and made a cup of her hand.

Something suddenly stirred in Bisa and she held out her hand. "Wait," she said.

Volustina turned to Bisa and saw a melancholic request in her eyes.

"May I ask you for one thing first?" Bisa asked. Her heart began to beat rapidly. "Well, it's of both of you."

"What is it?" Avery asked.

"I've changed a lot. I'm still changing. And I know there are things, really good things that will happen for me, and those around me, if I continue to grow like this. But I also know something is preventing me from becoming what I know I can be. And I worry that if I don't become that, if I let this thing in my heart rob me of that, I won't be able to forgive myself." Bisa's eyes were half ready to cry. She took a deep breath, and as she exhaled, her breath trembled. She had achieved a lot in life, but that didn't mean situations like the one she was in now would ever be any easier.

(do this for the right reasons, Bisa...)

Leo had been watching Bisa's every move as she spoke. He knew what she wanted before anyone else did. He just didn't want her to say it. Saying it would make it real, and there would be no turning back after that.

"I know that as a fairy, you can erase memories, or remove them," Bisa began as her eyes swayed over to Avery and then back to Volustina. "And you're the last of them, so this is my only chance to ask for this. Before you go, I want you to remove any—all—the memories with feelings for Leo. The romantic ones. The tender ones. All of those, I want you to remove those."

There was a period of heavy, awkward silence in the room. Of all of them, Leo looked the most flabbergasted. He could hardly believe she'd actually said the words out loud. He stared at Bisa, his heartache and hurt glaring at her from behind his eyes. When he finally digested what she had asked for so frankly, he let out a tortured gasp. "What?" he asked, bewildered.

"It might seem like a ridiculous thing to ask, or even to worry about, but I can't grow if I can't let go of this, because it's not good for me," Bisa said.

"We could try—" Ollie started.

"I've already tried Cord Cutting*. It just doesn't work. It's still there. And I feel it every day. Even when I'm not thinking about it—I'm thinking about it. I have to let that part of me go."

"How can you ask something like that?" Leo asked, half disgusted but more on the verge of wanting to cry, which was surprising in and of itself.

"I care about you, Leo. It's not about that. I don't really want to, because I can see how it affects me, how being around you affects me. I care about you, and I don't want to. I can't. I can't be in those kinds of shadows. I have to care for myself more. And I don't know if I can forgive you for all that you've done." She paused, and he knew. "Maybe one day I'll be able to try, but not now, not like this." Bisa turned to Volustina with desperation all over her face. "We won't accept your life force unless you do this for me," she said firmly as she looked over to Avery, testing her friendship and loyalty before all of them.

Avery had never seen Bisa so emotionally conflicted before, and she had listened to her retell stories from her past many times. For a second, Avery tried to understand how Leo could matter so much, but then she realized that it wasn't Leo, it was Bisa. There was something that Bisa just couldn't let go of. Maybe it was an energetic alignment, or something with her magical DNA, but Bisa needed to be free of it. Bisa had overcome many things in life, and this was something she hadn't planned for and needed a little help with.

Avery wanted to shake her head no, because she knew Bisa was a strong woman and it might just take a little time to release whatever hold Leo had over her heart. But she knew that if Bisa asked for help, she probably needed it.

Volustina turned their head to Avery and looked into her eyes. After a moment, Avery nodded. Ollie felt the shock and frantic emotion filling Leo without having to look at him. Leo grimaced at Bisa as if she were suddenly an enemy, which only proved Bisa's point even further. He was still the same energy as when they'd met, he just couldn't escape it, no matter how hard he tried. Ollie felt a bomb of thoughts erupt inside Leo's head as Leo replayed the choices he'd made and actions he'd carried out, and it made Ollie question whether Leo would even realize if he were faking emotions or genuinely feeling them.

Regardless of how sucker punched Leo felt, he didn't try to stop Volustina when they approached Bisa. On some level, he knew that what Bisa said had the ring of truth to it. He was the shadow, and she was the light.

Volustina stood but a few inches from Bisa, whose expression was both drained and passive. Her request and the emotions that followed had sapped her of the last bit of emotional energy she'd had left. *Perhaps she is right about this;*

perhaps she really can't let go…and she must if she is going to be who I know she will become, Volustina thought to themself. They lifted their left hand to the back of Bisa's head and cradled it with their palm.

"What do I have to do?" Bisa asked.

Volustina smiled politely and shook their head. "There's nothing left for you to do but close your eyes."

A wave of relief fell over Bisa's face. She looked at Leo out of the corner of her eye and turned away when his eyes met hers. She almost regretted it, thinking that she might change her mind if she saw him one last time. But—she didn't. Instead, she closed her eyes.

Volustina embraced Bisa's mind, and with their keen fairy eyes, saw all the energetic threads of her mind, body and spirit. A pool of tears began to collect in Bisa's eyes, but they never spilled over. Volustina massaged the back of Bisa's head and then saw the delicate cord that kept Leo inside her heart. There were parts of the attraction that even Volustina couldn't re-move—Bisa and Leo were starseeds, a type of soul mate that Volustina couldn't come between—but they could do what Bisa asked. Volustina drew their hand away from Bisa's head and caught the loose energy thread between their thumb and middle finger. They pulled, as if removing a stray hair from a coat, and released it into the air, where it dissolved instantly.

When Bisa opened her eyes, she was completely aware of what had happened but stunned that it had actually worked. The inexplicable draw and attraction—was gone. She looked at Leo, just to make sure. Her gaze fell over every inch of him, and still…she felt nothing. It was like the one day after months, maybe even years, of mourning a failed relationship…that you finally just get over it. That moment when you realize that the years you wasted in depression, hoping and wishing things would be different, were all for nothing and that you had to start living your life in a different way.

Volustina turned to Avery and grabbed hold of her hand. "Don't be frightened."

There was a hissing noise like the whisper of a breath, and the sparkle in Volustina's eyes seemed to fade. Then, before they could say any final words or take any final looks, Volustina turned to vapor. Avery looked into the palm of her hand, and all that was left was a pea-sized, flaky shard of violet lepidolite—Volustina's life force.

CHAPTER 37

Sad but grateful, Avery brought the newly acquired life force to Ollie. "Do you have any stormwater by chance? This needs to be infused in it before we can do anything with it." She turned the shard over in her palm with her thumb as she followed Ollie to his room. He rummaged through a few jars until he found the remaining stormwater he'd collected from an early morning storm in Louisiana.

Ollie poured it into a clean mason jar, set it upon the desk and called Avery close with a nod.

"How long do we let it infuse?" she asked with an eye roll, hating herself for a moment, wishing that she had thought to ask.

"Overnight?" Ollie replied, but more of a question than an answer.

Avery approached the jar and dropped the lepidolite inside. It sank to the bottom with a plop.

The lepidolite began to fizz, like an antacid tablet. The water slowly became a pale amethyst color as Volustina's life force dissolved. "I think we just have to wait until it's fully dissolved," Ollie said. "Let's just let it do its thing and we can check on it first thing in the morning." He pulled out a roll of blue painter's tape, ripped off a piece and placed it on the jar, then wrote *Volustina's Life Force Infusion* on it.

He looked around the room at the other various jar and plant labels. It was a trivial detail that most people wouldn't even notice. Ollie himself barely even noticed it. He probably wouldn't have if it weren't for the great significance that trivial detail held. At some point in time, his handwriting had changed. The way that he labeled had changed. The same was found in his journal. When he'd begun connecting more with Spirit and the natural world, honoring it, respecting it, he'd started capitalizing the names of all plants.

Ollie could do a great many things, but he had always wanted something that spoke to him. He found himself thinking of Nina and how she had told him that he was a healer. If someone had told him a few years ago that he would be a witch, a healer, and have a knowledge of and passion for plants that would rival that of prized botanists, he would have told them they were out of their mind. If he could go back and tell his old self one thing, it would be to not abuse or disrespect his own growth. His resume of skills and accomplishments, although diverse and interesting, was never something he wanted to be defined by. Even though the strongest pressure he felt from the world around him was to *be* his resume, he had always hoped people would appreciate him for how he saw the world rather than what he *did* in it. He felt a tremendous amount of gratitude for Nina in that moment. She had been the catalyst for his growth.

"What now?" Avery asked.

Ollie rapped his fingers on the desk as he thought. "I guess we should try to find an oak tree. That's the next part, right? The infusion has to be mixed with oak."

Avery raised her eyebrows. "*Powdered* oak. Powdered oak that has been struck by lightning first, and then powdered—actually."

"Well, Gambel oak does grow here. I know I've seen some chinkapin and bur oak too. Ideally any oak will work. Oak is oak, right? We just need to find some." Ollie looked out the window, as if he would see an oak tree from afar.

"We could scry, or do a spell maybe?" Avery suggested as she started looking at Google Maps on her phone.

(golden arrow road…)

Ollie looked up as he heard Nina's voice. "Can I see?" he asked. He took Avery's phone and checked out the location. "I think I know where to find one," he said as he traced a long road that led to a dead end only ten miles away. "Here"— he pointed out on the map—"tomorrow morning, we'll check this place out."

"How do you know?" Avery asked.

The two exchanged a look, and she knew that he just knew and to trust him. "Okay," she said with a grin.

"What about the lightning part? That…"

Avery nodded with full confidence. "I can do it."

They looked into each other's eyes like two mischievous friends.

"Can we get coffee first?" they said together.

The next morning, they checked the mason jar. The life force had completely dissolved, and the water had turned a lovely purple. The next thing they noticed was the scent coming from the liquid. It no longer smelled of stale stormwater, but of fresh-cut strawberries, pink peppercorn and honeysuckle, although Ollie thought it smelled more like datura than honeysuckle. They capped the jar and looked out the window. It was just the kind of morning that they had hoped for—mostly cloudy, but with a chance of Avery.

After a quick breakfast, Ollie and Avery told the coven to prepare for the rest of the ritual.

"Read through Rosemary's books and make sure we have a good handle on how to do this," Avery said. "The faster we get this done, the faster we can…" She realized that she hadn't given much thought to what would happen to any of them now, especially once (if) they actually succeeded in finding the rafkolite. Would they write a book? Open some kind of metaphysical store? Go their own way? "Do whatever it is that we do next," she finished.

Ollie and Avery stopped for coffee and dosed up on caffeine, although Avery didn't really need the jump start. Her nerves were already tingling with excitement. Ollie turned onto Golden Arrow Road and followed it through the open, snowy landscape.

"No way," Avery said as she nearly choked on her coffee. Her mouth dropped open as she stared at the large oak tree off the side of the road up ahead. She smiled at Ollie wholeheartedly, but he kept his eyes on the road. The corners of his mouth turned up into a cheeky, tight-lipped grin. *I just love this stuff sometimes*, he said to himself as he eyed up the tree. They pulled over, parked and walked out toward the large tree that was so seemingly out of place. Avery took a few swigs of her cooling coffee and set it at her feet. Ollie stood back and let her do her thing.

Avery pursed her lips for a moment and hesitated. Her confidence seemed to have taken a vacation since her big talk the day before. After a deep breath, she finally found it again. She lifted her hand and stretched it out before her. Her fingers began to wave, ever so slightly, as if she were petting an invisible animal. She closed her eyes and remembered Volustina's guidance in Kabare, where she was surrounded by lightning and consumed by both fear and fascination. She remembered the fear turning to respect, because Volustina believed that every part of nature, good or bad, is to be respected. Her hand found her face, and she ran her fingers across her mouth, letting her tongue lick the blade of one index finger. She glanced up at the tree and then raised her eyes to the sky. Her fingers followed suit. The cold air felt like ice against her wet finger. Then she called to it, ever so gently in the back of her mind, through the form of a mantra that only she and the sky could hear. Her hand jerked, like a limb just before one falls asleep, and she lowered her gaze to the tree.

Under the cloud-patched sky, Avery called to the lightning that was hiding. Suddenly her stomach turned and she could smell it all: the electricity, the energy, the condensation in the cloud. Without warning, a bolt of lightning formed in the sky and struck the tall trunk of the oak tree. It pierced with outrageous violence, three times over, in a bouquet of colors. First, a blinding flash of white, then sprays of orange, then violet, and finishing with a silvery white, brighter than any diamond in sunlight. Splinters of wood scattered away from the tree and onto the snow, still hot. Avery hardly batted an eye at the bomb-like sound that crashed before her. She stood still. The only thing that moved were the billowing ends of her handmade scarf that Mitch had made for her.

Ollie ducked for cover, surprised at the intensity of the strike. He looked around as the wood confettied to the ground, but no one else was around to see it. They approached the tree and searched the ground, a graveyard of smoking splinters. Avery found a piece that was light enough to carry. She lifted it humbly, and turned it between her hands. It smelled charged, charred black at one end.

"Let's go," Avery said, her voice soft and full of accomplishment.

As the coven ran through the ritual a final time and made a list of everything they would need, Leo studied for his own ritual. It didn't matter that, historically speaking, he wasn't a terrific student. He was now. It took him only five minutes to find the section of the book he was looking for. Perhaps he had inadvertently developed bibliomancy, or maybe he was just so determined that he willed it to reveal itself to him. He read through the ritual twice and started to lose hope. It seemed complicated, based solely on theory, and not only advised securing a protective amulet for the high risk of death, but also warned of a fairly low rate of success. He felt the urge to say "Fuck it" and just escape into a drug-induced fantasy for a while where he didn't have to think, worry or do much other than exist in complete emotional and mental paralysis.

But as he read through the list of ingredients for the spell, written by someone he had never heard of, in a stylized calligraphy, a light sparked inside him, and it wasn't just that it was incredibly dangerous. Near the bottom of the ingredients list was *essence of white dolphin*. It seemed too perfect to be coincidence. A few days ago he hadn't even known there was such a thing as a white dolphin, and now he knew exactly where to find the incredibly rare ingredient. All thanks to Grace's tour of her ASMR studio.

"We have to get the timing right on this," Mitch said aloud, his finger underlining the specific passage of the ritual. "It has to be done as the sun is setting, and the ritual has to be finished after the sun has set." Then he looked at his thumb, scabby and begging to be picked. So he picked.

Leo looked up at the group and, for a moment, felt caught. His eyes widened, and he waited for someone to look at him. But no one did. He looked down at the book and repeated the first line of the instructions mentally. *The ritual must be performed as close to the heavens as one can be, and commence just after the sun has completely vanished from the horizon.* Leo's heart jumped. If he was going to do this, he had to do it now, before his chance to escape was gone.

"Should we wait, maybe?" he said. "I mean, we don't have to rush this. We could always wait a few days…make sure we feel confident."

Bisa looked up and realized it was the first time she'd heard Leo speak since they'd sat down. "We talked about this. Today—well, *tonight*—is best. The magical timing of it, remember?"

Leo produced a series of evasive responses to cover up that he wasn't listening, and also had other plans.

"It's the day of the moon," Bisa said as if to challenge Leo's ignorance of magical timing, both to call him out and to establish who was actually in charge.

"Monday?" Leo quipped.

"Yeah. And the moon is waxing now. The new moon was only a few days ago, which ultimately makes this the best possible time to do this spell. It's not technically spring, but it's close enough. That would be just a little extra frosting on the cake. Magical timing is important."

"Is it? I—*we've*—done a lot without worrying about all that. Do we really wanna hassle with all that?"

"We do if we want it to turn out right. Nina would want us to. This is what we all came here to do. What we've been *called* to do."

"What's it for again?" Leo asked. Even Mitch looked up at him this time.

"Spiritual balance," Bisa said.

Avery and Ollie entered the room, carrying the piece of oak. "We've got the oak," Avery said, a smile spread across her face.

"All we have to do is powder it," Ollie said as he put his hand up to stop anyone from volunteering. "I can do that."

It seemed like hours passed before Leo looked up from the oak in Avery's hand. He knew that would be the next thing on his list. He wouldn't need all of it, just some of it. They would never even know some of it was missing. It would be just like adding a little water to the vodka bottle when he was younger. He broke out of his staring contest with the wood and combed his fingers through his hair, thinking, plotting.

"I say we get something light to eat before we meet up for the ritual tonight," Bisa said.

"Sunset, right?" Avery asked to verify.

Bisa looked over at Leo with eyes that said, *See...everyone else knows.*

Just then, Leo stood up. "Well, I'm gonna go into town, grab somethin' to eat."

"There's a ton of leftovers in the fridge," Ollie said.

Leo turned up his nose. "I don't want that. I'll be back."

"Be back in an hour," Bisa said. "I don't want to let the world dissolve into chaos because you wanted pizza."

Leo wanted to retort, but he didn't. He still felt a little residual pain from Bisa dissolving her romantic feelings for him, so it was best that he not say anything. And he hadn't even wanted pizza. But now he did. He took the advice written in the book and fashioned himself a protection jar with rosemary, lavender, frankincense, sea salt, cinnamon, artemisia, crushed amethyst and black tourmaline. Between Ollie and Avery's room, he found everything he needed, everything except a pinch of iron. His mouth tightened as he tried to think of how he was going to get the last ingredient. He didn't have to think too hard before the memory of ninth-grade chemistry suddenly surfaced. Leo laughed to himself as he remembered with striking clarity that he had told the teacher he would *never* ever in a million years use chemistry because he wasn't going to be a chemist. He snorted, shook his head and headed to the kitchen.

"I thought you were getting pizza," Ollie said.

"I still am," Leo said as he grabbed a handful of Wheaties. He popped some into his mouth and reserved the rest in his hand. When he reached the front door, he made sure he was alone and then looked into the handful of cereal. He thought about Mr. Mistry, who had taught Intro to Chemistry and re-ferred to it as Chem-Mistry 101 on the first day. He almost felt bad for giving Mr. Mistry such a hard time and saying he was allergic to random lab ingredients like sulfur and cornstarch, just so he could get out of doing an assignment. Leo was thankful he hadn't skipped out on the magnet and cereal experiment, because he never would have realized there was a ton of iron inside a bowl of Wheaties. He swirled his finger through the cereal a few times, with each pass pulling out a little of the iron inside. Like a bee collecting pollen, he eventually had enough to form a pinch, and then some. He added it to the bottle, fixed the bottle to a string and draped it around his neck. The rest he saved in a folded piece of paper, realizing that he had also found another one of the seven metals he'd been after.

Theoretically, the amulet was supposed to function like a lightning rod, attracting and absorbing the fatal flares of energy created from performing delicate magic like soul fusion. According to the book, the flares were a natural side effect of the complicated spell, and there was no way to prevent them. One just had to hope one wasn't struck and killed. It was just as risky as standing on top of a mountain peak in a storm, foolishly waiting around to be struck—which, inadvertently, was exactly what he was going to be doing. Leo was finally ready, and he felt like a gladiator.

CHAPTER 38

Leo stopped for a slice of potato, arugula and roasted corn pizza from Red Pie (it was on the way, he justified) and then headed to Ruby's. The restaurant was eerily quiet. A *Closed* sign was fixed to the front door, and the inside was empty. Leo peeked from around the corner of the restaurant and scoped out Ruby's house. His stalking breath steamed in the cold air. With a careful step, he inched over toward the door and tried the handle. Locked. He stared at the greasy fingerprints he'd left behind and decided he would just have to *unlock* the door himself. He cupped his hand over the lock and focused his intention. His eyes closed, and inside his mind, he visualized the mechanics of the lock with a little creative effort.

Leo was more of a jackhammer than a woodpecker. He didn't even know he could affect the lock until after he did it, albeit quite gracelessly. The lock was pulled and twisted out of the door in a matter of seconds as if melted, hammered and set under a piston. Not the most discreet operation, but did he really give a shit about that right now? He asked himself that very question and unfortunately arrived at—*No*.

Leo entered the restaurant and closed the door behind him. The emptiness brought a strange nostalgia rushing back to him. It reminded him of the days when he would arrive at the restaurant in New Orleans before anyone else to begin prepping for service. He would make coffee, have a snack, and bitch to himself about the list of tasks the chef had left behind for him, knowing that the chef wouldn't show up until halfway through service and that when he did, he'd take a nap. If only that chef could see him now. Although it was probably for the best that he didn't. Leo's line between right and wrong, although never very distinct, was nearly blurred out of existence, and he'd probably just snap his neck and then go out for pizza, and his body count was high enough.

Leo crossed through the restaurant and headed back to the ASMR studio. On the shelf was the bottle of white dolphin essence that he needed. He licked his lips and beamed as he retrieved, borrowed—stole—the bottle from its home.

Leo stepped over the mess of metal that used to be the lock and left the restaurant. He started off toward the closest hiking trail, thinking that people wouldn't be out and about, just like on the trails in Louisiana, where it was just too fucking hot and muggy—all the time. But people in Colorado were different. They were active, and they loved the outdoors no matter what season it was. That's what snowshoes and insulated gloves were for. When he saw more people on the trail than he was able to avoid, he tried his luck at Centennial Cone. The weather had been pretty mild lately, and there didn't seem to be a lot of snow to deal with, and when he parked, he was the only one there. *Meant to be*, he thought.

(stop...)

Leo trekked up the rocky slope, past the ponderosa pines and patches of Douglas fir, until he could look around and see the many rolling slopes that surrounded him. The windswept layer of snow swirled before him like it was alive. His eyes watered at the rush of cold wind, and he brushed the tears away with his hand. Finally, after all this time, never truly knowing exactly what his problem was, he was maybe, just maybe, about to fix it. He had raged on long enough, fucked up so many times, and screwed so many people over that it was time to mix things up. Then he could put the past behind him with the silver bullet of the soul fusion spell in his pocket.

There wasn't time to think about what would happen if it didn't work. But there was always the rafkolite. If the spell worked *and* he found the rafkolite, now, that would make him a real hot-shit witch, and the thought of that hooked him stronger than any drug he'd ever loved.

Leo took a deep breath and wondered if he was as close to the heavens as he could get. He could have snuck onto the roof of some tall building in downtown Denver, but he didn't really have time for all of that. There were cameras, people, and parking issues, and it was too far of a drive. He gave his hair an agitated tousle and looked out at the setting sun. It was almost time. He had to prepare.

"Where's Leo?" Avery asked as resentment started to build up in her yet again. "I didn't hear him come back. Is he even here?"

Bisa and Avery exchanged a look, and then Bisa felt her stomach twist. She knew he wasn't in the house; she could feel it. If she closed her eyes, she could feel the cold air blowing through his hair, the delicate flakes of snow melting on his skin, the rush of exhilaration in his blood. She had never felt so close to him before. She was truly growing into her magic, and it would have been something to celebrate had it been about someone other than Leo. Bisa couldn't be certain if it was her power or some kind of residual affection that she was supposed to have been emancipated from. "He's not here," she said.

No one needed her to explain. By now, they all kind of just trusted her when it came to things like this.

Avery checked the time. "Screw it, we can do it without him," she said, a dark bitterness in her voice.

"We should wait," Mitch offered. "I think that's only fair. We can spare a few extra minutes."

"Not really," Avery said as she started to draw a symbol in salt on the floor, meticulously scanning the book to make sure every inch was correct. "The book said the ritual needs *four* witches. There are four of us here. We don't need him."

Leo poured a bottle of rose petal essence over his head and shrieked as its cold rivers trickled down his skin into his clothes. He rubbed it across his face like a coat of primer and dug into his backpack to retrieve the rest of the provisions: the bottle of white dolphin essence, the jar with his soul, a plastic pipette, and a small knife. Leo placed the items by his side, stared out into the setting sun, and waited.

Ollie, Mitch, Bisa and Avery each dressed themselves with a necklace, a large chunk of raw amber hung at their chest. Bisa wore hers over Nina's amethyst pendant already around her neck. Next, they each dipped a finger in a small bowl of Transformation Oil and dabbed it on their third eye. Ollie placed a small cauldron of frankincense and amber resin, dried sweetgrass and cedar next to the symbol on the floor, and set fire to it. The smoke rose in long plumes that spread out into the air over their bodies. Avery brought over a nest she'd made of dried flowers and delicate twigs and handed it to Ollie. He leaned over the symbol on the floor, placed the nest in the middle and dropped a large piece of aquamarine inside it. Next, he poured a circle of Transformation Powder around the nest and adorned it with small rosebuds, fresh mint leaves, dragonfly wings and small feathers.

When he finished, Bisa handed out the ritual tools they had prepared earlier. Ollie received a set of rosewood claves; Avery, a crystal singing bowl; and Mitch, a large, flat, hand-made drum that had once belonged to Nina, and with it a birch drumstick, the head covered in fur salvaged from a dead wild fox. Bisa picked up a long didgeridoo and held it before her so the end faced directly at the nest. They each took a spot at the cardinal points: Ollie in the North, Bisa in the East, Avery in the South, and Mitch in the West. The sunlight painted the room, just barely, as the golden hour faded away.

"Begin," Bisa said as she looked out at the setting sun one last time.

The ritual began with a clack as Ollie banged the wooden claves together in a slow, enigmatic beat. After a few clicks, Avery lifted her mallet to the side of the crystal bowl and ran it along the outer rim, slowly, ever so slowly, until it woke up and sang back to her in a hypnotic, crystalline tone. After a few passes around the bowl, the ringing became a deep and constant humming, like the nudges from Spirit that manifest as a gut feeling that one can't explain but can only sense. Bisa blew into her instrument and produced a deep and cavernous bellowing. *If a ghost had a pulse, that is what it would sound like*, Mitch thought as he curled his fingers around the drumstick. He found Ollie's rhythm, and on the next clack, he struck the drum.

Bum...

Then again.

Bum...

Mitch didn't really think he would find the sounds, when combined, as soothing as they were. It was almost as if the music alone changed the very atmosphere of his heart. If even that were true, then surely the ritual, were it to be successful, would be able to do what it was intended to do.

Ten minutes passed, and the coven was in the trancelike state that the ritual required of them before they could proceed to the next part. Bisa looked out the window as the final sliver of the sun slipped out of sight.

Bum…bum…bum…

Leo watched the sun set behind the hills on the horizon, and then took a deep breath. It was time. He reached down to retrieve the white dolphin essence and opened the bottle. Even in the windy mountains he could smell the repugnant odor. He thought about something Avery had told him one evening, about how the things we hate about other people are just indicators of what we truly hate about ourselves. *Maybe I'm sickening. Maybe I really am just a really disgusting human being…as disgusting as this stuff smells.* The thought disappeared with the next gust of wind, and Leo picked up a dropper cap and stuck it inside the bottle. He gave it a squeeze and sucked up the essence into the dropper.

Bum…bum…bum…

Bisa stopped blowing air into the instrument and gazed into the aquamarine in the nest before them. *"Angeli, maiorum, ducibus, niversum. Quibusque gratias agimus tibi. Status spirituum nostri revertetur ad libratum."*

Leo picked up the plastic pipette he had stolen from Ollie's room, and dipped one end into the white dolphin essence. He gave the bulb a squeeze and sucked the fluid into the chamber.

There was an eerie familiarity to the process; it almost made him feel like he was shooting up. Leo's face fell dark as remembered what that rush felt like—almost like the rush he felt now—and he could only imagine what he would feel after the ritual was complete and he was whole.

"*Fenestris apertis,*" Leo said, not having any idea what he was saying, knowing only what the spell was for. He lifted the pipette over his head and tilted his head back. With his free hand, he pried open his eyelids with his calloused fingertips. He squeezed a single drop of the essence into his right eye, and then the left. His eyelids fluttered as he tried to keep from blinking the liquid out. Everything fell blurry for a moment as his pupils dilated. Leo felt the excitement winding up inside him. When his vision returned, he guffawed, then picked up the knife and made a small cut on his forearm. He squeezed more of the essence over his cut and let the essence-laced blood drop down into the jar with his soul.

Bum...bum...bum...

"*Sementi,*" Ollie said softly, and then looked to Avery.

"*Ad opprimere, mutare,*" Avery said.

Mitch nodded and looked down at the nest. "*Redi.*"

Then everyone all at once, "*Libra.*" A moment passed, then again, "*Libra...*" A pause, and this time loud, with conviction, "*Libra!*"

A snap came from the aquamarine stone in the nest. Their faces were hard with expectation. A small hairline crack split down the center of the stone. A thin wisp of powdery smoke sailed into the air, where it dissolved away. Then, out of the fissure in the stone, a sprout emerged. Pale yellow and delicate, and then rising higher and stronger, until it was a dark green. It rose fourteen inches high before producing a white bud that unfolded and bloomed into a gorgeous orchid with three long sepals and two petals of shimmering white extended like banners into the air. Its throat as pink as cherub cheeks, its lip and column like fireflies. The leaves that unfurled over the nest were covered in dust from the fractured gemstone. From where Ollie was standing, he could see straight down to the roots that had grown into the nest.

Bisa's breath broke as she marveled at the flower in front of her. She smiled, knowing full well that the ritual had worked and that soon, they wouldn't be alone. Outside, there was a whistling of wind, and then everything fell silent. Then, they heard it. Soft at first, like the flipping of pages from front to back, then growing stronger and louder, like a small electric current. Bisa could see it now, coming down from an energetic portal near the ceiling, a swarm of iridescent dragonflies. The cloud of violet insects droning into the room were of the fairy realm, the very same ones that were imprisoned in lanterns in Tengotodo, the ones native to Garland.

At first, the sound of the swarm put Mitch on edge, but he relaxed when he looked around at the coven and saw the look of awe slapped across their faces. They watched the swarm swim through the air in a tight ring, buzzing, whirring and hissing. The sound of them all together was so overwhelming, they could hardly hear the thoughts in their own heads. There were hundreds of them, and they were all there for one sole reason, to taste the nectar of the orchid. The nectar gave the dragonflies a revolutionary power to shift thoughts, perspectives and beliefs to benefit the greater good of mankind, through a single kiss.

One by one, they trailed away from the swarm and took the gift from the orchid before they flew out of the room via the energetic vortex. Each dragonfly, while invisible to humans, exited the vortex in the vicinity of a select individual. These chosen ones had the power to influence in a contagious way, through either their actions or their absence, however devastating it may have seemed. Those who received the bite immediately fell into a brief coma, a sickness that mimicked encephalitis. In that state of mystical unconsciousness, the bitten one was awakened and illuminated. Their perspectives, actions and manners of living, ruling, managing, governing, controlling, presiding, running, directing, overseeing, teaching, swindling, exploiting, scamming, abusing, profiteering and existing…were shifted to include one very important ethos…to be for the good of all and for their best benefit. Those who died from the bite did not die because of who they were, but because of who they were not. Change then affected those around them, those closest to them, making different choices, opening different doors.

When the last dragonfly left the room, Bisa knew that it would be quite some time before they saw any real results. But she knew that wasn't the point. Bisa understood that it might not even be something she witnessed in her lifetime, but that it was in the works for the collective. There was also no way of knowing for certain if it had worked. Rosemary had kept track of that, and she'd never shared how she did it. Was it a device? She had mentioned indicators, but what were they?

Maybe it didn't matter. Perhaps this was exactly how it was supposed to be. Was it?

Leo continued with the spell: *"Voco est anima mea usque ad me. Replete corpus meum. Facti sunt."* He began to feel weak and disoriented but also incredibly alive. He began to bleed from both nostrils, and a searing pain pounded from behind his eyes. He could sense how dangerous the spell was and could see the energy flares spiraling in the air around him.

He powered through the pain and past the danger. There was no other option. He reminded himself just how unhappy he had felt his entire life, and a life lived in unhappiness felt like the weight of forty lifetimes. What was a little blood and a headache if he could finally find relief from all that he had done to himself and other people? This was his chance, this was his time, he reminded himself. If not for himself, for his daughter, whom he had never deserved. If he could do this, maybe everything else would be different and he could be the person he should have been, someone who wouldn't have to remind themselves how awful they were.

A flare snapped past his head, and he flinched. It was so hot that his ear burned. He had only a little left to recite. Leo's hand grabbed onto the protection amulet around his neck and rubbed it like a lucky rabbit's foot. *"Iterum iterumque fieri unum!"* Leo said, and immediately thought, *I did it, I finally fucking did it!*

He closed his eyes shut at the sudden eruption of energy that exploded around him as he fell to the ground. He felt the heat of the flares on his chest as if it had cut straight through him. Blood was dripping onto the snow underneath his head. Leo rubbed his chest and checked to make sure he was still all there. His amulet was a broken mess around his neck. The contents scattered around him on the ground. It had deflected the fatal flare and saved his life.

Bisa put a hand on her chest and suddenly lost all control of her body. Her muscles tightened like a rubber band pulled too far, and her limbs jerked and shook, sending her right off her feet and onto the floor, where she landed with a heavy thud. Bisa's body rolled uncontrollably into the symbol on the floor, and her legs knocked over the nest in the middle, crushing the orchid. Avery first thought it looked like symptoms of the Exhauriat worm, from the spell cast on them by Merlot's coven, but it had come on so suddenly. The coven panicked, and they scurried to Bisa's trembling body and tried to figure out what was happening.

"What do we do?" Ollie said fervently, knowing there was nothing they *could* do.

Avery placed her hands on Bisa and tried to heal her in whatever way she could. But nothing was working. Bisa shuddered one final time, and then her body fell limp. Her hair a mess and tangled in her hands, and her eyes—empty. She was dead.

Leo pushed himself up from the ground and didn't even bother wiping the blood from his nose. He looked into the jar with his soul. It was still there. It hadn't worked. He had no words for how angry and disappointed he felt. Instead he just felt numb.

The amulet had worked, but not as intended. It hadn't absorbed the fatal flares, it had deflected them to the next most logical place—to Bisa. Leo and Bisa were bound by a psychic, magnetic, intense and tumultuous soul connection as a result of their soul being split into two bodies, each with a half. As twin flames, they were destined for each other—yet also toxic together.

CHAPTER 39

When Leo returned to the house, he followed the cries and panicked voices to find the coven standing next to Bisa's lifeless body. The anger and disappointment he felt from yet another failure in his life was replaced with horror. He wouldn't have believed it from their reactions alone, but he felt it. He knew she was gone, and he knew it was his fault. He couldn't explain that to anyone, it was something he just knew on a soul level.

Avery turned to look at Leo as he stepped into the room. He could see the hate behind the suffering in her eyes and knew there was nothing he could say to soothe either. A feeling of disgust shot straight through him: he was responsible for yet another death of someone he cared for—someone he loved, someone who no longer loved him. And Bisa had been right to decide not to. All he seemed to do was fuck people over to lift himself up.

The one person he thought deserved every bit of life was now dead on the floor in front of him, because of him. It had taken only one single selfish act, and the most creative artist he had ever seen in his life, the wisest and most compassionate woman he'd ever met, a mind that understood him better than he understood himself, the one who had seen and felt so much suffering throughout her life and overlooked his own shortcomings at her own expense because she believed he could change, would never take another breath and never be able to accept an apology that would've come too late. He had learned to live with this kind of shame before, but how much was too much, even for him?

Leo took a few steps closer, ones that seemed involuntary. He just had to get a closer look. Bisa didn't even look like she was sleeping. *They never do*, he thought. He was almost embarrassed for her because she was frozen in a state of hideous vulnerability, and it wasn't fair. She was beautiful, and he had single-handedly made her ugly. *I kill everything*. He wanted to cry, but he didn't have enough liquid in his body for the amount of tears that he wanted to shed, so he kept them all.

It wasn't supposed to be like this, it was supposed to be so different, Leo repeated in his head as he stormed off to his room and slammed the door behind him. His eyes snapped to the window that he always left partially cracked so the magpie had access to his magic nest. The magpie was there, staring back at him. In the nest were the remaining metals he needed: a tin handle from an old lantern and a shard of a lead pipe. He had them all, all seven metals. The silver coin, the vial of mercury, a copper wire, the gold wolf figurine, the collection of iron and now these final two. The magpie made a soft sound, as if to remind him that the task was complete, and then it flew off into space.

Leo had one thing left to do: make the talisman that would allow him to begin the Union of the Divine Dualities. He had the melted snow, he would lift Volustina's life force and the powdered oak from Avery's room, and he'd be good to go from there with all his metals. Maybe, just maybe, if he found the rafkolite, he would discover that it had all sorts of other powers too, and maybe he could bring Bisa back. He knew it was a long shot, but it was the only shot he had. Leo was running out of patience with himself, which he'd thought would never happen. Perhaps he *was* changing, or trying to change. Leo grabbed his backpack and started to fill it with everything he would need for the ritual. He wasn't sure if he would tell the coven. Maybe he would just go. But he would have to tell them something, especially now with Bisa lying cold on the floor.

He sucked in his breath as a thought ran through his mind. He replayed the events at the restaurant, the night Merlot attacked. She had said something about Corporeals that hadn't meant much then, but meant the world to him right now.

He stared into space and recalled Merlot's words. "Do you know what they can do?" she'd asked the coven. "The impossible. More than any of us could on borrowed powers. Think of all the people who could be resurrected!" Leo had never thought of such a thing—until now.

Alone, agitated and inspired, Leo made the choice to put off the ritual…just for bit. With a map, a black mirror and a bloodstone pendulum, he performed a quick locator spell and found Merlot without breaking a sweat. It was almost too easy, as if she wanted to be found. He didn't care. Whatever she knew, it was more than he did, and he wasn't about to wait, he wasn't about to find the answers on his own. He had to think outside the box, even if that meant turning to an enemy while the coven was crying over Bisa's death.

Leo transported himself into Avery's room. He was feeling stronger just from the rush of a new plan, and stole some powdered oak, the jar of melted snow, and the lepidolite that was Volustina's life force. Then he made it back to his room, where he shot himself straight into Merlot's home.

Merlot looked up at him without surprise, setting her cup of tea down on the table. "Good. You found me," she said.

Leo's pain and guilt suddenly disappeared, and he had the feeling that he had come to the right place. "How'd you know I'd come?"

"Ay yi yi, let's not waste time talking about things that don't matter."

Leo looked around the house and out the window, trying to figure out where he was. He wasn't the most skilled at sensory magic, but he could smell Merlot and her dark intentions. He suddenly considered that maybe she had brought him there with a spell, maybe he hadn't made the choice himself. He panicked.

"It's not a spell," Merlot said. "You decided to come here on your own. But I knew you would." She lifted the yellow mug to her lips and took a sip as if they had been casually discussing carpet samples.

"What do you want?" Leo asked.

"What do *you* want? *You* came *here*," Merlot said with a grin slapped across her face. She blew on her tea to cool it.

"I want you to tell me about what I can do. You know I'm a Corporeal. Can I bring people back from the dead? How does it work?"

Merlot set down her tea and took a few steps closer to Leo. She stared at him intensely, her eyes swirling with nightmarish chaos. "You're not trying to bring back Nina, are you?" she asked jokingly.

"Not her. But you know how? How do I do it? Can you show me?" Leo hadn't felt this insignificant in a while, but he didn't care. He was desperate.

"I can, yes. I can teach you how to do it, but you have to give me what I want. We can trade," she said—lied. There were no books, no records, no evidence that any witch, even a Corporeal, had the power to balance death and life and resurrect someone from the other plane. Merlot knew that, but Leo did not. She was never one to play fair—she hadn't played fair since she'd found out she was a witch.

Leo tilted his head back and for a moment wondered how sinister the cost of her help would be. "What can I do?"

"You can give me your blood. That's what I want," she said with full confidence. Merlot was in charge, and everything had been going exactly as planned. Soon enough, she would have Leo's blood and could accomplish all that she wanted and all that she hadn't even dreamed of yet.

(don't, Leo...leave...)

Leo heard Nina somewhere in the air and looked deep into Merlot's wild eyes. "What do you need my blood for?" he asked.

"Your blood is rare. Very rare. I don't think there are any other Corporeals out there...right now...and I'm not willing to wait. I'm like you, I'm not a patient person. I've been working on a way to manipulate your blood, strengthen the power within it. If I can do that, and I will...your astral fluid will become the strongest form of power that anyone has ever possessed."

"You mean like a drug? Like what you did with the coven that got them all killed?"

Merlot scoffed and shook her head. "Not even close. That was...recreational. This..." She reached her finger up to touch the crusted blood on the inside of his nostril. "This...can change the world."

Leo watched her retract her finger and stare googly-eyed at the dried blood before she slid her finger into her mouth and sucked the blood off. He had no idea what she was really after, and he didn't know that she had goals that seemed incredibly asinine: political aspirations, leadership, dictatorship, supreme living, control over everyone and everything. Being a powerful witch wasn't enough, she had to have the whole world on its knees. Merlot 2024…Her Majesty the True Queen…MEME…Make Earth Mine Eternally.

"Bisa's dead," Leo choked out.

Merlot turned the corners of her mouth down as though she were doing an impression of an emoji. "I had nothing to do with that—surprising, I know. She won't have to be if you help me. Help me first, and you can bring whoever you want back to life. Think about it. I won't want her dead if I have your blood."

Leo took a deep breath and ignored the second warning from Nina. What choice did he really have? If all else failed, there was always the rafkolite. Even if Merlot did try to cross him—and he figured that she might eventually—Leo was a murderous and self-serving witch. He was predisposed to always getting what he wanted, but he *was* trying to change that. He still felt pretty badass, and he could handle her in a magic scrap—if it came to that. He could break her neck, or make her eat her own tongue, or something a little more historic, like drop a house on her. "Okay. I'll do it. But I need to get clothes and a toothbrush."

CHAPTER 40

There was no cake, music or happiness of any kind when the spring equinox rolled around. Mitch had even had a birthday only a few days before, but he wasn't there to celebrate it or be celebrated. He'd packed up what little he'd acquired since his time with the coven and taken the first flight back to Salt Lake City to pick up whatever pieces of his life were left to collect there. It turned out there was a limit to the amount of trauma he could take, and he had reached that cap a long while back. He was there for less than a week when he decided to fly to California and visit his parents, who had moved into a smaller house in Cayucos. Avery had tried to get him to stay, desperately promising him that they would handle everything together. He didn't care. The initiation into the coven meant he had to show up and be present, but Mitch wouldn't be, not now, not after all that had happened.

Avery called Ruby after Leo snuck out of the house with Volustina's life force and the powdered oak and never came back. She did notice that some of his clothes were missing, along with his toothbrush, but she had no idea what to make of it. Ruby, being the next powerhouse witch in line, handled everything with Bisa. She used her power of influence to get her body out of the house with no questions, aside from the kind of casket they wanted. They buried her in New Moon Meadow, just a short walk from where Nina had been laid to rest.

It was when they returned from the funeral that Avery realized Volustina's life force was missing. She immediately knew Leo had taken it. She wasn't as angry as she was frightened.

Avery had never liked or trusted Leo, and if he was about to find the seven metals that she was unaware he already possessed, there was no telling what he would do with the rafkolite if he were to ever find it. He wasn't the brightest witch, but he sure was lucky and gifted. That combo could get anyone pretty far, she deduced.

Ollie played the piano to help calm Avery down. It worked. He segued into "Avril 14th," and as his fingers played the final notes, he noticed Avery had left the room. But he wasn't alone. Nina was there, standing by the window, watching him, haloed by the sunlight behind her, her curls glistening like black gold. Ollie smiled and stood up from the piano. He wanted to hug her, but he just knew that wasn't possible.

"I knew you'd come," Ollie said, so happy he could cry.

"I've always loved that song," Nina said with a smile that held some weight behind it.

"I've tried to connect with you so many times," Ollie said.

"I know. It's hard to explain in words. There's so much unveiled," Nina said.

"Do you know everything now?"

"There's too much to know everything. I know *more*, but not all. I guess I would still say I know…*some*."

"That's you just not giving yourself enough credit again," Ollie said with a smile.

Nina tried to smile, but didn't. She looked pressed for time.

"What's wrong?" Ollie said, now fully aware of the heaviness in her presence.

"Your ritual didn't kill Bisa. You did everything correctly," Nina said with a sadness in her eyes.

"What did?"

"Leo," Nina said with a heavy heart. "He didn't mean to. It was accidental. A freak accident, really, as far as spellwork goes. He couldn't have known that what he was about to do was going to have that result."

"That's what he was doing, casting a spell?" Ollie asked. "What about Leo? What about the Union of the Divine Dualities? What about the ritual we did? You said we did everything right, so does that mean it worked? Is it working? How do we know?"

Nina turned and looked up toward the sun, then turned back to Ollie. "Remember the shroud? The one we left in the window at the Barrow House? Perform that spell and leave the shroud hanging out my window. Spiritual balance has begun."

"Then what?" Ollie asked quickly, to quell his need for answers.

Nina pointed to a stack of books near the piano, with the one about the Union of the Divine Dualities on top. She said nothing.

Ollie looked over at the book. "What? The book?" He turned back to Nina, but she was already gone. He shook his head and sighed. His urge to have all the answers that he had felt only a few moments ago had totally gone. Ollie stood in thought for a few minutes as he stared at the book. He knew what they needed. They needed seven metals…but he already felt Leo had them. Perhaps the answers to how to proceed would come. He trusted Nina.

He and Avery bought a long piece of purple fabric, cleansed it with smoke, infused it with positive energy, steeped it in a tea of palo santo and rosemary and performed the rest of the ritual to charge and enchant the fabric so it was no longer just a piece of fabric. They opened the window in Nina's old room, tossed it out where it fluttered in the breeze, and closed the window on it.

Ollie and Avery shared a look, and then together they said, "So shall it be."

They returned to the piano and went over the Union of the Divine Dualities again.

"Oh, there it is," Avery said as she kneeled down to pick up her grimoire from the pile of books. "I couldn't remember where I put it."

Suddenly everything seemed to make sense to Ollie. Nina had meant for them to find the grimoire.

"Open it," Ollie said urgently. "Look in the back, I think."

Avery flipped through the pages, past the filled ones, the ones she had painted on, with spells, recipes, journal entries and rituals, until she hit nothing but blank pages. "What?"

Ollie frowned with disappointment and confusion. Maybe he wasn't interpreting messages correctly. "That's the end?" he asked.

"Yeah?" Avery continued to flip through the blank pages until she came across a single page that she scrolled past too quickly to see.

"Stop!" Ollie said as he took the pages into his fingers and found the one he'd seen. "There. What's that?" He pointed to a page with only tight lines and patterns that looked as if they wanted to make sense, but didn't—couldn't.

Avery shook her head, puzzled. "I don't know." She spun it around, looking at it from different angles, until Ollie placed it horizontally in line with his eyes and closed one. Then he saw it. He knew what to do next.

THE
ESOTERIC COMPENDIUM

A collection of key terms, places, spells & recipes

TERMS & PLACES

Amanita Feramignusa: A red-capped, flammable mushroom that grows all throughout Garland.

Astral Fluid: AFD for short. An organic substance present in all beings. A witch's powers and lifeforce are embedded in it. It can be extracted and used.

Bewalembu: A type of algae native to Garland with a slimy exterior and an incredibly foul odor. It is toxic to fairies.

Corporeal: The most recent type of witch to emerge, once thought to be legend. They can sometimes control the elements but cannot summon them. They are the energy alchemists, able to manipulate energy and matter. They possess varying levels of telekinesis, shapeshifting and auric manipulation.

Creamstone Township: A large, overcrowded, underdeveloped and impoverished area in Garland.

Flaming Flood Era: A period in which fairies were hunted for their life force by witches to near extinction. It began with the knowledge of the rafkolite among witches and ends in the closure of the majority of entrance portals to Garland by the fairies.

Garland: The realm of the fairies. Garland is a plane that exists within the natural world. It was formed when a shower of meteorites with unusual properties collided with earth and created an additional layer of existence.

The Land of Perpetual Midnight: The shadow realm. Existing under an open sky with more stars than one could ever see from even the most remote parts Earth, but no moon. There are occasional celestial activities in the sky that provide some additional light, with open fields of prairie-like grass, forests of evergreen and birch and a single mountain. There are no boundaries, no beginning and no end to its vastness. Access to the land, as well as other astral planes, can be achieved through ritual drug use, sexual trance, deep meditation, and repetition of words believed to contain power.

Nigrum Pullum: Translates to "Black Hen." A magically invoked animal that is the direct result of correctly performing the Union of the Divine Dualities ritual. The hen is the only thing that can locate the rafkolite, as no human, witch or spell is able to do so.

Primordial: The first type of witch to emerge, sometimes referred to as the Elementals. They can light fire, call storms, lightning and can manipulate water. They are especially gifted at using the elements for divinatory purposes. Heightened senses, can detect slight variations in voice pitch, mood and smell. They are physical healers and can communicate, summon and control animals to some degree.

Rafkolite: A vitreous silica projectile rock, silvery green with swirls of smoky purple bubbles that resemble moss. This rock fell to the earth as a meteor around 15 million years ago and is rumored to have many powers but especially known for its ability to create a butterfly effect of positive energy, when used by the right person or group.

Starseed: Souls that have origins in the stars and are all cosmically linked to one another. Similar to the energy of a Twin Flame, in which a soul has been split into two bodies and can exist at varying stages of spiritual evolution.

Tengotodo: The large and opulent palace where Jasper resides.

Transcendent: The second type of witch to emerge, sometimes referred to as the Spirit Witches. The empathic clairvoyants and the most in touch with the divine. They can communicate with spirits, astral project, and heal emotional wounds and trauma. Their strongest skill is their power to influence others.

Twin Flame: A challenging and powerful relationship between two people. A twin flame is the result of a single soul having been split into two physical bodies.

The Union of the Divine Dualities: An esoteric ritual designed to invoke the presence of the nigrum pullum.

SPELLS

Harmonious Passing Oil:

Magical oils are wonderful because they can be used in a myriad of ways. They can be applied topically to the body, carried in a vessel in the form of jewelry, or used to dress candles and other objects in spell or ritual work. The following recipe is a beautiful and uplifting blend that can be used to help ease the difficulties associated with loss, grief and passing. It can be used to help soothe in physical, emotional, mental and spiritual ways as a topical aid, and is a useful tool in any sort of funeral/passing/transformation ritual.

You will need:

1 T	dried lavender
1 T	dried lemongrass
½ t.	dried marjoram
½ t.	dried oregano
2 T	rose hips
1 T	hyssop
1 T	verbena
¼ t.	poppy seeds
¼ c.	pomegranate seeds, crushed
½ c.	grapeseed oil
2 drops	clary sage essential oil
2 drops	frankincense essential oil

- Charge each herb (lavender through poppy seeds) between your hands and infuse it with your desired intention. When ready, add it to a small pot. Add the crushed pomegranate seeds and the grapeseed oil.

- Place the pot over medium-low heat and warm the oil, swirling gently to combine. When the fragrance has been released, the oil is ready and can be removed from the heat. Let cool slightly.
- Strain into a clean bowl and add the essential oils, stirring to combine.
- Pour into a clean container. Charge the oil by holding it between your hands, closing your eyes and focusing on the feeling of harmony and peace while chanting "let this oil be infused with love, peace, harmony, and let it ease the passing for the good of all, so it shall be." Repeat the chant three times and the oil is ready to use.

Plant / Flower Essence:

Plant and flower essences are a natural remedy for the mind, body and spirit. The effect of the essence isn't meant to treat or dispel negative attitudes, but instead to transform the energy into something constructive. It is similar to making a magical tea. Choose a tree/plant/wild flower that is non-toxic and has the intended benefits you desire. It may even be as simple as a leaf from a place you enjoy spending time or from a place you meditate frequently.

You will need:

2 c.   spring water

1   leaf/stem/blossom

- Cleanse the water with your intention and set aside.
- Ask permission of the earth for what you intend to take and thank the plant for its generosity.

- Add the plant matter to the water and set the vessel in the sun for 6 hours.

- Strain out the material and store in a dark glass bottle. The essence may but cut with an alcohol like vodka to preserve it.

Dark Moon Elixir:

The dark moon (also called the new moon) is best for magic involving new beginnings, ventures, love, and mental, spiritual, emotional and physical health. This elixir is appropriate for driving out negative, unwanted energies and harmful, undesirable or unconstructive patterns that limit or hinder personal growth. This recipe includes black tourmaline to help shield the user from negative energy, promote creativity, physical vitality and overall practicality. Snowflake obsidian is an optional inclusion that can help sharpen mental vision and the realization of superfluous patterns. This elixir is a great way to realign the whole. This elixir is not for consumption.

You will need:

16 oz.   fresh spring or filtered water

1   chunk black tourmaline

1   chunk snowflake obsidian (optional)

1   chunk labradorite

2   chunks celestite (or one very large piece)

2 drops cypress essential oil

6 drops tangerine essential oil

6 drops sweet orange essential oil

- Pour the water into a bowl, glass or measuring cup.

- Cleanse all ingredients, apart from the oils, with your preferred method of cleansing (smoke, water or source energy). Charge the water with your preferred intention. Add the stones and the oils.
- Hold the vessel between both hands and chant, "Under the darkness of the moon, this elixir is made, infused with the power of shade. Strong and black as the moon's dark glow, new and fresh, as above so below."
- Let the water rest under the dark moon for at least three hours, and make sure to remove and bottle before sunrise. Store in a dark colored jar. The elixir may be cut with an alcohol like vodka to preserve the solution.

Cord Cutting Spell:

There are many ways in which to perform a cord cutting spell. Be sure to make adjustments, alterations and substitutions as you see fit. When we are involved with any relationship, even platonic, we form energetic attachments to those people—energy cords. If a relationship of any kind has ended, or needs to end, and the energetic bond—cord—hasn't fully been severed, it can have long lasting effects on your emotional and spiritual wellbeing, easily stunt your personal and spiritual growth, and even prevent you from moving forward at all. Some relationships are just naturally stronger than others for a variety of reasons such as: the level of intimacy, the length of time, mental connection, etc. It can sometimes be incredibly difficult to let go of a strong connection, even if we know we need to, must or should. This quick ritual can be used as a preventative but also as a way to help if you have found yourself having trouble separating yourself from the other person's energy.

You will need:

2   candles, color of your choice (be intentional)

8 in.   thread or twine

salt

fireproof plate or bowl

- Cleanse and charge each of your candles. You may designate one for you and one for the other person.
- Tie the twine around the top quarter of each candle, or alternatively, to the wick of each candle.
- Make two small mounds of salt at opposite ends of the fireproof plate or bowl and fix a candle into each one so they stand upright.
- Close your eyes for at least 3 minutes and focus your intention on severing the bond between you and the other person. Attune to their essence, their spirit, their energy. See yourself being free and released from their bond, with nothing but compassion for the severance and both people involved.
- Open your eyes and light each candle as you chant, "With this flame, I cut the cord. I call back what is mine and give back what is theirs, for the good of all."
- Allow the candles to fully burn out and extinguish. Discard any ashes outside into the wind.

RECIPES

Avery's Chocolate Chip Cookies:

284 g.	butter
180 g.	sugar
286 g.	dark brown sugar
8 g.	kosher salt
2	eggs
1 T.	vanilla
1 T.	barley malt syrup
36 g.	malt powder
200 g.	all-purpose flour
46 g.	cake flour
266 g.	bread flour
8 g.	baking soda
6 g.	baking powder
100 g.	semisweet chocolate
100g.	milk chocolate

- Sift dry ingredients into a medium bowl.
- Chop chocolate, set aside.
- Brown half the butter and set aside to cool slightly.
- Beat the other half of butter until creamy, then add the brown sugar and salt on medium speed for 3 minutes.
- Add the vanilla and barley malt syrup, beat 10 seconds. Scrape down bowl.
- On medium speed, drizzle in the brown butter. Scrape down bowl again.
- Add granulated sugar, beat 2 minutes.
- Beat in the eggs one at a time.

- Reduce speed to low and add the dry ingredients, mix just until flour is 75% incorporated. Add the chocolate and gently fold it in.

- Portion the dough using a 4 oz. portion scoop onto a greased sheet tray, flatten slightly to form a hockey puck shape, and chill the dough for 24 hours or at least 8 hours (will keep wrapped in plastic for 1 week or frozen up to 1 month). When ready to bake, preheat oven to 350°F and space the portioned dough 2 inches apart on a greased cookie sheet. Bake 16-19 minutes or until done. Edges should be crispy and the center should be just slightly underbaked. Remove from oven and let rest on cookie sheet for 3 minutes to finish baking with carryover cooking from the hot sheet tray. Transfer to rack to cool completely.

Ollie's Piri Piri Chicken:

10	fresno peppers, stemmed and chopped (or 8 jalapeños)
6	dried piri piri chiles or chiles de árbol, stemmed (or 2 serrano)
8	garlic cloves, crushed
1	4-inch piece of peeled fresh ginger, coarsely chopped
1 c.	cilantro leaves, plus small sprigs for garnish
¼ c.	apple cider vinegar
¼ c.	white vinegar
6	shallots, chopped
2	lemons, juiced and zested
2 t.	teaspoon smoked paprika
2 t.	sweet paprika
2 t.	thyme
1 ½ c.	cup extra-virgin olive oil
7 lb.	chicken thighs or (or 5-6 chicken breasts)
kosher salt	
pepper	

- In a food processor, puree the fresh and dried chiles with the garlic, ginger, 1 cup of cilantro, the vinegars, shallots, lemon zest and juice, paprika, thyme and the olive oil until smooth. Season with salt and pepper. Reserve 1 cup of the piri piri marinade.

- In a large plastic freezer bag, place the chicken inside and pour the marinade over the chicken. Massage into the meat. Let stand at room temperature for 30 minutes or marinate for 4 hours in the fridge or overnight.

- Preheat the oven to 450° F with the racks set in the upper and lower thirds. Set a wire rack over a large rimmed baking sheet.
- Transfer the chicken to the prepared baking sheet; discard the marinade. Season with salt and pepper and drizzle with 2 tablespoons of olive oil.
- Roast the chicken on the upper rack of the oven for 20 minutes, turn and baste with pan juices and roast the chicken for 20 to 25 minutes longer, until the chicken is cooked through. Transfer the chicken to a platter and garnish with reserved marinade and cilantro sprigs.

Nina's Stir Fry:

For the tofu:

14 oz.	firm tofu
4 oz.	butter
8	shallots, thinly sliced
8	garlic cloves, crushed
1 T	fresh ginger, grated
2 T	black soy sauce
2 T	tamari
2 t.	seasoned rice vinegar
1 T	brown sugar
2 T	black peppercorns, finely crushed
1-2 T	cornstarch

- Cut the tofu into large one-inch cubes. Pour oil into a large frying pan or wok and place over medium high heat. Toss them in cornstarch, shake off the excess, and add to the hot oil. Fry on all sides until they are golden brown and lightly crisped. Transfer to a paper towel and drain.
- Wipe out the pan and add the butter to melt. Add the shallots, garlic and ginger. Sauté on low to medium heat for about 10 minutes, stirring occasionally, until the ingredients have softened.
- Add the soy sauce, tamari, vinegar and sugar and stir, then add the crushed black pepper.
- Add the tofu and heat through. Set aside.

For the rice and cabbage:

4 T	grapeseed oil

2 T	fresh ginger, minced
4	cloves garlic, sliced thin
4	scallions, thinly sliced, whites and greens divided
4 c.	red cabbage, sliced
3 c.	purple kale, chopped into 2-inch chunks
¼ c.	low-sodium vegetable broth
1 c.	forbidden rice
1 t.	gochujang
1 T	tamari
2 T	lime juice
1 t.	seasoned rice vinegar

- Cook rice and set aside.
- Preheat a wok or large pot over medium-high heat until hot. Add the oil and tilt to coat the wok. Add the garlic and cook one minute. Add the ginger, garlic, and scallion whites, stirring, one minute. Add cabbage, kale, and 1/4 cup broth and cook, tossing until kale is tender, about three minutes.

For the brussels:

2 lb.	brussels sprouts, trimmed and halved
1 T.	Worcestershire sauce
2 T	seasoned rice vinegar
1	orange, zested
1 T	white sesame seeds
¼ t.	ground ginger
½ t.	poppy seeds
pistachio	

- Preheat oven to 450°F. Place one sheet pan in the oven while heating. Toss brussels sprouts and oil in a large bowl; season with salt. Remove the hot pan from oven and pour the brussels sprouts onto the pan. If you'd like, turn cut sides down. Roast brussels sprouts until brown and crispy, 15–25 minutes. Add to a bowl, add Worcestershire sauce, vinegar, ginger, sesame seeds and poppy seeds and toss to combine.

Assembly:

- Mix rice and tofu and heat through in a pan. Once heated through, mix in the gochujang, tamari, lime juice and vinegar.
- Top with brussels sprouts and garnish with scallion greens and toasted pistachio.

Mexican Hot Chocolate:

1 ½ c.	whole milk
½ c.	heavy cream
25 g.	dark brown sugar
25 g.	sugar
85 g.	70 % chocolate
55 g.	54 % chocolate
½	dried guajillo chili peppers
3	cinnamon sticks
¾ t.	salt
½ t.	vanilla

- Preheat oven to 350°F.
- Roast cinnamon sticks on a sheet tray in the oven until fragrant, 5-10 min. Remove, place in the center of a clean tea towel and top with another clean towel. Crush with a rolling pin.
- Heat cream and milk together with the sugars, dried guajillos, crushed cinnamon sticks and salt. Bring to a simmer, remove from heat and let steep for 10 minutes, tasting after 5 minutes to check on the level of heat from the guajillos. Strain through a sieve.
- Place cinnamon milk back on the heat and bring just below a simmer, add chocolate, remove from heat and whisk until fully melted and incorporated. Add vanilla and blend with an immersion blender, strain through a chinois, and serve.

Pancakes:

100 g.	all-purpose flour
60 g.	cake flour
1 T	baking powder
1 ½ t.	salt
1 T	sugar
1 T	malt powder
1 c.	whole milk
4 T	butter, melted
1	egg
1 t.	vanilla

- Sift all dry ingredients together in a large bowl.
- Gently warm the milk in the microwave or on the stove. Pour into a bowl and whisk in the melted butter and the egg until combined. Make a well in the center of the dry ingredients and pour the wet ingredient mixture into it. Whisk just until combined. Do not overmix, it's fine if it is a little lumpy. The batter is best if it rests overnight in the fridge.
- Place a clean, flat, nonstick skillet over medium-low heat. Add a little oil and wipe out with a paper towel just to leave a thin layer of fat. Dollop your batter onto the skillet, and cook 2-3 min on the first side, and 1-2 minutes on the flip side. Serve hot.

Bacon and Eggs Soup:

1	red onion, chopped
3 strips	peppered bacon
1	large russet potato, diced
8 slices	Canadian bacon
2 ½ c.	low-sodium chicken stock
¾ c.	whole milk
1	egg (per serving)

cayenne pepper

smoked paprika

Italian parsley

- Add 1-2 tablespoons of oil to a large skillet with high sides and place over medium-high heat. Add the onion and peppered bacon and fry until the bacon is cooked and the onions are wilted. Add diced potato, Canadian bacon, chicken stock and milk. Bring to a boil, then lower the heat and simmer for 30 minutes, stirring occasionally.

- Remove from heat and set aside to cool for 5 minutes. Pour mixture into blender and blend until smooth. Blend in batches if you have a small blender.

- Fill a small or medium sized pot with water and bring just to a simmer and remove from the heat. Crack an egg into a small bowl, and lower into the hot water. Poach an egg for 3-4 minutes. The yolk should spring back like fresh mozzarella when gently poked.

- Place a pad of butter in the bottom of each soup bowl, then place the poached egg on top. Gently pour soup over the egg and garnish with cayenne pepper, smoked paprika and Italian parsley.

- For a less creamy soup, omit the milk and increase the chicken stock to 3 ¼ cup.

Icelandic Rye Bread (Rúgbrauð):

200 g.	rye flour
80 g.	whole wheat flour
1 ½ t.	baking soda
1 t.	baking powder
1 ½ t.	salt
500 ml.	buttermilk, slightly room temp
160 g.	golden syrup

- Preheat oven to 350°F. Grease an 8- or 9-inch loaf pan. Line the bottom with parchment.
- Mix the dry ingredients together.
- Warm the golden syrup slightly and add to the buttermilk.
- Combine the wet ingredients into the dry and whisk until fully combined.
- Pour mixture into the prepared pan. Cover the top of the batter with another piece of greased parchment paper. Cover tightly with foil.
- Place into the oven and reduce the heat to 230°F and bake for 7 hours.
- Remove from oven and let cool in pan for 10 minutes. Remove from pan and let cool on a rack. The bread will still be quite moist.

Roasted Cauliflower with Yogurt Sauce:

For the cauliflower:

2	medium head cauliflower
3 T	olive oil
1 t.	cinnamon
1 ½ t.	cumin
1 t.	turmeric
½ t.	ground cardamom
¼ t.	rosewater
2 T	lemon juice
1 T	Salt

- Preheat oven to 400°F.
- Cut the cauliflower in quarters, discard the leaves and cut the florets from the stem.
- In a bowl, combine the oil, cinnamon, cumin, turmeric, cardamom, lemon juice and rosewater. Add cauliflower and toss to combine. Add salt and toss again.
- Place on a sheet tray and roast for 25-30 minutes, or until al dente.
- Serve with yogurt sauce.

For the yogurt sauce:

1 c.	walnuts, toasted
2	cucumber, deseeded and diced
5 c.	plain, full-fat Greek yogurt
2	cloves garlic, finely grated
2 t.	lemon zest
2 t.	lemon juice
1 T	crushed, dried mint leaves
¼ c.	fresh dill, chopped

1 T	olive oil
1 t.	crushed pink peppercorn
¼ t.	white pepper
4 T	whole milk

kosher salt

freshly ground pepper

aleppo-style pepper

- Preheat oven to 350°F. Toast walnuts on a sheet tray, until golden brown, 8–10 minutes, tossing halfway through. Cool slightly, then give them a rough chop.
- Mix together walnuts, cucumber, yogurt, garlic, lemon zest, lemon juice, mint, dill, oil, pink peppercorn, and white pepper in medium bowl to combine; season with salt and pepper. If the sauce is too thick, add a little yogurt to desired consistency.
- Garnish with Aleppo pepper and serve.

Butter Dumplings:

1 lb.	yukon gold potatoes
¼ head	napa cabbage, diced
½ c.	yellow onion, diced
1	carrot, finely grated
1 c.	shitake mushroom, chopped
½ c.	scallions or garlic chives, chopped
1 t.	fresh ginger, grated
2	garlic cloves, minced
1 tsp.	sesame oil
1 ½ t.	rice wine vinegar, or sake
1 T	black sesame seeds
1.5 oz.	unsalted butter, room temp.
1 t.	salt
¼ t.	white pepper
1 T	soy sauce
1 recipe	dumpling dough (or store-bought dumpling wrappers)

- Prepare a sheet tray with a light coating of flour. Set aside for later.

- Wash, scrub and dice the potatoes (keep the skin on) and add to a large pot of salted water. Boil just until these are fork tender, do not overcook. Drain in a colander and mash in a medium bowl with the softened butter. Add the salt, white pepper and soy sauce and adjust seasonings as necessary.

- In a small bowl, add the cabbage and carrot and massage a couple teaspoons of salt in with your hands. Set aside for

10-12 minutes. Squeeze out the excess moisture. Discard water.

- In a large skillet, add a little oil and then add the onion and mushrooms and sauté for 3-5 minutes over medium-high heat or until they begin to caramelize. Add the garlic and cook an additional minute. Remove from the heat and add the onion-mushroom mixture to the drained cabbage mixture.
- Add the vegetable mixture to the potatoes, then add the chopped scallion, grated ginger, sesame oil, rice wine vinegar and sesame seeds and mix together with a spatula until everything is homogenous.
- On a clean surface, lay out a few dumpling wrappers and lightly rub water around the edges with your finger.
- Spoon a slightly mounded, quarter-size ball of filling in the center of the dumpling wrapper. Fold the dumpling wrapper in half to cover the filling completely and seal the edge with your fingers, pressing out any air between the filling and the edges. With the folded edge of the dumpling facing you, pull the corners together until they just overlap, this will cup the sealed outer edge a bit. Pinch the ends together to seal. It should look like tortellini or a rose. (or these can be folded like traditional gyoza with pleats).
- Place the finished dumplings on the prepared baking sheet.
- Heat a nonstick skillet on med-high heat with about 2 tablespoons vegetable oil. Add as many dumplings as you can to the pan, starting along the edge of the pan and working towards the center. The fattest part of the dumpling should be facing down. Give the pan a shake to move the dumplings around so they don't stick.

- After about 2-3 minutes, carefully add ½ cup of water to the pan and immediately cover with the lid. Be certain to cover the pan quickly so the steam doesn't escape or burn your hands.
- Cook on medium heat until almost all of the water has evaporated, about 3-6 minutes. Remove the lid and let cook for an additional one minute. You'll be able to hear the crackling of oil when the dumplings are finished, they should be nice and crisp brown on the bottom and steamed on the top. Remove the dumplings from the pan with a spatula and transfer to a plate.
- Serve with black vinegar, soy sauce, la-yu, or any other dipping sauce you'd like.

Dumpling Dough:

12.5 oz.	all-purpose flour
1 c.	boiling water
Pinch	salt

- In a food processor, place the flour and salt and pulse to combine. While running, drizzle in the hot water, it should take about 30 seconds to come together. Dump out onto the counter or into a bowl and knead 1-2 minutes just to bring the dough together. Round into a ball, flatten slightly, wrap in plastic and rest for 30 minutes.
- Unwrap and divide the dough in half, cover one half with the plastic wrap or a damp towel so it doesn't dry out.
- Working with one half at a time, roll the dough as thinly as possible with a rolling pin, flipping the dough over after

every couple passes and to roll on the opposite side. Using a 3 to 3.5-inch round circle cutter, cut out circles. The remaining scrap dough can be wrapped, rested for 5-10 minutes, and then rerolled.

- Proceed with dumpling recipe, fold and cook according to recipe instructions. Extra dough may be wrapped and frozen for future use.

ACKNOWLEDGEMENTS:

This book, its characters, themes, events, design, atmosphere, energy, structure, darkness, and light, would not be what it is without the people who've helped me along the way. To all of you, I am infinitely grateful, some in ways that I would never be able to fully articulate in words, no matter how many I used.

To my mother, Carol Dahlen: the love I have for words and how they're used comes from you. You have always believed in and supported me, even when what I wrote just wasn't that good. I can't thank you enough for allowing me to be myself, for giving me proof that odds can be overcome, for raising me to think and see a little differently than most. I love you and will never be able to express just how proud I am to have you as my mom. With much love and gratitude, thank you.

To my stepdad, Eric Dahlen: one of the gentlest and generous spirits I've ever known, one who gives more than he takes. Thank you for always encouraging me with all my artistic endeavors and always being there to help me in whatever way that you could, even if you were exhausted, tired or it was to your own detriment. You've watched me grow, change and evolve, and have given me nothing but support. With love, thank you.

To one of my soulmates, David Petrusich: it would be horrifically unfair to say that you haven't influenced me, in so many ways. I remember the first night I met you; I said to you, "wow…you're like…a real artist," and I still think that to this day. You have taught me about love, hate, loss, beauty, spirit, psychism, *art, music, fashion*, but I owe a debt of gratitude for the collaboration that helped me develop the world, its themes, character traits and styles of magic. It began with you, me, and a legal pad in a dimly lit, honey-amber incense filled apartment in Chicago. Thank you for inspiration and creativity and teaching me that what is gray can be gold.

To my contrasting Libra, Erik McLinn: you know me better than most people in my life, and probably even better than I know myself, and even though that level of knowing is probably frustrating in a way that is somewhere between David and Moira Rose and Rebecca Bunch, you've been there when it matters and you still surprise me. You have always encouraged my artistic temperament, expressed frustration when my talents weren't recognized or appreciated, been free of judgement, been happy for my successes no matter how big or small they were, and have taken time for me to help me with whatever it is that I can't figure out, build, or do. Thank you for sharing your creative brain with me, forcing me to see things from a logical perspective and teaching me many lessons that have made a lasting impact on my life.

To my favorite Scorpio, Allison Layman: I adore your spirit, and your perspective on how we are all made of water will forever be burned into my memory. Thank you for being such a wonderful friend and for designing the beautiful book covers for this series. You somehow knew exactly what I wanted, even though I couldn't fully explain what it was that I wanted.

To my favorite Leo, Alexis Layman: I've been able to explore the depths of my characters simply from knowing you. For reading chapters and giving me feedback, and for sharing your thoughts, perspectives, life, habits and friendship with me, I thank you! I miss the days when all it took was a short train ride to see you.

To my beta-readers and squad of personal cheerleaders. Ellen and Laura O'Rourke: thank you for allowing me to be a part of Witches Magazine and for taking the time to review my novels and feature my work. Max Bever: for giving me an incredibly detailed, constructive and thorough analysis of my rough and first drafts. The compendium wouldn't even exist if it weren't for your suggestion. Your feedback has proven to be very valuable to my voice and success as a writer. Micaéla Royal and Sandra Szatkowski: your continued support is appreciated more than you know; thank you for reading, promoting and believing in my story. I'm incredibly thankful for your support and friendship, witches. You two are pure magic and I am happy we have crossed paths and gotten to know each other. Kellee M. Hunkapi: thank you for listening, reading, hearing and understanding me, especially when others can't or won't. Stephanie Trott: you've always been by my side and supported me regardless of whether it was making pizza dough at a restaurant that didn't' deserve either of us, reading rough drafts and providing me with questions and feedback, or just hearing my personal struggles. Thank you for all you've done. Brady Chiasson: thank you for being such a warm, loving and supportive friend, and showing up when it matters. Brandy Kenworthy: you know—more than most—just how important writing is to me, and the barriers and obstructions that I had to work through in order to make it to where I am. Thank you for teaching me to care for myself, value myself, and thank you for listening, understanding and above all—caring. You have helped me in more ways than you will ever know. Laurel Robinson: your editing really polished what I was trying to say and the message I wanted to get across. Thank you for all of your hard work and feedback.

To all the rest of you who have played a part in this story of getting me to where I am now: Michelle B McDonald-Ross, Sera L., Caitlyn Frank, Chris Galasso, Sara Holcombe, Cari Illa, Cody Torbert, Joanna DeVoe, Sarah Day, Sinisa Jancan, Penny C. Sansevieri and the many others that I haven't mentioned here or accidentally overlooked because I forget everything, and if I have—I apologize—it shouldn't suggest I am not appreciative.

To my angels, my ancestors, my guides, the natural world and beyond: thank you for allowing me to be here today. Thank you for guiding me through the peaks and valleys of my life. Thank you for the enchanting forests, the sandy beaches, the mystic deserts, the flowing oceans, the dark storms and the lightning that lives within them, the fire that I surround myself with in every home I've lived in, the sun with its cyclic light and a million moods, the enchanting moon where everything is blue in its light and outlined in its absence, the glittery stars, the swampy spell of the south, the mountains and the perspective it gives, the snow and the silence it brings, the universe and all that I will never understand, see, experience or comprehend while I exist here on Earth looking up into the cosmos. Thank you.

ABOUT THE AUTHOR

Ryan Kurr is an author, pastry chef, massage therapist, and mystic practitioner. *Powdered Oak & Seven Metals* is the second novel in the *Esoteric Alchemy* series. *Sage, Smoke & Fire*, the first book in the series, reached the #1 Best Seller spot in the LGBT Fantasy genre on Amazon. His debut memoir, *Sugar Burn: The Not So Hot Side of the Sweet Kitchen*, was released in 2015. His freelance work on spiritual and metaphysical witchcraft has been published by *Witches Magazine*. He currently lives in New Orleans.